Raised to be obedient by a stern grandmother in a blue-collar town in Massachusetts, Rosie Monroe accepts a scholarship to art school in New York City in the 1980s. One morning at a museum, she meets a worldly man twenty years her senior, with access to the upper crust of New England society. Bennett is dashing, knows that "polo" refers only to ponies, teaches her which direction to spoon soup, and tells of exotic escapades with Truman Capote and Hunter S. Thompson. Soon, Rosie is living with him on a swanky estate on Connecticut's Gold Coast, naively in sway to his moral ambivalence. A daughter—Miranda—is born just as his current con goes awry, forcing them to abscond in the middle of the night to the untamed wilderness of northern Vermont.

Almost immediately, Bennett abandons them in an uninsulated cabin without a car or cash for weeks at a time, so he can tend a teaching job that may or may not exist at an elite college. Rosie is forced to care for her young daughter alone, and to tackle the stubborn intricacies of the wood stove, snowshoe into town, hunt for wild game, and forage in the forest. As Rosie and Miranda's life gradually begins to normalize, Bennett's schemes turn malevolent, and Rosie must at last confront his twisted deceptions. Her actions have far-reaching and perilous consequences.

PRAISE FOR MELANIE FINN'S THE HARE

"A MOST HIGHLY ANTICIPATED BOOK OF 2021"
—ARIANNA REBOLINI, *BUZZFEED*; K.W. COLYARD, *BUSTLE*

"*The Hare*'s main character, Rosie, could be any of us. Imperfect yet formidable, she confronts patriarchy and expectations of womanhood in this smart... literary thriller." —KARLA STRAND, *MS. MAGAZINE*

"A novel that soars whimsically and lands with an unexpected stab in the palm of your hand; like a paper crane with a razor blade folded into its belly."
—ANDREA DREILING, *PAPERBACK PARIS*

"An elegant writer of unconventional thrillers, Finn has a gift for weaving existential and political concerns through tautly paced prose."
—MOLLY YOUNG, *VULTURE*

"Finn offers a chilling account of the ways women can be abused, with sexual assault, psychological trauma, objectification, and murder crossing class boundaries. Yet as she also shows, women often cannot escape the cages they have helped to build around their lives. A #MeToo tale that will also appeal to general readers."
—JOANNA BURKHARDT, *LIBRARY JOURNAL*, HIGHLY RECOMMENDED

"Finn's propulsive latest tackles power dynamics shaped by gender, age, and class... This lurid tale will keep readers turning the pages."
—*PUBLISHERS WEEKLY*

"A powerful story of female perseverance, strength, and resilience. This book has rare qualities: beautiful writing while being absolutely unputdownable." —CLAIRE FULLER, AUTHOR OF *BITTER ORANGE*

"*The Hare* is a brilliant, unflinching tale of gender, power, and entrapment."
—MARIA HUMMEL, AUTHOR OF *STILL LIVES*

"*The Hare* is a modern *The Awakening*. I'm convinced it'll go down as a modern feminist classic." —**MANDY SHUNNARAH, OFF THE BEATEN SHELF**

"[Finn]'s stories are beautiful and have a dark, suspenseful feel that will appeal to fans of literary mysteries." —**SARAH BROWN, *ST. LOUIS MAGAZINE***

"*The Hare* gives us an important, comprehensive picture of the stages of a woman's learning, suggesting, that over time, teachers will be rejected, new ones sought, and the student might herself become a teacher. The need to adapt, however, to be on guard, to figure out new methods of surviving will be life-long, the way it is for an animal in the wild, hyper-conscious of its vulnerability." —**MARTA BALCEWICZ, *PLOUGHSHARES***

"Finn is a master of complication made visible through taut and beautiful words. I highly recommend this book."
—**SAMANTHA KOLBER, NEW PAGES**

"Reminiscent of Amina Cain or Barbara Comyns... A thrilling story suffused with all rage of a feminist awakening." —**BOOK CULTURE BOOKSTORE**

"An unflinchingly honest portrayal of a woman who was denied the chance to become the woman she imagined in her youth, but thirty years later, is finally ready to try again." —**MARGARET LEONARD, DOTTERS BOOKS**

"A beautiful and powerful book—literature that reads like a thriller... It tackles big issues in an original way." —**ALANA HALEY, SCHULER BOOKS**

"Rosie Monroe, the protagonist of *The Hare*, is every woman and Everywoman... this is a powerful book and a powerful character."
—**KIM CRADY-SMITH, GREEN MOUNTAIN BOOKS AND PRINTS**

"Beautifully written literary triumph that you will want to treasure once you've dipped inside. It's full of art and female ideas and the kind of perseverance that lifts the spirit. I envy you your discovery."
—**LINDA BOND, AUNTIE'S BOOKSTORE**

MELANIE FINN, author of *Away From You* (2004), *The Gloaming* (2016), *The Underneath* (2018), and *The Hare* (2021), was born and raised in Kenya and the US. *The Gloaming* was a *New York Times* Notable Book of 2016, a finalist for the Vermont Book Award and *The Guardian*'s "Not the Booker" Prize. The writer and producer of the DisneyNature wildlife epic *The Crimson Wing: Mystery of the Flamingos,* she is also the co-founder and director of the Tanzanian-based charity Natron Healthcare. She and her family live on a remote hill in the Northeast Kingdom of Vermont.

THE HARE

A NOVEL

MELANIE FINN

Two Dollar Radio
Books Too Loud To Ignore

Two Dollar Radio

Books too loud to Ignore

WHO WE ARE Two Dollar Radio is a family-run outfit dedicated to reaffirming the cultural and artistic spirit of the publishing industry. We aim to do this by presenting bold works of literary merit, each book, individually and collectively, providing a sonic progression that we believe to be too loud to ignore.

TwoDollarRadio.com

Proudly based in
Columbus
OHIO

🐦 @TwoDollarRadio

📷 @TwoDollarRadio

f /TwoDollarRadio

Love the
PLANET?
So do we.

Printed on Rolland Enviro.
This paper contains 100% post-consumer fiber,
is manufactured using renewable energy - Biogas
and processed chlorine free.

100%   PCF   BIO GAS*   PERMANENT

Printed in Canada

SOME RECOMMENDED LOCATIONS FOR READING *THE HARE*:
Pretty much anywhere because books are portable and the perfect technology!

AUTHOR PHOTO→
Libby March

COVER ART→
"Princess Adelaide" from *Roses and Rose Culture* (Stecher Lithographic Co,1892)

For Kate

THE HARE

THE BOATHOUSE
1983

Bennett was a slow driver. He peered through the windshield.
The BMW was missing a headlight, and the single beam, alone
on this dark road, meandered like a shy child, head down. There
were no houses, just dark, dark woods over flat ground. In the
passenger seat, Rosie was trying to read Bennett's handwriting
with a lighter, as the interior lights did not work. She didn't want
to be lost. She wanted to be at the party.

"It says three miles past Hayley Road." Rosie's thumb was
burning from the flame. "Have we passed Hayley Road?"

"Jesus, I hate the countryside." Bennett lit up another cigarette, an expert choreography with one hand: the car lighter,
the cigarette, never taking his eyes off the road, his other hand
on the wheel. His hands were beautiful, Rosie thought, large,
strong, smooth-skinned, and it was absolutely true what was
said about hands.

"Birds," Bennett exhaled the smoke. "Cow shit. Farmers."

The party was at an old millhouse way out here in Meriden,
four turns off the Merritt Parkway according to the directions.
Mick and Keith might be there, Bennett had told her, and Rosie

played it cool by not asking *the* Mick, *the* Keith? She wondered what they were like, and if she'd get to talk to them, even a few words, "Is there any more ice?"

"Can you stop," she said. "I think I need to be sick."

Pulling over, Bennett rushed around to open her car door. He was insistent in this way, his old-world manners — doors, chairs, drinks, pulled open, back, delivered. He took her arm, as if she were an invalid, she pushed him away so he wouldn't get hit with the splatter.

Her stomach heaved and released. "It must have been that chicken salad."

When she was back in the car, Bennett offered to open the wine they'd brought, if she needed to rinse her mouth out. She had some gum somewhere in her purse. Bennett hated gum, he'd told her she looked like a cheap hooker. Secretly, she slipped a piece into her mouth now, letting it dissolve, allowing only the most furtive chew. He was pulling back onto the road: "It must be up here. He said there's a red barn with a big hex painted on the side."

He? Someone interesting, cultured, traveled, rich. Someone who might look at Rosie and wonder why Bennett was with her. At such a party with Mick and Keith, there would be beautiful girls — women who wore backless red dresses and spoke fluent French and modeled in Milan. Don't ever order maraschino cherries, Bennett had told her, not with ice cream, not with cocktails.

The only cocktails to drink are gin martinis or greyhounds.

They drove on. Sure enough, within five minutes, there was the barn. Bennett turned up the long, narrow drive, winding through pines. Eventually, they arrived at the house, on a river — a millhouse; but it was completely dark.

Rosie glanced at the napkin as if this might suddenly reveal new information: "Did we get the wrong night?"

"I guess the party was canceled." Bennett got out, stretched. He was a big man, tall and bulky with muscle, for he'd been a star athlete some years ago — lacrosse, Rosie recalled — and his frame held the shape. He got cramped in the small car. Ambling off toward the house, he peered in through the dark windows, then disappeared around the back. She saw his figure crossing the moonlit lawn to a barn tucked up against the trees. Briefly, there was the flare of a flashlight, and then he reappeared. He was carrying a small package.

Taking his place again behind the wheel, he tossed the package on the back seat, and opened the wine with the corkscrew on his key ring. This had belonged to his father, who'd brought it back from Berlin right after the war. Bennett was proud of its provenance: stolen from Himmler's private bar.

For several minutes, they sat in the car while Bennett drank and Rosie wondered about the package and if she could ask him about it. The river, visible through a stand of trees, toppled down a series of rapids, inky dark, the foam silvery in the moonlight. "It's beautiful here," she observed.

"It is bumfuck." He took another drink.

"Maybe they write sitting by the river."

"Who?"

"Mick, Keith."

Bennett snorted. "Whoever lives here crochets antimacassars."

"What is an *anti-massacre*?"

"Maccass-ar. Little doily thing you put on the arm rest and the back of the chair to prevent soiling of the chair's fabric."

Yet the image held in her mind of a bit of lace waving in the wind, so pretty and delicate that soldiers stopped killing women and children. "Why would anyone want a doily on a chair?"

"In ye olde days, middle-class people —" he said *middle-class* with a fancy English accent *clahs* — "middle-clahs people wanted to keep things nice in the parlor." *Pah-luh.* "They had all kinds of shit in their hair including grease and lice and didn't want the whole couch ruined."

Bennett was a trove of such information. He was an appraiser of fine art for a select few and spent his days steeped in paintings, jewelry, porcelain figurines. He knew what a soup spoon was — and that "one" must scoop the soup away from "one." Never slurp. He knew about shoe-horns, French cuffs, fish forks, Windsor knots, and the best bistro in Cap d'Antibes, France. Rosie assumed he came from money, but she didn't know where or how much; money, to her, was Gran at the table with a stack of bills, her lips set as she wrote out checks and put them in envelopes. Gran did not talk about money.

Rosie swallowed another bout of nausea. She was disappointed about the party and felt foolish for having had all the conversations with Mick and Keith in her head. The very notion that they'd even notice her to offer her a drink or ask her to pass the olives was absurd — a girl who had nothing to offer, not even beauty. At this very moment, they were at another party with famous actors. Had there even been a party here? Possibly, Bennett had been joking when he said, "Mick and Keith might be there." Probably, now that she thought about it; Bennett's humor came around blind corners.

"What is that?" She tilted her head to indicate the packet in the back seat.

"Jewels. Including a small, delicate piece from Tsarist Russia. The owner is a dear lady requiring a divorce. She has no money, only the family jewels, and she needs to procure the finest law-yer. So she's cashing in." He handed her the bottle, started the car.

They were on the road again, Rosie was drinking, too. It was good wine. Bennett knew his wine, a robust Bordeaux in this instance. She had found a Steely Dan tape and slipped it in the deck. *Rikki Don't Lose That Number.* Even if this wasn't the night they'd planned, at least she wasn't in her dorm room. She drank, she sang a few bars, she imagined the jewels — the rubies, sap-phires, diamonds nestled casually in the box in the back. Bennett might let her see them.

"Roll me one," he said and put his hand on her thigh, posses-sive, and she was possessed. She rolled him a smoke, adding in the tiniest bit of Mary Jane, just like he'd taught her, scooching the contents in, pulling the paper tight, then a firm roll, a twist of the ends. She didn't like either kind of smoke herself. She had the roll-up in her mouth, she was lighting it for him, when she saw a dark shape across the road in front of them. Bennett's hand lifted off her lap, she could feel his body begin to react, but as they were rushing toward the object — an old carpet? — and the road was ribboning it toward them, there was no time to react, he could not have swerved. He had both hands on the wheel.

The car lumped up and then down and Bennett kept going.

"Bennett —" she said.

Because something in the motion of the car going over the carpet, the lifting and descending of the wheels, the unexpected resistance, the carpet being more solid than she'd expected — this troubled her, she felt a tickling in her lower gut.

"Shouldn't we —"

"No," Bennett replied simply. He was hunched like a bear, both hands on the steering wheel.

He should though. He should stop, he should just check. She looked over at him, his gaze was straight ahead. Maybe she should insist, but how? Her voice would be strong and shrill in the dark car — her voice would be *loud*. Already they were moving away, they were scrolling forward through time, and the distance and the minutes made her doubt herself, so she listened to the scratchy groove of Steely Dan and she handed Bennett his smoke and she sipped the Bordeaux. *Any Major Dude Will Tell You.* Further and further on, the road rolled them casually homeward. If she'd checked her watch she'd have known only five minutes had passed. Her emotions were like a tide turning slowly and gently out on the reef, her agitation ebbing as the stronger conviction rolled neatly in: it was only a piece of carpet, of course it was, if there was any chance, any chance at all, that it *wasn't*, Bennett would have stopped, he was 38, he knew things, he knew how to navigate the Metro in Paris, the autobahn in Germany.

"Did I tell you about the time I got drunk with Truman Capote?" Bennett began. He and Capote had been the only ones in first class on a flight from London to Helsinki. Capote, wearing a large coat and long red scarf, had taken a shine to Bennett, slim and young in tight jeans and a tee-shirt — "Oh, I was pretty back then" — on his way to visit an Oxford classmate who happened to be Finnish royalty. They'd had a layover in Berlin and the stewardesses all disappeared. "Let's go and get a drink," Capote commanded, even though they were both already quite drunk. He and Bennett trotted down the metal stairs and onto the tarmac, no one seemed to notice them. They saw a bar on the other side of a chainlink fence, lit up "like Jesus in the manger,"

Capote said. When they climbed the fence, Truman's scarf got caught and he was almost strangled. He was hung there like a fat fly in a web and Bennett had just managed to set him free when airport security arrived. But because they were first class passengers, no one said anything, just ushered them back on the plane and a crew of fresh stewardesses brought them champagne.

Back at the boathouse, Bennett fell asleep cocooning Rosie's body, his semi hard-on pressing leisurely against her lower back. They had not yet used the word *love*, but surely she did love him. He filled up the lonely places of her life, the empty Sunday mornings, the yearning Saturday nights; he filled the hollows of her childhood and made her grown-up. Every day she was with him was one more away from her grandmother and the Sunday-brown house in Lowell. He was her direction into the world. His un-shaven chin grazed her shoulder. Again, she felt the car jolt over the carpet, the single headlight rise and dip then flatten out again. Yet, it was nothing more than the flickering of an old film, and though she wondered briefly about the package on the back seat, she fell asleep.

Bennett woke her with sleepy sex in the morning. He had this amazing technique which always made her come moments before he did. He liked to watch her roil under him and then pound into her. The light from the sea glittered on the ceiling above them and she could hear the water gently lapping. He rolled over and lit his first cigarette of the day and the smell of the tobacco layered with salt and seaweed. On this particular morning, there was also the scent of cut grass, as the gardener was again mowing the vast lawn, the burr of the machine entering her consciousness from the obscure shed near the greenhouses where such implements were kept and perhaps where the gardener even lived. She had never seen the gardener close up, she had never seen the owners of the main house — Bennett told her they were away in Lake Comma, Italy. Every day, people came and went from their house, delivering, cleaning, repairing. "Tradesmen."

"We have to go into town," he said, even though it was barely seven and he seldom used the imperative. She flung her arm over him, made a sulky face, "Want to stay in bed all day."

He rose up and away from her in one move so that she was tossed aside like a small boat in his wake. "Get up," he said and she was a child.

They drove down from Sasco Hill to the scrubbier end of Fairfield, where buildings were squat and square and telephone and electricity wires crisscrossed the streets. Edges were hard and sharp or prickly with antennae, and the road tar was already softening and off-gassing. The air was gooey with heat, it felt not like air but cake batter. Carly Simon took the place of conversation, a relief to Rosie, because when Bennett entered these moods he did not want her bright, inane chatter, he did not want her voice at all. Her voice seemed to hurt him. She was glad of the practice she had of silence, the years and years of not bothering Gran. The Carly Simon cassette was a live recording Bennett had made on Martha's Vineyard a few years ago, and it was gritty and uneven, people could be heard coughing and chatting. Carly and James — James *Taylor* — had an impromptu gig one night at a bar on the island and Bennett had been there. He used to sail with James.

Bennett pulled into Jiffy's Wash n' Wax, which had just opened for the day. A thin dark-skinned man — Jiffy himself? — was checking the three giant vacuums that squatted together along the far edge of the lot. Bennett drove past these, lined himself up for the wash on the designated track. The car didn't seem dirty. And yet Rosie sensed urgency, Bennett tapping his fingers on the steering wheel, and not in time to the music.

When Jiffy came to the window, Bennett slapped a twenty in his palm, "Hey, man, the super wash, please. And if you can really get under it, I'd appreciate it."

The tracks pulled the BMW into the flailing octopus arms at the entrance. The rubbery strips slapped and flapped against the car, over the windows and roof and Rosie felt a moment's intense panic of claustrophobia. She might be entering a horror movie or an episode of *The Twilight Zone* and something terrible and quick was waiting for her in the dark. A dead, run-over zombie-man perhaps. Jets of water now shot at the car, and soap blubbed over the windscreen. She stayed still and silent, Carly could not be heard, only roaring, whooshing. Bennett lit up a cigarette and the smoke, trapped inside, pricked her eyes. She gripped the seat.

Why are we here, she wanted to ask him.

She *knew* the answer but then she didn't, didn't know anything, the drop was precipitous, a ride at the fair without any safety harness. What might there be under the car? If it hadn't been a carpet. What needed to be washed off? Because if she was going to ask questions, she must be prepared for the answers. About what might have become lodged in the wheels or various joints and axle-whatevers underneath.

However. *However* like a foothold, a handhold, a hand up and out, so she gripped fast to the *however*: many things, other than carpets, might find themselves in the middle of the road at night. A deer, hit by a previous car. A duffle bag someone had accidentally left on top of their car as they'd driven off.

Cushions, part of a sofa, a small mattress. Plenty of things were soft, yet not squishy, things with an internal integrity. How accurately her memory retained the sensation.

She glanced back; the package of Tsarist jewels was no longer there. Possibly, last night hadn't even happened. She knew the way memory could feel spongy underfoot — a marshy uncertainty.

Then they were out in the blazing summer morning and she wondered why Bennett had brought her with him, he could have left her at the boathouse as he often did with a pile of Penguin Classics to read and her art materials. Did he want her to know the car was clean, they wouldn't have to worry about a problem with the police, just, *say*, if there was one? Or, better: that there was nothing to worry about in the first place, as they'd done nothing wrong?

"Are you hungry?" he turned onto the Post Road. "I'm starving."

Maybe, after all, he just wanted to take her to breakfast and give the car a quick wash on the way there. She put her hand on his large thigh, and he covered it with his, lifted it, kissed her fingertips. She felt the thrill of being chosen.

*　　*　　*

Rosie had been five when the clock had stopped and a neighbor collected her from kindergarten. The neighbor would not explain, but drove her to Gran's house, and she'd walked alone up the cracked cement path toward Gran, who waited at her front door. Gran's eyes like bruised plums had frightened her, her mouth opened, she said, "You'll live with me now." She did not say, *There's been a terrible accident. Your mother and father are dead*. Gran did not bend to comfort, but she'd made up the bed, put out a clean towel. Gran could not herself speak the words, so it took Rosie some time to understand her parents were not alive anymore. Even after the funeral, it was a year before she grasped the deadness of death. The full stop with nothing after it. Gran had refused to explain the manner of their dying, other than a car crash. Gran said details were maudlin, satisfying curiosity, and curiosity was a kind of greed. It was as if Rosie's parents had walked into a tunnel and had never come out, and no one went to look for them, no one even mentioned their names ever again. Yet Rosie stood alone at the hot, roaring entrance, peering into the darkness.

Her dead parents' life insurance money had been put aside to pay for her college education. There wasn't much, she'd have to go to a community college, work nights and weekends. Gran had told her: "Your father wanted you to learn a solid trade and marry a solid man." Rosie had wondered. Because she had been a small child when her parents died, and it seemed unlikely that they'd started to worry about her career and romantic prospects.

Parsons School of Design, then, was not what Gran had had in mind. Rosie had known this, and did not tell Gran she was applying. Instead, Gran witnessed her filling out applications for Worcester Poly and UMass. Parsons was a joke, a fantasy, because Rosie knew she'd never get in. The idea of studying art was wildly extravagant, like wearing velvet or hats with tall feathers. Gran wanted Rosie to study nursing or become a teacher. The aptitude test Rosie had taken on Career Day showed ambiguous results: carpenter, architect, sanitation worker. Yet when she put pencil to paper in art class, she understood lines, shading, shape, how to bend them, butter them, stiffen them — the process of taking something from inside her head and making it external was rudimentary. Easy. So much else — the peopled world — was intimidating, sometimes incoherent.

Was she stupid? Was there something wrong with her brain? The way ideas in math would seem clear and she'd be excited, but then try to apply what she thought she'd learned and find herself in the middle of an equation with absolutely no idea how x might $= y$. The equation broke apart in her hands like fragile china, and she'd feel panicked and hot and she could smell her own sweat. Or conversations began, someone finally decided to talk to her, and then she'd forget what she was saying, her sentence would halt, dead air

— Like that. As if whatever she'd begun to say wasn't important enough, the words themselves had run out of interest with her tongue, dried up, curled up, gone to sleep, run off, who knew where, and people would just turn away thinking she was a weirdo. Sometimes, walking home, she'd realize she had gone past her Gran's house, several blocks, or she'd turned too early and was in another neighborhood entirely.

Though there was Chris, a slim, nervous geek. They kissed and did minor sex things, first base, second base, and, from time to time, with a sense more of obligation than lust, he tried for third. They were together because no one else would have them. Each to the other offered a kind of protection, just as wearing a coat on a cold day was better than no coat. The coat of Chris had been warm and comfortable.

Gran hated New York City — she always used the entire name, *New York City*. New York City was an affront to her careful living, her fear of color and loud noises and garish behavior, her equal terror of greed and of poverty. New York City was full of vulgar people like Leona Helmsley and Donald Trump as well as criminals, discos, and homosexuals. Gran's frugality was the post-Depression variety: she put the car in neutral when going downhill to save fuel — even though the area around Lowell was relatively flat.

Her frugality of love had deeper roots that went generations back on her mother's side, into the mean soil of Scotland and the mean lives it barely sustained. Life had proved Gran's distrust of love correct: she'd loved Jim Monroe, and he'd died. She'd loved their son, also Jim Monroe, and he'd first abandoned her for a woman and then died. Gran was not, therefore, going to make the same mistake with her granddaughter.

Rosie's art made manifest this frugality: for her Parsons application she'd melted down all the wax crayons she'd ever had — because Gran assiduously kept every single one and they were the sale-price colors no one wanted anyway — and from the resulting vomit-colored blob, carved a tiny, exquisitely accurate sculpture of herself. She'd titled it: "This could be useful one day." The sophisticates of Parsons could not appreciate Rosie's complete lack of irony; they thought the piece a brilliant statement on the nihilistic angst of teenagers in suburban Massachusetts, and offered her a full scholarship including a stipend.

As a child used to playing by herself in a quiet house with few toys, Rosie had a talent for the make-shift and a skill for replication. Once at Parsons, she had struggled to be bold and grand, she infuriated her teachers who gave her gold leaf and pig's blood and broken crockery and glue. Sometimes, she felt there was grandness in her — a burning sun of creativity, and if she could reach in under her ribcage she'd find the buttons and undo them one by one, and out would come another girl entirely, who looked and acted more like Cyndi Lauper and she'd create the kind of daring works the school expected by dipping her entire head in buckets of paint and shaking it over canvas. In the meantime, she was a dull girl in the back of the class, studious and intent; she took careful bites of the raucous city, up to the Midtown museums, a walk through Central Park where she might buy a pretzel with mustard, and once, she took the bus all the way to The Cloisters to see the unicorn tapestries.

There, in the solemn stone hall, she had stared at the breathless animal surrounded by men and their dogs who wanted it for wanting's sake — not meat or fur. She understood the unicorn as a symbol of purity, but the men didn't even want to keep it, didn't want to put it in a cage to marvel at or try to tame, domesticate. No: they killed it with dogs and spears. The hunters were propelled by some dark, unquestioned instinct. Rosie felt the tapestries physically. Her mouth filled with saliva and her blood seemed to move from her head to her stomach. Was this revulsion? She stared at the tapestries for a long time but the feeling didn't abate; it shifted to her ribs, a dull ache, as if she was winded. The unicorn didn't really have an expression. Maybe this was the limit of the medium. Or maybe the artist had made a choice to portray supplication, acceptance. The unicorn understood its duty to men.

*   *   *

She'd met Bennett at the Museum of Modern Art, where she was filling one of the cavernous Sundays other, hipper students spent in bed, recovering from the night before at CBGBs or a party in a Tribeca loft with Keith Haring. The lesbians, two doors down in her dorm, for instance. They smoked a ton of weed. They'd triggered the fire alarm once, and the story went around that one of them had given the firemen head to keep

Parsons' administration from finding out. Rosie liked to believe this was true because those girls were fierce and wielded their sexuality like a mallet. They were bawdy. She wished she had their blood, even a pint of it, even a thimble-full so she could stare down the pervy guy selling *The Village Voice* on the corner. When she passed he'd make slurping noises. When the lesbians came in his direction, he walked briskly away as if he'd remembered an important appointment.

MoMA was empty at this hour, just after opening. The museum was familiar to her now, she knew where everyone was, Hopper, Rothko, O'Keeffe. Rosie sometimes felt her solitude in specific places of her body; today it was round and solid in her belly like an old donut. She felt the weight of it pulling her shoulders forward, so she straightened herself up. No one was watching, no one ever watched Rosie, she was not eye-catching, but she wanted the eyes of strangers to pause, to simply acknowledge her breathing existence, and then, maybe, wonder — for the briefest moment — if she was interesting. The feeling of sitting alone in the vast, noisy cafeteria back at high school in Lowell on a day Chris had been sick was always with her; the sitting and wondering which was worse: being alone and the other kids snickering at her aloneness; or being so invisible no one even noticed she was alone.

Shoulders back again, and out, along the hanger of her collar bone. Gran, at least, had taught her how to stand as a tall girl. She entered the Futurists gallery, Giacometti's wiry dog and skinny people. She was not convinced by Léger with his Lego-like colors and squat structures; he seemed to be trying too hard.

Perhaps she recognized the fault.

But Boccioni swept his images across the canvas, she could feel their movement across her face, like a phalanx of ghosts passing through a room, the way the past transitioned into the present and future: the whole concept of time being un-restrained. Once, she'd found the imprint of a bird's wing in the snow behind Gran's house — that was the idea, capturing the momentary in a way that didn't feel stolid, or like imprisonment. It was part of an on-going story outside the picture's frame. The frame was a restriction, a construct, no different to a camera lens that went "click," and the very word "capturing" was there-fore problematic.

"You are transfixed," a man said. "An acolyte."

And because she was in the middle of her idea, she was the person who'd chosen to be in MoMA due to her preference for contemporary art over eggs bennie, she spoke without restraint or shame, an entire sentence that even ran on: "He's doing with time what Picasso and Braque did with space, he's breaking it apart, de-constructing, he's saying there is no time, only what we impose."

Then she blushed, she could not even look at the man stand-ing next to her, though she could smell him, the sharp astringent of his aftershave, the starch of his shirt. When she did glance, she noted the smidge of shaving cream in his ear and a worn paperback copy of Camus's *The Myth of Sisyphus* in the pocket of his tweed jacket.

He was looking at her. "Do you work here?"

Which was flattering because the most happening people worked at MoMA, one of the lesbians had a summer internship. Rosie parted her lips, words came out. "Time is energy, we can't contain it."

"You agree with Boccioni, then?"

"I have no basis to disagree. But that's not the same thing."

"No basis?"

"I'm 18, I've lived in Lowell, Massachusetts, all my life."

"You have the profile of a silent screen actress."

Again, she felt the heat of a blush.

"But the point of art," he went on, "is that you can be from Lowell, Massachusetts, and still understand."

"No. That's not the point of art." Why was she speaking like this? What mechanisms were slipping into place? Perhaps because he was a stranger and it was Sunday and the lesbians were having brunch together in a café on Christopher Street and it was bitterly cold outside. Katya had a tattoo on her arm and May wore Doc Martens, they were acknowledged by other Parsons students as gifted performance artists, they knew Annie Sprinkle and were doing a performance around menstrual blood. The event was being held in an abandoned meat-packing warehouse just off Hudson. Katya had invited Rosie, and May had said, "Squeak," and Katya had elbowed May, who'd snorted out a laugh. Rosie'd had no idea how to interpret that laugh — laughing at or with? The next day Rosie found a drawing of a mouse on her door, the mouse was spurting blood from its rear end, presumably a period. The blood dripped down to the floor, where there was a ticket to the event. There were bloody finger-prints all over the ticket and the words *please cum*.

"The point of art," Rosie heard herself. "Is that you don't understand meaning, there's no 'meaning' or 'understanding' only fragmentary connection, where your consciousness connects with that of the artist. Because the artist, himself, herself, is working in an intense yet balanced dialectic of inner, personal space and outer experience of culture and society. 'Understanding' and 'meaning' are static, while art is continually evolving and synthesizing. Even as the paint dries, the work is already becoming something else for the viewer, the painter has already let it go."

The man considered, hand on chin. "Did you read that somewhere?"

"I —" she began, and ended. Ended where she always began. Stupid and dull.

Yet, miraculously, he waited, and when he realized she had no more words, he made a small, possibly sympathetic smile. She noticed the size of him, six feet, broad, with a lion's mane of hair. "What I mean," he said, "is that sounds didactic not visceral. Like something you've learned, but not experienced. Art needs to be *felt*. Don't you think?" He tapped his heart with his fist.

Rosie nodded. She thought of the unicorn tapestries.

"And I wonder," the man went on. "If we dragged the hot dog vendor on the corner in here and showed him any of these paintings what he might have to say."

She waited. She hoped he could not see the nervous dampness on her upper lip. The tag in her sweater was scratching the nape of her neck. She'd bought it in a thrift store on Broadway, thinking it was hip. But she suspected the bright blue didn't suit her, not just the hue but the noise.

Yet he did not move away, he regarded her, expectantly.

When she did not answer, he frowned a little: "Should we? Go and get him?"

"No." More of a breath than a word, a silly giggle.

"He'd be completely underwhelmed. Let me tell you. He'd laugh if we told him how much these paintings were worth, were revered, and we'd label him a barbarian, a dolt. A lot of this —" the man swept his arms out, around, and at that moment she focused on the small blot of shaving cream in his ear and she wondered why he was here, alone, on a Sunday morning without a wife, a lover to wipe it away. Was he like her? Pretending not to be lonely? "— makes us feel important because we understand it. But we're cheating because we've been told what it means. In books, by teachers, on the goddam pretentious little blurbs on the wall here."

"Not all great art is like that," she dared.

Yet: what if she honestly didn't know the unicorn was a symbol of purity, of Christ. Would she just look at the old-fashioned needlepoint and think, *Wow, that was a lot of work?*

He stepped up close to the Boccioni, almost put his nose on the canvas and Rosie saw the security guard shift and attend. "Some. Yes. There are artists who make you feel, even if you can't label the feeling, even if the feeling is discomfort. De Chirico, Turner. So much of the rest, it's just, just —" a dismissive wave of his hands "— decoration."

"Picasso —"

"Picasso!" He wheeled now to face her. "Perfect example, yes! He was brilliant. He upended all that stuffy realism and opened up a new way of seeing and creating. Art didn't have to be replication or even representation. Art could be anything. Everything followed on from Picasso — surrealism, dada, modernism, postmodernism, post-postmodernism, Julian Schnabel with his silly broken pots. But Picasso found out he could wipe his ass on a piece of paper, and it would sell for millions. My parents had a Picasso in the dining room, it was crap, and the reverence they held for it infuriated me, it was an altarpiece to all that's bogus and pretentious, and so when I was 13 I spray-painted a penis on it."

Rosie gasped and laughed, "What did they do?"

"Didn't matter, because I was right."

In front of her, Boccioni's men, his horses swept on, they were still moving a century later, vibrating ferociously. She knew the futurists were fascists, war was glorious progress to them, yet none of them fought in the trenches. If they had, their art would have certainly become contaminated personal experience. What she loved about Boccioni, even Léger and Giacometti, was their focus on the metaphysical. "Art is an invitation to participate in ideas, not feelings," she said boldly.

"I'd argue against such didacticism. Our conversation proves the point that good art makes you think, and thinking isn't the opposite of feeling — merely the opposite of intellectual posturing." He held out his hand in introduction, "Bennett. Bennett Kinney."

"Rosie Monroe."

"Rosie Monroe, why do you know so much about art?"

"I'm at Parsons."

"Rosie Monroe, you should read less and do more."

"I like the reading. Art is history, not battles and kings but the history of how people interpret the world. And anyway, I'm not very good at the doing."

"Who has told you that?"

She looked at him now, and he was looking back, as if peering over a pair of eyeglasses, with sincere expectation. He had beautiful eyes — large like a woman's with long lashes, and that thick dark blond hair, loosely curled. He was much older than her, he was a grown-up man. "I'm not an artist." She wanted him to know that she knew her limits, she wasn't conceited. "I'm a careful drawer, a painter of mediocre still lifes."

"You don't know what gifts the angels will bring." He leaned forward, continued in a low conspiratorial tone: "Listen, Rosie

Monroe, I have to go. An auction at Christie's, I'm bidding for a client. A tea set owned by the Duchess of Devonshire."

Rosie felt herself nodding like a normal person yet she was suddenly desolate. Her sweater was itchy, the crotch of her tights had sagged to mid-thigh and Bennett Kinney was going to leave her.

Then, as he was walking away, he turned, smiled: "I'll find you, Rosie Monroe." And he did.

*　　*　　*

The sea reflected light into the boathouse, wavering in morning, as if the building was underwater. The wood walls had been painted a deep sea green to amplify this effect. Rosie was a mermaid. A pregnant mermaid. The home-pregnancy test left no doubt. Since starting Parsons, her periods had been irregular, and she couldn't remember the last one — certainly before she'd come to the boathouse in June with Bennett. She'd been careful, but there had been a couple of times when she'd gone to remove the diaphragm and found it already dislodged. And a few instances when she hadn't replenished the spermicidal jelly between love-making. She had not anticipated how frequently she and Bennett would have sex. He desired her and it was grown-up to be able to fuck at will, she felt sometimes unsure but Bennett did things with his hands and his mouth and he wanted her to come, and she let herself roll on the waves of her orgasms while he watched and admired. Somewhere inside, Rosie had the idea, like a stone buried deep in the Presbyterian loam of her soul, this pregnancy was punishment for being greedy. Her orgasms were rich as chocolate cake or red velvet. Layers of sweetness and dripping icing.

Gran believed in Fate, a force far more powerful than God because Fate could not be appealed to. Gran's idea — drawn from the bitter experience of losing her husband and son — was that if you kept your head down and your mouth shut, Fate wouldn't notice you. You were the dull girl the rapist walked right by, the plain flower that kept its head, the unsmiling mother who kept her child. Fate kept score, like a golfer. Once, Rosie had told this to Bennett and he'd scoffed: "The score sheet is millions of years long and in a language unspoken by humans."

This was why she loved him. He was wise, he set her free. With him, her blood felt different in her veins, warmer, smoother, just as her hair was blonder from the sun. He told her to stand naked in the window, silhouetted against the sea, and raise up her arms, and slowly turn around.

He had brought her here to this light sea-place for the summer, which she'd otherwise be spending in Lowell, probably working at Dairy Queen and maybe seeing Chris, though she'd heard he was staying out in California. Bennett had given her an expensive set of pastels and charcoals and quality vellum paper because he saw her as an artist.

His mother had been an artist, she'd studied in Paris and been friends with Lee Miller and Man Ray. In her day, in her family, in her marriage, art wasn't encouraged as a serious endeavor, merely a hobby. "It was a great tragedy." She'd settled for watercolors, a medium devoid of drama or ambition. "Sail boats," Bennett said. "Thousands of fucking sail boats." Rosie wondered if his mother was still alive and when they might meet. But, except in anecdotal form, Bennett never spoke about his family.

An artist was a serious person, someone with visions and unique sensibilities, and every day Rosie aspired to visions, she waited for them through long, barren hours and she sometimes moved the pastels around in their box, rearranged the sequence of colors, and smudged them on her hands so Bennett would think she'd been working. She wanted to make up for his mother.

And now she was pregnant. Which should feel momentous — wondrous or disastrous. But felt, instead, improbable.

Rosie shifted on the bed to see the view out across the sound. The studio apartment perched high above the slips where Hobie and Mitzi kept an Atlantic and a meticulously refurbished lobster boat. She could hear the water below her gently slapping the boats. Elsewhere, in the gardens that sprawled between the boathouse and the main house: the ubiquitous droning of the lawnmower. The gardener was always mowing, the lawn short and thick as a high-quality wool carpet. The morning was breathless and hot, her skin damp with sweat, and the sea sprawled luxurious as Chinese silk, deep jade with hues of gentian further out. The sky was less interesting — a watery blue. Through the haze, she could just make out the distant cigar shape of Long Island.

The entire day stretched ahead of her, the same intimidating blank canvas she faced every morning since the start of summer. Bennett was out, a private auction at Sotheby's. Or perhaps an estate sale in Kennebunkport. An old chum selling off key pieces of her art collection to pay a blackmailer. A famous rock star — who must go unnamed, even though Rosie had no one to tell — needing to fund a stint at an expensive rehab in Switzerland. Sometimes, Bennett was away for the night, even two or three. It was easier than driving home. He stayed with his many dispersed friends, in their cottages and compounds, their penthouses and something he called *peed da tear*.

What to draw? Rosie stared out at the blue indifference of the sea and felt bloated with boredom. A shower would take

15 minutes, breakfast another 15. That would leave only seven hours before Bennett had said he'd return. She tried to read the books he wanted her to, but even the best of these eventually had her nodding off in the heat. At Parsons, her days had been so neatly collated, classes, assignments, studio time, homework. Was this adulthood? Great slabs of meaty time, hanging loose. Gran had always been busy, scurrying, tired, she worked at a school for special ed children, not with them — they were too needy, too noisy, too messy — but filing, answering phones. This work left Gran exhausted, a fragile exoskeleton, who sighed and placed cold food from the SPED kids' cafeteria on the table instead of dinner, the food jumbled together, the Jello and the beef stroganoff or what was supposed to be beef stroganoff but rather a fatty, gritty blob that smelled like an armpit.

If Rosie was an artist. Wearing only black. She'd be Georgia O'Keeffe in her red desert, staring through bones. O'Keeffe astride a motorcycle, looking back at the camera, was a woman in complete mastery of herself. She had shed all impediments to her art — the jealous Stieglitz, the noise of New York, the clutter of other people. Childless, she lived alone in a house with large windows and empty rooms in a remote corner of New Mexico. She was an arrow with a singular direction. She was heroic. Even in photographs of her younger self, there'd been no hesitancy — she'd never been a foolish young woman: she stared boldly at the camera.

Rosie lined the pencils up with the pad of paper. The dishes were done, the floor swept, bed made. These days were translucent like eggs without yolks.

She put her hand on her belly. Who was in there? A wayward seed. She decided to walk along the shore to the country club before the plastic heat melted everything. It was not a pretty walk, just hemming the golf course and a narrow, weedy beach. The sea was flat, a few boats bobbed about. The haze folded the water into the sky, giving the feeling of containment. She could just see the shore beyond Southport Harbor — a continuation of the large, leafy properties with private docks and boathouses. The views of the residents were only ever a reflection back of their own wealth, or of the sea. *Wealth* was Bennett's word; he'd said the very rich never say *rich*. "The wealthy don't live in ocean-front properties," he'd told her. "They live *by the sea.*" Rosie still had trouble understanding Bennett's idea of *wealth* because her only measure was Lowell, where the rich had big new cars and went to Florida for spring vacation, and had brick and cement gateposts and statues of Roman gods flanking their front doors. They were usually involved in construction or real estate. Yet Bennett dismissed such people as "the kind who wear white *after* Labor Day." His voice had lowered in mock horror: "And even white clothing with gold jewelry."

The beach improved on the other side of the PRIVATE BEACH MEMBERS ONLY sign. There was hardly anyone around this early, just a few nannies and their kids, a clutch of older women in tennis whites, their brittle limbs tanned to a roast chicken tint. Rosie ambled up to the clubhouse, hoping for a glass of water.

A short, tightly muscled man in tennis whites smiled at her as she attempted to sit in a chair on the porch. "Can I help you?"

"I was just —" she began. She thought about the pregnancy test. Bennett wanted to be careful, he'd suggested the pill. Why hadn't she just gone on the pill? She'd worried it might make her fat. Pregnancy would make her fat all right.

"Are you meeting someone here?"

"Just walking." She must have said something else — did she?

— because he left and came back with an iced water. He stood right there while she drank it. The water was wonderfully cold. Was he a member? A waiter? A tennis coach?

"I'm staying at the Wallace's boathouse." She thought he should know this.

He took her glass. "Should I put a day membership on their chit?"

Chit? What was a chit? It sounded like shit but Rosie was certain this wasn't about shit. Sweat pricked her underarms, she felt nervous, even though there was no threat, this tidy man, here on this warm day in full view of nannies. The lifeguard on the beach was rubbing thick white sunscreen on his face. But something was happening between her and this man — a low frequency transmission.

"Do you know Bennett?" she ventured.

"I know Bennett." His tone was obscure. She saw the slow sea crinkling in the sun. Long Island, a finger smudge. "But he is not a member here. Either."

She regarded his blank face. The *either* was said with a slight thrust. His smile remained fixed, exhibiting nothing but excellent dentistry.

"Thanks for the water."

"You're welcome."

In a way, she was fascinated by how words and their meaning could so completely diverge. She was not welcome at all. She wondered at the invisible power already moving her back down onto the beach, his mind like a leaf blower, getting rid of litter. She was trash. He was Uri Geller. Her face flushed, her mouth was dry as she gave him a little wave and walked back from where she'd come. He didn't return the wave.

When Bennett came home that evening, she told him, and he snorted, "Chip, what an ass."

"His name is Chip? Like chocolate chip? Wood chip?"

"It's actually Charles."

"How do you get Chip from Charles?"

Bennett opened the fridge and took out a couple of beers, handed her one. "It's a WASP thing. Chip, Skip, Pookie, Whip, Chat, Buffy, Muffy, Minsy, Miffy, Mitzy." Then he laughed that private laugh he had. "Matty, Twatty."

"I don't know what a wasp thing is."

"White Anglo Saxon Protestant. Although, occasionally, an Irish Catholic sneaks in the tradesman's entrance. My mother famously referred to Rose Kennedy as 'The Arriviste.' But then my mother married a Kinney, also a papist. Her father was not happy."

Often Bennett's sentences were a kind of lace — an antimacassar — full of pretty holes she didn't understand. "I'm a white Anglo-Saxon."

"You're not a WASP." He explained: "WASPs are tribal, like Jews. We intermarry to keep our money and our bloodlines, we congregate in certain places, dress a certain way, speak a certain *patois*. We have pugs but not chows, *never* chows. We have sensitive radars for interlopers and can spot a fake school tie from a hundred yards."

As this was intended to clarify, Rosie nodded. "How did Chip know I wasn't a WASP?"

Bennett laughed, "Aside from the way you dress, you have no native sense of entitlement."

Rosie had no idea what he meant.

"That," he pointed out, "is my point."

They took the beers down to the sea. The water moved slickly over the brick slipway, the daintiest tugging of the tides. Rosie had been to York Beach in Maine as a little girl, she'd gone with another family who'd wanted to be generous. The sea there had humped and smacked the sand, and Rosie was a fearful swimmer. While the others screeched and dove, she'd paddled only knee deep and they had jeered her from beyond the breaking waves. Now Bennett struck out, a fine, strong stroke, he barely made a ripple on the water's smooth surface.

"Come on," he urged.

Rosie was again knee deep. She felt a sudden surge of anger at not being good at anything; she was undefined, like a giant amoeba in the shape of a 19-year-old girl. Why did Bennett even love her? She wasn't beautiful or funny or interesting. He believed she was an artist, but she wasn't. She imagined his other lovers, blond and golden and bold — WASPs who sailed and skied and wore lime green and bright pink and certainly didn't get pregnant. He hadn't had to teach them how to give head or how to sit astride him *that's it, that's right, just liiikke thaaat* moving back and forth. They'd be out there swimming with him, stroke for stroke.

Bennett swam far out. He didn't worry about sharks or undertows. Rosie drank her beer — she shouldn't be drinking if she was pregnant, which she was, but hardly pregnant. She didn't need to be pregnant, she didn't even need to tell Bennett and she'd get unpregnant.

Small birds bobbed about in the frill of surf, pecking and skittering. "I envy the bird at home in his garden" — a line, a poem from one of Bennett's books, he was so well read, he'd studied at Oxford. Modern Literature. Or was it History? She wasn't envious of the birds, for they were small and flew through wild storms; but she yearned for their sense of purpose, their ergonomic design. The loose, gelatinous shell of her wobbled around her narrower, psychic self. She had no idea even how to occupy her own body, and now a little, polyp thing was burrowing into her flesh, nesting.

Bennett had turned toward the shore, his arms arcing in perfect rhythm. He was an excellent swimmer, the muscles on his sun-freckled shoulders bunched and released. He suddenly reared out of the water and ran at her and caught her, she screamed as he dragged her into the sea. The cold water surged around her, she clung to him in terror. He did not hear her terror, only her excitement, and this urged him on, he plunged her and tossed her, ravishing her like Neptune. Finally, she bit him hard on the shoulder and he let her go — he threw her aside. "What the fuck, Rosie?"

"I can't swim, I can't swim." Her voice at a strange high pitch.

His face contorted, he took a step back. "Everyone can swim."

"I'm sorry —"

He rubbed the teeth marks on his shoulder.

She was shaking. He watched her, repelled by her. She turned and ran up the stairs, she shut the bathroom door behind her. Of course she could swim, she could swim, just not very well. She'd bitten him! He would send her back, he would send her back like a dog from the pound. Rosie put the toilet lid down, sat. Her teeth chattered as if she was cold. Bennett had turned on music — Dire Straits. She heard the screen door as he moved out onto the deck to drink another beer. *Money for nothing and your kicks for free.* What was wrong with her? She was demented, faulty. She must go back to Gran of her own accord, she would take a bus, she would walk the streets, the lefts and rights until she was there, she would bow her head and knock on the door.

Gran waited therein, with her crossword and her one glass of sherry. Oh, she'd always been waiting, she'd always known Rosie would come back, unwanted by the outer world.

Bennett knocked on the bathroom door. "What's going on, Rosie?"

She leaned against the door, her hand encircling the handle.

"Open the door."

Gran wouldn't even look up, Rosie would walk past her and up the stairs. Not her bedroom on the right. But the one at the end of the hall. The lodger's room.

"Rosie?" Bennett persisted. He knocked louder.

Now she back-tracked to the toilet, sat down again. The tone of his voice was becoming angry, he was battering the door with the flat of his hands, "Rosie! Goddamn it, Rosie, open the fucking door."

Briefly, she regarded the window, but it was too small and dropped 20 feet. So she sat and watched the door as it thumped, rattled.

Minutes like ants, marching on tiny tiny feet.

The clock downstairs was ticking and Rosie was half-remembering the white gloves, the feeling came upon her now like a pressing weight on her ribs, the half-remembering wasn't forgetting but more like the lurking, squatting of some dark, living toady thing, and the long hallway in Gran's house and the man at the end of it.

The framing around the door began to tear from the wall and then the door itself flew open. Bennett hurtled in, screaming, "What is wrong with you, what the fuck is wrong with you?" And she waited for him to seize her, she shut her eyes, and it was silent and blank, his hands would fall on her, he wore the gloves because she was dirty, she had no fear at all, only the pause the —

Sunday light — Sparrow song outside, the clock downstairs, *Do you like it when I do this.*

Gran always went out, her handbag over her forearm.

And he grabbed her and lifted her and she was lightest bones, and the white gloves and he was saying *Rosie-Rosie-Rosie* and then at last, *at last*, she understood *Bennett*.

Bennett was sobbing. "I thought you were dead I thought you were killing yourself."

His body covered hers, arced over her, her face buried in the meaty part of his shoulder so she returned to the smell of his skin, his deodorant, the sea salt. "Thank God, thank God, thank God." His face was tears, wet with snot-slime, he now held her face in his big hands. "My mother, my mother," he wept, "killed herself, cut her wrists in the bathroom and I thought I thought —"

"Oh," Rosie whispered, she stroked his big head, her fingers in his thick hair. "Oh."

On his knees, his head falling to her lap, his arms around her thighs: "I found her, I found her, Rosie, Rosie, don't ever do that don't ever do that again —"

"No, no," she murmured, soothing. "Never, never, I love you, I love you." Rosie pictured the small boy and his mother's lily hands out-stretched on the bathroom floor, her life unfurling, unspooling, and he'd tried to gather up the satin red ribbons of her blood.

Rosie wanted to tell him that she understood, she understood about the bewilderment that followed and the loneliness. But instead she held her man, her lover, kissed him and soothed him, and in this moment she loved him with a red, swelling heart, the feeling was almost violent in its force, and the love was woven through with the desire to protect him and the idea that she knew him, maybe not in every way, but deep down in the shadowy well of the man. He had chosen to share with her this secret — to open his hands to her like a child showing a small injured animal that must be placed carefully in a box with water and food and bedding. Rosie loved him, and the love and the desire to protect him made her feel like a grown-up woman.

"You must never leave me, my girl," Bennett was whispering. "I need you to promise that you will never leave me."

"I promise, oh, yes, I promise, I promise."

He pulled her onto his lap, his sobs transforming to kisses, and she moved her hips to take him inside her as he'd taught her, as she wanted.

*   *   *

"We are going to lunch," Bennett announced. "At the club."

"But we aren't members." Rosie worried about Chip.

"My club has an agreement."

What club? Where? An elegant building with white rocking chairs aligned on a broad porch that overlooked a lake. A lake with trout. A private lake. Or the sea, the harbor, where his family kept their boat. Bennett pulled on his seersucker jacket, then carefully selected a tie — a garish yellow with little embroidered ducks. Rosie felt she should understand the tie, it was a message but she lacked the cypher. He handed her a brown paper bag. "Here, wear this."

Inside was a Perry Ellis chambray cotton dress, expensive and not something she'd wear in a million years. She wondered why he had this dress and where he'd gotten it, new but without the tags. It flattered her.

"Shoes." Another bag: white Ralph Lauren espadrilles with low wedge heels. The left one fit perfectly, the right squeezed her toes.

Finally, he dug into his pocket and pulled out a gold locket on a narrow chain. The locket was decorated with delicate filigree. "I'll need this back, though," he said as he fastened the clasp.

The BMW squealed as they turned off the road onto the club's drive, and kept squealing until Bennett parked. He opened her door, attentively took her elbow. They entered the cool gloom of the clubhouse. It was surprisingly shabby, the brown carpet scuffed and the woodwork over-layered with gobby paint. There was a smell of cooking grease — French fries and hamburgers, like a seaside food shack. Through the dingy entry hall, Rosie could see the dining room: tables with white cloths clustered under a low ceiling. The walls at first appeared to be covered in mold, but this turned out to be wallpaper decorated with a sea-weed design. Lights with tiny red shades — the size and shape of the hats that pet monkeys often wore in old-fashioned children's books — jutted out from the weedy walls.

Chip stepped forward, menus under his arm. He smiled like a ventriloquist's dummy, glanced at Rosie. He recognized the trash he'd swept off the beach. "Mr. Kinney, how are you?"

Bennett patted him on the shoulder, "Great, Chip, great. And you?"

"Which guest are you meeting here today, Mr. Kinney?"

"Just me and my girl. We suddenly got a hankering for sub-standard food."

The smile ironed itself out so that it became just lips and

teeth: "You're not a member, Mr. Kinney. You're aware of our policy."

Rosie felt herself wince. But Bennett held onto her with one hand and with the other deftly pulled the menus from Chip, stepped forward, "The table over here, you said? By the window? Number 10? Doesn't Barky Decatur usually sit here? Oh, that's right, he's got cancer of the balls. He won't mind then. Super, thanks, Chip."

A few of the docile guests glanced up from their soup. Spooning it, Rosie noticed, away and not toward. With soup spoons. They smiled vaguely at Bennett, an old hand rose in a wave. The men wore bright ties sporting black Labradors or tiny anchors. Bennett cut a swathe through the tables, Chip followed, "Mr. Kinney, Mis-ter Kinney."

Bennett was so tall he was merely inches below the ceiling. He pulled a chair out and Rosie sat down in it. Then he sat himself. "What are the specials, Chip, old boy? That runny canned pea soup with lumps of old pig gristle in it, hmmm?"

"You can't do this," Chip whispered. Was he going to get the police?

"I'll have a Heineken, please, very cold, and my girl will have a greyhound. Use the Stoli, not the moonshine Willie gets on discount from the Ukrainian in Bridgeport." With a flourish, Bennett put the starched red napkin on his lap, and waited.

"Mr. Kinney, as you know there is no cash payment here. Only chit. You are not a member, you do not have a chit."

"Put it on your chit, then, Chip. Chip's chit. Now go away and bring us back the drinks."

"Nice necklace," Chip noted to Rosie as he swept past. "Looks just like my mother's."

"Everything is disgusting here," Bennett said. "Stick with the club sandwich."

Resigned, bearing the drinks, Chip returned. Bennett ordered two of the clubs.

"*This* time." Chip snatched the menus.

"Whenever I fucking want, Chip. And whenever my girl here wants." Briefly Bennett watched Chip attempt a nonchalant strut away. "Mincy little douchebag. Brought me his mother's jewelry and her collection of vintage Hermès scarves to sell. She's not even dead yet but he's got a bad drug habit." Bennett put one finger to a nostril and sniffed hard.

*   *   *

Paper boxes, paper bags, suitcases came and went from the boathouse, items shrouded in tissue paper, in velvet draw-string bags, in leather boxes embossed with faded initials. Bennett was storing them, safe-keeping them, appraising, he was away for a night or two, an auction in Chesapeake, old family friends in Ardsley. "These people really only trust one of their own," he'd explain. He showed her Chip's mother's stash of Hermès scarves. Rosie didn't like the designs that were mainly horse bridles in bright colors. But the silk was glossy, slippery, thick. Bennett took a scarf in each hand and began waving them about. "Semaphores," he grinned. "How Buffy and Winky communicate across a crowded room." One scarf in his left hand moved up and down, he assumed a high, posh voice, "Just been to Paris, Buffy, old girl, got a new one!" His other hand moved in frantic circles, accompanying a different voice, "And while you were there, Winky dear, I fucked your hubby and he gave me this one!"

Rosie laughed, and he kissed her. "My girl," he said. "My Rosie Monroe."

*　　*　　*

She had drawn a pair of white gloves.

She stared at the sketches, the only thing she'd drawn in two entire months.

The gloves were beautifully rendered, the soft texture of the white fabric. The prominent ridge of knuckles beneath, the width and bulk of the hands were distinctly masculine.

She had really tried not to think of him.

She remembered-forgot. There wasn't a word.

Sometimes, an image of him, or just a feeling of him might shout or flash, in the way of loud music in a passing car. In the next moment, she couldn't be sure. It wasn't forgetting, like someone's birthday, but slipperier.

The lawnmower stopped. Had been stopped for some time, she realized. For the sun had shifted around the boathouse so that its shadow cast outward upon the green shallow afternoon sea. More accurately, it was 6:25. Standing, Rosie realized how her hips and lower back had tightened from the long sojourn in her chair. The table was covered with dozens of sketches of gloves. She had no recollection of drawing so many or the way they articulated his fingers curling and extending. They moved, like a Boccioni, with a relentless momentum. She felt a little insane, or as she imagined insanity to be: a confusion between the selves, as a child resolutely denying knowledge of a broken cup while holding the pieces. Looking at the drawings, she wondered if this is the way memory works, not as film that replays in perfect replication — but in shards or swatches and these are embedded in a dark, frantic scribble of somatic feeling. As if the purpose of memory is to inhibit the act of remembering. Her brain seemed to refuse to disinter the event in its entirety. It wasn't doubt; she didn't disbelieve herself. She knew he had been a lodger in the room at the end of the hall and she had called him The Giggle Man. And when Gran had gone out, her bag upon her arm, Rosie walked down the hall and into his room. He pulled on his white gloves. The clock, the light through the trees, and the way, when he was done, she felt sad and —

Helpful.

*   *   *

Ida Shultz studied the drawings. She looked like Gertrude Stein, or how Rosie imagined Gertrude Stein. Cubist, dressed in brown.

"Zay are good," Ida growled in her smoker's voice, her heavy European accent. Rosie had heard she'd survived the Holocaust. "Togezzer, a strange und powerful ani-mation."

Rosie did not smile, though she was happy; she kept her expression serious. Ida had agreed to meet with her in the city, having given all her students her number in case they needed her advice over the summer.

"You are accessing zee interior." Ida was regarding her with the dark, unblinking eyes of a curious bird. "Vat are zay?"

"Gloves," Rosie said.

Ida smiled, because that much was obvious. "Vat I feel ven I see zis work, it iz not casual. It iz not a *bagatelle*."

If there was anyone to tell, it must be Ida. Her corporeal solidity suggested unlimited absorbency; Rosie's secret would enter into the brown pleats of her smock, Ida would keep it safe.

"The Giggle Man," Rosie mumbled and the mere sound of

his name summoned him and he opened the door and pulled on his white gloves.

"Zee gig—?" Ida leaned forward. "Forgiff me, I haf terrible hearing."

She had gone willingly up the stairs, along the hall, she hadn't run away, she hadn't screamed or cried, she had sat on the bed.

Ida was looking at the drawings again. "Drrread. Zat is vat I feel. Vill you tell me zee story?"

"There's no story," Rosie said.

"Just gloffs?"

"Just gloves."

Ida shifted on her chair, making it creak. She shrugged and made a "Hmmmph." She was drinking black coffee with four spoons of sugar. They were in a dingy coffee shop on Varick, just around the corner from Ida's studio. The studio was really where Rosie had hoped to meet, but the coffee shop was its own reward. Men slopped in smelling of blood from their meatpacking jobs. Ida smelled of paint and turpentine. The coffee shop smelled of coffee and onions. It was fantastic. What if you could draw a smell? Rosie wondered. She knew she was destined to live here one day, to become a regular in this very spot. "Hey Joe, Hi Mack." Just like Ida. "How's it goin', Ida?" She painted their lives in the warehouses, vast, dripping canvases, the ribs and backs and skulls of butchered animals.

Sliding the sketches back into Rosie's portfolio, Ida ordered the bill, refusing Rosie's offer of payment — the grubby dollar bills she'd fossicked from Bennett's laundry — and then folded her huge hands. They were slabs of flesh. Suddenly, the left sleeve of her shirt inched up and Rosie glimpsed a set of tattooed numbers on her wrist. Ida Shultz quickly pulled her sleeve down. There was a moment of church-like silence when Rosie could hear the sounds of the kitchen, clacking plates and voices. Then Ida said: "Rozee, zese are personal. Zis is vere you must start und leaf quickly. How can you transform zis — zis fear, zis mal-ignunce — into art? Rozee, art is not about vat you feel but vat you share. Wizzout connection to a greater experi-unce, art iz pusillanimous. It's a diarree for leetle girls." She patted Rosie's hand. "I look forward very much to vorking wiz you in zee autumn, yes, yes."

Back at the boathouse, Rosie had to look up the word *pusillanimous*. Cowardly.

They were walking up the garden to the main house. Hobie and Mitzi were back from their trip to Lake Como (not Comma, as she'd thought, a huge blue lake appealingly shaped like a comma), they were having *drinks* and at last Rosie would meet them. The house was alight in the evening, the doors open so the sound of laughter and conversation fluttered merrily upon the air. The gardens around them exploded with fat peonies and roses, the tidy beds were dense with frothy flowers, daringly color coordinated, and winnowy plants Rosie thought might be foxgloves. Wisteria draped itself along the *veranda* — not patio — and drooped over the arbor. So much effort had been put into the garden to make it appear casually robust.

"How did they make their money?" Rosie wanted to know.

"Make it? Oh, no, no, no. Nothing so *gauche*. Money is inherited, carefully channeled through the DNA, like a sixth finger. Though, it's true, Mitzi owns half of Phoenix. She bought land when she first went to rehab in the '70s and now it's worth a fortune."

Even though the house had been in her view every day for the past month, Rosie hadn't seen it up close. It had seemed unreal, a movie set looming at the top of the garden, four stories up and at least 1,000 feet wide, layered out and up. As they closed in, she noticed the fine brickwork and the meticulously painted shutters. Nothing was cracked or peeling or chipped. She thought of Gran's moldy house. The mold still clung to her, the rust, the rot, the damp.

"Do I look OK?"

"You're lovely."

But the right espadrille was still too small and the heat made her hair frizzy. Her Perry Ellis dress bunched under the armpits.

"Then what do they do then?"

"Do?" Bennett laughed his secret-joke laugh, only he knew where he'd put the whoopee cushion. "They dabble. They travel to their properties. They lunch, they dine. The Algonquin. The New York Yacht Club. They sit on boards. They found foundations, they are on the committees of charities. They have other people take care of their money — bankers, accountants. They have other people cook their food, buy their art, and eventually, wipe their assholes. The very wealthy are, essentially, decorative." He seemed pleased with this assessment, for he chuckled lightly and then squeezed her hand, giving her confidence. "They may dress well and have nice hair, but they are dull and they are cheap and some are even stupid. Don't be intimidated, my girl."

A dozen guests mingled on the veranda, sparkling and murmuring. Rosie could see they were perfectly coiffed.

Bennett steered her up the steps, leaned in, "Just remember, polo never refers to water."

"Hello!!" A male voice came through the crowd. Rosie looked to see a trim, silver-haired man in his mid-fifties, hailing them. He had a glass in one hand.

"He's wearing a scarf," Rosie whispered.

"That is a cravat," Bennett corrected.

Hobie shook Bennett's hand, eye-to-eye, bass-toned greetings mumbled, then he took her hand and when she made an odd bobbing curtsey, he smiled as if he knew exactly how foolish she felt and forgave her. He looped his arm through hers. "Come, Rosie, and let me get you a drink."

He led her inside, where everything was beautiful, exquisite, there was even a bar with a barman in a white tuxedo and maids in black uniforms with silver trays serving *drinks*. Rosie took the glass of champagne as Hobie and Bennett drifted away from her, talking about boats and racing, the time Bennett crewed with the America's Cup, and Rosie recalled that boats meant yachts, though you never used the word *yacht*, but ketch or boat or skiff or yawl, just as polo was for ponies, and the ponies decamped to Boca in the winter. Rosie kept moving with her glass of champagne, slipping like a silvery, silent eel between conversations so that no one noticed her.

In New York, she had often wondered what the apartments along Fifth Avenue and Central Park West looked like inside, and if Bennett's family lived in one with their Picasso above the dining table. Because he had not, of course, stayed with her in the dorm at Parsons. He had moved, even then, mysteriously beyond her purview, in an adult world she had not yet entered. Sometimes, she felt that Bennett was in an elaborate play, there was the stage, and there was off-stage, but she didn't know which one she inhabited.

Rosie gazed at the velvet sofa in bright bottle green against a citron wall, plush cushions with pink silk fringe and orange tassels. Oil paintings. She recognized some of the Hudson River school, and, incredibly, a Miró above an elegant antique desk. Persian rugs on polished cherry-wood floors, looming vases of cut flowers, heavy drapes in peacock blue. She loved the confident riot of colors, she could not imagine being so bold.

"Yoohoo!!!" The high trill belonged to a tall, brittle blond in a black dress, waving, the many rings on her fingers glittering. "There you are!" Rosie watched as this woman threw her charred arms around Bennett. Her lips were bright peach. "You are adorable! Thank you for coming! Oh, you do look like your mater!"

Her appearance was entirely constructed. Her movements jerky and imprecise. She was a kind of puppet, and inside there was another woman, perhaps a tiny, quick brunette, busily working the gears and levers.

"Mitzi, darling, you look spectacular!" Bennett kissed her taut cheek.

"And you are Posie!" Mitzi pivoted to Rosie, who imagined she could hear the mechanical whirring and clacking.

"Rosie."

"Of course, *Rozzzeeee*. Is that Rosemary? Rosalind? You prefer *Rozzzeee*. How sweet! Welcome. How is everything at the boathouse? We're so glad you're staying there. We do like to have it used. No point in leaving such a divine little place to rot." Mitzi smiled, the little woman inside her frantically pulling and pushing the levers, locking them into the smile position. "Do you need another drink?" A twiglet arm extended into the air with a clatter of gold, diamonds refracting like a disco ball. "Selena! *Selena*!" As Selena abruptly turned and approached, Rosie noted the little white cap she wore to match the white frilly apron over the black uniform. "Posie needs another glass."

"No, I —" Because the first glass was fizzing the cauldron of her stomach.

"Or would you prefer something else?" Mitzi began to speed

up, something was wrong inside her. "We have a full bar bourbon Scotch gin and of course wine *very* nice Napa Chardonnay *surprising* what is coming out of California these days though my father would roll over in his grave he was with the 82nd Airborne and would only ever drink French wine absolutely banned Riesling bloody Krauts he'd say though didn't think much of the French either they fight with their feet and fuck with their face he'd say so no Riesling even with pudding and brandy if that's your thing vodka —"

Rosie looked to Selena but Selena's expression remained blank.

"Ouzo Grappa a fruity Beaujolais —"

"Water," Rosie blurted.

"Water, Selena."

Selena turned on a dime like a soldier, and Mitzi's crazed eyes locked on to Rosie. "Water? You're not pregnant, are you? Good God! Bennett as a father!" She laughed in a short, hard spurt, then her gaze shifted abruptly. "Do excuse me." Her hand briefly perched on Rosie's shoulder, and she marched into the crowd, performing again and again a flawless turn, pivot, twist while chiming "Yoohoo!!" like a faulty doorbell.

In the quiet eddy of Mitzi's wake, Rosie caught her breath. Then she turned, surveyed the room. She did not see Bennett and noted the hallway to the left. Escape, she thought, and eased through the crowd. Here, the decorator had picked up the peacock blue on the walls in a vibrant wallpaper print, contrasting with a bottle-green carpet. The carpet was so plush that Rosie took off her shoes to feel it against her feet and to relieve the squeeze of her right big toe. Hunting prints lined the hallway — caricature horses with spindly legs, arched necks and bulging shoulders leapt over ditches or pranced against a screen of autumnal woods. Midway along, a table with delicately turned legs displayed a cluster of photographs in silver frames. Rosie scoured the images: attractive people in white Victorian ruffles with tennis rackets; in riding clothes with hounds; a debutante's ball — a pretty girl with a chin like Hobie's; sailing (was that a Kennedy at the helm? Certainly the teeth); a couple on a tropical beach (was that Princess Margaret?). Gran had managed to stick Rosie's school portraits onto the fridge with free magnets from an insurance company. Her father and grandfather, Jim and Jim, looked down from plain black frames in the hallway. And her mother, her mother? "You're her spitting image," Gran had declared. "I hope you will be more sensible." Rosie'd looked in the mirror, trying to see her insensible mother, for there was no photographic record, and sometimes Rosie felt Gran wanted to wipe her away as well. Then there'd be no trace at all.

The hallway smelled of lemon and silver polish, of the freesias in the vase by the photographs, of Mitzi's perfume, and, she thought, of shoe polish. She dug her feet into the carpet and felt the real wool, thick and soft: *plush.* Could she recall one plush thing from Gran's house? One of the lodgers had been a woman with a satin wash bag. Rosie could even now recall the wonder of it in the second-floor bathroom, the pale blue glimmering fabric, a tuft of lace and sequin on the front, and inside, pots of fragrant cream and make-up. Rosie had licked the satin as if she might assuage the hunger it made her feel — the coveting. The blue washbag mocked the rough towels, the tacky linoleum, the polyester sheets that snagged on the tiniest hangnail. Yet Rosie had feared for the woman. No good would come to someone with such an indulgent washbag. Fate would see it, glowing like a flare, and stamp her out.

"Are you looking for the double u c?"

Hobie, drink in hand, the ice gently clinking.

"Yes," Rosie waivered. "No."

"Usually, one's not ambivalent about such things." He smiled. She was suddenly aware of how clean he was. He was white linen on a breezy day. Maybe money made you cleaner than other people. His hand rested on the pretty wooden table — nails, neatly trimmed, the cuticles obedient.

"I don't know —" Her words wandered away, dandelion seeds in the breeze.

He smiled, kind, and what lovely teeth. "What a double u c is?"

Instead of a nod, she pressed her lips together.

"Ah." Another smile. "W dot C dot. W.C. Water Closet. Toilet, bathroom, john. Loo if you're from across the pond."

Rosie could lie, that would be easiest, but then she would have to go to the bathroom, and she'd have to come back from it and he'd expect her to re-enter the party. "No. I don't need the *W.C.*"

Hobie leaned in, a co-conspirator, "I hate parties, too."

"Your house is so beautiful."

"Mitzi is a genius."

"I love the wallpaper."

"Ah, the wallpaper." He chuckled privately. "And you're at college?"

"Parsons School of Design."

"An artist. I say! Are you any good?"

As she faced him, she wondered if he was attracted to her. "I'm not sure."

"Are you working on anything this summer? Painting the sea?"

Rosie flushed, lowered her gaze. Her body reacted to him — she wanted to curtsey again. "Not the sea. Gloves."

"Globes?"

"Gloves. A pair of gloves."

"What kind of gloves?"

"White gloves," she said.

"Interesting!" He gave a short laugh. "We used to have to wear those to dancing school. The waltz, the cha cha cha. Had to escort the debutantes, you see. I used to wonder about the gloves. Were they to keep me clean or the girl? I rather think, as a sweaty boy, it was the latter."

Rosie hadn't thought of this, she hadn't wondered at all why The Giggle Man wore the gloves. Now, she considered the purpose, and the purposefulness. Gloves were a barrier. And why white? Not rubber gloves, washing-up gloves, winter wool or even the kind doctors wore. She said: "I think the gloves were like masks for the hands so his hands weren't his hands."

"Hand masks?"

"The gloves create an objectivity."

"I never thought of that." Hobie now thought. "It's a way of creating the impersonal while doing something as intimate as dancing. You are clever."

Rosie pressed her lips together, she didn't want to smile. Hobie put his hand lightly on her arm, a moment only; then he released her. "Let me show you something."

He led her down the hall, turned right into a large drawing room. This was not a room for drawing, she knew, but for *withdrawing* from the dining room after dining. The walls and ceiling were crimson, huge windows overlooked the gardens to the sun-dimming sea beyond. The overstuffed sofas were pale blue satin with maroon trim — a daring contrast to the walls. What must it be like to walk in these rooms with a sense of complete possession? *Mine.* Everything was perfect, beautiful, tasteful. Here, too, were fresh flowers — tumbling roses among a twisting dark creeper and a wild ruff of Queen Anne's lace.

"What do you think?" Hobie was saying, standing in front of a small painting hung discreetly on a side wall. "I just got it last week."

Rosie stepped closer, and Hobie stepped aside. "That's not —"

"Yes. It is."

The low, bland light of a Dutch winter, the claustrophobia of a life lived primarily indoors — how the black and white tile flooring and wood paneling narrowed that interior space so it pressed upon the thin, upright couple who stood deep within the framework. The husband seemed bored — something about the focus of his eyes, as if he was looking beyond the artist who'd been working in the foreground. But his young wife, much younger — pale, almond-eyed — stared boldly and immediately at the viewer, as if in challenge. The artist had chosen to maximize the interior, possibly to show the couple's wealth through the quality of the woodwork and flooring. Yet, the effect was a subtle sense of imprisonment. Just glimpsed in the background, a maid stood by an open door. In the sunlit outer world, she held a dead hare by the ears.

"You have this in your house." Rosie was breathless.

"Would you like to touch it?"

"No!"

"I'm giving you permission."

"I can't!"

"Go on!"

Rosie lifted her hand, her fingers lightly caressed the paint.

"Mitzi doesn't understand." Hobie had put even more distance between them. "We had a terrible row about where to hang it. She says it ruins the pink."

"I can see her point."

"Really?"

"I mean, this is the wrong room for it."

He tilted his head to one side, waiting for her to continue. She felt a rush: this incredibly rich man was listening to her.

"You never come in here. Or you come in here only to see the painting. And that's not enough. Look at the girl." Hobie looked. "She wants you to look at her. Maybe vanity. She's proud."

Hobie nodded.

"But she doesn't see the house is a kind of prison for them."

Hobie looked closer.

"See how he's contracted the space, used lines to create a kind of claustrophobia."

"There you are!"

Rosie and Hobie were standing several feet apart. They had never touched, only his hand briefly on her arm in the hallway. There was nothing to hide. Mitzi glanced down at Rosie's bare feet and smiled — slowly; as the wires seemed to catch on the little levers behind her face, so that the smile stopped then started, stopped then started, requiring effort to have it achieve full height. "Bennett's looking for you, Rosalee."

*   *   *

For their first date, two weeks after meeting at MoMA, Bennett had taken Rosie to The Stanhope Hotel on Fifth Avenue for tea. The maître-d' led them across the room to a table in the corner. The room was unexceptional, pea-green wallpaper and fusty furnishings, and the patrons were mostly old ladies. Two of them knew Bennett, and he stopped to fuss over them and they kept touching him, one of them murmuring something about poor, sick Pookie. The woman spoke in indulgent sing-song, "Poor widdle Pookie-wookie." Bennett was very sorry to hear about Pookie, he had kissed her hand.

The maître-d' had pulled Rosie's chair out and she didn't know why, she thought she'd dropped something, so she looked down.

"Rosie," Bennett had whispered. "Just sit."

Expertly, the man put the chair under her ass and she gave a little laugh. A waiter was already there, and even as he held out the tombstone-sized menus, Bennett told him, "The usual, please."

"What's wrong with Pookie?" Rosie asked in a low voice.

"Lung cancer."

Rosie had said, "I didn't know dogs could get lung cancer."

Bennett's eyes had sparkled, his mouth stilled a smile. "Pookie is her husband. Smoked three packs a day."

The tea came. Not the tea Rosie had ever seen — a Lipton teabag in a mug — but in a china pot with china cups, saucers, side plates, silver spoons, tiny silver forks and tiny round knives like dolls' cutlery. A jug for milk. A silver dish for the butter, beading with cold. A tiered tray of pastel-colored cakes and scones. Bennett poured the tea, which curled out of the pot and into her cup with a smoky aroma.

"Lapsang souchong," he'd told her. "Have it with the tiniest dash of milk."

As well as the table, he had reserved a room with a view of the park, and after tea he took her there, which was presumptuous and also thrilling. He took off his clothes while she sat on the bed, remembering to keep her shoulders back. Bennett had the bulky body of a man, he was tanned even though it was midwinter, and when he moved to stand in front of her she traced the line of white around his waist with her finger.

"Use your tongue," he said.

Afterward, when he saw the dab of bright red blood on the white sheet, he touched her face, "I had no idea you were a virgin."

Virgin had sounded odd, old-fashioned, Mary in her blue robes, clean and pure.

"Hey." Bennett had kissed her. "Don't cry." He had held her, cloaked in his body.

*   *   *

"Rosie? Hello. It's Hobie."

She scrambled out of bed, almost dropping the phone.

"The gent who lives in the big house up the hill," he prompted.

"Of course, *Hobie*." Did he really think she'd forgotten him?

"I keep thinking about what you said, about the painting. And you're right, it needs to be elsewhere. Are you free at all this morning? Could you come and help me hang it?"

Clearly, there were professional people — tradesmen — to whom Hobie might turn, if he could not wield a hammer and nail himself. What did he want? She recalled his caution when they'd been alone together. Maybe he genuinely wanted her opinion? He even liked her, as a person, found her interesting? He'd actually said *Interesting*. He actually said *You are clever*.

"That would be lovely," she said, because she knew her art, didn't she, she had instinct, and he was going to recommend her for a job at a gallery, a museum, Sotheby's. Maybe he would even ask to see her art, and he'd become a benefactor, a patron, not necessarily a lover, or perhaps a lover in a sophisticated way, he'd appreciate the arterial quality emerging in her work, and there'd be a year in Paris, an attic studio in Montparnasse where the artists lived, or a light-filled loft near Ida Shultz.

Rosie stood in front of the mirror. Her belly was only slightly convex. Still, she felt a heaviness in her pelvis, like a bad period, and her waist had thickened. She went through her clothes, she didn't have many, she couldn't afford them on her student's stipend and was not one of those women who instinctively understood clothes, who threw this on with that and looked chic, iconic. Sometimes, she caught her reflection in the mirror or a shop window and was crushed by how disordered she appeared. She was slim and long-limbed, but clothes did not flatter her. Even Bennett said she looked better naked.

Blue leggings, she decided at last, Bennett's blue Brooks Brothers shirt with the French cuffs over a white tank top. The Ralph Lauren espadrilles. Even though one was too small, she had only sneakers otherwise. Hair up in a clip, trace of mascara, no other make-up. She studied herself in the mirror, then pulled a tendril of her hair loose. If someone reached up and undid the sliver clip, such hair would tumble down, cascade into their hands.

Ascending along the line of cedar trees that bordered the gravel track from the boathouse, Rosie then cut through to the gardens that spilled over lawns and terraces. In the hazy summer morning light, these were voluptuous, impressionistic — subtle constraint countered wild abandon. The profusion of flowers and greenery obeyed the unseen gardener who tamed them gently — one of those cowboys who whispered to their horses instead of beating them into submission. She could just make him out, by the shed, fixing one of the mowers.

The veranda door was open, Hobie standing in the door, framed by purple wisteria. "Thank you for coming, Rosie."

"I wouldn't miss the opportunity to see that painting again."

"And the older gentleman who owns it?"

Her armpits prickled, she was suddenly wary. But also flattered. "Is he here?" She gazed around enquiringly. "Can I meet him?"

Hobie laughed. They moved inside. Somewhere, there was the sound of a vacuum cleaner — Rosie doubted Mitzi was at the helm. They reached the main reception area as Selena appeared in her maid's costume.

"Selena, dear, could you bring us coffee in my study?"

Hobie's study was on the lower level. In a normal house, this would be the basement. But here it was a kind of Bat Cave replete with pool table, card table, dart board. Nothing so trashy as a wet bar, but a hand-carved, antique mahogany bar along one wall and sofas and chairs covered in a masculine dark hunter-green plaid. The same green covered the ceiling and walls above darkly stained wood paneling, but with the light from the ocean and sky, the room avoided being gloomy. Folders and papers smothered the surface of Hobie's vast teak desk. No doubt from his bankers, his board members. Books spilled out of the book shelves, stood in piles on the floor.

He swept his hand out. "What do you think?"

She bit her lip. "The light isn't good in here, though."

They went back upstairs — almost colliding with Selena and the coffee. "We'll have it in the drawing room instead," Hobie told her.

"I can take it," Rosie made an attempt on the tray.

Selena's eyes widened and she tightened her grip. "Miss, no —"

"Really, I can —"

There was an awkward tug-of-war. Hobie touched Rosie's waist, "Selena can carry the tray."

Triumphant, Selena led the way. She settled the gleaming silver tray on the coffee table and fluffed a few of the cushions before exiting.

"Don't mess with Selena," Hobie mock-whispered.

"I just wanted to help."

"She is the help."

"Right."

"We pay her well. Don't feel guilty." He poured the coffee. Even the cups were exquisite — green and gold dragons frolicked on a pale orange background. There was a side plate of delicate ginger biscuits. Homemade. The silver tray was covered with a starched white cloth. How did it get so white, so clean, Rosie wondered.

"You're very wealthy," she said.

"I am."

"What's it like?"

"What do you mean?"

"You can have anything you want."

"Not true."

She waited for him to glance at her and say, *I can't have you.* Instead he said: "People like me can buy anything without thinking about what we might really want. Let alone need. And then we just end up feeling deeply unsatisfied but with lots of stuff."

"Why did you buy the painting?"

"I didn't know. I was just drawn to it. And then you said what you did about the couple being imprisoned, and I understood my attraction."

"Are you imprisoned?"

Hobie regarded her. "I can't tell if you're fearless or naïve. I suppose, being young, you are both."

"I'm sorry."

"For what?"

"I have bad manners."

"Did Bennett tell you that?"

"My grandmother."

"I'm suspicious of manners," Hobie went on. "Especially good ones."

"But you have good manners."

"Exactly."

Without warning nausea welled up Rosie's throat, and she stood, needing immediate escape. She banged the tray with her knee and the coffee clattered and spilled. "I'm so sorry —" The coffee was dripping from her onto the plush cream carpet. She pulled off Bennett's shirt.

"No, leave it —"

But she kept dabbing at the coffee with the hem of the shirt, apologizing, "Sorry, sorry, sorry, oh —"

"Selena will —"

At last he grabbed her hand. "Leave it!"

Was he going to kiss her? Were they about to become lovers?

But he let her go. Abruptly, he said: "What do you know about Bennett?"

Rosie felt the wet dark stain of the coffee on her thigh. Having charted this course, Hobie was bound to continue, and Rosie sensed this was why he'd brought her here and not because of the painting at all, not because of the job at Sotheby's.

Hobie sighed as he spoke, "He's troubled, you know."

What did that mean? *Troubled.* Like a boy who hurts cats.

"We help him. Well, Mitzi, really. It's her sense of loyalty. She's very loyal."

The coffee stain seemed to come from inside Rosie, as if she was leaking this dark fluid, staining the sofa. What would Mitzi say when she saw the mess?

"But there's only so much we can do."

Rosie thought of Bennett with his head in her lap, weeping about his dead mother. She loved him, and she wanted to heal him.

Hobie was speaking, she tried to listen. After all, he'd invited her here so that he could speak to her, at her. So that he could say things like: "I don't know who you think he is, though I can see he might be attractive to someone like you." And: "The family has cut him off. Though it would be indiscreet of me to say more." And: "Please take this in the spirit of my concern, you're very young, very inexperienced. You should ask yourself why he isn't married and why he isn't married to someone of his own age and background, or at least dating —"

"I'm pregnant," she said because it was the only thing she had in her head to make him stop.

Hobie was quiet for a moment, considering. His voice was surprisingly gentle. "Do you want to be?"

"I don't know."

"Have you told him?"

She shook her head, bewildered, suddenly, as to why she'd confessed to this man.

Hobie said: "Go back to school, Rosie. Figure yourself out. You'll have other chances with a far better man."

She heard herself sob, and then sniffle.

They sat for a moment. At last, he picked up the thread. "I just wanted to warn you."

"Warn me?"

"He's just —" Hobie searched the ceiling. But within the filigree plaster was neither the word nor a speck of dust.

"I love him."

"You love him. Oh dear. You're like a peasant girl in a 19th century novel. He's a rake. He'll ruin you."

"Isn't he your friend?"

"Mitzi and his mother were great pals at Groton, you see."

She did not see. What was Groton? Groton, fish forks, shoe horns. Hunters. Hunters were a type of horse that you rode with hounds. Shooting was not hunting even though you shot animals, birds and killed them. Hunting was something rich Texans who owned car dealerships did. Rosie regarded the van Eyck now, the pompous man, the precocious young woman, perhaps younger than her. Fastened into her winter clothing, fastened into her life with all the windows shut, she had not yet realized her predicament. But the artist had: the dead hare in the maid's hands.

"Do you need money?"

"For what?"

"To get rid of the baby."

"And how would that look if I took your money for an abortion?"

"No one is looking."

Hobie was holding his money clip. Because the very wealthy don't have wallets, they have crisp-as-fresh-lettuce cash or accounts or chits.

* * *

Rosie walked from the boathouse toward Southport train station where she could get a taxi. She hoped to assume the casual air of someone out strolling. The road along Sasco Hill was lined with huge maples and high walls. It was poorly paved, rutted with potholes, belying the wealth on either side. The road also cut cleanly between two types of money, for the WASPy wealth occupied the sea-side and the aspirational rich the landside. Their houses were just as large — perhaps larger; but the sea was the premium status: the inherited money, the old money. Here lived the Daughters of the American Revolution, Bennett had explained, the debutantes, the members of the Pequot Yacht Club and the Country Club of Fairfield who knew the difference between Fishers Island and Block Island, Aspen and Vail, Palm Beach and West Palm Beach. On the other side: those who thought a scull was a Halloween decoration.

Cars drove past. Mercedes, BMWs, Jaguars did not stop. She didn't mind, the walking felt surprisingly good, the striding. There were squirrels in the trees, they chided her, and unknown birds. Who might know their names? She could smell the sea and fresh-cut grass, for the wealthy kept their lawns meticulously mown. A trickle of sweat worked its way down her spine as her leg muscles lengthened and contracted. She was even a little out of breath when she came to the bridge that crossed the Mill River. Beyond, the road tilted uphill and inland, past ornate Victorian homes on small, carefully tended plots. This was still pricey real estate, yet Rosie wondered at the panoply of money, the way the rich — and the wealthy — must self-order. Like files in a cabinet. Where did Bennett fit in? He always told her not to worry about money, he seemed not to worry about it himself. Yet his family had *cut him off*.

A tradesman's truck honked twice, whether the honker intended to flatter or to warn her out of the way, she couldn't know. The road went downhill only a short distance to the station. In five minutes she was there, knocking on the window of a cab. The driver didn't want to go to Bridgeport.

"Please," she said.

"You gonna tip?"

He grumbled most of the way there, a diatribe against black people and Puerto Ricans. Rosie knew she should tell him she didn't agree, but she was afraid he'd stop and make her get out.

The clinic was a low-slung building in a neighborhood turning sour. "Can you wait for me?" she asked the driver.

"Sure. But you gotta pay me now."

"I don't know how long I'll be.

"Honey, you know how many times I sit waiting for a fare and they never come back?"

She thrust a hundred at him.

Inside, behind the bullet-proof glass and the bullet-proof steel doors, a dozen women were sitting on hard mustard-colored chairs, focusing on the tattered back copies of *Good Housekeeping* and *Time* as if these contained stories of deep interest. Rosie had thought it would be mostly young women like her who didn't want to mess up their lives with a baby. But there were older women, too; one had a child with her, a boy who incessantly banged his toy car on the floor.

No one looked up, the women seeking invisibility, for even here, among strangers in a similar situation, Rosie felt their weary shame. The fault was theirs — as it was hers: the missed pill, the slippery diaphragm, the sexual abandon. The consequence was absolute, a hard, singular fact in a foamy, relative world. You're either pregnant or not pregnant, Rosie thought as she sat.

Had any of these women been raped? Rosie didn't see any obvious signs, black eyes or bruises. Katya and May went to protests, STOP VIOLENCE AGAINST WIMIN. They'd stuck fliers under her door that said "No, means NO." And in smaller print: "My body, my consent. YES, PLEASE. Otherwise, it's rape, asshole." Was it, though? Wasn't it something else — some other word, like the co-pilot taking over the plane? A kind of duty?

One by one, women were called, meekly following a nurse through a door. Nothing could be heard, though Rosie imagined machines sucking and sucking, vacuuming out women's wombs. She wondered where the contents went, the *waste*. Down the sink? Into a special vat? Ten minutes passed and the boy began driving his car into Rosie's foot. His mother grabbed him roughly by the shoulder. "Quit it, Michael."

"It's OK," Rosie said. Their voices were loud in the quiet room.

The boy didn't quit, he moved the car up her leg.

"Can you imagine bringing a child somewhere like this?" The woman sighed, pulling him back. "It's the only time I can get here."

With dark, solemn eyes, Michael looked up at Rosie and began licking his car, extravagantly rolling the wheels against his tongue. The other women were glancing furtively over their magazines. Suddenly, the woman gathered up her boy and her giant handbag and hurried to the door. The handbag slipped off her shoulder, almost causing her to lose her balance. With one hand on her child and the other hand dragging the bag, she crabbed around the reinforced steel door.

For a moment, Rosie sat. Her turn was coming up. Like the line in Baskin-Robbins on a summer day. Only she was going to get an abortion. An *abortion*. Then she'd go back to New York, she'd finish her degree, she'd learn what it meant to be an artist and it would be the beginning of her true journey, Ida Shultz would be her mentor, she and Ida having coffee, painting together, and this summer would fold up behind her, as others had done, those with Chris, those of her childhood — the still, hot, untended days she'd waited it out in Gran's house. There would be another man, as Hobie had promised, another lover, even *lovers* like weeks or seasons, and one or two in Paris, in Venice, on wide beds with white sheets and rain outside, the smell of gesso and turpentine, a tray of coffee, a bottle of wine.

"Rosemary Monroe," the nurse said.

Rosie stood, she hovered between the seconds, between the skin of time, and then she turned and ran out the door.

Outside, the taxi was nowhere to be seen. Perhaps this was a sign, she wanted a sign, to help her turn back into the clinic, to the art, the lovers in Venice, the marvelous beginning of her life. Then she saw the woman — Michael's mother — shoveling him and her handbag into a rusty Ford Fairmont. The recalcitrant bag caught on the side mirror, disgorging various items onto the pavement — a wand of mascara Rosie knew was a cheap brand, .scraps of papers, keys, a hair brush, a packet of cigarettes, a packet of gum. The woman scrambled to collect them, and now the child was crying, pulling at the seatbelt. Should she offer to help? Yet Rosie refrained, she sensed a despair she couldn't fathom or counter; she wanted to run away from it, appalled, it wasn't what she wanted — which was a wise, calm, know-ing friend, perhaps Ida Shultz and not the way the woman was shouting at the child, "Shut up, shut up! God's sake!" and now the car wouldn't start, the woman kept turning the motor over and over, rurrrrr, rrruuuurrrr, and the abortion she'd decided not to have, or maybe wanted to but now couldn't and there'd be another child to be shouted at or was she just going to get someone to take care of the child and come back? There was a smell to this, the way Gran's washing machine smelled, the stagnant-pond, wet-dog lint that got caught somewhere inside. She'd always thought of it as the damp debris of the lodgers. It had been Rosie's job to wash their sheets once a week.

The woman leaned her head against the steering wheel, the boy screaming behind her, his fury at the injustice of the seat-belt. Rosie saw the mascara on the ground, near the wheel. She ran, picked it up, knocked on the car window. "It's yours," she said.

Perhaps she'd expected crying, the woman's face wet with tears, maybe even relief that she'd decided to keep her baby. Or simply gratitude for Rosie's kindness with the mascara. But the woman merely turned her head, her eyes dry, the whites red-veined, Rosie could see, and the smears of dark beneath them. "What?"

"Your mascara."

The woman's hand came out, took it. Now, they'd be able to share the bittersweet choice they were making. A sense of kin-ship rose in Rosie like dough. This woman would help her, they'd help each other. Rosie could see inside the car, the mess on the floor, on the seats, an odor of sour milk, of rotting apples. Now, they'd go and get a coffee.

"Thanks," the woman said.

"Your car," Rosie noted.

"What about it?"

"Can I help?"

"You a mechanic?"

Obviously not. The child's screaming reaching a pitch, so Rosie had to raise her voice. "I have some money."

"What?"

Louder: "I have some money."

Rosie saw the boy kick the back of his mother's seat, a determined thump-thump, and she turned and slapped his thigh. "Knock it off, Mother of God, I can't take it!"

"Here." Rosie suddenly thrust the rest of Hobie's money at her. The woman looked around, searching for the trick, the joke. "You think I'm selling?"

"I just want you to have it." Rosie smiled.

The woman seemed uncomprehending. Then she gazed at the money with a hungry, animal stare. The notes were clean, green, peeled off a brick of notes, a brick among other bricks in a vast shining vault of money — clean rich-people money, not coins, not wrinkled by time or softened from being left in a pocket in the wash. A moment's hesitation, and then she grabbed it.

"Would you like to get a cup of coffee?" Rosie suggested with a smile.

The woman frowned. "What?"

Rosie realized she couldn't even offer to buy one, she'd just given all the money she had. At that moment, the Fairmont's engine finally caught, it jerked backward, the woman hauled the wheel around, then the vehicle lurched forward, exhaust billowing from the tail pipe, and out of the parking lot with gathering speed, the magnetic pull of a future that did not contain Rosie or her pity or her confusion.

The pity felt remarkably good. Pity made the pitier powerful.

But then Rosie thought: What if she uses the money to buy drugs?

Briefly, Rosie saw herself from an objective perspective, as a passerby might: a girl, alone, in the parking lot of an abortion clinic on a summer morning. She felt bereft for herself, to undertake this sad pilgrimage alone, to err so wildly in her attempt at connection, and now to have found herself without a choice to make, having given all her money away. What had possessed her to pursue a fantasy that coffee with a stranger might help her decide whether to have an abortion? Her thinking was like a scribble by a child: it started at one point then went scribble scribble sribble scratch scratch scribble loopy loop and then stopped. She was penniless, she hadn't had an abortion, and she was a dozen miles from Sasco Hill. What a fool.

She began to walk.

Her right heel blistered. At first, she tried to walk with her toes pressed hard against the toe of the shoe, but this made her shuffle. So she folded down the back of the espadrille, which was better, though now the shoe flip-flopped and would soon be ruined. Few people remarked as she passed through the broken neighborhood. It was like sections of Lowell she'd always avoided, flat and low, boarded up, weedy.

"Where you goin', honey?" A guy yelled. He was drinking beer at this time of day.

"You lost?" An old woman with a shopping bag demanded.

Kiss kiss whistle whistle commented some men on a road crew filling in potholes. She didn't want to smile, but she did, she felt the trap, the thrill of their flattery because she had a vagina and breasts and wasn't 72 years old. She saw pigeons eating an old bit of fried chicken, and considered their cannibalism. They couldn't know what the piece had been as a whole, or even that it was part of a whole. Which was true of many things in life, you saw the piece and did not understand the greater context, the entire chicken. You could not, because you lacked information, you lacked perspective.

By noon, she'd reached I-95, and she was wild with heat and thirst. But there was nowhere to get water — not a store, not a restaurant, only houses, many boarded up, as was the only gas station. She remembered Chip and the ice water, how the droplets of condensation shimmied down the outside of the glass, and the cold metallic tang of the water on her tongue. Her toes had been rubbing for some time, and she realized the gooey sweat she was feeling in the shoe was, in fact, blood. She considered walking barefoot, but the sidewalk was littered with splodges of gum, bits of glass, coils of dog shit. Occasionally, there were needles and syringes.

The air clung to her, a tight plastic wrap of sooty-sludge.

In the lee of the roaring interstate, she turned onto Fairfield Avenue. She assumed this was the most direct route, as she couldn't take I-95 itself. The pain in her foot did not diminish, but she realized she could go for long periods without attending to it, so she focused on what techniques she'd use to render her surroundings in paint or charcoal or pastel, and she wondered why no one painted such shabby, lonely places. In photographs, they appeared crafted — line, shadow, mood, narrative. Hopper's paintings were gentrifications. Art couldn't help but glorify, art was a singular trajectory from the glory of religion to the glory of the self. Although Ida had said art needs to be about something other than the self — it paradoxically required an enormous ego and self-interest to imagine and execute provocative work. Even Ida's bloody, muscular canvases glorified the struggle of men and meat and blood in the Tribeca warehouses

— sanctified it, for as Rosie really considered the life of those men, and the death of the animals, they were without glory, they were mired in dirt and excrement and offal, the terrified animals skidding in their own blood. The grubbiness of the reality was absent from the art. And if art reflected society's values, then society did not value the banal side-streets of Bridgeport, CT, or Lowell, MA. These storyless, unlovely wastes existed only as a map, out the window of a speeding car, or from above, the plane flying elsewhere, fast. Art was a product for the wealthy — only they could afford it — and it reaffirmed their view of the world. They did not ever see the scuffed, the soiled, the stinky, the dull, and so it did not exist for them.

She thought about Bennett defacing his parents' Picasso. It was like the ducks on his tie: he was defiant; and that's what made Hobie uneasy — a sense that Bennett was pretending to be inside, but was in fact, outside, giving the finger. Rosie wondered if she was part of Bennett's provocation. Had he chosen her because she wasn't what they all expected? And did this mean that she merely represented something to him — she was a kind of prop? She remembered she'd already had this idea of a play, and she now reflected on how a play depended on the intensity of the acting, which was actually lying, lying sprouting from the heart so it sounded like truth and felt like truth, and everyone was fooled despite the cardboard set and the velvet curtain.

Fairfield Avenue melded with the Post Road, and Rosie paused in the shade of a hardware store. Her foot throbbed, her head throbbed. She might have a miscarriage from the walking and the heat and what that would be like, warm, lumpy blood and relief that the decision had been made for her. For a few minutes, she watched customers coming in and out of the store, mostly men in work clothes. They didn't seem to notice her, intent on pine cabinets and plumbing. They had pencils tucked behind their ears. Their sense of purpose amplified her lack of it, and she felt again her vagueness and transparency. Hobie had said, *a girl like you* and she'd assumed he meant *poor* but perhaps he meant insubstantial. He hadn't flirted with her, he'd summoned her and dismissed her, like a disappointing employee. The money was nothing to him — bits of paper to him, and yet it was life or death for the unborn child within her. It was her entire future.

She could phone Ida. It would have to be a collect call, and how would that go? Would Ida be excited and tell her to keep the baby, and come to live with her in New York, she'd be a grumpy but loving godmother and the baby would play on the floor as Rosie and Ida painted? No. Ida would wonder why a student, one of hundreds, was asking for advice on getting an abortion.

Rosie thus continued on, miles in the Saharan heat, then she turned onto Station Street, down Rose Hill, carried on to the bridge over the river, and up Sasco Hill. Despite the low light of evening, the heat stubbornly remained. Her shoulders sagged, she could not affect an effortless stroll. She trudged. She felt dizzy and unsteady and sticky with sweat. She looked at the golden sea and thought of Bruegel's Icarus and the relentless forward motion of life. With every second, the summer was closer to being over.

Reaching the country club, she decided to take a short cut, past the clubhouse, along the shore. As she turned down the club's drive, she saw a dead squirrel, its lower body completely flattened, but the upper portion and the head intact. The death had just happened, for the blood was bright, and the squirrel still retained a look of surprise. Maybe she'd even seen it here alive in the morning. Rosie hurried past. But then she stopped. She turned and bent down. The perfection of the animal, she noted, the clean fur, the eager eyes and nimble hands, and then the exploded pink sachet of its stomach, the mutilated spine and legs: the absolute fact of what a car does to a body. The frailty of skin and bone and form. Rosie thought about the carpet on the road, the night now months ago. Tart bile rose in her throat.

The driveway descended, parting the cartoon-shaped greens, and slithered toward the white clubhouse and the glittering gold sea. She began to run, either away from the dead squirrel or toward the boathouse, or both. Her breasts bounced painfully, she hadn't worn a bra and they were bigger with the pregnancy, and her right shoe came off. She veered from the tarmac, onto the links, directly toward the boathouse. She was stumbling. Her eyes were open, though her vision was hazy, the dark grass, the yellow sea, and she was in the car with Bennett all over again, her memory had not reshaped the object in the road, the motion of the car had not altered. Bennett had run over a man. Maybe a woman. Maybe already dead, maybe, maybe, maybe drunk, a tramp, a lost child, a woman, and Bennett had not stopped and she had not insisted. She'd listened to "Rikki Don't Lose That Number," she had sipped wine, rolled a joint, she'd wished there really had been a party with Mick and Keith.

Golfers watched her as she ran. She heard vague shouts, protests, she kept running. She had to call the police and explain, they would understand, she was very sorry, it was an accident, an oversight, a dark road, an easy mistake to make.

Tripping into a bunker, she collapsed in the sand. She was filled with wishing; wishing like a runner needing breath at the last mile, wishing so hard, so-so-so hard her guts hurt, wishing that it wasn't true, praying — even, praying to either no God at all or a God who certainly wouldn't be sympathetic, praying that it hadn't happened, hadn't happened surely, surely had not happened, not the carpet, not the baby. This wasn't supposed to be life, not what she'd fled Lowell for, not how it was for the lesbians who were probably at a party on Fire Island or rehearsing their new performance. Rosie gritted her teeth and sucked in, wishing somehow time would scroll back, she dreamed, imagined, deluded.

Maybe a really bad person had been in the road, a wife beater, a child molester. Maybe someone already dead. Maybe —

"Hey, are you OK?"

A man in an outfit of circus colors stood above her, golf clubs slung across his shoulder.

"Do you need help?"

She could tell him right now, she could say, "Call the police. I've killed a man." She would be brave. Not pusillanimous.

The golfer extended his hand. Another man was behind him. Rosie thought she heard him say, "Is she on drugs?"

Rosie stood of her own accord, sand fell off her, she could feel the grains rubbing into the blisters on her toes and her heel, and she was glad of the gritty pain.

"This is private property," the clowny one told her.

The other said something about calling the police, and Rosie almost laughed, or perhaps she did because the two men stepped back as she rose up. They were unsure, she wasn't what they expected out here golfing on a summer evening. Yet she rose, Rosie-rose, a shabby Botticelli's Venus, she shook loose the sand, shook loose her long, sweaty, clumpy hair, and she stumbled away from them. They snickered in her wake.

It was dark by the time she reached the boathouse. The lights were on, the French doors open, she could hear the rambling notes of Miles Davis, the meaning remained incoherent to her, irritating to be honest, but Bennett loved it. "Listen, listen!" he would demand. "The complexity! The cohesion! The beauty!" Up the stairs she staggered, her throat was dry, and she felt the sting of sunburn on her shoulders and face. Through the glass of the door, she saw Bennett inside, reading a thick book, drinking wine.

Hearing her, he turned, assessed. "Rosie, Jesus Christ —"

"I want," she said. "I want to talk about that night in the road."

"What night?"

"You know, *you know*. When we went out to that place in Meriden. And on the way back —"

"Meriden?" As if he'd never heard of the place.

She persevered: "On the way back you ran over something in the road. She caught his eye. "What was it?"

Then his focus shifted. "Are you OK? What's happened?" He put out his hand, a gesture of concern. But, also, she knew, of obfuscation. She pushed him away. He said, "I don't have the faintest idea what you're talking about."

"We must go to the police. It will be all right."

"The police?"

"We'll say we thought it was a carpet."

"Rosie, you're not OK. Look at you —"

"Stop it!" she heard herself shout. "I was there and you were there, and we ran over something in the road, maybe someone, a body, and you kept going, we kept going and the next day you went to the car wash and told Jiffy to clean under the car, specifically under it."

Bennett stared at her, a Minotaur in his tunnel. She took a step back, she gripped the hard, certain table edge.

He countered her, moved to her, his hands on her arms. He could do anything to her. "What's this about, my girl?"

"Just tell me what you think it was."

"You're really upset, sit down and tell me —?"

"The thing in the road."

"Rosie —"

"You know, you know it was a body, you know it!" She could hear herself shrieking.

He tried to pull her into him, against his big, safe chest, but she resisted.

"Ssshhhhh," he held her. "It's OK."

And then she smacked him, not hard, because she didn't have the range, she was pressed up against him, so it was an awkward swipe at his face. Now he let her go. He turned his face, and she couldn't see his expression. He made a small nod. Then regarded her, calmly. "Eggs," he said.

She didn't understand, and he smiled gently, maybe lovingly.

"Scrambled eggs, Rosie. That's what you ordered. A side of bacon, coffee, whole wheat toast. You remember, don't you? After the car wash, we went for breakfast." He released her completely, she wouldn't run away. "Rosie, Rosie, my girl, we sat in the window of Denny's and ate our breakfast."

She stared at him. She was slow to grasp his point; but then she could recall the way he'd chatted with the waitress, he'd liked her earrings, little hanging baskets of flowers, and she'd made them herself. Bennett had been amazed; he had his way of charming women of a certain age simply by noticing them. He had made a joke — slightly off-color — and Rosie and the waitress had laughed. Oh, laughter like a little bubbling stream.

Ladies and gentlemen of the jury, what kind of person laughs after they've run over a dead body in the road?

"We should have stopped." Rosie wasn't even sure anymore if she was saying this, or whispering, or only thinking.

Bennett poured himself more wine. "Can I get you anything to drink? You look like you've had a terrible day."

And this is the way decisions are made. The day unfolded and Rosie stumbled through it, and she grasped only that turning left or turning right changed nothing. Fate absorbed such details, it hardly noticed, lumbering forward in its steady and ancient gait, and the best she could do was stay out of its way and not make a fuss.

MIRANDA
1985

Rosie had crafted a way to carry Miranda on long walks. She'd taken her old Parsons backpack and cut two holes in the bottom for the baby's legs. In rain, she had a poncho to cover them both. In sun, she fitted a canopy made from a wire coat-hanger and a pillow case over Miranda's head. They often went down to the sea, along the beach to the country club's boundary. Rosie sat on the handkerchief of sand between the *PRIVATE MEMBERS ONLY* sign and the rough, scratchy wild grass and pebbles of the native shore. Chip stared at her, the little man in his tidy whites, and she would wave cheerily. Miranda sucked on rocks as Rosie watched the white seabirds skimming the water.

On this particular morning, as Rosie returned to the boathouse, she saw Hobie waiting. He and Mitzi had been away for nearly a year, Aruba and skiing in Switzerland, Bennett had said, and then a sojourn in London for Ascot followed by a stint in Marbella — which, Bennett noted, had done wonders for Mitzi. "She looks years younger and you can't see the scars at all."

Miranda was fussing, Rosie jiggling her on her hip.

"May I come in?" Hobie's teeth seemed too big for his mouth as he smiled.

Rosie opened the door, he entered, but only just.

"How are you, Rosie?"

"I gave your money to another woman who needed it."

He blinked, nonplussed. He couldn't remember the money, it was so unimportant, a mere four hundred bucks. Then his eyes settled on Miranda; oh, *that* money. He'd paid for her not to be alive. "What's her name?"

"Miranda."

"She's beautiful." He chucked her cheek but Miranda turned away from him, sniffling. "I need to tell you, Rosie, I need to ask — do you have someone else — someone, somewhere else you can go?"

No, she did not.

"Are you sure? No one?" he pressed.

She touched Miranda's cheek. "No."

"I really regret that it will be unpleasant for you."

"What will?"

He looked sad, or perhaps disappointed that she hadn't taken his advice about the abortion. The baby bothered him. He took out his money clip. "Let me give you something so you can call a cab, get a room at a motel."

"Why would I need to do that?"

"Or we could get you a job. Can you clean?"

She couldn't understand him, he was speaking WASP.

He looked from her to Miranda and back again. He was almost pleading, "Mitzi knows people."

"People? What kind of people?"

"People who need cleaning."

Obviously, he didn't mean this literally, dirty people in a line.

"Go away," Rosie said and tried to shut the door. But his foot was there.

For a moment, he stood regarding her through the door. The skin around his eyes had tightened but otherwise he was expressionless. "I came here to help. I felt sorry for you." Hobie retrieved his foot and started back down the stairs.

In one of Bennett's novels — she couldn't remember which because they were all thick and had paintings of wistful women on the front, usually by one of the Pre-Raphaelites or Degas or Sargent — Rosie had read about droit de seigneur: the right of the wealthy landowner to sleep with any woman who lived on his property. But Hobie didn't want to fuck her, she was a cheap thrift-store girl, and he pitied her. Instead he had loomed in his tailored shirts, smelling like daffodils and lemons, showing her his gleaming teeth. She didn't belong in his house, didn't go with the magnificent décor, he was moving her around, she was an object, an unattractive chair or a lamp, and he was putting her out on the sidewalk. This was what Bennett had meant by entitlement. Rosie shut the door, hard enough for him to hear. But he didn't turn — couldn't be bothered, as he strode back to his vast house through his garden.

She tried to stay awake to tell Bennett. Miranda snored softly by her side, sleeping at oceanic depths. The Marianda Trench, Rosie called it. The weeks since her birth had passed with quiet consistency, flitting like a cartoon calendar, and the only way Rosie could track time was the incremental changes in nature on her walks. The arrival of certain migrant birds on the drizzly brink of rain storms; the buds that hesitated for weeks then popped like fireworks — forsythia, dogwoods, apple, cherry; the wild grasses along the shore pressed forth their own humble flowers, miniature folds of purple or pink attended by noisy bees. The summer heat had colonized the days, diffused the colors to a Monet haze, and the gardener resumed his tours of duty with the lawnmower.

If it wasn't for Miranda, Rosie might imagine nothing had changed: her life remained contained within the miles she could walk. Bennett lapped around her in his wild ellipses, returning home with bags of groceries and good humor. He was happy, he swept Rosie into his arms and kissed her, he took Miranda on his knee: "Do you see how strong her legs are? She's going to be a lacrosse player."

Rosie felt a truce between the fierce, bright moments of love she had for Bennett and the doubts that crouched in certain dusty corners — where he went, what he did, the source of his money. She suspected he wasn't doing quite what he said he was. The art dealing seemed more about the *dealing* and she wondered if it was *dealing* pot or if the provenance of the art wasn't quite proper. He couldn't bear boredom or stillness, he needed amusement, to find the edge of situations. Beneath the quiet exterior of her days pulsed a kind of electrical charge — an anticipation, at times a foreboding. Sooner or later, something was going to happen, like a trip wire, and maybe that was Hobie.

Rosie woke.

A door. She heard and waited. Footsteps on gravel, and also the shushing sea and the baby breathing. Bennett was not in the bed. She got up and went to the window. He was outside in the night.

Below her. Lit only by the interior light of the BMW.

Putting a suitcase in the trunk.

"Bennett?" she said.

He looked up, his expression difficult to discern in the dark, then he put his finger to his lips. "Sshhss. I was just coming to get you."

"What's going on?"

"Hurry, you must hurry."

Thus, Rosie flew, she threw things into a garbage bag, what came to her hand, what was in her direct path, and she lifted Miranda, drowsy, sucking at the creamy teat of sleep, and ran down the stairs.

Within seconds they were in the car, Bennett was reversing fast, and Rosie saw the boathouse — windows and doors open, Bennett's clothes were strewn across the deck, a single Docksider left in the driveway, she hadn't noticed.

"My art," she said, and began to open the door.

But he jammed the car into first, the gravel spitting out from the rear wheels, and they were already halfway up the driveway, already hitting with speed the lip of tarmac as they spun onto Sasco Hill Road. Rosie had always thought the reason he drove slowly was the age of the BMW, but it was clearly capable of sprints.

They could hear sirens, so Bennett swung right onto a side-street, then slowed to his usual speed limit. He carefully wove through the night-empty streets, Rosie's ears pricked for the sirens, she scanned for police cars.

"Light me a cigarette." Bennett checked the rearview mirror.

"Not in the car with the baby."

"*Jesus,*" he muttered, opening his window, snatching the pack from the dashboard and doing it himself as he segued onto 95 north. They drove on without speaking, through the toll at Stratford. The hot outer air hummed and whistled as it battered the windshield and bounced in through the open windows.

Rosie's hair snapped and twisted, Medusa-like. She didn't even have a hair tie.

"Bennett?" The furious sound of the wind and passing cars made conversation difficult — for most cars were passing them, Bennett holding to the speed limit with the accuracy of Apollo coming in for the moon landing. Except this was no conversation, merely Rosie yipping against the air currents. "Bennett? Is this something to do with Hobie?"

The cigarette had begun to calm him, so he lit another one.

"Why were there sirens?"

Still he said nothing, he was ruminating, far, far away, in his Minotaur cave.

"Why are we running away from the police?"

He glanced at her, "Police?"

"There were sirens."

A short laugh: "Maybe a Jew was trying to order a drink at the club."

They drove among the streaming tail lights, smearing red ribbons in the dark, and at last, he put his hand on her thigh and announced: "Great news! We're going to Vermont!"

"But the police —"

"A brilliant new career opportunity has come my way!" Another inhale of another cigarette, another glance in the rearview mirror, there was almost a rhythm now. "I am very tired of dealing with trinkets and baubles, my girl, the flotsam of divorce and death. Sad, angry people are so unreliable. We need something more stable and I've been offered a teaching job at a small liberal arts college located near the Canadian border. It's where the wealthy send their less palatable children, those rejected by well-endowed alma maters, after all even Dartmouth must draw the line some —"

"Bennett," she said, then screamed, for he swerved into the adjacent lane. "BENNETT!"

"Asshole!" he yelled at the neighboring car. Another cigarette, he was practically eating them. He turned on the radio, classic rock, shouting, *"My blood runs cold."* And began drumming his hands on the dashboard. *"My memory has just been sold!"* Now he slammed his fists. *"Ba da da da da My angel is the centerfold!"* This delivered with seething mania, the vocal severity of a dog barking.

Rosie brought her knees to her chin, wrapped her arms around her shins and held on.

Then he was laughing, the raucous Bennett laugh, turning the radio off. "Did I ever tell you about the time Hunter S. Thompson and I tried to steal Fidel Castro's underwear in Cuba?" His cigarette dangled from his lips. "Hunter's doing a hush-hush piece for *Rolling Stone*, and I just happen to be there because I'm on a Hemingway lark, I'm obsessed with Hemingway, and on an island like Cuba, a few years after the Bay of Pigs, it doesn't take long for the only two Americans to find each other. It was a wild ride, that's for sure, I had just turned 18 and I'd only ever had a couple of tokes with Willie Kreitler behind the field house, and there's Hunter with this tool box — I'm not kidding you, an actual tool box — of pills and drugs and paraphernalia. It's all beautifully arranged, color coordinated, so all the red pills are together and the white pills are there with the individual packets of coke and green pills with the weed. Hunter's a real old lady in the beginning, the drug taking is very ordered, very systematic."

Had he forgotten that he'd already told her this story? Should she interrupt him *and then you and Hunter decided to steal Fidel Castro's underpants.* Should she finish the next sentence, *we woke up and there were pills and shit everywhere, the tool box looked like it had been attacked by angry monkeys.* Rosie already knew *the shit was literal shit, greasy little turds smeared or set in neat mounds like Jello molds and then we realized monkeys, factual monkeys, I didn't know Cuba even had goddamned monkeys but the monkeys had been at the drugs and the monkeys were outside and they were fucked up, they were looping through the trees, they were falling like fruit, they were screaming and festering and moaning.*

Rosie hugged her knees tighter, her head down, so her knee-caps pressed firmly into her eye sockets, but she could still hear him *and we were electric, man, we were running through the hot soup night with the smell of frangipani punching our nostrils and a bottle of cheap rum in hand, we were super-human climbing over the wall, any saner and we would have been scared but we felt no fear, no pain, Hunter and I, the quantity and quality of drugs had seen to that, and fearless we were also invisible, and we fell into the dictator's garden, we saw his boxers hanging on the washing line like bunting, fine white cotton, made in France, so much for communism.*

*   *   *

By dawn, they were arcing around Boston, passing Route 3 to Lowell, and Rosie imagined Gran waking up. Rosie had never seen Gran actually *waking up*, she had always been already awake, dressed, in the kitchen making breakfast for the lodgers. As a child Rosie had wondered if Gran slept at all, or merely folded herself up like a bat and shut her eyes for brief minutes. In the middle of the night, Rosie had sometimes heard the TV.

She hadn't phoned Gran in over a year and in that brief conversation had given Gran the impression that she was still at Parsons. Rather, she hadn't admitted that she was shacked up with an older man and pregnant. There had been nothing to say, there never was, the weather, general health. It was strange how little Rosie felt for the person who'd housed her and fed her for more than a decade; she was, perhaps, just another lodger. Not even that, because Rosie had cost Gran money, not just the outgoings on food and clothing and shoes but the occupancy of a room that might otherwise be generating income. Gran had once said — one anniversary of the car crash — that Rosie was "an accidental pregnancy." At the time, Rosie hadn't understood, not just how sex could be an accident — from the little she knew, sex definitely involved awareness of certain body parts; but why Gran would tell her this. Chris put her straight: "You weren't planned." Then added, "That doesn't mean you weren't wanted." As there had been no legal abortion at the time, Rosie had no real way of knowing if her parents had stayed together out of love or lack of option. She couldn't remember them together, not in a single frame of her memory. Chris thought he was also an accident because his parents didn't love each other at all, they fought and spewed all kinds of hatred and this spattered out on him, he sometimes came to Rosie wrapped in silence, and it seemed to Chris unlikely that his parents had come together for a moment of love. "But they still had to do it," Rosie had noted. "Drunk," he said. "They do stuff when they're drunk, I hear them, and it's disgusting. Sandra and me, we're the hang-overs that won't go away." Chris's parents constantly reassured him of his trespass, they actively un-loved him with words and even bruises, while Rosie felt instead the cold, steady drizzle of Gran's resentment.

The week before Rosie left for Parsons, Gran told her to clean out her room, she already had another lodger lined up. It wasn't much: a Ziggy Stardust poster Chris had given her, shells from the trip to Maine, her art supplies. When she walked away from the house — Chris had given her a ride to Boston's South

Station — Rosie hadn't looked back, there'd been nothing to see, certainly not Gran having a last-minute change of heart. Certainly not The Giggle Man looming down. He'd long gone.

As Bennett turned north on I-93, and then, entering New Hampshire, Rosie felt a wild rush of gratitude. Exits drifted by, turnings to towns exactly like Lowell, filled with Grans and dull, yearning girls like Rosie. Only she was here, fastened into the car seat, escaping a second time. They passed Concord, passed the signs for the Maine seacoast, and the first mention of Canada to the north. For an hour, the highway cut through a flatland of forest, the trees straight and solemn, the lack of horizon felt claustrophobic; then the landscape suddenly opened out in the morning sun, so Rosie had a sense of the wild, high mountains she was entering, and she was amazed that this rising tumult of rock and sky existed only hours from Lowell, and Bennett was saying, "We had a Picasso on the dining room wall. From his later period. Even genius runs out. It was a doodle, probably while he was on the phone or taking a shit, but my father had decided we must have modern art in the house. He never had good taste. It was true what my mother said, the Irish sense of style is limited to potatoes and popes and she once served him a potato in a little pope hat to make her point. The Irish are impressed with fancy dressing. James Joyce is just Hemingway in a frilly shirt for 500 pages. Have you ever read *Ulysses*? People *say* they have. People *say* they wash their hands after going to the bathroom."

Rosie turned to regard him, his handsome profile, and as she watched his face and hands mobilizing the anecdote, she realized the telling soothed him, and maybe the stories and the asides, the Picasso on the dining room wall, the drugged-up monkeys, were the way he re-invented himself when he was lost. This big, strong man buried his fear in bravado.

The highway narrowed now, funneling between a high peak of dark pine and a sharp granite plinth. Beyond, Rosie could see more mountains, endless green forests over recalcitrant hills, on and on. It was another country, and she felt the liberty of the traveler.

*   *   *

Bennett pulled off in Franconia, they had breakfast in a diner. He had to make a phone call, he told her, and staked out the phone booth near the men's room. It was many phone calls, and waiting for return calls, and the manager of the diner frowned as Miranda's squalling disturbed the other customers. So Rosie went outside and found a stream just beyond the parking lot, and she and Miranda dabbled in the clear, chilly water rippling beneath the dappling leaves. No Chip leered out to drive them off. There were rustlings instead, among leaves and underbrush — chipmunks, small brown birds, and a bright blue bird she thought might be a jay watched her intently from a high branch.

At dusk they drove on, another two hours, and where the signs promised Canada 20 miles northward, Bennett turned off the highway. Just across from the exit ramp, a motel squatted, low and toad-like, under a single blinking street light.

Rosie's body still shuddered from the car as she sat on the bed, and her ears hummed with the wind of the open car windows. Bennett went back outside, shutting the room door quietly behind him. For a moment, she panicked, thinking: he has the car keys, he's going to leave us here and disappear. But she could see him out the window, leaning against the pillar of the motel's overhang. His shoulders were hunched, and she felt a wild, lurching sympathy.

In the bathroom, the soap, cup, towels were arrayed on the sink, an altar for the traveler. Rosie soaked a flannel in warm water and cleaned Miranda as she slept. Vomit had congealed in the fat wrinkles of her neck — it had been a mistake to give her ice cream. Rosie gently wiped her child, tracing the small, perfect body with the cloth. A rash was beginning to sprout between her legs from the long hours of damp confinement, though she had not complained. Rosie wiped on cream, sliding her fingers between Miranda's soft labial folds. Once her own mother had done this. Her own mother, not even a ghost, not even a disturbance of the dust, she'd left no impression, not even a photograph. Yet Rosie felt her now, leaning in against her, guiding her hands over Miranda's warm skin. Once Rosie had been thus lulled and loved and *wanted*, Rosie was sure, and that love had entered into her, a particular osmosis, stubbornly lodged deep in her cells, never to be bartered.

*　　*　　*

"Rosie."

He mumbled in the dark.

His hand moved along her shoulder, around her waist, he pulled her to him, onto him, just like that. She arched her back to take him deeper. After, when he'd fallen asleep, she went to the bathroom to wipe away his wetness, and then, for a while, she stood at the window.

Beyond the motel's fluorescent glow, she could see nothing in that charcoal dark. There was the murky smell of water and mud, the sound of unknown creatures pipping — night birds?

Insects? Every few minutes a car or truck sped by on the interstate, heading to or from Canada, she assumed. A town of some
kind lay not far away, but its lights were off, its dogs asleep. She
had no other sense of the topography — hills or lakes or rivers.
She was hovering above the earth, as if in a spaceship, unteth-
ered from both gravity and time; the world had paused for her
on this warm August night. In a few hours it would roll forward,
and she and Miranda and Bennett would tilt and fall with it.

THE WOODSTOVE
1985–1986

The leaves were already turning this far north, russet, red, flame-thrown across the high-humped hills they drove along the ribboning road. How did Bennett know the way, the roads had no signs, they branched off indifferently, tunneling into the riotous trees — some had already thrown down their gauntlet of bright primary yellow. Madness, she thought, that nature can produce color this intense and pure. The sky moved above, a sailor-blue backdrop for the white clouds, fleet despite their plumpness. White houses, red barns, yellow houses, grey barns, cows in green fields, a white steepled church, the steady hem of hills always emboldening the horizon. The trees rustled like crinoline above her.

They had long ago left the tarmac for the dirt, a wide dirt road for a narrow one, passing yet another dairy farm, and then no farms only rough woods and wild meadows. Bennett said, "Here." At the dead end: a small white house with a green door and high gables, the garden overgrown with brambles and golden rod, two apple trees drooping with fruit, gold and red.

Bennett no longer opened her car door, for he tended

Miranda, holding her in his strong arms. Rosie stepped out into the grass. The smell of leaves, the hum of bees. Squirrels were feasting on the wind-fallen apples. The steps needed repair, the door was not locked, Rosie noted, as they entered the house.

In the rooms, furniture loomed under white cloths. There was faded floral wallpaper, and underfoot wide floorboards painted dark green. "Whose house is it?"

"Family friend," he said.

"Buffy and Wally?" she suggested. "Or Binky and Monty?"

He laughed, a deep, appreciative laugh, inviting her in so that she laughed with him, a comrade. At last they looked at each other. She half-expected an apology, but he was incapable, she knew. He had passed the exit for Lowell, and that was sufficient.

"Let's get these covers off." He pulled at the first one, revealing an armchair in chintz. Miranda had fallen asleep in his arms, so he placed her on the chair with exquisite tenderness. They went around the rooms, the sofa, the dining table, the sideboard, the kitchen. Bennett took her and turned her onto the kitchen table, his fingers found their place, opening her. "You're always so wet, Rosie, you're always ready for me."

Upstairs, the beds were made up, tightly cornered with crisp cotton sheets and wool blankets. Who had made them, and how long ago? A bed, she thought, stays made for years. When they climbed into the double bed that night, between the cool pressed sheets, they found — however — that a congregation of mice were living in the bottom half. They'd buried into the mattress, scattered seed shells and droppings. The house was infested.

* * *

"Yull be needin firewood?"

The man had knocked at the door. He did not introduce himself in his odd, high voice. He was short and broad and dirty, an insect odor hummed about him that Rosie recognized as unwashed flesh. He had a massive tumor in his left cheek and no teeth, no teeth at all.

"I don't know," Rosie replied, trying not to fixate on the tumor or the smell. Bennett had left for the college wearing his Harris Tweed jacket, so nervous he'd packed an extra deodorant in his briefcase.

"Ya leavin before tha winta, then?"

"I think we're planning to be here."

"That roight?" The man chewed, looking thoughtful.

"Will it be very cold?" Rosie asked.

"Reckin will know come April."

It was perhaps a joke, but the man didn't smile, so Rosie pressed her lips together.

"Ya goin through tha winta withou heat, then?" He chewed some more, then deftly moved the tumor to the other cheek. Rosie realized it was tobacco.

"I'm sure there's heat."

"Must be some special kinda heat they got down theah in tha flatlands." This insect man, dark-hair as a beetle, tipped his hat and walked back toward his pick-up.

"Wait!" she stepped out after him. "Do you have a number? I'll have to find out."

"No phone. Yain't gotta phone neitha."

"Then how will I —"

"I'm ya neighbah. That shithole with tha hounds."

Yes, Rosie recalled it, a jumble of a place almost eclipsed by brambles. She made a little goodbye wave. The man tipped his hat. His pick-up crabbed away down the road, the entire back-end of the vehicle moving at a 45-degree angle to the cab.

Back inside the house, she regarded the wrought-iron stove, sitting sturdy and spinster-like in the corner of the living room. There were two latches — one on top, and one on the front. These accessed the inside of the stove, which was scrupulously clean, just a trace of ash on her fingertip. A lever on the outside worked to open or close a small hatch near the stove's chimney pipe. At the bottom was a drawer to collect ash that fell through the grate. It was as mysterious as an Egyptian tomb.

The boathouse had had radiators along the walls. Despite a thorough search, Rosie couldn't find any here. There were no thermostats, either. Bracing Miranda onto her hip, she made her way down into the basement. The low-watt light bulb illuminated a grubby dirt floor, a metal box she suspected might be something called a "fuse box" and a large cylindrical tank covered in rust. She put her hand on the tank — it was warm and burped softly at her; she was fairly sure this was the hot water heater — though *hot* was an exaggeration as her shower had made evident. The warmish water warmer, then. What might "heating" look like? Was it connected to the warmish water warmer? But nothing connected, no machine or device suggested the potential for heat.

"Heating? Of course there's heating." Bennett put his hand confidently on the wood stove when he came home. "This'll have the place warm as a sauna." He gave her twenty bucks for firewood.

The next day, Rosie walked with Miranda in the backpack to beetle man's house. The drive was rutted and brutal, terminating in a muddy opening among the brambles. Within this bristly thicket, she could see uneven stacks of logs, piles of scrap wood, rusted machines with arms and jaws, at least six dogs on chains, snowmobiles of dubious functionality, a count of four cars that, clearly, were not going anywhere. A seventh dog lived in one. The house was encased in part by flapping plastic. She squelched forward, charting her way through the dogs. They leaned out at her, their full weight against their chains, snarling and bouncing. One was almost suicidal with rage, leaping at her with such enthusiasm that the chain snapped it back, choking its bark. Closer to the house, she called out: "Hello?" Her voice sounded foolish, girlie, as if she was selling cookies.

The door swung open, the man stumbled down to her. From ten feet he stank of sweat and booze. The stench intensified so that by the time he stood before her, Rosie had the taste in her mouth of rancid butter.

"Ya want tha wood, then?"

"YES." The mud was seeping into her sandals, oozing between her toes. She was shouting over the barking of the dogs.

"How many cads?"

"WHAT?"

"CADS! HOW MANYA WAN?

The man reached into his back pocket and pulled out a handgun. Rosie shrank back as he raised it skyward and fired. Miranda jolted with surprise and let out a brief wail. With a whimpering transition, the dogs silenced. "Theyah eagah ta getin tha woods, is all." He put the gun away. "Huntin."

"Hunting?"

"Beah."

Beah? *Bear?* Do people hunt bear? Maybe he wanted to frighten her, she was soft as a kitten. "What is a cad?"

"8 foot by 4 foot by 4 foot o' wood."

She offered him the twenty. He squinted at it. Then, in practiced sequence, put away the gun, pulled out his tobacco, stuffed a wodge in his mouth. "Seems opta-mistic. Yav got no insulation 'n tha ol stove'll make more creosote'n heat."

Rosie did not know about creosote. "We'll be all right," she said.

Was he smirking, she wondered, or just chewing? He took the money. "I dont stack."

She turned to face the gauntlet of dogs.

"Why dont yar husband drive ya?"

The dogs were howling now, thrusting against their chains. One weak link, she thought. But she kept her gaze steady, shouted: "I LIKE TO WALK."

The cold came without warning, the cold came at noon, a storm bending down from Canada in the first days of October. The morning had been warm, almost balmy, and Rosie had the windows open, letting in the yeasty smell of dry leaves, the moist life-smell of the cows from miles away; for, at last, she was banishing the sour musk of mouse piss from the house. She had cleaned each room over weeks while Bennett was at work. At first with squeamish trepidation; but now, with the cunning and indifference of a seasoned hunter, she had set traps. SNAP SNAP SNAP the traps went in the night, like gnashing teeth, and she'd find the soft tawny bodies in the morning, heads clamped, small eyes slightly popped, whiskers stiff. Death had been quick. Twice, though, mice had been caught by their back legs. The first one Rosie had thrown outside in the long grass, alive and still in the trap. She'd been repelled by her cruelty, and then amazed at how quickly she forgot the suffering she could not see. The second mouse had peered up at her, bereft of self-pity, neither fearful nor pleading. Tiny leg bones poked through the grey fur. Rosie'd taken the fire poker and smashed in its head.

The cold came on a silver sledge of cloud. Within an hour the sun had vanished, and the wind began, mean and prying so that Rosie soon knew how thin were the walls of the house — *Yav got no insulation.* And how the doors were not flush in their frames and windows loose on their sashes. The roof lacked sufficient nails as did the siding on the north side. Something clanged but she could not find it. The wind laughed and howled and danced and drummed, a band of gypsies surrounding the house, trying to get inside not for profit but for jest. The wind came through the cracks like knives. Then the rain lashed, the kind of hard rain that in summer lasted only minutes; but here, now, lasted for hours. The house leaked, and Rosie ran from room to room with pans and buckets as Miranda clapped her hands and gurgled to see such fun.

Outside, Rosie saw, through the great woolen blankets of rain: the pile of wood, where it had been left, in the middle of the driveway. She and Miranda only had summer clothes — what she'd grabbed in their flight from the boathouse. Now they were wearing these in layers: tee-shirts, dresses, multiple thin cotton socks.

As the temperature dropped, ice slicked the inside of the windows upstairs, ice on the buckets catching the water, her breath exploding into the air with each compression of the lungs. Then the lights flickered and the power went out. Rosie stumbled through the dim house, thinking of the matches that lit the propane cooking stove, thinking of candles she did not have and how useful a flashlight would be. Grappling with the cooker, she got the burners alight, the blue flame threw off a marvelous heat. Why hadn't she thought of this? She turned on the oven, opened the door, and pulled one of the armchairs close.

When the door burst open, she thought it was the wind or a fairytale bear; but it was Bennett and the beetle man, arm-in-arm, stumbling like drunks in, somehow the small dark man supporting Bennett's weight.

"He'd gone off tha road, those tayahs are shit," Beetle said sighting Rosie in the blue propane glow. "Haf froze in tha fancy car."

The man and Rosie guided Bennett to the sofa. Their breath huffed the air. Then Beetle glanced at her, he strode to the cooker, turned off the burners. "Ya got no sense! Yull blow tha house roight up!"

"I just needed to get us warm."

"Warm in a coffin, more loik."

Shaking his head, he made for the door. For a moment, he paused — Rosie sensed his disapprobation; then he merely raised his hand, a gesture of limited effort, and walked out into the storm.

Rosie stripped Bennett of his wet clothes. Shivering, eyes half-closed, he stood child-like at her command as she wrapped him in blankets and sheets. Then she made an igloo of covers on the bed. We don't even have warm socks, we don't even have boots, she thought. She made him coffee, held the cup to his lips, and he began to sip. Gradually, his shivering subsided and he was able to grasp the cup himself. "I can't remember," he mumbled. "I must have passed out."

He reached for her. "Rosie?"

"I'm here."

Bennett mumbled: "What if we've made a terrible mistake?"

"No, no," she stroked him. "We'll be happy here."

"I'm the dark wood, Rosie, in the middle of my life."

She kissed him, kissed him, caressed him, she had the strength for him, she knew. The storm raged through the night, snow and freezing rain, a wild tempest filled with hungry wolves and evil queens. In the morning, the kitchen tap did not work, and Bennett slept on.

Rosie dressed herself and Miranda in most of their clothes and wrapped them in blankets like sarongs. She tied plastic bags over her sneakers and inserted her home-made baby back-pack into a garbage bag. With Miranda on her back, she went out to the woodpile. The wind had torn every leaf from the trees, and they stood newly naked, vulnerable, against the bleak sky. The day was glum and grey and frigid. The snow was only ankle deep but after a few minutes of clearing it from the wood, Rosie's bare hands were freezing. Back inside, she fashioned mittens from a pair of Bennett's thick rag-wool socks by stabbing holes in the wool for her thumbs with a kitchen knife. She marveled that he had managed to pack several pairs in his haste to leave the boathouse.

Or were these brand new?

After an hour, she'd moved a quantity of wood inside and set about trying to start the stove. Through its window-eye, the stove regarded her suspiciously. A pox on you, too, she aimed her thought back at it.

How was it that she was 20 and did not know how to light a fire? In movies it involved paper and dry twigs. What dry twigs might there be after a dozen hours of rain and snow? Vaguely, she recalled a couple of broken chairs stashed in the basement.

Retrieving them, she smashed some of the larger pieces on the back step until they splintered sufficiently. An elaborate sculpture of crumpled paper and broken chair rose from her hands, and she admired her work before lighting the match. Instantly, the pile ignited, the bits of chair catching quickly. Now she reached for the larger logs, selecting two that felt the least wet. These she placed on the fire and shut the stove door.

Her triumph was short-lived. Smoke seeped, then quickly billowed from the stove and she ran to open the doors of the house, the smoke so thick she could no longer see the stove. Coughing and spluttering, she grabbed Miranda, they waited outside in the cold until at last the blue haze cleared to a mild fog and she could open the stove. The paper and kindling had burned completely, the log lay, un-scorched, in a wet mush of ash.

She tried again, more paper, more chair, a different log. But the result was the same — the log was not even warm to the touch. As she made her third attempt, there was a knock at the door.

The beetle man greeted her impassively. "I seen yar smoke signals."

"I'm trying to get the wood stove started."

"Ya wanta keep troiyin?"

Rosie pulled open the door, Beetle stepped in and immediately took off his huge boots, which were about half of him. His red wool hat stayed on his head. He gestured to Bennett, still asleep, warmly cocooned on the sofa, "Dont reckin he's gonna live." Miranda had crawled to the stove, stuck her hand into the ash mush and put it in her hair. "No, no," Rosie said, scooping her up.

"I'll get ya some wood'n kindlin, enough fortha week."

Boots back on, he left.

Ten minutes later, he returned on his tractor, a stack of logs in the front-loading bucket. Together, they carried the wood inside. If he noticed the plastic bags on her feet, he didn't say a word.

"This heah's yar dampah." He fiddled with the knob on the side of the stove. "Ya wanta open it ta start, then ya close it once tha fiya gets goin good." He'd brought a feed bag of newspaper, too, and this he scrunched into long, tight wands. On top of this, he layered kindling of different sizes, and like the cherry on an ice cream, a small log. "Ya want tha wood to clink loik yer grandma's china cups. Heah that?" He knocked two pieces together. "Then ya know it's good'n droiy."

Within minutes the fire blazed. Rosie instinctively placed her hands open and palm down to feel the rising heat. Delicious. "Oh!"

"Yer gonna feed this beast till May," he nodded at the stove. "Reckon six cad'll do ya."

"Thank you," she mumbled again, bobbing like a demented bird. "Thank you." She followed him to the door. "Can I pay you for the wood you brought today?"

He looked at her, perplexed or insulted, she could not discern. "No."

"But the cads?"

"This heah's a welcome gift."

"How much for a cad of wood, then?"

"Fifty."

"You'll need that all at once?"

"Pon delivery."

Rosie thrust out her hand. "I'm Rosie."

"Billy Mix."

It was only when Rosie took the hand, felt the hand, she

acknowledged the fine bones within and she looked again at Billy's face, saw the smooth cheeks and the smooth throat, and she recalled the voice. Billy was a woman.

Billy, for her part, threw one last look at Bennett, still slumbering. It was an inscrutable regard, yet, as if by a visual trick, Rosie briefly saw Bennett as Billy must. Hadn't his hair been thick and lustrous? In reality, it ebbed back from his forehead. The skin on his face collapsed against his arm, his mouth partly open to emit a soft snore. For too long they both stood watching Bennett sleep.

"Shhhiiit," Billy hissed. "Titsonna bull."

Titsonna. Bull. Rosie took a moment to process. Then nearly burst out laughing, because it was really how she felt about Bennett sometimes.

The next morning, Rosie found a pair of winter boots on the front porch, used, too large, but thickly felted.

While Bennett huddled like an old woman in layers of blankets by the stove, Rosie pulled on the boots, stuffed Miranda into the backpack, wrapped in the trash bag, and set off down the hill. Town was seven miles there, seven miles back, the day was fine and clear. The first mile had been rough-plowed by Billy, the snow banked up and grubby as it hadn't snowed in a few weeks. Kirby Mountain to her east drew a hard line against the blue sky, and to the west she could see as far as the Green Mountains that ran like a spine up the middle of the state. As she passed Billy's house, the dogs, curled up against the cold, awoke with wild and sudden outrage. Turning onto the paved road, she noted that trash lined the way: beer cans, cigarette cartons, Styrofoam cups, fast food containers. The jetsam of the lazy, she thought; or perhaps these litterers were marking the route like dogs, asserting possession of their territory. Halfway down the hill, she came across a bundle of junk mail and unpaid bills addressed to Williamina Mix. Most of the beer cans were probably hers. They were exposed, like an archeological dig, in layers of plowed and melted snow, the weeks of winter drinking and driving.

Along the slow, descending curves through farmland and woods Rosie walked, and onto the wide flood plain of the river that began near the Canadian border. The town ambled out to meet her: houses clustered along the roadside, three or four to a group, with enough land out back for a small holding. Walking, Rosie saw what she could not when passing in the car with Bennett: decrepitude under the decorative cloak of snow. Sway-backed barns, windows boarded up with plywood or swathed in plastic as Billy's house. Briefly, she thought of Bennett at home, warmed by Billy's firewood. What did he mean: I'm in the dark wood in the middle of my life?

A fabric store going out of business, a lumber yard, a gas station. Further on, the supermarket, the library, a pizza joint, a car dealer, the post office, two banks, a bar, a Dunkin' Donuts. This, she decided, was her best bet for a quiet, working phone. In her bag, she had $4.25 in quarters, pilfered quietly from Bennett's pockets — enough for the phone call, a coffee, and a donut. She dialed, she knew Gran would answer, the phone ringing in that quiet house like a rare and alarmed bird.

"It's me," she began.

"Yes," Gran said. She was standing in the hall, the black phone on its own table, her bag looped over the bottom bannister. "Where are you?"

The surface of the moon. Timbuctoo. "Vermont."

"Vermont."

"I'm a bit short of money."

"Why are you in Vermont?"

"Could I borrow —?"

"Why Vermont?"

Rosie pressed on: "Just fifty." Then she thought it would be good to buy herself and Miranda some clothes. "A hundred?"

"A hundred?"

"I'll pay it back." Though how, Rosie couldn't imagine. Money was like lighting a fire: she didn't know anything about it. She didn't even know what most things cost. Except abortions and firewood. "I have a child now," Rosie continued. "I need to buy firewood to keep us warm."

She could hear breathing. And then, at last: "You have a child?"

"A little girl. Miranda."

"You're in Vermont and you have a child and you want to borrow money."

These simple facts, laid out in a row, suddenly seemed outrageous, and Rosie felt her face flush. "I just need a hundred. That's all. And you'll never hear from me again."

"What do you mean by that?"

"I won't ask again, I promise, just this once." Rosie went on, summoning conviction. "I'm in this house and all it has is a stove."

"Why aren't you at Parsons?"

"Because," Rosie exhaled. "I met a man, and then I got pregnant."

"And you think fifty dollars will solve this mess?"

"It isn't a mess, Gran."

Rosie called into the speaker, "Gran? Gran?"

Rosie heard the softest shuffling, perhaps a crumpled Kleenex being pushed back up the sleeve of a sweater.

"Gran?"

"You had a scholarship, Rosie, a full scholarship."

"But you didn't want me to study art!"

"I wanted you to have opportunity."

Rosie did not like how she felt, disembodied and flushed and uncertain. "Just fifty for the wood. That's all I need." The phone was heavy, the plastic slightly sticky. "I love him. We're happy." She imagined the mouthpiece smeared with germs and despair from all the others who'd stood right here imploring into the punctured mouthpiece, whatever their needs — a ride, money, love. Who else uses the phone at Dunkin' Donuts? The needy, the drunk, the abandoned, those with error-filled lives.

Gran said: "What makes you think I have money to spare?"

This was all about money. The money Bennett mysteriously had, his magic tricks. Hobie buying paintings. Gran: Gran hunched over the kitchen table, the calculator in her hand, envelopes, bills, stamps, and the lodgers who came and went with their dog smells and dirty sheets, Gran knocking softly on a door, saying a name, making a demand that was more like an apology.

The memories were an abacus, and Rosie could align them in their rows, she could draw out a certain sense or story, and she suddenly understood the cold grey food Gran had brought home from the cafeteria, not out of spite or laziness, but imperative. And on the row of counting beads was The Giggle Man. Rosie felt him, then, his gloved hands upon her ribcage. *Do you like it when I do this.* He gave her money, rolled tight as a cigarette. *For your Grandmother*, he'd say. *Good girl, there's a good girl.*

"Did he pay you?" Rosie challenged.

"Who?"

"The Gig — the lodger. He wore white gloves."

"There were many lodgers. Dozens."

Something about how Gran had answered that too readily, how she hadn't even paused to flick through her memories. "You knew about him! You knew what we was doing and you did nothing. You did nothing to stop it. Maybe you even let him, maybe he paid you for me, too, so when I ask you for fifty maybe you owe me because of what I did, you sent me up the stairs —"

"Who?" Gran's voice was rushed and shrill. "Who are you talking about? What did he do —"

But Rosie hung up the phone. Miranda started grizzling, her teeth were bothering her. "There, there, my sweet," Rosie said. "There, there."

The Giggle Man. Her name for him because he tickled her and she giggled. That's what he did. He tickled her and tickled her until she ached and sobbed with laughter.

But she kept laughing, she kept giggling, and he kept tickling her.

Do you like it when I do this.

It was dusk by the time she returned home — if she must call it home, the destination she'd found herself at the end of a road halfway up a mountain mid-November. Bennett had gone back to bed, he'd let the fire die down and the house was bitterly cold. Rosie heard his somnolent breathing and had the urge to poke him, a bear through the cage.

She unclipped the bottle opener from the BMWs key ring — there'd be time to make an excuse; she could say, for instance, that it must have fallen off when he went into the ditch. Miranda was restless after the hours in the backpack, so Rosie started back outside quickly.

Billy's dogs set up their insane alarm, though it was insufficient to invoke their owner. Rosie banged on the door, again and again, until at last it flew open. "WATHAFUCKYAWAN?"

"I need good firewood," she said.

The dogs were howling, Miranda screaming. Billy frowned, confused by the cheap bourbon of which she stank, the noise of her half-starved dogs, the improbability of a girl with a baby coming to her home after dark.

Rosie held out the bottle opener. "This is from Himmler's private bar. It must be worth something. You can trade it."

Billy squinted at the opener. "Ya wanta trade a bottle opena for fiyawood?"

"Himmler's bottle opener. A genuine Nazi artifact."

"Looksa reglar bottle opena ta me. Fifty cents downna tha redemption centa."

"This one's worth a lot of money."

"Is tha roight?"

"Hundreds," Rosie stated. "Bennett is a dealer in art and antiques. He sells this kind of thing for hundreds, three-four hundred, to collectors."

"Reckin yull be lookin' for a collecta, then."

Billy stepped back, she began to shut the door. Rosie grabbed the handle. "Please." Then softer, leaner: "Please."

The next day, Billy helped Rosie stack the wood, showing her how to brace with crosspieces. Billy told her about dry wood, seasoned wood, green wood, shit wood, pisswet wood and goodfa fuck all wood, and how you had to know your stove, which wood to start with, which to fuel the heat, and which to last the night on a slower, cooler burn. She told Rosie about kindling. Without good kindlin', a fiyas nevah gonna start. She showed Rosie how to split wood with an awl. When Rosie asked her in, she refused. "No, thankya koindly."

In the kitchen, the kettle was whistling madly as Bennett stood at the sink watching Billy's truck depart. "Will we be having him round for evenings of cribbage and fine Spanish port?"

Rosie almost corrected the gender. Instead she took off her sock-mitten, her warm boots. Bennett had let the fire die down so she stoked it. The kettle shrieked on.

"Look at this sofa," he sneered. "It's put me off chintz for life."

And Miranda had taken the lid off the jar of flour, she had flung flour in Kandinsky-like arcs, she had stuffed it in her mouth. Rosie squatted down and began to clean.

"Not an arabica bean fora hundred miles."

The kettle blared and steamed inches from his hand. He seemed not to notice. He was wearing three cashmere sweaters and two pairs of wool trousers. On her knees with the sponge and the flour, Rosie glanced up from the floured floor and the floured child.

"I heard wolves circling the car. It was a Hemingway moment. Like the hyenas in *The Green Hills of Africa*. Death was right there, right there!" He had to raise his voice over the kettle. "The college has offered me a room during the week so I don't have to risk the drive."

She heard the lie and stood and turned off the kettle.

Over the winter, Bennett came back on the weekends and they went into town to do the shopping and the laundry, he paid for everything from his money clip, those crisp lettuce bills, wherever they came from. They ate what they could buy at the supermarket — "Alas, no brocollini, I fear the locals would think it deformed broccoli, unaccustomed as they are to anything not wrapped in plastic. And I thought this was a farming community."

Bennett complained that the house was too cold, she could never get it warm enough. He always fucked her from behind now. She wanted tenderness, she wanted love like rain in the desert, she wanted Gran to kiss her goodnight and tuck her into bed, she wanted her mother and her father and time to rewind, undo, do over. But she had, instead, this threadbare lust. Bennett moved his fingers around her, inside her, and she wondered who had taught him, a Parisienne call girl, his family's maid, the Duchess of Devonshire? And then on Sunday afternoon he would leave and she'd wonder at the stopped-clock silence and the way time would begin again with the drip of the tap or the whine of Billy's chain saw across the white fields or Miranda's chiming laugh. Then relief, like a scullery maid off duty at last in the large house of a rich man, alone with her own soft hours.

* * *

In the middle of the night, when Rosie got up to feed the stove, the house was still and timeless and cold. It was never really warm, unless she sat right by the stove, practically embracing it.

She had moved the bed downstairs and into the dining room, and she took to sleeping in her clothes so she wouldn't have to dress and undress. The upstairs was horrifically frigid — Miranda's old diapers were frozen in the pail in the morning, and a pipe burst in the shower. Billy had told her she'd better shut off the water entirely up there and gave her directions for how to do this.

Sometimes after stoking the stove in the night, Rosie sat in its proximity and sketched it. In one version, the stove loomed ominously, black and solid: the compression of shadow. In another, the stove glowed with life-warmth, with magical power. She wondered who else it had warmed in its lifetime. Simply by shifting the perspective, she could change its moods.

Outside the night was still or restless. There were clear nights, diamond-sharp and diamond-cold and in the morning the snow squeaked underfoot. Storms slammed down from the north or stampeded from the west, all the way from the Central Plains and the Great Lakes. Sometimes they slithered up from the south, warm and sloppy, spattering the windows with a batter of snow and ice. She had never thought about weather in Lowell or New York or Southport, the weather was merely more or less convenient, more or less comfortable. Here, it changed everything — the landscape transformed with a storm, the dark pines huddled in the wind and the freezing rain or illuminated under the fierce touch of an ice storm, the glittering branches tinkling in the wind.

She was aware, her eyes were opening, she gained a new quality of sight, and in the days, she walked into the winter world with Miranda on her back. Billy had given her an old pair of snowshoes, and now she left the road, plunged into the fields and woods. The walking in deep snow kept her warm, she could feel and hear her heart, and had a distinct sense of her anatomy — tendons, sinew, muscle, bone within the firm package of her skin. She was strong.

Winter laid bare structure — the rocky granite bones of a hill, the limber skeleton of a tree. She loved the red spike of bramble against white snow and painted this in her mind because she had no paints, they'd been left behind, and sometimes she wondered who'd thrown her things away, maybe Selena, crumpling up the glove sketches. The winter light this far north was low-angled, casting sharp shadows, and upon the snow, she saw a new geometry.

The snow itself was never white, not when she really looked at it, but dappled with blue and violet or tinted umber, gold, rose. In the moonlight, it turned navy, aubergine. Upon the snow, she found the tracks of creatures, and took to sketching these. One day, she and Miranda had walked into town to the library, and she'd checked out a tracking guide. She had then learned the spoor of bobcat, coyote, weasel, squirrel, turkey, crow, deer mice, chipmunk. When the snow was firm and fresh, she could read their stories, their itineraries, and she wondered at their business, so much went on, unseen.

On this day, she turned into the woods on an old logging track, wanting to see if she could connect beyond the beaver pond to the snowmobile trail, and then loop back homeward. After several hours walking, she sat down on a log and took out a snack for herself and Miranda. The sun, gathering strength in March, fell upon them in the clearing, so warm Rosie took off their jackets. Snow melted from the trees, the sound of the dripping in the otherwise stillness had an almost metallic precision, and Rosie felt the gift: this was hers, she would carry it within her, no matter what happened, she'd have this moment in the sun. Some things could not be stripped from you. A crow chided her from a spruce, and Rosie chided back. Back and forth they went, the gentle *cah-cah, cah-caahhh* arguing about which had the better position, the log or the tree. At last the crow lifted her obsidian wings in three beats, into the air, *But I can do this!* And Rosie laughed, calling after her, "All right, you win!"

Coming back along the road, she was surprised to see Bennett's car in the drive. It was mid-week. Stamping the snow from her boots, she entered. The house was chilly from hours without warmth.

He was sitting in the chair by the stove. She walked past him and tended the fire in brusque movements. "Can't you at least keep the fire going?"

Even with her back to him, she felt the dissonance of him. Turning, she saw that he had not slept, his eyes were deep within his sockets, yet his pupils were bright and hard as brass thumb tacks. His hair was lank, and she became aware of his sour smell. Miranda crawled to him, swarmed up his legs. He buried his face for a moment in his child's body.

"You like walking," he said.

"Yes." Rosie was trying to calculate this new tone, this strange mood.

"Who gave you the snowshoes?"

"I found them in the basement."

"No, you didn't."

It was a flat disavowal, like a slap. Rosie looked out the window. If she was to paint the snow at this time of day, she'd use hues of orange. "Billy —" she began.

"Billy," Bennett said savagely. "Does Billy even know who Ezra Pound is?"

And yet the house was warm because of Billy, Bennett was alive because of Billy.

Bennett sighed, he was out of cigarettes. "Where is my bottle opener?"

"Your bottle opener?"

"My father's bottle opener."

"Why would I know what happened to your bottle opener?"

"Maybe Billy does. He had the perfect opportunity."

"Billy drinks from cans."

Bennett smiled. "Not bad, Rosie. I must give you credit. But you have a lot to learn."

She watched him: he was standing still; yet, within him — that off-stage man — she sensed movement, erratic, chaotic. She felt frightened. For now he stood, Miranda at his hip, and moved toward Rosie, he very gently kissed her, and with a low voice that was the opposite of the gentle kisses, he said: "This is how you do it, Rosie, this is how you lie." His hand went down into her trousers, into her underpants, his fingers into her vagina. She tried to back away but he hooked her, and he leaned in close: "The college, Rosie, the college has awarded me a fellowship in Paris. My work with Sartre and the other existentialists and how I'm synthesizing their philosophies with those of the Civil Rights Movement. It's an incredible opportunity, I'll be gone for at least a fortnight."

Letting her go, he put thirty dollars on the table beside her. "Here's some money." Then he started toward the door, Miranda still firmly on his hip. Rosie grabbed his sleeve, she heard herself utter little, bouncing No's: *no no no no.* He was taking her baby. With all her weight she tried to counter him, but he pulled and she was on her knees, and he was dragging her. Miranda, alert to the anxiety in her mother's voice, began to cry. Thus Bennett edged toward the door, the screaming baby, the crying woman. Instinctively, he tried to fling Rosie off, but she was stronger and quicker now and she held on and Miranda screamed and flailed about; unforgivably, she was reaching for her mother.

"Shut up, shut up!" Bennett shouted at Miranda, holding her in both hands *Shut up shut the fuck up* he had come undone, Rosie saw he was without restraint and she saw into the future, the fractional seconds ahead, in which he would shake their child, her head upon her narrow neck battering back and forth in the terrible wind of his rage.

A new voice came forth, a low growl: "Bennett."

He was still far away, his muscles were already beginning to tense, his hands tightened their grip and the neurons in his brain were already beginning to shake his child.

"Bennett," Rosie uttered, placing her hands firmly on top of his. His eyes lifted to hers, and she wondered if this stranger was the real man, at last he was here. Then she felt him soften, retract, he stepped back, leaving the weight of Miranda in her hands, and he turned and ran out the door.

*　　*　　*

Cheddar cheese 1.76
    Bread .55
    Can of tuna .59
    Can of tuna .59
    Can of tomatoes .69
    Campbell's soup 3 for 1.00
    Potatoes 5lb 1.23
    3 boxes of spaghetti 1.28
    Milk 1.59

Dozen eggs .80

Ground beef 1.47

Frozen green beans .29

Frozen spinach .29

Bag of oranges 2.31

Butter 1.59

Peanut butter 1.49

Coffee 2.13

Shredded Wheat 1.29

4 jars baby carrots 4 for 1.00

4 jars baby barley and beef 4 for 4.00

4 jars baby banana and strawberry 4 for 1.00

Tampons 3.69

Frozen chicken drumsticks 2.34

Vegetable oil 2.59

Rosie arrived at the checkout, slid the items onto the conveyor belt. She'd made a rough estimate in her head, yet the cashier told her "$35.85." She felt herself scroll inward, tighter and tighter, and she suddenly had an intimate connection to her stomach, could feel its dimensions, its rubbery exterior and the pooling yellow acid welling within. "I don't have enough," she mumbled.

The cashier regarded the 30 dollars in Rosie's hand. She was not unkind, just matter-of-fact, there were three people waiting. "What you wanta put back, hon?"

Rosie didn't know.

A large man in dirty sweat pants emblazoned with the NASA logo stood behind her. Breathing.

The cashier handed Rosie a coupon flier. "Somma this'll help ya."

Apologetically, Rosie shoveled all the items back into her cart as the NASA scientist shuffled forward in his flip-flops. His terrible feet were the color of plums, mottled and peeling and he smelled of dampness, of folded skin. Such were the denizens of the supermarket; they had rotting feet and missing teeth, they were over-weight — they moved like sailors carrying heavy cargo on an unsteady boat: legs wide taking timid steps, their hips tilting back to counterbalance the volume of their torsos. Their diet was mostly the extra-large size of anything nutritionally useless. The food of the poor is not the food of the rich, it is sweeter, saltier, creamier, cheesier, softer, brighter, it has rainbow sprinkles and pink frosting, it has the visual subtlety of cheap greeting cards or free calendars from the bank. How Bennett recoiled from what he saw in this market, sneering at bread labeled "French baguette," marveling at the giant people buying giant bottles of soda. "How do they wipe their own asses?"

Yet as Rosie saw them today — a few were even familiar, the woman with the dyed red hair and arm tattoos, for instance, the baby in her cart eating Oreos — she thought: this is what you have to comfort you instead of fine art, instead of the Paris Opera, instead of winter in Aruba. You have marshmallows, you have white bread. Beauty is not made for the poor. The poor don't have money for dentistry, podiatry, dermatology. Billy, for instance, had explained her lack of teeth, *Givin me trouble, couldna pay tha bills, fuckin doc takin them out one atta toime, loike drillin holes in chahk tha doc says so we figured best to do is take-em-all out in one go.*

Rosie held the box of tampons in her hand. A luxury item, it was also subject to sales tax. She put them back on the shelf. She'd find some rags, wad up toilet paper. With the coupons there were cheaper eggs, and cheaper milk. On the discount rack, she could get the day-old bread for .33. She realized she was poor.

On the way back, the weather turned sloppy and Miranda was already sniveling with a bad cold. Struggling to carry the baby and the groceries, she was just beyond the flood plain when a truck slowed.

Billy.

"Ya needa roide?"

Pushing aside a pair of jumper cables, Rosie bundled herself in with Miranda. The cab smelled of engine oil and it was wonderfully warm, a special car oven that baked engine oil bread.

"Long walk."

Rosie nodded.

Silence.

The truck groaned through its gears.

Silence.

Silence.

"Ya can borrow tha truck anytime ya want. Ya got no needta be walkin inta town with tha baby."

"I don't know how to drive."

Tears came, though Rosie did not know why, she was not remotely sad. They were onion tears and they dribbled down her face, plopping off into space below her chin. She had the idea that she was crying about something open or empty, but could not elaborate.

"Shhhiiit." Billy pulled over.

"No, no, it's fine, I'm OK," Rosie protested; her snotty nose, her sniveling baby all evidence to the contrary.

Billy handed her a rag that smelled of oil. "Ya got any money?"

Rosie shook her head. "Just what I had for groceries."

"The one bag?"

Wind rattled the truck and Rosie felt grateful to be in the warm interior. She wiped Miranda's snotty nose with the oily rag.

Quietly, Billy chewed.

Then said: "We're gonna jacka deah."

Salt. Billy put down a big square red brick. She also had a bag of old apples, windfallen from the trees that grew in wild profusion in the woods. "Usta be orchards, usta be fahms, sheep, Christmas trees. Not even in my day, tho. Now's jus loggin' n' dairy, tho theyah fucked ovah by the big outfits Midwest. Corn maybe, hay n' silage."

Two mornings later, Billy showed Rosie that the deer had found the salt, their high-heeled prints daintily engraving the mud around the block. "Molasses in tha fall, salt in tha spring. That's what theyah needin'. Ya gotta luah them from theyah habits. A deer'll go tha same place, tha same way every day. Gotta be somethin' special to pullem off track."

That dusk, she came to collect Rosie but refused to bring Miranda. "She'll croiy. A child croiyin'? Leave 'er ta croiy, she'll learnta quiet herself." Rosie locked Miranda in the dining room. She walked away from the crying, and then in the truck she couldn't hear it.

The truck bumped across the rough field behind Billy's, the lumpy residue of summer's golden rod, bramble, milkweed, and tussock grass. Billy tucked the vehicle under a cluster of wild apples and pines and cut the engine. There was to be no talking, and as Rosie waited in the dark, she came to learn about the quality of sound, not the cluster of noises or the background rattling that she'd always taken to be sound: but the single note of a squirrel's feet pattering across the leaf litter, or a car passing on Wilder Hill Road several miles away. Her ears seemed to vibrate, the tiny hairs within the coiled interior stiffen with the anticipation of listening. An owl. An unidentified snuffling. Rosie entered a different dimension.

Thus she heard the gentle pinprick step of hooves in damp grass, she heard the fabric of Billy's coat rustle. But she could see nothing, the moonless dark was absolute. And then: a wild blast of white light illuminating the salt lick and a doe as Billy flared the truck's headlamps. The deer slowly raised her head, she did not seem the least alarmed, looking directly into the light so her eyes gleamed blood red. In the peripheral light, Rosie watched Billy shift out of the car, leaning her rifle on the open window of the open door, her finger slid to the trigger. For a moment, Rosie wanted to shout to the animal, or to yell at Billy to stop; but already the bullet had left the chamber, already the doe was dropping, knees first, then canting to the side. Billy put her rifle up to the deer's eye, but it did not blink.

They lifted the doe into the back of Billy's truck, and back at her house, Billy slit open the belly and the garlands of intestines slipped smoothly out. Her dogs smelled the blood, howled and agitated on their chains, and Billy tossed them the guts. An argument broke out, loud protests by the dogs who hadn't reached the guts in time. Then she hoisted the deer by its hind feet onto the overhanging branch of a tall tree. Rosie saw from the wear of the rope that this had happened regularly. Billy held the body with the familiarity of a lover. Swiftly, she drew the knife down, peeling back the skin, so this hung in a cape around the deer's head.

The scene is cruel and beautiful, Rosie thought, the chiaroscuro of Caravaggio from the headlights, the deadness of the animal, like a crucifixion or one of Ida Shultz's meat-packing

canvases: the body both dull and bold, objectified and personi-
fied. Yet who would make art of this awkward womanless-woman
and her illegal deer?

Billy severed the hooves, cut off the head. These she threw
to the rest of her dogs.

"So hungry I ate 'em once," she said. Rosie thought she
meant the head and feet. No, Billy clarified: "Tha dogs."

Her knife flashed in quick, sure cuts, the slabs of meat off the
flanks and ribs and neck. The spine was exposed — she cut this
also for the dogs — so that only the hind legs remained, hanging, swaying slightly.

*   *   *

A hunk of back strap in the skillet, the blood oozing from the
tissue. Wild onions Billy gave her, a basket of dried boletes. *The
woods'r a lahda if ya know them.* The meat browning on the outside, interior still red and moist, the sharp smell of the onion.
Rosie pre-chewed small pieces for Miranda and then ate her own
steak with her hands.

A week later, Billy brought them a hare, already skinned and
butchered. It seemed so rudely naked. She set it in a broth of
dandelion greens, ramps, and potatoes.

*   *   *

Mud is its own season in Vermont, it is no simple transition.
Rosie's previous idea of spring was a brief gap between winter
and summer, a mere fortnight of unsettled days and blossoms.
But mud this far north colonizes three entire months. Mud

oozes through the seams of frost. Mud congeals like cold oatmeal. Mud slips like silk. It clamps onto boots and the wheels of cars so they screech, it clomps onto the axles so they wobble and judder on the highway. The smell of mud is the earth's own and oldest smell, the first smell the first olfactory sensor ever detected. Mud is the smell of earth time. Rosie sat on the back porch and inhaled.

The trees were still without leaves, brushed with tones of umber and the palest green — a teenage fuzz, more tint than color. She'd grown accustomed to their nudity, she even felt a trepidation for the foliage that would hide the mountains from her, obscure the woods she'd mapped on her walks. She liked things spare. Today, dozens of robins bounced about Billy's overgrown pastures, and red-winged blackbirds perched on the electric wire and the brook that ran through the woods behind the house unfastened its icy corsets and she listened as it *rush rush rushed* downhill, excited and eager as a birthday child. Miranda toddled in the grass, which was just green by this mid-May. The temperature was still below freezing at night, barely breaching 50 in the day, but the little girl demanded bare feet. Rosie took off her own shoes, her feet so pale they were nearly luminous. Miranda ran, and Rosie followed. The puddles in the driveway lured them and they flattened their feet into the silt and curled their toes through it even though it was icy cold. Miranda patted it with her hand.

"Mud," Rosie explained.

"Mudah," Miranda agreed, plumping it. "Mudah!"

Dimly, Rosie heard the car as it turned onto the road by the gravel pit. Dread rose in her like sap, flushing every vein in her body. She had half a mind to grab Miranda and run across the fields like refugees avoiding sniper fire.

Into the mud Bennett returned, the BMW slogging and skidding. The way the noise of the engine filled up the air, the smell of the exhaust, and then the wind once again looping in when he cut the engine: Rosie was so used to the quiet that foreign noise now squeezed against her ears, an uncomfortable pressure. Bennett stood by his car, he seemed hesitant, almost awaiting a command from her. Rosie scanned him, head to foot. He was shabbier, his clothes not quite flush with the frame of him. Wherever he had been, whatever he had done had reduced him. This new vulnerability had a wildly ambivalent effect on Rosie: she was glad of it, yet she felt a swell of compassion.

He was standing in the mud. "How are my girls?"

Miranda examined him, too, confused by her inarticulate memory. He must have seemed like a dream to her.

"It's Daddy," Bennett smiled. Miranda pumped her arms up and down, made a breathy noise like a fire bellow, and stepped forward. Just one child step yet Rosie felt the roaring of her daughter's treachery. Rosie blinked, turned away, for she was the traitor, too selfish to desire her child's happiness; if only her own father had come home.

Bennett came upon her as she was making supper: fiddlehead ferns in butter, deer liver. It hadn't occurred to him what she'd accomplished. For in the months of his absence, she had found her way to the dairy on Wilder Hill where she could get milk and eggs in exchange for sluicing out the milking shed; sometimes, too, she got meat when a cow died. The farmer and his wife had older children, and they gave Rosie bags of old clothes for Miranda. And Billy — Billy had taught her to drive the icy roads, the blind corners.

"I missed you," Bennett said, his hands on her hips. Didn't he notice the taut muscle of her lower back, the firm obliques of her waist and belly?

"Don't," she hissed.

Surprisingly, he fell away. "I understand. I'll wait."

Now she spun, the short chopping knife in her hand: "You understand? You left us here for two months with nothing, your child — with nothing!"

His large, beautiful hands splayed out, then came together in something like prayer. "I came back."

Outside, the earth was rolling slowly into space: Rosie felt herself to be miniscule upon the surface of the planet, of time. She was unimportant. She could disappear and nothing would change. Who even knew she was here? Bennett, Billy, the dairy farmers. This was the way she'd felt in Gran's house, looking out her bedroom window at other families, other children, they feathered carelessly, ceaselessly through the afternoon air in loud flocks, on bikes, skateboards, Myra Foley on her roller skates, her mother pushing yet another Foley in the worn-out stroller. They ran with balls, they ran with sticks, with ropes around their waists playing horses and they never glanced up, they didn't even think of her except as the orphan child with the creepy grand-mother, a character in a cautionary fairytale.

Bennett was one of them, wasn't he? Running with his sticks and his toy gun, and he had chosen her — not for inclusion with the others, not to join the running and the shrieking, the hide-and-seeking, but for his own private purpose. He had seen her, that morning at MoMA, in her solitude and scuffed shoes. Perhaps it had been curiosity or sympathy that set him toward her at the museum; though she wondered now, about a darker intention: when a man evaluates a lonely young woman, he knows exactly why he chooses her.

"I came back because I love you, Rosie." His hand on her face was hot with need.

And this is love, what all the fuss is about, the wielding of love to make you do what you don't want to, up the stairs, along the dark hall, swooning with gratitude for human touch, the intervention of a hand, to wear the bright halo of one who is chosen not discarded or ignored. She'd gone to The Giggle Man willingly, up the stairs, up the stairs, and now she stood obediently, obligingly for this other man.

*   *   *

While he was sleeping, she went through his things, yet there was merely: a gas station receipt from Portland, Maine; a packet of cigarettes; a lighter; matches from the Algonquin in New York; a copy of *Going After Cacciato* by Tim O'Brien; his money clip. He did not have a driver's license. In the car's glove compartment: no registration, no papers, only a wad of paper napkins, another packet of cigarettes, rolling papers, a leather button. She noted, too, a new smell like the damp sawdust she swept from the corner of the farmers' cow barn where the rain leaked in. Perhaps Bennett had spilled a drink of some kind, a yeasty beer.

As she fed the last of the wood to the stove, she considered Bennett's presence, his absence: the wavering quality of him. He might be a small-time dealer in art and antiques, he might be an intellectual teaching at an elite Vermont college. He might not. Bennett cultivated his obscurity, it was a mindful curation; he did not want her to know who he was. Nor did he want to know who she was. In Southport, this anonymity had seemed daring to her, a liberation, not having to explain Gran. Yet now she realized he might be anyone, anyone at all.

A friend of Bennett's was coming for dinner.

A colleague from the college.

"Wheezie. Teaches French and Canadian History."

"Is Wheezie a WASP, then?"

"He's an old friend."

The whole world was Bennett's old friend.

Rosie bought a chicken from the dairy farmers, an old layer hen, and the wife told her to brine the meat to tenderize it. She stuffed it with wild garlic, colt's foot, and dried wild cranberry, and rubbed dandelion greens with a tiny bit of oil, then salt. Bennett had foraged on his own in town — a passable wine, a bag of Florida oranges for dessert. The evening was sleek as an otter: warm, slippery. Rosie laid the picnic table under the maple with a white linen tablecloth she'd found folded neatly with the sheets in the linen closet. In the center of the table, she placed a jam jar stuffed with wild flowers while Bennett dressed Miranda in the farmers' hand-me-downs. As they worked together, Rosie felt the reverberation of some other life they might have had together, the one in which they were happy.

"Close your eyes," Bennett said, and she obeyed and felt the weight of soft fabric in her hands.

Dark green silk, a slip of a dress. Even though it was crumpled, Rosie could tell it was new by the smell. The clothes she bought in the thrift shop, the blue-tag-three-for-a-dollar, stank of detergent, and deeper in, nestled within the very molecules, of other people's lives. Bennett was dancing around her, "Put it on, put it on!" She noted the hemming. The pearl button at the neck. The way the fabric moved over her hips and breasts, the way it hung in loose pleats. It felt like warm water slipping over her body. It wasn't the kind of dress you could buy around here. Even if you had the money.

"And your hair. Wear it up." He admired her. "You're beautiful, Rosie."

Wheezie was a small man, narrow as a boy. He wore Wayfarers so Rosie could not see his eyes, and tight black jeans, a white tee-shirt, Stan Smith sneakers.

"Lovely to meet you, Rosie."

He handed Bennett a bottle of wine and offered her a bouquet of cut flowers that certainly did not come from the local supermarket, where the carnations were dyed bright blue and purple. He glanced at her dress, or seemed to — his head making an up-down motion: "Fabulous dress."

Rosie had a whiff, then, of sawdust.

Miranda tottered out holding her stuffed bear.

"Buggy," she told him seriously.

"Hello, Buggy." Wheezie offered his hand to the bear, whom Miranda engaged to return the gesture. "What a pleasure to meet you."

Dinner was served on the white tablecloth. The chicken had a gamey flavor, more like Billy's wild hares. Bennett kept touching Rosie, his hand on her shoulder, caressing her neck. Glancing at him, she saw only his easy smile, his open face. Wheezie kept his dark glasses on and told gossipy stories about the college — fellow teachers screwing each other or students, the revelation of the art teacher's criminal background.

In the kitchen, she sliced the oranges, distracted for a moment by the exotic color. Oranges came with Bennett and went with him; alone, she couldn't afford them. Through the window she watched Miranda, plump and content on Wheezie's lap. He had at last taken off his Wayfarers, for Miranda was chewing on the ends. His eyes were periwinkle, extraordinarily bright, like the eyes of a doll. As Rosie cleared the plates, she watched Bennett in attendance, his body swiveled to Wheezie. The narrow, little man is so convincing, she thought, with his stories, how neatly he embroiders with detail, and his instinct for the salacious.

But she was alert, as in the middle of the night, when she heard snuffling and pawing at the back door. It was only coyotes smelling the garbage, but long, long ago, it would have been wolves.

*   *   *

Once, driving Billy's truck, she saw Wheezie walking down the main street, his Wayfarers on, so she could not tell if he saw her back. Even though it was mid-day, mid-week, he wasn't at college. "College" — she added the quotation marks in her head.

And then, on a warm day in mid-July, she saw Bennett.

Just as she pulled the pick-up into a parking space under the trees at the supermarket, Miranda fell asleep. Rosie had wound the seatbelt around her with vague deference to the law — though, just this morning, she'd seen three different cars with small kids in the front seats, unbelted. Miranda chewed her fat cheeks like an old man at a cigar. Her eyes shifted back and forth beneath the lids, deep-dreaming. "Miranda," Rosie cooed, then louder for good measure: "Are you awake?" The little girl sighed, settled deeper.

Winding the windows down a few inches as she'd seen people do for their dogs, Rosie slipped out, locked the door. She was about to bolt for the entrance, when Bennett crossed from a parking space at the center of the lot. He was tilted forward with intention. At her remove, she studied him as a stranger: a man now in his 40s with thinning hair, a handsome face, a dapper wardrobe. He was getting fat. He carried a small paunch before him with the pride of an early pregnancy.

Inside the store, Rosie edged along the aisles until she spied him perusing the cheese. He had once brought home a Wisconsin gruyere "in a pique of optimism." But it had tasted like the sole of a new sneaker — of nothing but bland, white chewiness. Here he was picking up the plastic-encased slabs of American Swiss and discount parmesan as if, genie-like, he might transform them into the delicacies available at Balducci's in Greenwich Village. Why was he buying cheese? Why was he now looking for wine — the top shelf with the more expensive labels?

Items in hand, he headed to the checkout. Rosie, sliding behind the newspaper rack, heard the cashier call out the fantastic tally of thirty-three, seventy-two. Drafting out the door amid a pod of teenagers, she hustled back across the parking lot. She realized she was muttering to herself. The money Bennett was spending on cheese! The way she used rags instead of tampons, the cheapest soap that never lathered! And she accepted, accepted it! And here's Bennett buying *thirty-three-dollar cheese*!

A police cruiser was parked perpendicular to Billy's truck, and as Rosie approached she saw the male officer, Miranda inside — her furious shrieking only just audible.

"Is this your car, ma'am, your baby?"

"Yes," Rosie stammered. "I just needed to run in and get some diapers."

He cocked his head. Obviously she wasn't carrying anything. "You know it's illegal to leave your child unattended in the car."

"I was just a couple of minutes."

"At least 15, ma'am."

"I just went in —"

"We got the call at 10:23, and it's now 10:45."

"But she's fine, she can't get — the door was locked —"

Rosie unlocked the door and pulled Miranda close; almost instantly the shrieks subsided. Other shoppers were peering as they wheeled their carts past. Rosie felt the sting of their gazes. She hoped the officer didn't ask for her driver's license.

"Do you have a car seat, ma'am?"

Bennett drove past, he did not even see them — a police car with flashing lights, his own girlfriend and child — oh, no, Bennett was gazing ahead, already at his destination, that higher ground, where he was eating the Northeast Kingdom's very finest cheese and drinking wine with a cork.

"Do you know what happens to a child when it hits the windshield?" the policeman was saying.

"I just needed — I borrowed the truck from a friend —" Suddenly Rosie was crying, aware that her tears were partly fake, partly real, reflecting the tension she felt between the live wire of anger within her and her sense of how quickly and badly the situation could go wrong. Either way, she was at the mercy of this law man, this cop. He could take Billy's truck, he could take her child. "I'm just doing my best," she murmured, head down. Was this contrition sufficient? She kept her eyes on his heavy black shoes. He could make her do anything. "I'm so sorry, officer, I won't do it again."

He nodded in agreement, then stepped back. He dealt with messy people all day long, they spilled their lives like sticky drinks. "Just go," he told her and she went, slowly, orderly, intending to turn left. But as she checked right for on-coming traffic, she saw Bennett's BMW creeping away from her. He was obeying the speed limit as he headed for the southbound entrance to the interstate.

Tailing him was tricky because drivers on the highway simply overtook him, leaving her exposed. Even though he had no idea she could drive, she kept back as far as she could. Three exits down, he got off, merged toward Barnet. She let distance accrue, glimpsing him on the straighter stretches, but then, around two corners, she realized he wasn't ahead of her. Doubling back less than quarter of a mile, she pulled into the only alternative: the Shady Lawn Motel. Bennett's BMW was parked around the back.

Rosie turned off the engine. For a long moment, she simply sat in the warm sun, the leafy quiet. She could simply drive home. If she pretended she knew nothing, she would actually know nothing. But, of course, she would know *something*. Pretending not to know is willful self-deceit. The choice, then, was whether or not to be complicit in whatever elaborate lie Bennett was going to tell. *You've got it all wrong, Rosie, Rosie, this isn't an assignation. This is Matilda. Matilda is my old friend, Andy Warhol's daughter.*

When another car pulled in beside the BMW, Rosie ducked down. What would she look like, Rosie wondered, Bennett's cheese-and-wine-loving lover. *Matilda.* Or perhaps *Celia*, his never-before-mentioned cousin from Bermuda. Perhaps a student. Some off-campus tutoring. An enamored, silly young girl. Perhaps a little on the plain side, a poor dresser who looked better naked.

She heard the motel door open, muted voices, the door close again, and she sat up.

For a long moment, Rosie stared at the motel. Even denial has consequences. She got out, hitched Miranda onto her hip, and walked around the front of the motel. The old woman at reception was hooked up to an oxygen tank. Rosie told her that her husband had accidentally locked the key to room #23 inside.

"Dint know he hadda woife," the woman wheezed. "Nora a choild." Not much surprised her after seventy years on this side of the counter; she knew exactly who was in the room with Bennett. She gave Rosie the key.

It made a jaunty sound in her hand as she walked, and she slipped it into the lock and turned, the door opened. The wine was on the table, the cheese not yet un-wrapped. Bennett sat on the bed, Wheezie in a chair. What Bennett referred to as a tete-a-tete.

He turned, regarded Rosie and Miranda briefly, then refocused on the cheese.

"Come on in, Rosie," Wheezie said at last.

But she did not move.

Were they lovers?

"Rosie," Wheezie repeated, standing now, gesturing to a chair. "Have a seat."

He offered her a chair, gave Miranda a little smile and a wave.

Rosie stood on the threshold, failing to understand.

In the winter, snowshoeing with Miranda on her back, she'd found herself lost in the woods. She'd kept the Kirby Mountain ridge to her left, thinking that if she continued to bear right, she'd eventually come onto the mountain road. But it was difficult to see the mountain through the tall trees, and she'd thought to tell direction by their shadows, but the clouds moved in. At last, gratefully, she came across another set of snowshoe tracks. She'd thought they must belong to a trapper — who else would be up here? All she had to do was follow these back, and she'd come out somewhere. For the next hour, she dutifully backtracked, and then came upon a second set that joined this first.

These were clearly all her own tracks, and instead of bearing right, she'd made a huge circle *to the left*. There was no trapper — just her. She had a small baby on her back, she was lost and alone in the woods: she understood this intellectually. But physically, she had felt dizzy, as if someone had spun her around and around. Her internal compass had jammed.

She glanced at Bennett. *He's gay*, she thought.

The red compass arrow kept jamming at this point.

Didn't gay men want a certain kind of sex?

And he'd never
never tried
the other
hole.

She was lost in the woods, the trees were tall and dark. She'd thought she could count on the mountain staying still, but the mountain was liquid, the mountain tilted and drained from one side of her vision to the other, she could see it sliding through the vertical lines of the trees as the earth shifted off its axis, and she felt a terrible vertigo. The snow was deep, she might die in the woods, for no one knew she was here with her child. She had read that dying from cold was easy, you grew sleepy, you submitted to sleep with relief, you slept. And such a tiredness had been upon her, the tiredness went both backward and forward in time — the exhaustion of her past and the fear of the future, how uncertain the way. She could not trust her own tracks to lead her out, she had to make new ones through fresh snow across uneven terrain.

She saw a glass pipe of some kind on the table between the men, and the air of the room held a low smell of burning plastic. Bennett lifted the pipe, lit whatever was in the bowl and inhaled. He held his breath like a diver, then exhaled slowly.

"Oooooffff, maaaan."

"Join us, Rosie." Wheezie smiled, though his doll eyes frightened her or reminded her of a certain fear like white gloves so she turned, her arm tight around her child, and ran away.

The hills folded into valleys, richly embroidered in green, braided with sparkling rivers, a marvelous summer tapestry, the road threading through. What if she imagined a different life? What if she simply left? Took Billy's truck and just kept driving, her own Manifest Destiny. California, Arizona, New Mexico. She'd become Georgia O'Keeffe, live in an adobe casita on the edge of sagebrush with north light for the studio. She'd look through bones at the blue sky. Somewhere else, the life, her own life, and she'd slip into it like a green silk dress.

Yet today she found her way to the elite fine arts college, the entrance under an avenue of maples. Being July, the campus was quiet, though Rosie could imagine the scholars in pleated skirts and penny loafers inhabiting the lawns and pathways, the elegant brick buildings and white clapboard dormitories. Discreet signs provided direction: Calvin Morgan Library; Mildred Crawford Evans Memorial Auditorium; William Forsythe III Gymnasium. Rosie held Miranda's hand, and they toddled together toward Administration. Miranda announced, "Buggy wants moon."

The office was cool and dim, the walls lined with cabinets displaying awards, trophies, photographs. Briefly, Rosie studied these — the bright faces of students, clever, athletic, white, rich. *Wealthy*. Old money. Where were they now? In the Senate, on Wall Street, touring the Amalfi Coast in a red Fiat convertible. *This adorable pensione just east of Naples.*

"Can I help you?"

Rosie already knew. But she asked anyway, about a professor Bennett Kinney.

The receptionist tilted her head to the unfamiliar name. "Kenny?"

"Kinney."

"What does he teach?"

The whole Potemkin village, shoddily erected. He'd made so little effort — just cardboard and poster paint, a card trick that would fool a child, a coin taken from behind an ear. There she'd been, standing in MoMA, alone on a Sunday morning, not pretty, not clever; a bumpkin.

"Literature," Rosie said.

"I'm sorry, I don't have a record of him." The receptionist was flipping through the filing cabinet. "What years was he working here?"

"May I use your bathroom, please?" Because Miranda's diaper hung down, fully loaded with two hours of urine.

"Just down the hall, on the left."

In the bathroom, Rosie regarded the floral print wallpaper. Who designed such dreck? Was the artist instructed: take a living flower, provider of nectar to countless bees, and reduce it to decorative banality?

Miranda resisted the diaper change, scampering away half naked. "No! No!"

"You have to. You can't just pee all over yourself and Billy's truck."

"Bees fuck!" she gurgled, and made a vrooming sound.

"Truck."

"Fuck!"

Wrapping one expert arm around her child, Rosie fixed the diaper in place even as Miranda struggled.

"Liar. Can you say 'liar,' my love?"

"Liyah."

"Liyah," repeated Rosie, hissing the word through iron teeth.

"No!" Miranda told her.

Rosie's hands were too tight on Miranda's arm. "Don't you dare defend him." She quickly let go, stepped back. She turned on the tap and splashed her face with water.

"It's where the wealthy send their less palatable children," he'd said.

Miranda was looking up at her. "Mumma?"

The receptionist fretted that she hadn't found any record of Professor Kinney. Rosie mumbled her own apology, it must have been Middlebury or Bennington where he worked. Then, as if casually walking out, she glanced at the awards' cabinet, the photographs, black and white, the shaggy '60s 'dos and side-burns. Lacrosse, she recalled. A large silver trophy. Regional Champions, 1969. She read the team's names: Tucker, Forsythe, Forbes, Biddle, Harriman, Hartley, Wallace, Bentley, Tollemache, Carrington, Worth, Whitley-Burns, Kreitler. *Kreitler.* And there, beside Willie Kreitler, in the back row, with his broad shoulders and confident smile, was Bennett Kinney. He would have been about her age — 20. His thick, tousled hair fell across his fore-head, his arm rested on Willie's shoulder.

There was an ease about all these young men, Rosie observed, not just their physical strength and obvious health. They had money, they had good teeth, they had summer homes on Martha's Vineyard and winter ski cabins in Stratton. Their years ahead would be charted among family connections — whatever they wanted or needed, jobs, marriages, cocktails, Christmas in Aruba, and, eventually, obituaries in *The New York Times*. "I see that Skippy Pierce is dead," Bennett would say, reading the Sunday paper. "My mother used to hunt with him in Old Chatham."

Hunt. Not bears. Rather: foxes, with horses, to hounds.

Peering through the glass, Rosie compared this Bennett to the current Bennett, and could see not simply his aging, but an interior degeneration. Perhaps she should have some sympathy. Somewhere, somehow, between then and now — within that arc of blue time, within the assurance of his entitled trajectory — he had stalled. In that silent, gravity-less moment of suspension, he had looked down and seen the Icarus-swallowing sea.

Billy was at the door, a chicken of the woods fungus in her hands. She only came when Bennett's BMW was gone, and she would never enter the house.

"He stayin away this toime?" Billy spat her chew to the side.

Rosie shrugged. Bennett always came back.

"Ya wanta practice targit?"

They walked through the gauntlet of dogs, only one of whom had accepted Rosie, an older bitch with one eye — *beah tookit, hookt her claw n poptit lika fuckin grape* — who lifted her nose to gently sniff Miranda on Rosie's hip. Billy had no shortage of bottles and cans. The fragments and shards gleamed in a pile perhaps two feet deep under the wooden beam she'd set up against the berm behind her house.

"Ya wanta breathe, keep soft."

Rosie held the rifle, the rigidity of it still felt unfamiliar in her hands, she still anticipated the bang and the kick, and Billy wanted this to become second nature, for her body to take the movement as routine, no more than turning on a tap or lifting a cup to drink.

The problem with target practice was you didn't learn how

to account for movement. With an animal, Billy said, "Ya gotta know tha animal, wheresit movin,' howsit movin, straight or zig-zag, left, roit? Shootin' birds ya gotta aim down to flushit then up to gedit, boom-boom."

On Billy's command, Rosie fired. She was a lousy shot. "Good, good," Billy said, "Ya gettin it, ya gettin it." Then Billy scooched her chew to the other side. Spat. "May be a turnuv e-vents, ya gotta be prepared."

Rosie lowered the gun until it drooped over her forearm. She glanced at Billy, questioning. *Turnuv e-vents?* Turn of events.

Billy wanted Rosie to have a gun in the house; she worried about e-vents.

"Ya cant count on tha cops ta do nothin but scorn ya."

Billy went to set up another round, Rosie watched her — the way she moved with her shoulders like a man and hid her breasts and hips so deliberately. Billy Beetle, Rosie thought, burrowing into an invisible life out here on a dead-end road. No one comes to visit.

"Feel ya belly, make shuah it's soft'n loight, yar not holdin."

Rosie lifted the gun, sighted, softened her belly.

"Events turn, men turn 'em."

Rosie looked at the beer cans, lined up on the beam.

"Cops'll come out quicka for a roadkilled deah than they will forah woman with a fistin her face. Breathe, Rosie, fuck's sake, ya can't neva shoota gun if yur not breathin, can't do a fuckin thing if yur not breathin."

Rosie came back from a walk with Miranda. She was heavy to carry now, and restless, so Rosie's walks were shorter, less satisfying. Wheezie and Bennett were cozy at the kitchen table.

"Well, well." Wheezie was smiling. "What can we do about this trés awkward shituation?"

Bennett laughed warmly. "It's really not a problem, my man. We don't have to talk about this now."

Wheezie's hair was slicked back, he was slightly damp with sweat. His smell was sawdusty.

"You remember Wheezie," Bennett at last noticed her standing there. "He's just stopped by about a business matter."

Wheezie's Wayfarers hid his eyes, his clip-on, taxidermy eyes, which perhaps are not there today, only holes, Rosie thought.

"A business matter," she said, flatly.

"I'll have it for you on Monday, my man."

"You have said that for four Mondays."

"A minor liquidity problem, I'm having words with my banker?"

And how is he, Rosie said to herself. *How is your banker? Gorham-Chase, IV? We haven't seen them since the croquet match in Montauk.*

Crossing his narrow legs, Wheezie scratched his chin. Bennett plunged on, "I just don't understand how we got so far behind, Wheezie, my man. It seems like we were giving you stuff on a regular basis. Treasures, items of quality."

We? Rosie pondered. *Treasures?*

"Bennett, *my man*, that was always on contingent of sale. I can't move that kind of upscale schwag around here. Boston,

New York, Montreal, *my man*, I've had to travel. I've had to use my own funds."

"But more than two grand?"

Wheezie gave a low laugh, "This isn't an accounting issue."

"What about the dress? Rosie, go get the green dress. It's Lanvin. Worn only a couple of times, still worth a hundred at the very least."

A couple of times? Rosie had worn it once. Who else then?

Leaning in, Wheezie fingered Bennett's shirt. "This is quality but it is your costume only."

Rosie thought of Billy. Should she go and summon her? Billy would stride in with her gun and banish Wheezie. But, no, Wheezie was a small, fast, sly creature, he was hard and bionic.

"Come on, we're friends." Bennett's smile was beautiful, sincere and for a moment Rosie's heart pitched. "Buddies."

Wheezie sniffed, "Hours of listening to your bullshit stories. Vietnam? Viet-*nam*. That is what did it for me. I might've let you slide. But to lie about that." He made a motion to spit. "I was there, *man*, I lost *buddies* there, *man*."

Bennett seemed to be trying to say something about Vietnam "— Alpha Company, Kai Lam —"

"You read it in a book, that's all."

Rosie suddenly felt braver than a gun. "You want to fuck me?" She was matter of fact: "You can fuck me."

Now Wheezie pivoted his focus to her. "That's sweet of you, Rosie, dear. But no one fetches that kind of moolah up here. Not even the cherries."

"The cherries?" Rosie was tilting toward him, a kind of attraction or fascination.

"The farmers bring their daughters. They've got meth debts you would not believe. Those guys are getting up at 3:30 a.m.

and going to bed at midnight. The only way they can keep doing that is to pipe in the speed. And believe me, they are all mortgaged to the hilt. The dairy industry is in the shitter. All the big ag outfits in the Midwest get the government aid, and these local guys get totally shafted. It makes my heart bleed for them. You have to get their daughters young, though, before the uncles and the cousins have a go. In some cases the dads themselves. You're bugging hard enough, any port in a storm, right? So I must get them very young, ripe, very very —"

Young, Rosie heard. *Five or six. Four is even better.*

"What," she said.

Little cherries.

Wheezie did not have a face, it was a black sucking hole and it led down his throat and into the indifferent universe. Around the hole were small white teeth, like Tic Tacs. The teeth were opening and closing in a rhythmic way. There were sounds from the universe, howling space sounds, galactic winds that shattered the human body, and the teeth were somehow modulating the sounds. "Miranda" was echoing from therein.

Bennett was stuttering, "Is a toddler."

"Just photographs," Wheezie was saying.

Rosie leaned over and grabbed his ears and bit his nose and did not let go until she felt her teeth meet.

Bennett held them as they lay on the bed, Miranda asleep on one shoulder, Rosie awake on the other, the taste of blood still on her tongue. She wondered if Wheezie had gone to the hospital and if so would the police be summoned, he was so obviously the victim of an attack. If he didn't go, his nose might become infected. He might die under a bridge, like a wounded dog. Or he might be fine, wounded but absolutely fine.

She turned her face into Bennett's chest. He smelled of dry cleaning and cigarette smoke. The hot, still afternoon seemed to stick at three o'clock. Three o'clock would linger forever, the world would stop just this once. Darkness would not pad down from the mountain on its silent paws and cross the overgrown lawn and lean its hungry jaw on the window sill. Bennett kissed her head and his confession came at last: he'd stolen from Hobie and Mitzi — the dining silver, jewelry, and these he'd sold over the winter months. He stole from his rich friends, a kind of compulsion, a bit of a lark because they never suspected him, always the staff, the tradesmen. It wasn't a business plan but a way to make money and keep moving. He couldn't bear to be still. And then he met Wheezie and the coke, some freebase, a bit of meth, the odd smoke. He'd been so unhappy, the winter cold, God, how he hated Vermont, and he just hadn't realized Wheezie wasn't sharing out of generosity. "I needed someone to talk to," he said: "I thought we understood each other."

She rolled onto her back. "You never told me you were in Vietnam."

"Oh, Rosie. A soldier doesn't speak of such things."

She heard the shrill ttzzzeeeeoop of a red-winged blackbird. They often perched on the fence posts where the field was marshiest. Miranda sighed in her sleep. A car was coming up the valley and Rosie thought she should be afraid. But she wasn't. Not of a car. Because when Wheezie came back he'd be silent. She said: "We should go, we should leave now."

"How? We have no money."

"But you used to. You used to have a Picasso hanging in the dining room."

In one motion, he stood, braced himself against the window, framed by the soft round copper of late evening.

"It was all lost."

The car droned down Wilder Hill, carried on. The night was warm, so she opened the window and saw there were fireflies.

He flung his arm out. "Fabulous riches. All lost."

The apartment in New York, the house in Kennebunkport, the boat, the tailor, the concierge, the tea at Claridges in London, the estates, the compounds, oh, the invisible pathways the wealthy travel, never by bus or subway, instinctively turning left when boarding an airplane. Unless by private jet. Economy refers only to finance. The particular Venn diagram of first names shared by WASPs, drug dealers, and dwarves: Babbity, Babs, Wheezie, Sneezie. The last names carved on libraries, museums, cancer wings of hospitals. Tiffany gift boxes in pale blue with ribbons. All lost.

"My father. Dear, old Pap-pah. You'd think it was impossible for one man to make so many bad decisions — all the money, the incredible *all* of it — but he did. A sort of mad hubris took over him after my mother died, he believed he was a genius investor. Friends tried to tell him, 'We hire other people to touch the money.' And even when he started losing — crazy investments, scams, a tunnel between Ireland and England — he thought he was visionary, and he just kept going. He didn't understand what broke was until he couldn't pay for lunch at the Algonquin and Bunty Speer had to pick up his tab. Aunt Bee had married a minor Mellon, and they tried to help him, they'd staple on a tie and brush away the dandruff and put him about as a consultant. But losing is catching. And it smells. He drank and lived in their pool house and died of a heart attack."

Blink blink blink went the fireflies.

"And Vietnam?"

Bennett sighed with loss, with the pain of remembering.

"I wanted to be brave. A young man. It was all happening. Woodstock. Kent State. I used words like *honor* and *duty* as if they meant something. Oh, they were shiny like King Arthur's sword. And I believed nothing would happen to me, I was special, I was protected. Money protects you."

The bulky muscles of his shoulders flexed when he shifted, and the light showed all the lines in his face, especially the finer ones she'd never seen or noticed that pulled at his mouth, that frayed downward from the corner of his eyes.

"Shards of teeth," he said. "You have to watch out when a body hits a Claymore mine. Charlie Duck was blinded when a piece of Pete O'Brien's molar lodged in his right eye."

He lit a cigarette, and she thought the pause effective, he didn't let it go on too long. "Sometimes I get scared. The glitches in my soul, Rosie, the glitches in my soul," he clicked his fingers. "The glitches, glitches, you know, like fuses blowing."

Or fireflies glowing.

Rosie stood, she went and made supper, a can of tomatoes, a box of spaghetti. She chopped the garlic. Pete O'Brien, she was thinking, and the book she'd seen in his car by Tim O'Brien. *Going After Cacciato.*

*   *   *

In the end, there was no shroud of mist, no horror-film theatrics — the single knife missing from the knife block, the cellar light that doesn't work. Instead: a knock on the front door and she opened it, for it must be Billy with a luna moth for Miranda or directions to a patch of chanterelles. Instead: the smell, beneath the old apple of Miranda's that must have rolled under a chair, beneath the tang of his aftershave and the brine of cigarette smoke: the loamy stink of wet sawdust.

In a movie, she would have slammed the door and leaned her back against it, wide-eyed, panting, searching the room for a weapon to wield in self-defense. But in real life, this actual place from which she could not escape and from which she would not be saved, she stood and regarded him. Her guts roiled. A scream began in her throat, a mechanism to carry the fear from the cavern of her stomach to the surface, yet when she opened her mouth, the horror shapeshifted into reasoned words: "Come in, Wheezie."

Because he would come in, one way or another, he had been waiting to come in for weeks, she was certain now, not sneaking, not breaking and entering or leaping from a dark corner, but invited. He took a seat at the kitchen table, leaned back in the chair and removed his Wayfarers. The scar was impressive, a raw arc across his nose. He smiled. A mere movement of the lips.

"I'm not sorry," she said. "I wish I had bitten your nose off and spat it back in your face."

"Understandable. My mother tried to castrate me when she found me with my sister."

"This is all about your unhappy childhood?"

He tilted his head, "Au contraire. I'm grateful. It has given me an unsentimental perspective."

"It's made you a drug dealer pedophile."

"Made me? Or did I choose?" Seeing something in her face, he made an odd expression, a downturn of the lips that was either mocking or sincere, she could not tell. "Ah," he continued. "It happened to you."

"What did?"

"Who was he? Helpful neighbor? Kindly uncle?"

"How could you possibly know?"

"Oh, goodness look at you, tying yourself to a dope like Bennett. Don't try to tell me you love him. The damaged don't love."

"That's not true. I love my child."

"You should note that you only contradict the love part of that equation. Not the damaged."

"I hope you die a slow, painful death."

"You were a vulnerable child, lonely and unprotected by adults who were otherwise pre-occupied. It's always the same."

Rosie flushed, hot blood through her cheeks to her ears. She turned away.

"I wanted to be an architect," Wheezie went on, casually. "A large office with a corner view, worthy projects, designing houses for the poor. I'd wear nice suits, Italian shoes. But it didn't work out that way."

Damaged, she thought. But not *ruined*. Not yet.

"How did you know Bennett wasn't in Vietnam?"

"Only the poor go to war." Wheezie was looking at her, and she saw, for a moment, another version of him, and he was tired and sad and pathetic.

If things were different — looking-glass different — Rosie considered that she might value what he knew. Wisdom doesn't only come from the good. But he was a wicked elf, he moved within people's very worse intentions. He was a pedophile.

He said: "You don't have a phone. So I came to tell you. Out of the kindness of my heart. Bennett has been arrested. Up on Derby Line. The CBP busted him bringing in a car-load of cheap prescription drugs from Montreal. It's an open-and-shut case, five-to-seven, three hots and a cot."

The cracked linoleum: Rosie studied the spidery fractures,

one led to another. "You're here for something, aren't you? Not just to tell me about Bennett's arrest."

Sucking briefly on one arm of his Wayfarers, almost insouciant: "There is still the matter of his debt."

"It's not my debt."

And right then Miranda toddled in from her nap. She glanced shyly at Wheezie, then buried her sleepy face in Rosie's skirt.

He put his Wayfarers back on. "You have a self-sufficiency I admire, Rosie. You're like a wild animal. It's quite beautiful."

*   *   *

The car was a sun-faded silver Subaru Forester registered to Samuel J. Dinkins of Sheffield. It was exactly the kind of car Rosie saw other mothers driving around. In the back was even a high-quality car seat. The gas tank was full. By 9 a.m., she was on the road. Miranda chatted contentedly to herself. The radio, playing soft rock, began to crackle near Barton and snatches of quacky French broke through. For a moment, she forgot what she was doing, and imagined herself merely a tourist, in fact, traveling to Montreal for a day of shopping.

At the border, entering Canada, she showed the driver's license Wheezie had demanded she get and Miranda's birth certificate. The border agent looked French, dark-eyed, olive-skinned, and he spoke with a heavy accent. "What is your purpose in Canada?"

"Shopping."

"You have no shops in Vermont?"

"A friend recommended a children's boutique near Montreal. There's nothing near where I live, I'd have to drive all the way to Boston."

"How many days will you be in Canada?"

"Just today, up and back."

"You have the baby's father's permission to leave the United States?"

"Yes. Absolutely."

He looked sternly at Miranda, now fast asleep in the back seat. Rosie hoped this relaxed state would indicate all was well. For long minutes, the officer disappeared. She frowned and began looking impatient, as she supposed an innocent person might.

At last he returned. "We have to be careful. There are many kidnappings across the border."

"Really?"

"Custody cases." He handed her back the license. "Bon voyage."

Wheezie's directions were exact, and by noon she was entering a lowland of shopping malls, by-passes, and housing estates — the specific, soul-less way humanity flattened the life out of the land. Humans simply sat the earth with a giant cement bottom and this was the imprint. Beyond, she could just see the steel balustrade of Le Pont du Champlain and the spires of Montreal. Spires, like New York. She could not even imagine the young girl who had once lived there.

At hand was The German Sausage, exactly as Wheezie had described. With some effort, the square cement building had transformed into a Bavarian mountain chalet — dark beams, white paint, geraniums hanging in baskets, a looming wooden door with huge metal studs. She carried Miranda inside, encountering a strange Heidi-land of wooden chairs, checked tablecloths and photographs of snowy mountains. She was the only customer and the waitress — buxom, of course, in an embroidered dirndl — showed her to a wooden Heidi seat. The meal was pleasant, other customers filtered in, and by the time Rosie had finished an hour later, the lunch rush had started in earnest.

The car felt no different, parked in the exact same spot. Had it even moved? Were there even drugs in it? Or was this a fool's errand — Wheezie's idea of a joke? She buckled Miranda into her seat and spotted the shopping bag in the footwell of the front passenger seat. Peeling back the layers of pink tissue, Rosie lifted out a dark-blue velvet party dress with a sequined collar. It was beautiful, Miranda's size and color. A filthy image flashed through her mind of Miranda in the dress, Wheezie pulling up the hem to tickle her, and she stuffed it roughly back into the bag.

Heading east, only several miles since she'd returned to the highway, she saw an exit for I-89/Vermont — the other entrance to the US. To return via Derby Line, she'd need to simply continue straight. At the very last minute, she swerved south. Perhaps this would make no difference — if the border was alerted to her vehicle, they'd surely be alerted at every port of entry. Perhaps she was even making it worse, for Wheezie had a contact on the inside at Derby Line who'd make sure she passed through without trouble.

Yet, she crossed the border without incident. The US Customs Officer merely glanced at the receipt and at her passport. She drove south, through Burlington, then onto Route 2 at Montpelier, east for another hour and a half until Kirby Mountain enfolded her. With relief, she unlocked her door, entered the cool, quiet kitchen. Miranda had been brilliant all day, the perfect accomplice. Rosie lifted her child into her arms and murmured into her soft hair, "Thank you, thank you, thank you." The warm smell of her child triggered in her a great wash of relief and her eyes began to tear up: she'd done it, she'd done it, safe and sound!

From the living room, a polite cough.

Wheezie was sitting in an armchair, drinking a cup of coffee. He gave her a round of applause. Blank-faced, she handed him the keys. "So," he said. "Only three more runs."

"No."

"Wasn't I clear? I'm giving you a good deal, Rosie. A special deal because I know your situation. Five hundred *a run*."

"I can't do that again. I will not."

He put down the cup. "This coffee tastes like old shoes." Then he sighed, immensely patient. In the drug business, he had to deal with recalcitrant and unreliable people; he should have stuck to architecture. "Did she like the dress, the little darling?"

This time he was ready for her. He caught her just as her hand grabbed the coffee cup and began its arc toward his face. He held her wrist, twisting it so she cried out and dropped the cup. "What is wrong with a few photos? Just pictures. No one will know it is her, she herself will never know."

Rosie spat, but again he had experience, he ducked and the spittle hit the back of the chair.

"On your knees."

She almost laughed as he torqued her arm up behind her back. Only this? She prepared herself to smell his musty crotch, she hoped his penis might at least be clean and small.

"Lick the floor."

"What?"

"I don't like old meat."

Rosie got down on her knees, examined the floor. The feeling was familiar to her, as she had once raised her foot upon the first stair, and the second, the way up to The Giggle Man's room, the heavy wet-dog dread, another step. "I'll be back in a few hours," Gran had said. She had called up from the hallway so those remaining in the house would know they were alone. With her handbag upon her arm, her shoes on her bunioned feet, she had walked out, shutting the door behind her.

Generously, Wheezie did not make her lick the entire floor, merely around his chair. When she was done, she sat upright on her knees. He patted her cheek like a dog.

Good girl, there's a good girl.

"What was done by that man, it's not you. Not you, Rosie. That's what you need to understand. Me, on the other hand, I am defined by it. Don't you see? Strangely, I'm the victim. Every day, every hour, like a wolf dying of hunger I obsess. I obsess."

*   *   *

His skin was grey, his eyes red. Bennett peered at her through the glass partition. "Hello, my girls." His lion mane lay flat, exposing the recession on his forehead. Rosie wondered if early baldness might have made him a better man. He made a silly face for Miranda, bobbed his head. "Hello, little girl, Daddy's little blub blub! Hellllooo!" Miranda batted at the partition. Bennett gave his best sheepish grin. "I guess Daddy screwed up."

Rosie made a dismissive noise in the back of her throat. Bennett did not ask: *how did you get here?* He did not consider her car or lack of car or what needed to be done to simply not die in the winter. He did not consider Billy, for Billy didn't know Yeats or Hardy. He didn't know how to light the stove. He was still waiting for tea and scones with rose petal jam.

He began to cry. Fat tears dripped down his face and off his chin, a drip of sad snot leaked from his nose. With all the weight he'd gained, he resembled a very sad bear. How he repelled her, she felt ill considering the fact that he had touched her, licked her, been inside her. She had never loved him, love had vaporized retroactively. Yet she had only herself to blame. Less pusillanimous, she would already have moved to Santa Fe and gotten a job waitressing, she'd already be painting the rose and ruby-colored land. Oh, cowboy boots and silver bangles, skulls and sage! Oh, Georgia O'Keeffe on a motorbike. Rosie had lacked vision. She had failed to see she could have had the child without the man.

"The arraignment is tomorrow." He pressed his hands against the window. "Please. Please. You have to help me, Rosie."

She swallowed the spit that still tasted of floor.

"Please." He was sobbing wet, childish sobs. "Ask Hobie — Mitzi — ask my sister. I'll give you her number —"

But Rosie was furled, she was curled, she was thinking only: *I hope you die in here, you lying sack of fucking shit, I hope your lies crawl out of the rotting sockets of your skull.*

He did not notice her silence. Grief and sorrow were upon him. "I'm sorry I'm sorry I'm sorry I'm sorry so sorry so so so sorry I'm so sorry Rosie Rosie Rosie Rosie Rosie Rosie please sorry sorry for everything everything I'm so sorry please don't leave me please don't leave me here."

Rosie looked at him, this one last time, there was so much to say but what she decided was this: "Now you'll really have something to tell stories about."

And that was that, the buck had finally stopped, she stood up, she was raising her eyebrows to the guard, who lifted his in return — an entire conversation taking place between sets of eyebrows. All she had to do was lift her eyebrows and he opened the door. She hoped Bennett was watching the ease with which she moved out into the free world. Then the door slammed shut behind her, and she heard only a muffled droning of despair, which might not have been Bennett. Some other mug.

In the hallway, in the white scorching light, she stood for a moment, bracing herself against the wall. Miranda was drooling through the gap in her teeth, so Rosie crouched down, dabbed it away with the hem of her skirt. She saw the floor, smeared with the filth of those who walked in and out, gathering whatever on their shoes, dog shit, mud, urine from the floor of the men's room. How might this floor taste? Different from her own floor? She'd licked the cracked linoleum, she'd licked Wheezie's shoes, she'd swallowed back the gagging in her throat — the floor had had an oddly neutral taste, gritty, dusty, slightly sour. She did what women do and have always done, because the laundry still needs to be folded, the children collected from school or the fields or the workhouse, the dinner has to be made or gathered or harvested or butchered. Women do what needs to be done, they do what is expected, the obligation of their gender. For centuries, for thousands of years, tens of thousands, millions of years, women have been sucking cock and licking floors and going up the stairs just to keep men from making any more trouble. Men mistake the act of submission for the condition of submission. But they don't know that women split themselves right down the middle, the submitting part and the *fuck you* part.

When did this splitting begin? Rosie regarded Miranda. Had it already, in this small girl-child? She'd received, aged twenty months, her first sexual proposition. How many more to come? Women had holes and men believed it was their right to fill them. Not content with the physical holes, they tried to make existential ones. Drilling, drilling, drilling.

Rosie could not possibly protect Miranda from this, she was

completely unequipped for motherhood, the mothering of a porous girl. She'd entered a foreign country, a terrible Gulag, Ivan Denisovich in his broken boots, dreaming of hot potatoes by the fire.

"Dadda!" Miranda reached back toward the door. "Dadadadad." The word Rosie herself could not remember uttering. Dad. Daddy. The first word a child learns. Not Mama. Because the "D" is easier to form in the mouth. Dadda, the first claim.

"We won't see Dadda for a while, my love."

"Bap bap bap." Miranda swarmed up Rosie's body, her small, fat hands tapping her face. "Mummumumumumum."

Outside, Billy waited in the truck and she started the engine and they pulled away from the prison. Through the gate, onto the road of this obliterated place, a landfill on a bog, devoid of trees where only wind and mosquitos dwelled. The ubiquity of such a cubist cement structure upon a stripped land provided a grotesque kind of democracy. Bennett was absorbed, now, into a classless system; or, rather, a system of different classes, where the violent and the hardened were the entitled ones. Rosie was suddenly filled with wild joy — and she let it run through her veins, she allowed herself the illicit, savage pleasure of vindication. Quickly, though, she let her hair fall across her face so Billy'd not see her bright glow. Not just Billy, but Gran's Fate who patrolled the earth on the lookout for such delirium.

"Howaboutan icecream?" Billy began. "There'sa place in Derby —"

"Just home." *Home.*

Rosie watched the trees along the roadside, the road itself bending and looping like a dog through the loping land.

Five-to-seven, Wheezie had said, five entire years, six or even seven, how many days — more than a thousand, possibly two thousand, and these days ran ahead of her on the road, uncharted, aimless in their multitude. She saw herself, clearly now, Miranda's hand in hers, striding toward the distant mountains. Purple in the summer noon they rose, softly contoured against the sun-diluted sky. So fixed on her horizon, Rosie hardly heard Billy, who was saying something about building a greenhouse, a plan she'd had for years but *nevah godup offa moiy fat ass*, and givin up tha drinkin and maybe tha chew and sortin out them apples, a bounty was to be had if we'd getta prunin and we can store em all winta in tha root cella, no pointin jus leavin them all far tha beahs and tha deah and tha child'll need-tah gotah school less yor thinkin a home-schoolin'.

Through the drab town, and Rosie was cheered by the effort made to hang baskets of nail-polish pink geraniums on the small white pavilion in the park. Children were playing in the fountain, though a sign said not to, they were splashing and laughing, and the water scattered into the air, droplets hanging like a silver net in the heat.

The truck rattled homeward, the tar yielded to dirt, and past the rough fields rife with burdock and milkweed and black-eyed Susans. Miranda was fast asleep, her head improbably kinked against her shoulder, mouth open like a trout. *Mine*, Rosie thought. All I need, all I have in the world, this child, my child. Even the house with its treacherous roof, the broken window and the rotting doorframes, even the house is *mine*. Bennett is gone, gone, a far ellipse, catapulted into deepest space. Pluto.

"Wouldya liketa —"

Rosie turned, surfacing.

"Come for a bar-bi-que, kinda celebratin'."

Now Rosie saw Billy's new shirt, or clean at least; and, oddly, earrings — a dainty pair of butterflies in the plump lobes of Billy's clean ears below her clean hair.

"Oh," Rosie heard herself say, a sound like a stone dropping in water.

Billy blushed fiercely and retracted — not her body, which remained stolidly in the driver's seat, the small hands with the scrubbed nails gripping the steering wheel — but her heart. Billy pulled in the white lace of her heart, the delicate material she'd hidden away, carefully, fearfully sequestered in tissue paper, it was stained but still pretty, and the mending had been done with small, dutiful stitches.

"I mean," Rosie tried. "Not tonight, maybe tomorrow."

"Yep. That'd be foine. Ya let me know."

Rosie got out, cradling her still-sleeping child, this weight in her arms was all she ever wanted, it wasn't too much, and she bowed her head as the greedy gods stalked on by.

THE CEMETERY
1991

A deer trail cut through the woods, faltering and veering within the dense understory of ferns, brambles, and hobblebush. Rosie paid attention, for animals always took the way of least resistance. Here, in the early spring, when stubborn patches of snow clung to the shadows of the spruce, she harvested fiddleheads. In late summer, she picked firm-fleshed bolete mushrooms, puff balls, hedgehog fungus. Dozens of these were now stored in the basement, sliced and dried and packed in brown paper bags, ready for use in venison stews and soups. Ahead, where two streams intersected in a flat area of marsh, she knew there were marsh primroses in May and lady slipper orchids in July. In this late November, she was the brightest object in the wood, dressed from head to toe in hunter's orange. She had not been up here for more than a month, for it had been rifle season, and fools were about with guns and beer and the need to compensate. For the weeks through November, she'd hear the sharp retorts echoing around the peaks and valleys of Kirby. She always hoped for one shot, which meant the deer was dead in an instant, or one shot, a pause, and then the mercy shot. But often enough there was blasting, bang-bang-bang, then long, long minutes passed and more bang-bang, so that she knew an incompetent was killing the deer slowly, gut shots, broken legs. Some let it run off to die the animal way. Rifle season ended after Thanksgiving, and it was musket now, which required greater skill — therefore fewer hunters. Rosie had learned with Billy's rifle, but she preferred musket simply because she wanted to be alone in the woods, not fearing for her life, some Masshole in a Filson jacket and Timberland boots mistaking her for an eight-pointer.

A grouse suddenly flew up from under her feet, launching upon the air with whirring wings and an outraged squawk. She watched it flee, amazed as always by the ability of such a dowdy, plump bird to navigate at speed the tight macramé of branches. Otherwise, the forest was still, the early winter light fragile, pallid.

Before Billy's knees had turned to grit, she'd taught Rosie how to be in the woods, and that entering them required a different attitude, nothing sacred or religious or even mystical, but a re-focus. The smells of animals, the temperature of their scat, the broken branches or flattened bracken or scrapes against a tree: here began other stories: deer yard, moose in rut, bear territory. Once, they found a coil of still steaming guts: "Beavah," Billy whispered and made a dramatic cutting motion across her throat. "Kiyoat." Billy sniffed, Rosie sniffed. Upon the air: currents of musk, the spice of blood.

Her stand was beyond the marsh, near an old apple which bore small, tart fruit even after the first hard frosts of mid-October. The taller trees had crowded out the other apples. Once there'd been an orchard and a homestead. Rosie had found the foundations of the high barn, and a rusted stove slowly disassembling at the base of a paper birch. The birch was at least a century old, which made the stove a few decades older. At that time, all the land would have been cleared for sheep — the now deep-wooded hills would have been bare-assed as highlands, criss-crossed with stone walls that even now dredged through the leaf litter. Rusted barbed wire remained to trip up the unwary, the narrow strands embedded within the meaty trunks of maples and pines. The trees absorbed the cruel wire, grew straight and tall, regardless.

There had been a road here, too. The earth still held the depression where wooden carts had passed, and even further on, a small cemetery with a dozen headstones. Rosie knew these almost by heart now. She liked to sit among the quiet, unremembered dead. These slabs of marble and slate had cost someone dearly, a gravestone purchased instead of a pair of new winter boots or a new blade for the saw. And to what end? The dreary annual trips to the graveyard with Gran had never felt like a communion with her mother and father, Rosie had no connection with the two headstones and their administrative facts, their drab chrysanthemums. Her parents were not there comforting her with a gentle breeze. They had absconded, they had left her without love, and what she often wanted wasn't to grieve but to harangue. *Why did you leave? Why did you leave me? Why did you leave me with Gran?*

Two years ago, when Rosie first found this cluster of graves, she thought she would like to be buried here, and then considered how absurd, for this place would mean nothing to her dead. Soon the trees would reclaim the earth, upend the gravestones, weave their roots through the catacombed bones.

Billy told her there used to be farms all over the mountains, schools and tracks, and the cemetery had been busy. But then the descendants of the descendants died or moved away. Even the Mixes were newcomers — they'd come to Kirby to farm Christmas trees in the 1920s. Billy didn't like graves, the idea of the dark, suffocating earth, she said, gave her *the hebemajebees.* "I'll be foddah, I reckin, for tha kiyoats and fishers, beahs and the loik. They're oweda pieca me. Payback, yep, for the killin' of them I done. Fair's fair."

Climbing up to her stand, Rosie opened her thermos and drank the dark coffee. The warmth in her hands and throat was beautiful. Then she waited, a hibernation that was also a coiled preparation. Within her physical stillness, she listened and watched. The coming of a deer, the punch of narrow hooves on near-frozen ground, or the flickering of an ear, a tail.

At last, at last, a young buck appeared, a second-year male, she was lucky, for last week she'd had only does. He slipped through the woods, his movements silken and spare. She'd tried to learn from the deer how to move without wasting precious energy, how to imagine the land beneath the undergrowth so she did not stumble, how to step over, under, threading through with a sinewed continuity.

The buck approached, tentatively, as if suspicious of anything so sweet as apples. He scented the air, but on this still morning, he would find no trace of Rosie, the breeze carried her smell away from him. He flicked his glorious tail, he reached back and scratched his hind leg with his teeth. Rosie could see the boot-polish wet of his nose, his dense eyelashes. She could almost hear his breath as he moved directly beneath her, his nose to the ground, his mouth upon an apple. Billy had told her she shouldn't think about being slow, or trying to move so incrementally that the deer wouldn't notice, because the deer would see the slightest movement, such was their design, their eyes mounted on the sides of their skulls to see behind and above. Billy said she had to stop thinking about the gun and the movement altogether, to practice at home again and again until the motion was thoughtless. "They see ya thinkin'," Billy said. "They heah ya thinkin'. It's the thinkin,' the ruckus in yer head like a circus parade."

The buck dropped, the sound of the shot continued around the hills, ringing the clear morning air, around and around like a bell. Jumping down from the hide, Rosie squatted to pee — the release of coffee and tension made the pissing intensely sensuous. From her low position, she admired the morning, the tones of cool blue and pale pink, heavy frost still sheathed the startling cerise of the wild blackberry canes and the bright citron of the bunch grass. The sharp tang of gunsmoke prickled her nostrils. She felt ancient, as if she put her hand down on the earth, she might reach right through and grasp a cord that connected her directly to another hunter who had squatted here on similar terms on a similar morning centuries ago. Nothing felt this complete, not even Miranda in her arms. She was entirely happy.

The buck's blood melted the frost, began to congeal in the cold air. She stroked the soft head, her bare hand on the fading warmth. It was a beautiful animal, entirely driven by purpose. From her belt, the unsheathed her knife and field-dressed it. The guts made a neat pile, still steaming with the heat of the living body. Skunks, coyotes, weasels would find them soon enough.

Tucking the hind legs into her elbows, she began to drag the buck. It was a good size, probably 150 pounds without the guts. Now she began to walk back down the hill, perhaps a mile, over rough ground. Sweat soon streamed down the narrow of her back and the cleft of her buttocks. Her lungs heaved in her chest, yet her heart obeyed, her heart loved this, her heart whirred and pulsed with the joy of the effort, she had a soul, for the soul flew down the hill, leaving the mortal carapace to struggle through the brambles and over the debris of fallen trees and rotting logs.

Two hours later, her thighs and shoulders aching, she neared Billy's. The dogs began to bark. Billy hobbled out of her house, squinted: "Ya find tha on tha road didya? Some real huntah forgot to close tha tail gate, I reckin."

They lodged the buck on the hook and hoisted it up on the hanging rack. For the first time all morning, Rosie felt squeamish. Still she hated the leaden deadness. To have the deer strung upside down was a kind of humiliation, his neat furred testicles on display. The buck had survived the brutal winters and the cunning, hungry springs, and now hung neutral as drying laundry. The first time Billy got her over a deer, Rosie had missed, relieved to see the buck bolt into the thick bush. But two things changed her mind about the order of life: Billy told her that there are no easy deaths up here. "Wacha think? Tha deah jes lay down and go ta sleep when theys too old?" No. They die slowly from disease or winter or "they get gimpy and the kiyotes take 'em, apieca ata toime."

Death and *hungah*. "Ya evah bin starvin?" Rosie had not — whatever Gran's failings, there had been food. Growing up, Billy had endured lean winters, leaner springs, because by then the salted meat was done and nothing was growing yet, the root cellar empty, they were scraping the last of the berries from the preserve jar, and Billy did not believe a deer felt less worry than a child — the peculiar anxiety of chronic hunger, the pain in the belly and the way muscle disappeared, the shape of your own skeleton emerging beneath the skin. "Ya see ya own veins throbbin in ya feet and ya cant nevah get wahm."

Billy knew how life slipped, snake-quick. Her father'd died of exposure, falling on the ice while going to feed the pigs, knocked himself out and no one realized until the morning. "I thought ita pilah rags, someone'd dropt tha laundry." Billy also knew how to survive on residue, like some kind of Saharan antelope. Tuesday was when the thrift store in town put out the newest donations — the boots and good shoes and coats went fast. She knew the supermarket handed out expired food if *ya go ta tha back doah, if ya ask fa Donnie.* You could get oranges, bananas, meat and chicken, bread and milk. Billy refused to take state assistance because then "They" would know where she was, and who she was and that wasn't anyone's business but her own. The very poor don't have many choices, and Billy didn't want some nosey *pakah* from *tha town comin up heah* with a clipboard, *pryin, tellin'* her her house *weren't upta* code or why hadn't she paid her taxes. Neither did Rosie.

After dividing the deer, Rosie slung a haunch across her shoulders and took the shortcut back across Billy's fields. She remembered the first time Billy had given her a whole deer leg and she'd had no idea how to cut it up. She'd wrestled with the meat, thinking it should be sliced, perhaps like a pineapple, lengthways, and finally taken an axe to the joints. Now she knew how to filet and debone with the expertise of a butcher.

It was barely eight, the palest sun broaching the mountains. Now the cold came to her, her toes like stones, her hands aching. Her fingers fumbled the lock to the front door, and inside the latch for the dining room.

"Mama?"

Rosie swung open the door, reached down and pulled Miranda into her arms. Her child held tight, regardless of the deer blood. "You were a long time."

THE CELLAR
1993

Rosie was almost out the door — Miranda already in the car with her backpack and coat. She did not recognize the number, it was local, she picked up. For a fraction of a second, she imagined that it was State Farm telling her she'd missed a payment on the car insurance.

"Rosie."

Not a question.

If an elevator suddenly lost its traction and plummeted, the occupants must feel exactly like this. The squealing gravity, the falling almost too fast for fear.

"It's me."

No point in pretending, no point in asking *Who?*

"I'm at the Gulf station in town."

She coiled the phone cord around her fingers, said the only thing she could think of: "Why?"

He made a soft laugh, weary perhaps. "You ask why, my girl?"

Rosie peered out the door. Miranda was looking back at her, pointing to a make-believe watch on her wrist and mouthing, "We're late!"

"Come and pick me up," Bennett said.

"Right now?"

"Yes, right now."

Rosie said, "I need to be at work." There was a pause. She heard him huff, as if of displeasure. "Tell them something came up."

"It's not that kind of job."

"Tell them."

"Yes, Bennett." How odd his name on her tongue, the syllables dead-ending with the hard 't.'

"Where's Miranda?"

"On a field trip."

"For how long?"

The lie was smooth. "Three days. A nature center. In upstate New York."

"I have ached in my bones for you."

Rosie wound the phone cord tight around her wrist. "Give me an hour. Two hours."

There was silence, as if he was considering what there may be to consider, the full array of options before him. "If that's the best you can do."

Rosie thought of calling Billy. Perhaps she could take Miranda away for a few days. But she didn't want to put Billy in the middle.

At school, she parked rather than simply dropping Miranda at the front door. They walked together, Miranda's warm hand in hers. Soon Miranda would tear away from her, veer into her group of friends.

"Bye, my love." She kissed Miranda's forehead, and her daughter embraced her.

"Love you, Mummy!" Away she flew.

Inside the school office, Rosie found Karina, the school

secretary. "I don't know if you can help. My grandmother died and I need to go to her funeral. It's not a family-friendly event and so I'm hoping I can find someone for Miranda to stay with for a few days."

"I'm sorry to hear that." Karina frowned. "But —"

"I just don't know any of the other mothers," Rosie rushed on. "I'm always working so I don't get to meet them. Or I'd ask one of them."

"I wish I could help —"

A woman's voice from the hallway, "Miranda can come with me."

Rosie turned, and the woman continued, "I know Miranda, she's in Margo's class. She can come home with me. She can stay the night. Two nights. Whatever you need."

"Are you sure, Ginny?" Karina sounded relieved.

Ginny held out her hand to Rosie, "Ginny Benoit."

Rosie exhaled. "Thank you."

She arrived at the care home five minutes late. The job was minimum wage — bathing the elderly residents, changing their diapers, helping serve meals; but Mary, the owner, was teaching Rosie how to do the book-keeping. And as Rosie didn't have a drug habit or a drink habit or a criminal record, Mary cut her some slack. She didn't mind, if, on the odd snow day or sick day, her employees brought their kids to work, provided they didn't get in the way. Mary had raised five boys on her own. Today, she fastened her lips over her fake teeth. "You've got three showers lined up this morning."

"I wouldn't ask you, if I could avoid it. Mary, please."

Mary sighed, "Just do Roberta, then. She cooperates for you for some reason."

The reason being that Rosie took care. She soaped the old

backs, some smooth and white, others mottled with cancer-
ous patches. She cleaned old feet, between their toes, the stinky
cake of dead skin, she trimmed the yellow claw-like toenails,
she wiped between the sagging buttocks the smears of shit and
dried urine, she rinsed between the folds of exhausted skin. The
bodies had neutrality, like butchered deer, they were parts that
needed tending. Ball sacks, pendulous breasts, scars, creases,
grooves, niches: Rosie felt no repulsion, though the decrepitude
scared her, the inevitability of the body's failure, the terrible
loneliness and abandonment. Yet she couldn't see herself in old
age, the old were another species altogether.

Roberta sat curved forward, her knitting almost up to her
face.

"Bath time," Rosie began.

"I jes wanta die."

Rosie said nothing, simply folded her arms across her chest
and stood. She'd learned this from Big Sal, one of the nurses
who'd grown up on a dairy farm. Big Sal was 5'2", but she was
used to moving cattle around. "You just stand n' glower, don't
be noice or hava chat, then they see maybe you're soft n' they'll
make a run at you."

Roberta was 94, she'd broken her back ten years before,
though no one in her dysfunctional family had noticed. The spine
had healed curved as a fiddlehead. Grumbling as she pushed her
walker, head angling down from her back at 90 degrees, Roberta
marked her progress to the bathroom according to the swirls on
the carpet beneath her feet. "I want to die."

"We're nearly there," Rosie replied.

"Why cant I jes die?"

"Watch the door. I'm sorry you're so sad. Here we are, a few
more steps."

In the bathroom, Rosie helped Roberta out of her clothes, exactly as she had once done for Miranda, taking of the pee-soaked diaper one leg at a time. Roberta smelled — body odor, urine, probably feces, certainly the foul stench of her rotting gut that roared up her throat and out her mouth, so Rosie made sure to evade Roberta's face. Gently, she pulled her shirt over her head, and held her under her armpits to maneuver her into the shower stall. When Rosie turned on the water, Roberta began to cry. "They're ol dead," she whimpered. "I jes wanta join 'em." Her son in a car crash, her husband of heart-failure, one granddaughter to cancer another to drugs, a great-grandchild to pneumonia. Life seemed a high tide that had taken the people she'd loved out beyond the reef, leaving Roberta on a lonely shore. Sometimes Rosie wondered that if she ever made it to 90, what might have happened to her. Sometimes she wondered about Gran's grief, what it might have done to her — losing a husband and her only child.

She ran the warm water over Roberta's body while she wept, for the shower stall was to Roberta a kind of chapel where she could express the grief she refused to otherwise show. When Rosie was done toweling down the arched back, Roberta sighed and sniffled. "What's for lunch?"

"Tuna noodle casserole."

"I hate tuna noodle casserole."

"There might be some soup from yesterday."

"I jes wanta die."

After tucking Roberta into her chair by the window Rosie found Mary in the nurse's station sorting prescriptions into paper cups. "I'll be here tomorrow."

"And this weekend?"

"This weekend?"

"I left you a message," Mary said.

Rosie shook her head, there'd been no message. Miranda, perhaps, playing with the buttons. "When do you need me?"

"To cover for Doreen from six to midnight Friday and Saturday night. Her husband's in the hospital, she can't make the whole night shift. You can bring the kid."

In the car, Rosie flipped down the visor and regarded herself. Touched up her mascara, softened her hair. Her eyes looked back, just that section of her face, like an Arab woman who showed only this part of herself to the world; her eyes were pretty, greeny-blue, the iris rimmed with a dark wheel, thick lashes, nicely arched brows. Suddenly, roughly, Rosie smeared off the mascara with saliva and the edge of her shirt, pulled her hair sternly back.

Bennett was sitting on the guard rail that separated the Gulf station from Trader Bill, who repaired chain saws, lawn mowers, and snowmobiles. Trader Bill had once asked Rosie out when she brought in her chain saw blade for sharpening. She'd politely rebuffed him, and when she went to use the blade it snapped and would have cut her face to hell if she hadn't been wearing a visor. Bennett stood as he saw Rosie in her car. He was bulkier, his hair very much thinner, greyer. Was he buffed from muscle — or was the bulk merely fat and a cheap jacket? He was old, she realized, in his 50s.

When she pulled to a stop beside him, he walked over, looked down at her in her car. "Hello, my girl."

Rosie had ignored this moment, she'd denied it. She'd imagined Bennett would be absorbed like a splinter into some dark corner of the world. Yet, here he was, the Universe had boomeranged him back. Stripped of his Harris Tweed, his Brooks Brothers French cuffs, he wore a grubby flannel shirt and ill-fitting stone-washed jeans, worn sneakers and the dirty jacket. Jail had coated him with seediness; he was now the kind of man who'd do his supermarket shopping in his pajamas and flip-flops.

Miranda thought he was dead, everyone did: he'd died in a car crash. It was a tragic and short story, and far better than Miranda being labeled a drug dealer's daughter. Rosie had assumed that one day she'd have to tell the truth, or a savory version of it. She'd assumed she would do it on her terms. Miranda never asked about her father, she had no need of him, stuffed as she was with Rosie's love. Sometimes, it had really seemed as if Bennett had gone from the world.

Yet here he was. Reincarnated. Evenly, Rosie said to Bennett, "Let's go and get a cup of coffee."

Bennett gave her a breezy smile, not one she recognized. He drummed his fingers on the hood of the car as he walked around, keeping his eyes on her. In the seat beside her, he touched her face. "You look good, Rosie."

She snapped her head away. She wanted to say, "I don't care what you think of how I look." But she just started the car. He lodged himself into the passenger seat, ignoring the bleeping of the seatbelt alarm. "I want you to know I've changed."

Her mouth was dry but she didn't want him to see her licking her lips. She turned onto the road, toward the town's diner. His seatbelt alarm bleated on. His voice was soft, generous. "Hey, it's OK that you didn't write. I understand, I do, you're busy and I know what I put you through. I've had a lot of time to think. I want to make it up to you. So, we're going to move to Maine, to my family's summer home. It's right on the ocean, so beautiful, so wild, Rosie, my girl, you won't believe it. And we'll take long walks on the beach and eat lobster and watch the sea in all its vagrant moods and, Rosie, the way the gulls move within the webs of air, and the storms will surround us on dark winter nights but we'll be inside, you and me and Miranda, we'll have the fire, we'll have each other, we'll be playing backgammon."

Rosie found a parking spot, grabbed her bag, and opened her door before he could. He followed her across the lot, then pulled the entry door just before she got there.

"After you," he said with a cheery flourish.

They sat in a booth by the window. Bennett immediately opened the menu, surveyed the options, most of which came with the kitchen's thick, grey, oily gravy. He looked wolf-hungry. When the waitress came, Rosie ordered coffee.

"Get something," Rosie said. She had part of her paycheck in her wallet, she was showing him how things were different now. "Whatever you want."

"Tall stack with sausages and eggs. Sunny-side up, please. A side of bacon. And coffee. Thank you so much." When the waitress left, he smiled at Rosie. "The food in prison, there's something spiteful about what they do to it. It's not tasteless. I could live with that. But what can you do to meatloaf that makes it taste like an old man's leaky ass?"

The coffee came. The sipping gave their conversation a rhythm, the mugs kept their hands busy. They appeared a normal couple having a conversation. She nodded, she sipped, yet she felt the old exhaustion braided with new, raw anxiety. Her tone was scrupulously neutral, "How did you get here?"

"Hitched."

"You hitch-hiked?"

He nodded. "Trucks mostly. St. J is a big depot. I got a ride all the way from Trenton."

"Trenton?"

"I was transferred down to Pennsylvania a few years ago." He cocked his head. "I sent you a letter."

She looked back at him. "I threw them away."

"Unread?"

She nodded.

"And the ones for Miranda?"

"Don't pretend, Bennett, don't pretend you wrote to her."

The food came, and for a while they didn't speak. Bennett focused completely on the food, mouthful upon mouthful, his manners still impeccable. He used the fork and knife correctly. His elbows were not on the table, his mouth was closed as he chewed. At last, he drew knife and fork carefully together in the center of his plate. "Famished! Haven't eaten since yesterday!" Leaning in, he spoke in a stage whisper: "I stole a bag of groceries from a woman's car as she was returning the cart." Then, an unfamiliar, lilting laugh. "A jar of Fluff, two bags of Cheetos. My luck to rustle a culinary heathen."

So here was this person, this Bennett, sliding in and out of focus, who stole food and hitched in trucks. His arm went into the air, his fingers elegantly rang an invisible servant's bell. He ordered another coffee. *Please could I, thank you so much, it's wonderful coffee.*

Rosie said: "Why are you here?"

"You're my family — my wife, my child."

"We're not married."

He seemed surprised, and so gave his warmest smile. "Then let's get married! Marry me, marry me, Rosie."

She began to push back her chair. He grabbed her wrist. Their eyes met. He'll make a scene, she thought. She sat back down.

"Listen, listen, Rosie, Rosie. I know, I know. Unforgivable.

I do not ever expect you to forgive me. But I love you, I love Miranda, she needs a father."

"She hasn't so far."

"I am her father. I have a legal right to be her parent."

"What will you do for a living?"

"I'm making decoys."

Rosie laughed.

"Seriously. I have a talent. Don't laugh, Rosie, my girl, don't laugh. I make decoys — duck decoys — and sell them. I learned in prison."

"What kind of ducks?"

"Eider. Harlequin. Whimbrels."

"Whimbrels aren't ducks."

He glanced at her — and there it was, glinting, what had always been there but hidden from her, the way the light shifts on a vernal pool and there — *there* — is the quick, sly movement within the dark water.

Bennett's smile twitched: "So, you're a birder now?"

"A whimbrel isn't a duck."

"Decoys are the only truly American folk art. Did you know that?"

"No."

"The Native Americans made them, and the settlers learned from them. Europeans didn't make decoys."

Rosie studied at his thin, lank hair. The loss of it must have pained him. "I don't give a shit about decoys, Bennett."

"Tell me about Miranda."

How dare you, she thought, and she felt a fierce coveting. My child, my child. Mine, mine, mine, mine, mine. Bennett was looking at her over his cup of coffee. Rosie opened her mouth, moved her tongue: "She's happy, she does well at school, she has friends."

"And this field trip to Boston?"

He was trying to catch her out. "Plattsburg."

"Plattsburg, that's right. And, ah, what have you told her about me?"

"I didn't want her to think you abandoned her."

"I didn't abandon her."

"Whimbrels are not ducks, Bennett."

"What did you tell her?"

That you're dead. But out loud, she said, "That you made a mistake."

Bennett was looking at her — looking for her, the old Rosie, the silly, young girl. But she was murkier. "What mistake?"

What mistake?

Leaving the toilet seat up, putting the forks away with the knives. Rosie was silent a moment.

"What mistake?" he repeated.

"You tell me, Bennett. What mistake?"

Leaning forward, he crabbed his hands toward hers, then smothered them before she could move away. "We can even pick her up tonight. Surprise her. I know it'll take a while, there'll be an adjustment —"

Rosie tried to move her hands, he held fast. Finally, she wrenched them away. "Your touch makes me sick."

"Be sick then."

But he released her, he leaned back, stretching, and his shirt gaped open to reveal his hairy belly, a cavernous belly button. What might be in there? Bits of old food, sweat, the lint of unwashed clothes, little lies like lice crawling out. She turned away. When she turned back he slid a sheaf of papers across the table to her.

"It's the house. I'm giving it to you."

"How is it yours to give?"

"It was always mine."

"Not Pinky or Perky's?"

Again, he reached for her hands, but when she snatched them into her lap, he lowered his head. "I can never atone. I lied, I stole, I abandoned you — *I abandoned you*, I exposed you and my child to a disgusting, utterly reprehensible person. I was arrested, I'm a felon. There it is, there it is. I don't expect your forgiveness, I don't expect your love. But, Rosie, Rosie, I have been so lonely and I have been afraid and all I want is a small life, a humble life. With you, with Miranda."

Rosie could not suppress her incredulity: "This is still about what you want."

"OK," he said. "OK." His eyes began to water. "I have a psychological problem. An illness. I clearly recognize this. In prison, I had the opportunity to go to therapy. A really wonderful therapist, and she helped me get in touch with myself. My childhood, my parents, my mother's suicide." He took a breath, then added. "'Nam."

She waited, there was more. Always. Jack Nicholson was his brother. They'd robbed the Metropolitan Museum of Art together.

"It's been tough, it's been revelatory. The things I had to remember. Consequences I have to face." He wiped away a solitary tear. "The people I love whom I've hurt so very, very badly. The terrible, terrible things I've done."

So many, many adjectives.

"I've seen bone poking through living skin, Rosie, in Lai Mai, my second tour was the roughest. The inside of bodies suddenly on the outside, like turning a jacket inside out. I've shot a family's only pig." He shook his head as if it was heavy with the memory. "Their only pig, they loved it like a pet. And I laughed when I wounded it. Shot its front legs off. Can you imagine? Can you imagine?"

A long silence descended, Bennett held his solemnity. "I'm wounded, Rosie."

This, at least, was true. She did not know the shape or source of his wounds, but she was now aware of their festering, perhaps even the faintest gangrenous smell of them.

Then Bennett threw out his arms in exclamation, loudly; other customers turned to look: "How can I make it up to you and Miranda? How can I? Tell me! Tell me, Rosie Monroe, and I'll do it."

"Leave," she whispered. "You can leave and never come back."

"Alas, alas, that is the one thing I cannot do."

She felt his weight upon her, the way she'd once borne him as a lover, now he was stones, he was granite ledge.

He tapped the papers, he implored, "Rosie, this is the title to the house, you'll see the notarized letter giving it to you. I want you to have it, I want you to feel secure. Whatever happens in Maine. You'll have your own place."

Her voice was even, she was calm, she grabbed the paperwork: "Nothing will happen in Maine." Getting up, she put a twenty dollar bill on the table, not even waiting for the change. In the car, she fumbled for the keys, her hands were shaking. The coffee gurgled rebelliously in her stomach.

A storm moved in from the west that night. The wind and rain came clawing at the house, the darkness absolute so that she could not see the lights of town down the valley. The storm felt staged, as if Fate had decided that it needed not only to make manifest Rosie's inner turmoil but to create the creepiest conditions possible for her to be alone in the house. She was grateful that Miranda was safe, and grateful for the lights in Billy's house. Beside her bed she had placed her flashlight. The batteries worked, the implement was heavy in her hand.

Yet she could not sleep, the surrender was impossible. Her blood was electric in her veins, her heart raced. Why was there not a God, a useful God who might be persuaded to intervene and turn Bennett into a tree or a swan or constellation — far, far away, twinkling at night? She had phoned Ginny, and Ginny had reassured her. "Miranda is just fine, she and Margo are having a great time."

Rosie was waiting for Bennett to come. He would always come, always, always. They would sit at the table, speak as adults, sensible, practical. Other children at school had divorced parents; they managed their loathing, they even sat together at school plays and stood together on the sidelines at softball matches. Custody, child support, the long summer holidays — these could be negotiated. And Rosie would find a way to explain to Miranda the resurrection of her father.

Dawn sun slipped into her room. Outside, the fields were gauzy with low mist. Birds sang. The chickadees, white-crowned sparrows, and vireos exalted the new day. Billy's dogs set up a howl. They had been restless in the night, there must be a bear nearby. For a while Rosie lay still, it couldn't be more than 4:30, there was no need to rush. For the briefest moment, she indulged herself: Bennett had left, vanished, forever.

Then: the creak-creak of the floorboards downstairs. At first, Rosie was certain she'd misheard. The storm had loosened a gutter, the screen door had blown free from its latch — the usual disintegration of the house. But the next sound was distinctive: water running from the tap, on, then off.

She was certain she'd locked the door.

A lazy little lock.

Rosie jumped up, pulled on her dressing gown, ran downstairs.

Bennett was just putting the kettle on the stove. "Want some tea?"

"What are you doing here?"

"Making tea."

Bennett calmly made himself a tea, he knew where everything was.

"This is my house now. You gave it to me."

"So I did." He got the milk from the fridge. "Call the police, then." He gestured to the phone. "Oh, wait, the power's out and you've got one of those electric ones with voice mail."

Suddenly, she recalled what Mary had said about leaving a message, and there'd been no message. Bennett. Bennett had been here. Possibly for days, ghosting in and out of the house. Listening to her messages. Poking around. With his *droit de seigneur* he handed her a tea.

And because something very ancient was stirring within her, she took the tea. She was walking like a deer through the dark forest, aware of every movement and sound, the predators woven within the very tapestry of the trees. And she heard Billy's dogs, heard them in this heightened context, and their howling was not hunger or greeting; it was full of distress. Rosie sipped her tea — he'd made it for her exactly as she liked with plenty of milk — and looked out at the fields, toward Billy's.

"I have to be at work early today," Rosie said.

Bennett got down on one knee before her, though he did not try to touch her. "I want you to marry me."

For the briefest second she was profoundly sad — that this might have been the truth, a beautiful second chance, the story they'd tell their grandchildren, *when Grandpop came home from jail and Granny took him back and they got married.* However, that required not just delusion, but an entire rewriting of their story — what had happened, who she was, who he was, not could be might be, but as a fact, like a stone, like the blade of a knife: Rosie, Bennett.

"I have to go to work. We'll talk about it later."

"Who taught you to drive, Rosie?"

"I taught myself."

"Not that little freak?"

Rosie looked blank.

"You know," Bennett said. "That fat little dyke."

Rosie simply turned back upstairs. Dressing quickly, she considered Bennett's choice of words — *fat little dyke*. He'd always thought Billy was a man.

She moved down the steps to the car, she heard herself breathing. When she glanced in the rearview mirror, Bennett was watching her, leaning casually in the door frame with his cup of tea.

Once she'd rounded the corner by the gravel pit, she parked and back-tracked through the woods, approaching Billy's place from the river. She was afraid to call out, she could not be sure how far her voice would travel on such a still morning. If she could hear the dogs at her house, then Bennett could just as easily hear her voice. Breaking from the woods, she had to cut across open ground. She could not see Bennett, and thus she convinced herself he could not see her, a flash of mere seconds as she ran.

Never had she been inside Billy's house. It was untidy but not dirty. Piles of unopened mail, newspapers, clothes; tatty furniture covered in old blankets — where Billy nested in her evenings. It was quiet, no hum of the fridge, no tick of a clock. As Bennett had pointed out, the power was out.

"Billy?" Whispering, from room to room. "Billy?"

Up the stairs. It was a surprisingly big house once you were in it, built for a large farming family a century ago. With only Billy, three of the bedrooms were empty but for their worn furniture. The remaining room, under the narrow eaves at the north end of the house, must be where she slept, though it was the smallest and the darkest.

Entering, Rosie immediately understood why Billy chose this room for her own: the view fell directly onto her own house. A chair faced the window. Billy had sat here for hours, for years, watching their lives — the kitchen where Rosie cooked, the small garden where Miranda played and Rosie hung up the laundry. It wasn't repulsion that Rosie felt — anger at Billy, outrage at Billy; but a creeping sense of dread. Billy would never have willingly let her find this shameful coveting.

Bending forward, Rosie peered out the window. And there was Bennett.

She jumped back, almost falling over the chair. Of course Bennett couldn't see her, he didn't know she was here. She returned her gaze, watching him move around the kitchen. He was looking for something. At last, he came outside, marching in his belly-carrying way to the small woodshed Billy had helped her build. He reappeared with her shovel, went back into the house. Rosie could just see him open the basement door and descend.

Billy, she was certain — those cold words, *dead certain* — Billy had been sitting here and seen Bennett enter her house. Maybe even days ago. And she'd gone over there to challenge him.

Turning now from the window, Rosie opened the drawer beside Billy's bed. Took out her handgun. Think. She sat on the bed with the gun. Think clearly, think *well*. But her brain was buzzing, too much was happening too fast. She checked the gun's chamber. A fat, full round. Billy had told her to keep a gun in the house because "events turn." But Rosie had always refused. Guns were for food. Billy laughed, "Salts fa food, peppahs fa food. Condimunts not gonna fuckin impress who needs impressin."

Rosie stood, she went downstairs and out the door.

Across the field, along the path she and Billy had worn over the years, *founda patcha morels, We had some leftover stew, Could you help with the woodshed, Figah'd this jacket'd suit for Miranda.* Conversations fell between them like leaves, simply, delicately; they had divided their lives, an intuitive choreography of separation and gentle interdependence. They never shared too much, they never entered each others' houses. Yet in this lonely place, they had relied on each other, honoring a quieter friendship. Rosie had thought this was what Billy wanted, too. But now she understood — not the secret of Billy's salacious desires or some dark pedophilia — but her longing to be among the clattering evening kitchen and to help hang Miranda's clothes on the washing line and sit at the table with Miranda's homework. Rosie remembered the day when Billy had driven her back from prison up in Newport. The pretty butterfly earrings. Billy had never worn them again.

Stop the ruckus in yer head, she thought as she walked, the circus parade, and she balanced into herself, her breath, her heartbeat, the way her legs propelled her, muscles bunching, extending. Into the house, smooth with snakelike silence. Reaching the open kitchen door, she could hear Bennett in the basement, whistling a jazz tune. She moved, soundlessly across the floor, and she was at the top of the stairs when he turned and looked up. Billy's body was at his feet.

Because he had his way of seeing her fixed in his mind, Bennett seemed not to note the gun. He remembered her vulnerability, the drab girl in MoMA. He could not see *this* Rosie, hardened, burnished, sharpened. His face had no particular expression, he might as well have been gardening with the shovel in his hand. His eyes met hers. What did she see? Only the form of his eye, the iris, the pupil, the white shot through with red veins. The eyes were not the windows of the soul, they were a mechanism for viewing out, they belonged entirely to their owner. What she saw was Bennett looking at her. That was all.

His gaze shifted to the gun in her hand: he was amused, dismissive. "Rosie, my girl," he chuckled. "Is that yours?" Rosie felt the beautiful winnowing of purpose, the stillness within her, how she'd locked Miranda in her room in order to hunt and how she'd let the guy at Tire World in Littleton fuck her for a set of snow tires, she'd cleaned the toilets of junkies in a motel, she knew the names of every bird in the woods, she gathered mushrooms and wild plants, she loved the first scent of mud in the spring, she knew green wood from seasoned, she'd driven home from work so many late nights with Miranda asleep in the back of the car, she'd saved up for Miranda's skiing lessons and orthodontics, she'd learned to use the snow plow on Billy's truck, and she washed the feet of the dying with great tenderness. *A girl like you, a girl like you:* Rosie felt the fit of her skin upon her flesh, the shape of her skull, her ears, eyes, lips, and she knew her form. Bennett was still smiling, and she stopped the ruckus in her head, she saw briefly, Bennett with his expensive cheese, his bottle of wine, coming out of the supermarket, then she breathed this image aside, she did not move, the gun floated up, Bennett did not notice, still only saw a girl who looked better with her clothes off, a girl who would never leave him no matter what he did, and she shot him, the loud retort reverberated around the basement, and for a moment she blinked as her ears whined. It was a clean kill.

Billy was smaller than Rosie had thought, for she wore her clothing in layers — two pairs of jeans, three tee-shirts, two flannel shirts, and this even in the warmer days of late spring. She had died either from falling or from Bennett smashing her head, Rosie could not tell, there was only the open wound, a surround of shattered and protruding skull, blood on the basement's earth floor. Kneeling down, Rosie shrugged her shoulders under the body, hefted herself up like a weight-lifter and climbed the stairs. Her thighs were shaking, burning by the top stair, yet Rosie knew the worst thing she could do would be sit down to rest.

Outside, she staggered, up the trail into the rough woods. Behind her, Billy's dogs were wailing. Into the woods, they folded behind her and she climbed up. The briar, tree roots — all these she had to sense beneath her stumbling feet, beneath the dense layer of obscuring leaves; the mud, the sudden depression of a woodchuck hole, the winter's deadfall. Saplings caught on her jacket or hair and whipped back into her face with a spiteful snap. Crossing the stream and up the steep bank besotted with sumac, Rosie slipped to her knees, dropping Billy. She was exhausted, she couldn't heft Billy to her shoulders. So, she stood, hooking Billy's feet in her elbows and dragged her like a deer. At last, she reached the cemetery. In the quiet afternoon, the busy chickadees and grosbeaks flitted through the clearing, and the broad oval of a pileated woodpecker with the telltale swoop-snap-snap-swoop of her flight.

Here, amidst the mossy, crumbling headstones, Rosie left Billy. Small creatures would find her first and eat the soft tissue of her eyes, her lips, her genitals, and then the larger scavengers, coyotes, ravens, crows. Within days, Billy would be scattered, disintegrating, she would be among the wild cranberry and within the hobblebush, under birch roots, aloft in the bellies of turkey vultures. Maybe one day a hunter would find part of her, a hand bone, the gentle arc of her skull, maybe soon, maybe never and Billy would be absorbed within the mountain as all the other unaccounted dead. Rosie wanted to cover her with ferns, she wanted to build a monument, but Billy would have told her, *them mountains'll be moiy bed and tha skoiy's a blanket.*

It was dark by the time Rosie got back to the house. Adrenaline had suppressed her hunger but she was thirsty and drank long, cold glasses from the kitchen tap. Then she scooped the water over her face. The tap dripped and she listened to the drips, drawn out like a single note on the piano, clinking in the sink.

She was not done.

Down the stairs, narrow and dark, beneath the warm water heater and the frazzle of electrical wires, lay Bennett. His shirt had come open, revealing again the pothole of his belly button. He was soft bellied, she could see that now. Fat. He must weigh well over 200 pounds. How then, how then could she move him? Could she haul him up the stairs with a system of pulleys? But that would be a visit to the hardware store, a receipt, someone seeing her. Already there was the waitress in the diner, perhaps others who'd seen Bennett. Rosie looked down. The tidy rosette on his forehead might be a joke, it might be a lie, and briefly she felt a jolt of fear that he would rise up — he was not gone, he was returning and in his fury, he would place his hands around her throat and kill her. She nudged his hip with her boot, his belly jiggled, and then she knelt and tried to lift his arms above his head, thinking she might drag him incrementally up the stairs.

His body, though, had stiffened with rigor mortis and the arms would not move from their position, one across his chest, the other to the side as if waving "Hello." His body was bulky as a large wooden bureau, rigid, with no desire to cooperate. Rosie almost laughed. How could a dead man retain the intransigence of his life?

Then she considered: if you need to move a bureau, you need to make it lighter and you take out the drawers, you carry them one by one. Thus, she'd have to cut him up, take him out in pieces. Like a deer. Just a deer, no different to a deer, the body, the meat, the tendons: she knew exactly how to dismember.

Rosie kept her butchering knife in the very back of the kitchen drawer. The blade made a slick, silvery sound as she wiped it back and forth over the stone. Night surrounded the house, and she was aware of a new solitude, for Billy had always been just across the field. Part of her brain stubbornly insisted that Billy was still there, the day hadn't begun, Bennett hadn't returned, and that she was immersed in a dream. There was a wall of probability around her, a padded buffer, and for long moments she was reassured that none of what had happened had happened. Surely, if Billy was dead, she would feel grief; if she was about to carve up her old lover in the basement, she would feel fear or at least trepidation. Or she would at least consider her options, such as going to the police. Yet she was filled with calm and a profound sense of disconnection from herself.

In this state of mental objectivity, physical sensations were particularly intense. The sound of the blade was extraordinarily loud, and when she sniffed, it sounded tidal. Her exhales boomed and her heart thumped — though not fast, not a stampede, but a steady, certain heavy-booted march. Her mouth tasted of tin, a childhood memory of sucking on a metal pencil sharpener and the tart mineral flavor on her tongue, and she could smell the house around her, as if it were an unfamiliar house, the smell of mouse, of laundry soap, of something damp, and the cheesy insoles of Miranda's shoes that she insisted on wearing without socks. And Rosie could smell the cellar, the earth, the copper piping, the distinct tang of blood.

When the blade was sharp, Rosie descended into that cellar. The disbelief was like a magic cloak that would allow her to do the necessary. She remembered the first time she'd butchered a deer, the feeling of the knife slicing through the skin and flesh. Billy had told her to grip fast, cut sure, like it was pie. Only Billy pronounced it *poy* and she'd wondered what a poy was, as she'd once been confused by cads and beahs. But flesh wasn't like pie, more like ripe avocado as long as the blade was sharp. And Billy had taught her exactly where to dismember the joints, the way to slice the tough sinews. In one quick swoop of the blade, to disembowel the animal, and clutch the hot, slippery guts in one hand so they didn't unravel. Rosie could butcher a field-dressed deer in an hour and twenty minutes.

Now she knelt beside Bennett and pressed the blade below his ribcage, for here was the place to start with a deer. Yet, perhaps she should simply cut off his limbs, carry legs and arms and then wrestle his amputated body up the stairs. As she squatted, she contemplated the blood. Bennett would of course bleed all over the place. She'd have to deal with the quantities of his blood. She'd have to get garbage bags and line the floor, she'd have to get towels and sheets, all the bed clothes to soak up the blood, then she'd have to bury those or burn them. And still some blood would soak into the earth floor, more than already had, and the flies would find it. She and Miranda would be having supper in a few days' time and a fly would buzz above the table, and it might land on the butter or Miranda's broccoli, and Rosie would know what Miranda did not, that the fly was fat from her own father's blood.

And where might she bury the pieces of him?

Among the apple trees? No, further out. In the woods beyond Billy's fields? Somewhere Miranda would not go. Deep, deep underground, she must encase him in drums of cement like radioactive material, a thousand feet, perhaps, or seal him within a mine shaft on a mountainside. It wasn't simply that Miranda must never know about her father's death, but that, in her innocence, she must never come within the proximity of his body.

Laying the knife across Bennett's body, Rosie rocked back on her heels and she covered her face. Not grief, not horror; she was exhausted and her eyes felt as if they'd been pushed back into her skull. And then her hands fell to Bennett. She pressed her palms against the coldness of him, the irreversible, immutable, deaf-blind-dumb deadness of him. He had defeated her. She would have to go to the police and try to explain why she had carried Billy's body into the mountain and left it for animals to eat, and, oh yes, explain how she'd shot him. The explanations could not possibly suffice — who would understand the sense? She would go to jail, Miranda would be placed in foster care, and she'd move forward in her life with the story of her mother as the killer of her father.

There was another body, of course, on the road to Meriden. Years ago. Perhaps Rosie should be in jail, she was *damaged*, and the best thing for Miranda was for her to be removed, placed far, far away. Perhaps the best way to express her love for her daughter was to leave her to the safety and measured care of strangers. Yet Rosie knew the lunar loneliness of the abandoned child, and it was no mitigation but a different kind of hell.

Though the light in the cellar remained as it had for the past hours, outside the dawn chorus had begun. Down here, Rosie could hear the wild singing of robins and goldfinches, buntings and sparrows. Still she felt nothing — neither regret, nor shame, nor grief.

And yet, the singing of the birds stirred her, they were there on branches demanding the sun and the warmth of the late spring day; the songs, when the listener attended, were aggressive and passionate affirmations of territory and love. They weren't pretty, they were mighty and irrepressible.

Into this particular moment, memory came like an arrow. Rosie remembered, with absolute clarity, The Giggle Man. Not his face, but the Balthus-like impression of him. *Sit on the bed*, he said. He pulled on his white gloves and slid his hand up her thigh and tickled her. Not a playful tickle but an act of violent trespass. He tickled her and tickled her and she writhed in agony and laughter, and he would not stop. She couldn't breathe for laughing, convulsing from the agitation of her nervous system. She had no control. Time had been impossible to tell. How long did she stay in that room, minutes or hours? *Do you like it when I do this.* The light through the trees outside, the clock in the hall downstairs. She had ached with the pain of laughing. Her ribs and thighs and armpits felt bruised, but there were never marks. *Please stop, please stop*, but she was laughing, she was giggling, and so he kept going, her aching body truant with joyous laughter, and every week she returned, every Sunday she went up the stairs and along the hall and she sat on the bed and he tickled her. When, at last, he was done, he gave her money. *The rent, for your grandmother.* She'd straighten her clothes. *Good girl, there's a good girl.*

And then, one particular Sunday, she had pissed on him.

Pissed all over him. Squirting hot volumes of urine as if she'd horded it for days, weeks, as if she'd connected a fire hydrant to a garden sprinkler of piss.

It had not occurred to her that she had any defense because it had not occurred to her to defend herself. She was *that* open. Her body was for him — *for him* — to play with, his possession that she kept all week, carefully within its skin case for him, for him to lift up her shirt, pull and bare, to pry apart, her ribs cracking, so open, she'd been so open, he could reach in and take out her heart. *Do you like it when I do this.*

She had not meant to piss on him.

She had meant to oblige, the ancient tenet of her gender. To not make a fuss. He was only tickling her.

But some rebel force within her — oh, her angry little bladder! Her red-faced, furious, rubbery, redoubtable little bladder — had fought back, had turned and charged back down the hill toward the enemy.

He had thrown her off in disgust, hard, against the wall, he was soaking and stinking *you filthy, you disgusting* but then next Sunday he was gone.

So now Rosie stood, knowing that she was fierce, had always been, and she took up the shovel Bennett had brought down to bury Billy, and she took off her clothes and continued his job. Naked, swearing, she dug. The earth was hard and packed for the first few feet, but deeper down it crumbled and darkened and turned loamy. She dug for three hours, a proper grave, the length and width of him, six feet deep. Getting down on her knees, she braced her back and pushed and pushed and rolled him in.

Rosie looked at Bennett's face as she threw down the soil. She breathed into the rhythm of the labor, the blistering of her hands, the sweat flowing over her naked body. By seven, she was done. She showered, scrupulously scraping the dirt from her fingernails. Billy's dogs had set up a fresh round of howling, and Rosie dressed and set out across the field toward them.

HOOK
1993

The dogs: she shot them in quick, unsentimental succession. No one would want the dogs; Billy-centric, too old to be re-trained, certainly no one's pet, they'd be killed anyway. The dogs had tried to get away from her, they had grasped her intention even before she shot the first one. But the chains held them. They had pulled away from her, they had whimpered. Rosie had done the very best she could, she shot fast, she shot true, one, two, three, four, five. Reload. Six, seven. She knew what the police would think.

But one dog. Hook. Hook had put her head under Rosie's hand and pushed up, and Rosie's fingertips had felt the sleek fur, the hard skull beneath, the knob on the crest. She'd never had a dog, did not know their language or even what they ate other than deer guts.

Rosie led Hook home. She phoned the police and she set a tremor in her voice: "My neighbor is missing. Her dogs are all shot dead. I'm worried that something has happened to her."

They came, in no particular hurry, without lights or sirens, two careless cops, and they saw the dead dogs in the yard, and in the house, the drawer open and empty by the bed where a hand gun was likely to have been. They saw Rosie, pretty and distressed and the way her shirt fit snuggly over her young breasts. They asked Rosie how well she knew Billy, if she'd seemed depressed, and Rosie had said *Kinda* and *Maybe*. The lies bloated within her, like a foul pregnancy — a deformed ball of cells and hair and fingernails and teeth. And, yet, Rosie felt Billy would expect no less, for this was a fight for survival, you ate your own dogs because you were starving. Events turn.

One of the cops was somewhat acquainted with Billy, she was his cousin, he said she was "strange and crazy" and Rosie had not disagreed. It was obvious — wasn't it, for look at the dead dogs — that Billy had gone into the woods with her strangeness and her craziness and her gun and would not be coming back. The dogs were already attracting flies in the sun. Then they drove away, the two cops, they went to get coffee and donuts or whatever, and they never came back.

No one did. Not even to bury the dogs. So Rosie buried them.

And then in the afternoon, she sat on the sofa in her house. Her hands were raw from digging. The new sense of isolation felt oceanic, a particular part of the ocean where there is no wind, no current, a slow gyre where you die and no one finds you for days or maybe never. Hook whined and regarded Rosie with her single yellow alien eye. For a moment, Rosie thought the dog might attack her — having witnessed the massacre of her pack, having a mysterious understanding that Rosie was in some way responsible for her owner's death. But Hook stepped forward, bowing her head and pressing it into Rosie's knee with slow insistence. Rosie let her hand move down the dog's back, she was too thin, Rosie thought, the knuckles of her spine protruding, the hip bones angular and mobile beneath the skin. Hook wagged her tail.

"It's okay," Rosie whispered, and the wag engaged Hook's rear end, the hip bones shifting steady as a metronome. Slowly, Rosie slipped off the couch and onto her knees, and Hook moved her chest in against Rosie's shoulder, and in this way Rosie found her face in the crook of the dog's neck, the smell of the dog was earthy and clean and oily and she wept.

THE HARE
2019

Rose regarded herself. She needed to know what she looked like, if only this once. She believed that a person — a woman of 54 — should be acquainted with her naked physical self. And so here in the changing room of JCPenney with its merciless prison break lighting, here and now was as good a place as any.

This is what she saw: her neck in loose folds, so if she pulled the skin with her fingers it remained pinched into a peak of skin for long seconds, then slowly softened back to its original sag. The skin itself was pocked like a plucked chicken. She leaned in, tilted her chin to the side, that single dark, bristly whisker had grown back. Insistent little bastard. She moved on, down her neck to the wide, boney rack of her shoulders from which the rest of her body hung, pale as a fish belly. Things had gone horribly wrong. Her breasts looked as if someone had shoved tangerines into panty hose, her nipples faced the floor. Her arms, when she held them out, jiggled, flop-flopped, the muscle like pizza dough. She realized her analogies were to food items, and wondered if this was because food rotted, food was fresh and plump and then it moldered and stank and bit-by-bit disintegrated. Her belly rounded and pooched above her pubic mound — again, food: the "muffin top."

Her pubic hair was getting sparse. One day it would disappear altogether. What irony that young women — she'd been one once — spent a fortune manicuring this, ripping it out with hot wax, right there alongside the delicate labia. Some women even took off all the hair, so their privates resembled those of a child. What kind of man wanted to have sex with a child? What kind of grown-up woman would encourage this?

Sex, however, was no business of hers. No one would touch her again, no hand slip across her hips, no kisses upon her neck. She might live another 40 years with not a single touch other than her own.

Her thighs dimpled, pale and lumpy, as, yes, oatmeal. Clusters of burst veins resembled bruises, so the oatmeal looked mottled, indeed *moldy*. More skin gathered in a crease above her knees. Pastry. Her lower legs were a relief. Her calves were still slim, tapering to nice ankles, and her feet had so far evaded the ravages of bunions. Her gran had had those, they had hobbled her, deformed her. She must have been in considerable pain.

Rose now braced herself to turn, to angle herself in the 3-way mirror, and there it was, her ass. Not so much like food, but wax, melted, the whole structure dropping down as if subjected to great heat. Her ass was vertical, flat. Her ass connected directly to her thighs and her back, straight up and down. It was no longer an ass, no one would call it an ass, she was missing an entire section of her body; what she now had instead of an ass was — basically — a toilet seat. Further up her back, around the red marks of her bra, were handfuls of back fat. She could grasp them, fully, with both hands. Why did she have fat on her back? She was not a fat person. Her shoulders were bony, muscular even, so what *was* this fat? And why was it not on the other side of her body, filling her breasts, where it might look OK? It was all a terrible joke, her boobs migrating to her back, her round ass swapping places with her flat belly.

What was the *point* of a woman her age?

She felt sad, but her sad expression wrinkled her forehead, deepened the crease between her eyes, and she appeared even older, even less attractive. Was *ugly* a word she might use? *I am ugly.* Slowly, she pulled on her underpants, swung her breasts into her bra, slipped into her clothes. A big puffy neck-to-knee fake-down parka covered everything, a winter burkha.

Clutching a Liz Claiborne blouse, she opened the dressing room door, walked solemnly to the cash register. The woman at the till was at least 100 pounds overweight and her grey roots were showing through the hard brunette dye. And yet she was wearing lipstick and mascara and jaunty yellow earrings. And yet she was wearing a wedding ring. Someone loved her.

"Did you find everything you need today?" She smiled at Rose.

"Yes, thank you," Rose replied, smiling back.

"I love this blouse!"

"It is a wonderful color."

"Do you want to use your JCPenney Rewards card today?"

"I don't have one, and I don't want one. Thank you for the offer."

"That's twenty-six dollars and eighty-one cents. You saved sixteen dollars today!"

"Did I?" Rose took the bag, releasing her smile again. Here we are, all smiling. "That's great, thank you."

It was drizzling outside, the snow turning sloppy and she slopped across the parking lot, slop, slop, slop, her stupid boots, supposed to be waterproof, were already damp. Slop slop. She got in her Toyota Tercel, and she drove out onto the main road. The slop splattered her windshield; the wipers obviously needed replacing as Rose leaned forward to peer through a low arc of clean glass below a gritty brown smear. She had to pee, she should have peed at JCPenney. Now she had to make it all the way home. Plus — *Fuck!* Plus! — her feet were cold from the leaky boots and the Tercel's feckless heating.

The day was suitably mournful, the way only early April can be in the far northeast. Dumpy, grey skies, squatting low on the land, obscured the mountains and their sense of distance and drama. On such a day, there was nowhere other than this small, cold town. The temps hovered in the low 30s, enough to keep the drizzle from turning to snow and the slop from freezing. A sharp-tongued wind screeched down from Canada.

Once home, she found the stove with only embers. She was down to the last of her firewood. If she was careful, she'd make it through the month. But if May proved cold, she'd just have to be cold, too. With prodding, the stove soon roared to life, and she sat with tea and reached for her book club book. It was about a woman fashion photographer. She had no interest in it and thought the writing was poor. It was one grade up from the pulp that got sold at the Rite Aid. She should probably quit the club, but the other ladies would guess it was because she thought she was better than them. There was a look she saw pass between Bev and Jean and Laurie and Connie, a look that slipped like a coin, one to the other, if she happened to make certain comments. She could not say, outright, that she didn't like a book; this would be taken personally by the member who'd suggested it. This was unspoken courtesy, for they never criticized her choices, though Rose was sure they didn't

like them. *The Power and the Glory, Play It as It Lays, My Ántonia.*
Strange books, unsettling, she often couldn't understand what
she felt when she finished them, and she liked that emotional
ambiguity. That was the crux of the problem, she wanted to feel
muddled, the others in the group wanted to feel certain.

Except for Ginny. Ginny understood. Ginny chose *Madame
Bovary.*

Quite suddenly, Rose pulled open the stove door and threw
in the book.

She watched the fashion photographer burst into flame, and
felt briefly, wildly happy.

*   *   *

Bob was a chain smoker who would die at 104 or he'd be hit by
lightning. But the smoking wouldn't touch him. Rose wondered
if meanness might be healthy, just being an asshole boosted your
immune system. Look at Dick Cheney, look at Donald Trump.
They didn't get cancer.

Bob liked to light up whenever anyone came into his office,
it was his special way of putting you in your place. "If the state
or whoever wants to come in here and arrest me for smoking
in my own damn office, then they can go ahead and try," he
liked to say, opening his desk drawer a few inches. This is where
he kept his gun. He played himself out as a hard ass. "Nothin'
that a match and a gallon of gasoline won't fix," was another
favored line. He wore tight jeans and ironed shirts and probably
would have worn cowboy boots if he thought he could get away
with it in Vermont, which he couldn't, no one could, unless you
were a teenage girl or in costume for Halloween. He liked to
think of himself as a rancher, maybe one of those heroes who'd

take a stand against the government, on horseback, in the sage-brush, holding an American flag. But he was an egg farmer in the Northeast Kingdom.

His wife, Margie, had been responsible for building the business from her ambition, acumen, and 20 laying hens. Margie had formed partnerships with the big supply chains, marketing her eggs as "family-owned" with a photo of herself in a gingham shirt cuddling a perky chicken. Her wholesome image came just as the state of Vermont was marketing itself as a place filled with Margie-like people who made maple syrup in their own woods, cheese from their own cows, socks from their own alpaca wool. She died of a heart attack, and Bob took over the business. It was an indication of her talent that she'd created a solid foundation and all Bob had to do was not fuck with anything. Perhaps she'd banked on his laziness. She must have known exactly who she was married to: a man who wore his muddy boots inside and left the mess for others to clean up.

"There's just a couple of questions I have, then we can sign off and get these to the tax man before the 15th." Rose placed the spreadsheets in front of him. "You'll see where I've highlighted on the pages."

Exhaling luxuriously into her face, Bob flipped through the printouts. "Looks fine."

"Except if you look here," she leaned in and felt him retract away from her — recoil as if she smelled bad, and maybe she did, the hot flashes made her sweat like a boxer, mid-match. "These costs here, and here, aren't tallying. So, either the numbers are wrong or we're missing receipts or the receipts we have are somehow inaccurate. Or."

"Or?"

"There's something funny going on."

"*Funny?*" Bob snorted.

"Well, money's missing."

"It is not."

Rose said, "It is. Nearly seven grand."

Bob tilted back, blew his smoke so it wafted between them, a way of making her retreat with a small cough. "Look, Rose, if you can't handle the accounts — I mean you said you could and I want to give you that chance and I get that this is your first year with us and everything — but Andy never had any problems. If you can't figure it out, maybe Andy can recommend someone else."

Rose was very careful to focus her gaze on the wall behind him, on the many photographs Bob had of himself with a variety of dead animals and fish. She felt the sudden blooming of heat. Her head was in an oven, her body in the Sahara. In August. Actual sweat pricked her scalp. *Jesus Christ*, she was hot. She breathed in, out, in, out. She knew exactly what tone was required, there must not be a trace of sarcasm. "With all due respect, Bob, the numbers simply don't add up. It's not that I don't know what I'm doing, but that I do."

"So? What? Andy didn't?"

"I haven't looked at the accounts from last year. Maybe it wasn't a problem last year."

"Honey, why don't you do that. See how Andy did it. Copy the master."

"Don't call me 'honey,' Bob. I'm 54."

"Gee, I thought you were older."

Rose retrieved the spreadsheets, turned and walked out. She should quit, of course, of course. But she needed the job and she wasn't some delicate flower. She wasn't Christine Blasey Ford wilting because a drunken boy had groped her 40 years ago. The whole Kavanaugh hearing irked Rose because it seemed to tell people they couldn't change — not Christine, not Kavanaugh, they were epoxied to that moment in time when they hadn't even been adults. Dumbass teenagers. The women in her book group looked at Blasey Ford and saw a rich, educated woman with a career, a loving family, and really expensive hair. Hardly a victim they could identify with. And Kavanaugh? He was a greasy, spoiled pig who'd get away with whatever he'd done because rich men always did, so why even bother to argue about it? Connie had said, "Rich white men have always run the show and they always will. Enda story." Kavanaugh maybe didn't even remember Christine, what he'd done had been so unimportant to him.

Back at her desk, Rose pulled up Andy's accounts. Sure enough, the same item columns were out of alignment — "Incineration." And for the same amount. It was an interesting amount, perhaps carefully chosen; high enough to clearly show up in the accounts, but if the company was ever audited, low enough to explain away as an error and pay without serious penalty. "Incineration" was a clever choice, for the dead birds were taken by shed manager, Silas. There was never any paperwork, and it wasn't as if the IRS would have any real idea of how much it cost to incinerate chicken carcasses, there wasn't exactly a blue book value. No paperwork simply meant it was easier to *find* paperwork.

Seven grand was a nice chunk. Rose wouldn't mind seven grand, a holiday, a new used car, a new roof on the house. How did Bob spend it? She turned her attention back to the statement of accounts, she saw exactly how Andy had hidden the loss. Again, it was sly. A cursory audit would expose it, so it didn't look purposefully hidden and it would be easy to explain. But if there was no audit, the waters folded smoothly over it.

A knock at the window startled her. It was Nick.

"Front gate!" he was saying, thrilled. "Cops!"

Genetics had miraculously created Nick from Bob and Margie. Nick was tall and lean and dark, he was beautiful even in baggy blue overalls and Bogs boots, and Rose felt relieved to be so removed from lust, for she was sure that even a decade ago she would have fallen for this boy. "They want to talk to Dad!"

Rose glanced out; the cops were standing in front of their cop car, on the other side of the steel mesh gate, a man, a woman. She felt a chill of panic, she always did, like a spooky, cold wind, in proximity to cops. But they were here for Bob. What had Bob been up to?

"Do they say why?"

"They do not say."

"Let me go tell him."

Rose shut the door behind her, stood for a count of ten inside the hallway. She could hear Bob down the hallway on the phone talking about his golf game. She re-opened the door to Nick, "He says, sure, invite them in."

She watched Nick stroll toward the gate, slide it open. The cops followed him into the compound. Rose met them at the bottom of the steps. The woman was hefty but she wasn't bulgy, so Rose figured she lifted weights. A lot. She extended her hand. "Hi. I'm Detective Lieutenant Pamela Fornier. This is Detective Sergeant McRae from the Vermont State Police. We're here to see Robert Booth."

"Sure. Let me take you to him." Rose led them up and into the trailer, then directed them down the hallway. There was a lot of stuff on a cop, Rose noted as they passed, their belts like cop charm bracelets: flashlight, club, taser, gun, something in a Velcro pouch, cuffs, keys. Their heavy boots thumped on the rickety floor.

"My wife buys your eggs," McRae said. One of his boots was squeaking, so every other step there was a mouse-like *eeeek*.

"I can get a couple of dozen to take back to her," Rose offered.

"Thanks, but we're not allowed to accept gifts."

As if anyone would try to bribe a cop with eggs. Rose knocked on Bob's door, he was midway through a narrative about a tricky tee-off.

"Hey, Bob, Detective Lieutenant Fornier and Detective Sergeant McRae from the state police are here to see you."

"What?" He fumbled with the phone. "Gotta call you back."

Rose stepped aside, allowing the cops to breach Bob's doorway.

"You're Robert Booth," Fornier said.

"Ah, yeah, sure, that's me. What is this about?" He gave Rose a quick poisoned look, thinking she'd called them in because of the accounting irregularities, then he delivered a rubbery smile to the cops. "Take a seat."

As Fornier made for the unstable swivel chair, Bob said, "Just watch that chair, Detective Sergeant —"

"No," she corrected. "I'm the Detective Lieutenant."

"That's right. I really approve of affirmative action, it's so important."

"Isn't it, though?" Fornier agreed. "Being a woman is the only reason I got the job. I'm not qualified at all."

"Just, yeah, hey, Rose, get another chair, get us coffee."

"It's OK, we'll stand." Fornier braced her legs like a sailor, McRae folded his arms. He lifted, too. Maybe he lifted her, maybe she lifted him, while the wife stayed at home with her eggs.

"Right. Sure. Rose, shut the door on the way out." Demure, Rose obeyed. But in her office, she opened the heating vent by her desk. Normally, she kept this closed as it fired scorching hot air at her legs. Open, it was an intercom. She could hear everything said in Bob's office — which, normally, was of no interest to her because she already knew he was a bore. Golf, an appointment with a proctologist for his hemorrhoids, more golf, complaints about Nick, and golf. She could also see, through the glass partition. Total audio-visual.

Fornier was speaking "...your whereabouts on April 11th, between 6 p.m. and 1 a.m."

"That's, ah, last Friday?"

"Yes."

"I, um, I was, I'd have to check."

"Go ahead."

"Now?"

"Sure. Now is good for us."

"Can you let me know what this is about?"

"A crime."

"What crime?"

"We're not at liberty, as this moment, to reveal the details."

"Is this those animal rights kooks again? We totally complied with the state. They can come and look for themselves."

"We can tell you that it isn't related to animal welfare. We're with the Major Crimes Unit."

The words *Major Crimes* seemed to hit him like a wet fish. "Uh," he said, "So, you just want to know where I was and that either makes me guilty or not-guilty."

Now McRae clarified, "This is very preliminary, Mr. Booth. We just need to know where you were. Information."

"I don't remember."

"You don't remember? Last Friday was three days ago."

"I have a lot going on."

Rose could see Fornier making a show of looking around the office as if genuinely trying to appreciate the frantic pace of Bob's life. She let the silence settle like the dust on Bob's dead animal pictures. A long moment. Rose wished she could see Bob close up, she imagined tiny beads of sweat forming at his temples.

Then Fornier: "Would you like to come down to the barracks and speak with us there? Perhaps in a less, er, hectic environment, you'd be able to remember."

"Give me a couple of hours, and I'll call, I swear. Obviously I don't want to give you the wrong information. Incorrect, I mean. Incorrect information."

"Here's my card, Mr. Booth. We'll wait for your call. Later today."

Detective Sergeant McRae on the way out: "We're in the process of obtaining a warrant for your computer. Don't delete anything."

Bob was looking directly at Rose through the glass partition as the cops moved down the corridor, clomping and clacking. Rose held his gaze, her unapologetic manner suggesting complete innocence, then she swiveled her chair, lifted the slats of the window blind, and watched the cops walk back out to their car. To Bob, she said with polite concern: "What's the matter, Bob?"

Ignoring her, he hurried from his office, stabbing his cell phone. She heard only snatches as he moved toward the front door — "warrant... how long will it take... what if I just delete..." Peeking through the blinds again, she saw him get into his car and speed toward the gate, just as Nick was closing it.

"Open the fucking gate!" he shouted. Nick complied but gave him the finger.

When he'd gone, she stepped outside. The smell hit her — it really felt like that, being hit in the face by a solid physical force, not just an odor wafting, but a skillet. *Thwack.* Chickens. If she had to break it down, she'd distinguish feed, feces, feathers, and fear. She glanced over at the sheds, she never went inside. The chickens could not be heard, the huge ventilation fans drowned out their constant clucking.

"What'd they want?" Nick leaned on the trailer. He looked like something on the cover of a romance novel.

"No idea."

"Probably his pervy stuff."

"What pervy stuff?"

"Chat rooms." Nick made a retching expression. "My dad thinks the girls he's talking with look like their pictures."

"What do they look like?"

"Young."

How young, Rose was about to ask. Then Nick's phone rang, he spun away from her into this new conversation, and she ceased to exist.

*   *   *

Ginny pulled on her gloves and hat. It was their weekly walk, and they took it regardless of weather and often to be belligerently defiant of the weather. "Larry won't let me drive to Hanover by myself anymore because of the murders."

"What murders?"

"Didn't you hear? It's awful. On 91. This last one was near Bradford. There was a story in the paper over the weekend. I think they found her on the Friday. A young woman."

They started up the path behind Rose's house. It would take them across the road, into thick woods, around, and at last out into sprawling long-fallow fields. From there, to the north they'd see the granite bread-knob of Mt. Pisgah and the Willoughby Gap; to the west lay the Green Mountains, and far, far to the southeast, on the clearest days, they could see the Presidential Range in New Hampshire. It was an unsettled landscape, tilting at all angles, and mostly wild with dense forest cover. The big old farms were cut out from the burry grey of the woods in hard geometric shapes, the hayfields, cornfields, and pastures. Tourists thought it pretty.

"It's the second in two months," Ginny continued. "The first was in the lookout just before Wells River."

This was south, maybe 20 minutes on the interstate.

The climb was steep on this part of the path. Ginny stopped to catch her breath. "They found her in March. It sounded like she'd been there all winter and they found her in a snow bank when it started to melt."

As the forgiving cloak of snow drew back, the refuse of winter lay exposed — mostly beer cans, dog shit, old tires. Rose had an image of the dead woman surfacing with the trash; she remembered Billy describing her father as a pile of laundry on the ice.

"Didn't anyone miss her?"

"You hope, right? That people have connected lives. Someone

knows you haven't come home. You're not at work. But maybe there was no one for her."

In the years after Billy's death, Rose could easily have died, the way people do in banal ways, falling off a ladder, slipping on ice, and no one would have known, Miranda wandering for days until the coyotes found her or she died from exposure.

"If you ever need me to drive you —"

"Thanks. But, oh, Larry enjoys being chivalrous. He can't come into the treatment room, though. He gets too upset. I told him to replace the word *chemotherapy* with *cocktails*."

Rose knew she should ask how the treatment was going, and when it would end, and when Ginny was going to be better. But it was like talking about summer in the middle of mud season. And then Ginny said: "I can't quite get them out of my mind. Those women. They were young. That highway is so dark and lonely and there's no cell reception for long stretches. I keep wondering how it happened. Did their cars break down? Did they stop to help someone? Did they know him? I have this feeling he chose them and he was following them. He was purposeful."

"How does someone get it in their head to go out and kill like that? To decide and plan and follow through? It's incomprehensible."

"I did a residency rotation in a mental hospital years ago, and there was a girl who'd cut off her baby brother's arms. I just didn't have the chops for it."

"Jesus," Rose said.

"That was just one case. The hardest part was walking around in the world after that. Knowing what people could do to each other. That's why I married Larry."

"Because he wasn't a psycho killer?"

"A pretty low bar, right? Don't tell him. He thinks it's because he was so good in bed." They laughed together, walking on until they crested the ridge and stood on a granite slab overlooking Victory Bog. Below them a burred conglomeration of trees and marsh.

"It's so wild," Ginny said, inhaling. "I wish I was like you and could just plunge into it and not immediately get lost."

"I've been lost plenty of times."

"You always found your way out. Me, they'd have to come in with dogs and helicopters and they'd find me twenty feet from the road. I'm hopeless."

"You help people find themselves. That's your job."

Ginny shrugged. "Maybe. Though I think it's a self-sorting process. The people who come to me aren't the ones who are really lost. Those who are just carry on, moving helter-skelter through life like those big shit spreaders that fertilize the hay fields, just spraying shit everywhere."

Rose could see Bennett at the wheel of his giant shit-spreader, veering wildly from side to side.

She said: "Look at fiddleheads coming in." They stooped to admire the intricacy of the delicate green curls just breaching the dark earth. "I used to collect these all the time. I should come up here with a bag tomorrow. They're so delicious with butter."

"I was always worried I'd pick the wrong kind and poison myself and Larry."

"Look at the shape — they come up earlier than a lot of the other ferns. And they have this delicate little gold gift wrapping. There's another fern that looks similar, but the wrapping is much thicker and coarser. Once you know, you don't forget."

Rose thought of Billy, who'd first shown her these insistent coils of green, suddenly there among the dead leaf litter. *The woods'r a lahda.*

"A long time ago," Rose began, and considered changing course. It wasn't too late to make the story about fiddleheads and morels. She was less sure when she continued, speech was almost a bodily process she couldn't quite control. "A friend of mine was killed."

There. She'd said it. Ginny glanced at her, intent.

"I knew the man who did it."

Minutes passed in silence. The wind swept up from the bog.

"Killing someone — not by accident — he planned it, not like going to the hardware store and buying duct tape and rope, but with clear intention. I think it was a kind of revenge."

"Was it frightening?" Ginny asked in her quiet therapist's voice.

"What do you mean?"

"Not just to lose someone you cared about in a violent way but to be in proximity to the person who took your friend's life? We think we know people."

Rose often thought about what would have happened if Bennett had lived. He might have killed her and taken Miranda. He might have vanished and haunted them for years — he'd be haunting them still, unsettling their lives with unexpected visits, his random shit-spreading. There certainly would have been no round of Happy Families. Now, Rose contemplated the possibility that Bennett had been capable of killing — not just in the broken end, but all along. The body in the road had been a pattern not an aberration. Killing Billy wasn't the culmination but a direction. She felt cold and pulled her jacket around her.

"Are you OK?" Ginny asked.

Rose was surprised to find her fists bunched in her jacket

pockets, and part of her breath seemed lodged under the diaphragm. She exhaled, smoothed her palms on the front of her jeans, and then worried that Ginny would note her tension. "We should get back."

Ginny put her hand on Rose's shoulder for a moment as they entered the woods, then let it drop when the path narrowed to single file and Rose went first. The tall trees created an intense sense of the vertical, Rose felt very much surrounded, not in a fearful way, but of being among or within. This early in the year, the sky was still visible above them, pale and feathery with light cloud. Way up there, the leafless branches swayed gently in the wind that Rose couldn't feel down here. It was so still, she could hear her breath and even Ginny's.

At length, they came out into the fields and the wind found them. Ginny pulled her coat down tighter. "There was these two teenage boys from somewhere around here and they murdered a couple in Hanover. A lovely couple, professors at the college. The boys slashed their throats open. And when the police began investigating, they realized the boys had this whole story they'd told themselves, about how they were going to get money and move to Australia. They'd ordered knives. They'd staked out this couple's home for days. And yet to meet them, you'd think they were just average kids. And probably they were, in one part of themselves. 'A' students, on the soccer team. But in the shadow, they'd found another set of clothes."

"And they put them on," Rose said.

Ginny nodded. "There are many mechanisms of denial and emotional subterfuge."

Rose imagined that right now she'd tell Ginny the story. All of it. That Rose had her own set of secret shadow clothes and that Bennett was buried in the cellar. What would such a confession feel like? And what purpose might it serve? For Ginny to deliver atonement? Would Ginny justify her action — or tear down the justifications? Ginny would wonder, "Why didn't you just call the cops?" No phone. Fear of Bennett. Self-protection. All these were viable. But Rose knew why she'd killed Bennett, and Ginny might guess. It was like getting rid of mice.

Instead she said, "I was with him in a car once, and he ran over someone on the road. It was late at night. He didn't stop."

Ginny made a small, thoughtful frown. "And you, what did you do?"

Rose watched her breath cloud the air, the heat of her interior meeting the cold exterior. "It felt unreal, it wasn't happening, and even afterward — even now — it feels like it didn't happen. And yet I know, *I know* that it did."

"Were you the driver?"

"No." Then more emphatically: "*No.*"

"Do you have a question, then, for yourself about your culpability? Your guilt?"

"I was young. Is that an excuse?"

"If it's an excuse you want, then sure. We're young, we're so incredibly stupid. We don't have the data to make informed decisions, so we make bad ones."

"Miranda wouldn't have sat there like I did in the passenger seat, so passive, so weak."

Ginny smiled. "Take the credit then, you raised her. Miranda *kicks ass.*"

"Is that it? Everything comes back to our childhoods?" Rose burst out: "We're nailed there!"

"Oh, I don't think we can admit defeat that easily. Despite my profession, or maybe because of it, I'm a great believer in free will. I see it all the time." Ginny put her hand on Rose's arm.

"It's the point, isn't it? Of carrying on, of bothering at all. To get to the place where you can at last say, 'I'm truly myself.' And *like* that person."

"Look," Rose urged, pointing to the human-baby print of a yearling bear.

"I love how you show me these things," Ginny said.

They followed the scat for several hundred yards before the bear turned off into dense undergrowth. Their path now bled into the top of Rose's road, and their talk turned to Ginny's son's difficult transition out of a long-term relationship. The girl didn't want to let go and Ginny was afraid she'd "accidentally" get pregnant.

"Ironic, isn't it, this equipment we have," Rose said. "We think we can weaponize it. But we can't really, we're the ones left with the crying baby and the lost opportunities."

Rose was surprised to see a car parked outside Billy's house. A young couple came around from the back, talking excitedly. He had a dark beard and coal-black eyes, she was round-faced, apple-cheeked, her hair in dreads. They both had various piercings. Rose tried not to judge, but still she did, wondering if they'd regret the holes in their skin when it began to sag and wrinkle. "Hey," the girl said. "D'you live around here?"

"The house next door."

"Wow. Cool. D'you like it? Are you happy? This place has great feng shui."

"It does?"

"Sure! The river, the mountains, everything is, like, in align-ment with ley lines. It's really powerful." Then she allowed a small frown. "The only thing is the road, being too straight, it can carry money away."

Rose nearly burst out laughing but she merely nodded and made a non-committal, "Huh."

"We'd have to put in, like, some really powerful plantings, a garden right in front of the house and maybe even a fish pond to make sure our profits don't get carried away."

"Maybe I should have done that," Rose murmured.

"You're a gardener, then?" Ginny queried.

"Hemp," the boy said. "We're doing CBD."

"How long have you lived here?" The apple girl turned to Rose and Ginny. "You live together?"

"No! Ginny's just my friend. But I've lived here for over 30 years."

"So you know what happened to the guy who used to own this place? Billy someone."

"Billy was a woman."

"Oh? I heard some weird story."

"To be honest, I'm surprised the house is on the market," Rose countered. "It's been empty for years. It's barely standing up."

"I'm good with my hands," the boy held them up as proof. "We reckon we can fix it up, we're in no hurry and it's got good bones. We'll restore it bit by bit. We're going to start with the barn so we can grow inside all year 'round."

"I hope it works out for you." Rose smiled, began to turn away, Ginny drafting in beside her. "It will be great to have young energy here."

"Thanks," smiled the boy.

"And about the Billy person," the girl persisted.

Rose glanced back.

"It's just the vibe, or something. You know, someone dies, they die, you can, like, deal with the spirit, even if it's restless, you can call it up and talk to it. You can help it get some peace. But when someone disappears? Like, what is that? Like, that person just vanished? Super creepy."

"I'm sorry I really don't know what happened," Rose told her.

They left the young couple to leap like puppies back toward the house: they were talking about the best color for the front door — lucky turquoise.

Then Rose suddenly turned, called out to them: "Billy would be happy that you're here. She was the most beautiful person I've ever met."

The girl smiled, put her hands together in prayer and made a little bow.

"Look how old we are," Ginny laughed as she and Rose walked on, arm-in-arm. "Young people are now growing pot for a living, and it's totally legal. All those years Larry and I spent hiding our joints in the coffee tin!"

"Want to help me plant a big garden and giant pond and then we'll buy a sweepstakes ticket?"

They giggled, tilting toward each other, as they turned into Rose's driveway.

*   *   *

The bed was the shape of her, the depression in the mattress bore her exact dimensions. Rose lay on her back in the dark, wide awake, her eyes dry, gritty, and her heart pattering noisily in her chest like a restless mouse under the floor. Billy. She thought again of her friend, and felt the loss with the same shock and intensity. Billy would be in her sixties. She'd seemed ancient to Rose at the time — but she'd only been a decade older. The finality of death was still incomprehensible, like trying to understand infinity. There remained the stubborn burr of doubt that a mistake had been made and if Rose phoned the old number Billy would pick up, tentatively, for the phone was a new and strange device, "Yep?"

And with the memory of Billy always came the rush of alternatives, avenues of possibility pin-wheeling off from the hours around her death. If Bennett hadn't come home at all. If she had surrendered to him — submitted — and moved to Maine. If she'd found some other language, a new and sweet tongue, to speak to him and persuade him to leave. She couldn't quite pinpoint the chronology — when, exactly, the gears slid into place and she decided to stay and raise the gun and shoot to kill. These possibilities tailed back into the distant past. If she'd never met Bennett, if she hadn't gone to MoMA that Sunday. If she could undo the knot of time and place.

If she was an entirely different person.

Rose had never returned to the graveyard where she'd left Billy; all she could imagine was the rotting corpse, the infestation of beetles and maggots, the tearing decimation of the small, light body. And how she herself was an agent for that ruthless thanatopsis. There should have been a search party, if anyone had cared or if Rosie had given the cops any doubt or prompting. But she didn't. She let the narrative prevail: Billy had taken her own life, she went into the woods with her gun. Miranda hadn't been able to understand the idea of self-obliteration and she had insisted that Billy had been happy, Billy had been her friend, didn't Billy know that, how could Billy be sad when she was loved?

"How could she shoot her dogs, Mama?" Miranda had demanded. "She wouldn't do that, she just wouldn't."

Sometimes, Rose could see right through her ceiling, through her roof to the obsidian-dark northern sky. The sky hangs above as a vast fabric, the dark banner of heaven, and the sky will one day come unpinned, the cloth drooping, dropping, the weight of it bearing down on the earth, this vast, heavy blackness, smothering, smothering and everything ending.

* * *

The car had been making unhealthy sounds for some time and had nearly failed the last inspection. Something about the catalytic converter. Rose did not want to be one of those women, helpless in the face of the mechanical; she'd merely been hopeful. But at last the Tercel sputtered, coughed like a tuberculosis patient, and then began seizing. She edged it onto the shoulder. At that very instant, the rain began.

For a long moment, she merely sat, the rain sloshing down on the windshield, slapping the sides of the car, urged by a vigorous wind. When the storm's intensity increased, she opened the glove compartment and pulled out her insurance card, flipped open her phone and called the roadside assistance number on the back. A woman told her it would be 45 minutes. Rose waited. It was chilly, her feet were freezing, so she stamped them on the floor. Occasionally, other cars would pass, but they were blurred by the heavy curtain of rain. She was thinking about the women found murdered on the interstate. How a car felt so safe, gave you independence and mobility, you could lock the doors, you could drive away. But then, suddenly, it wasn't safe, and you were far from help, you were too far out.

At last, the tow truck loomed into view, the taillights smudging in the rain. The driver dashed out, exactly the man she'd expect a tow truck driver to be, generic middle age, overweight, ruddy complexioned. Should she be taking closer notice in case he was a murderer, and, escaping his clutches, she'd have to give a detailed description? Women needed to be vigilant at all times. She'd always wondered about those police sketches, watching cop shows on TV when the victim said things like, "His chin was wider, and his eyebrows a little closer together." Rose therefore stared at this man, noting rheumy blue eyes, searching for any significant scars — *Yes, officer, he had a jagged scar on his right cheek.* But nothing distinguished this man. He was like her, utterly forgettable.

"You gotta ride up front in my truck. I'll hook 'er up."

Rose scuttled through the rain and climbed in the cab. A few minutes later, the driver joined her. "Ya know what they say about spring in Vermont. If ya don't like the weatha, wait a minute," he laughed. "Where we takin' ya?"

"Boudreau Automotive, you know it, on Village Road?"

The prognosis was not good, replacing the catalytic converter was akin to a kidney transplant. Tony Boudreau sucked in his breath when he told her the estimate came in at just under two grand. He could do the work now, it would take a couple of days.

Rose felt her gut tighten, as if someone was pushing her belly button all the way in until it touched her spine. What could she do? She had to have a car.

"Can I make payments?"

It pained him, she could see that. He knew how people struggled with their vehicles, the tough inspections, the problems with rust caused by the salt on the roads in winter, the rough roads that stripped bearings, tore apart suspensions. He twisted his mouth left then right, and at last: "We can work something out for the labor. But I can't take on the cost of the parts."

Which were going to be nearly $1500. Plus, she'd need a rental car for a couple of days. "OK," she said. "I really appreciate it."

"I have to take payment now, though. For the parts."

Because, obviously, he'd been screwed over before. Not by liars and cheats, but people just like her who couldn't afford to fix their cars and couldn't afford not to. She reached into her purse, lifted out her wallet and took out her credit card. Suddenly, she was wildly hot — heat surging up from her drying womb, through her chest, setting her neck and head on fire. Sweat prickled her scalp. Her face was burning.

Tony noticed. "You need a glass of water?"

"Just ah —" she fanned herself. "Hot."

"Yeah," he gave her a gentle smile. "My wife's the same. She suffers."

As the heat drained from her, she wanted to burst into tears. She wanted to lean against this big, kind man and have him just give her a hug while she cried and cried, the desire to sob was like thirst or hunger, a purely physical craving. But instead he tapped into his computer, and turned the credit card reader toward her. She slid in the card. *Processing...* it read mercilessly. *Processing...*

"Can be slow." Tony scratched his chin.

Processing...

Processing...

At last the answer came. *Declined.*

Rose frowned earnestly. "They must have not yet got my payment."

"You want to try for a smaller amount?"

"Could you? Then I can get a cash balance from my other account." This sounded plausible. *My other account.* Because she had a number of them, and she merely had to contact her *banker* and have him move some money around.

Tony tried a number of times, and, at last, the machine accepted $750.

"I'll go to the bank, then come right back."

"You got a friend coming to give you a lift?"

"Yes," Rose nodded, smiled confidently. Tony went back into the garage, leaving her in the empty office. The problems were multiple, the car, the lift, the money, the lack of money, the bank, the rental car. She had once borrowed two hundred bucks from Ginny; she could not ask again because this would skew the one friendship she had. She couldn't even ask Ginny for a lift, because Ginny was on the way to Hanover to mainline toxic chemicals. What about the book club ladies? Connie? To ask for help was to admit need; but with them it would be worse: she'd be admitting to all of them that she didn't have anyone else to ask. She couldn't possibly expose herself like that. Dumbly, Rose stared at her phone. She dialed the office.

"Margie's Farm Fresh Eggs," came the cheery answer.

"Nick?"

"Yeah?"

"It's Rose."

"Heya, Rose. What's up?"

"My car, Nick, it's broken down and I need a ride."

"Where're ya?"

She told him she'd need a lift first to the office, because she had to pick up her car insurance card which was in her desk, and then to the Enterprise car rental in St. Johnsbury.

Ten minutes later, Nick arrived. His car — a late '90s Subaru Outback — could not be street legal. White smoke farted from the tailpipe. The left rear window was duct-taped with clear plastic. She ran through the rain and got in. There was trash all over the floor. She carefully tunneled her feet inside the mass of soda cans and fast food wrappers. Sitting, she felt the engine's vibration jarring up her spine.

Nick smiled. "Like my rig?"

"Hey, it's moving. Which is more than I can say for mine."

They peeled out onto the road and Rose clung to her seatbelt, laughing despite herself. Nick turned up the volume on the radio. "I love this song!"

Golden Earring's "Radar Love." Still playing decades later. She watched him singing, the tendons in his jaw visible beneath his skin. She watched his hands on the wheel, they were beautiful hands, like those of a sculptor. She watched the soft skin at the base of his throat rise and fall with his breath, his singing, and she felt her humiliation ebb and her feet warm with the furnace blast of the Subaru's unsubtle heating. Soon, they were at the compound.

He waited for her in the car while she rushed in *to just grab my car insurance from my desk.* "Hello?" she called out. No answer. For good measure, she checked Bob's office. He wasn't here, perhaps out grooming 12-year-olds. Which wasn't funny. Rose was quick, she went right for the petty cash in the safe, she took nine hundred. She phoned the credit card company and begged Ivan, a reluctant customer service advisor with a Southern accent to extend her credit just this once for the car rental.

Out the window, she saw Nick in the Subaru on his phone. He was in no hurry.

"Let me speak with my supervisor," Ivan told her, as she watched Nick in the car, laughing at something his friend was saying. All that life, all that joy. All that *time.* At long last, Ivan agreed, a temporary extension and Rose felt a flush of victory. She'd gotten the credit card company to give her more debt! Hurrah! She hurried back out, down the steps and through the rain. Nick was waiting for her. He has a fast car, she was thinking, fast enough for them to drive away.

"Check it out!" He thrust his phone at her. "This new aging app, I can make myself your age and visa versa!"

He showed her a photo of Bob. "But that's your dad."

"Freaked me out! That is me in forty years."

Rose peered again: she discerned now, the difference, Nick's nose was straighter than Bob's. The app couldn't quite capture what happened to your eyes, however, only the skin around them. The app didn't show how the eyes dimmed and narrowed. The app didn't show the cosmic skillet in the face that was life.

Taking the phone back, he snapped her, then applied the app.

"Here's you at my age!"

Rose regarded her image, the smooth skin and lustrous long hair. But the eyes told the truth: conversely, they were the tired eyes of a middle-aged woman, and in the face of a 17-year-old, they became the eyes of a girl who'd suffered immeasurable trauma.

"You were a babe," Nick said.

"Really? You think so?"

"Didn't you look in the mirror?"

Rose urged: "We'd better get to the rental place, they have weird hours."

*　　*　　*

"The tap's still leaking." Miranda stood with her hand on the offending item.

"It's the washer, I keep forgetting." Rose was plumping cushions, even though they would never be plump enough for Miranda. Miranda's entire adult life was a reprimand to Rose

— to show her how single-motherhood could look if you did it right. There was no concrete evidence of this, apart from Miranda's success. The rebuke was insidious, like an odorless toxin that kills families while they sleep. Rose could not fault her daughter. She was dutiful, she checked boxes. She called, she sent photos of Anika, and invited Rose to stay, and Rose went to the show-off house overlooking the sea in Marblehead, the en suite guest room, the thick cream carpeting. Once a year, Miranda and Anika came to visit Vermont. They stayed at the Darling Hill Inn because Rose's house was too small, though it was the same house Miranda had grown up in. Miranda didn't want to be a burden, and Anika loved the animal sanctuary behind the inn. So they came, but didn't really come, they ate out, they slept elsewhere, for two nights only.

Rose would watch her daughter in the house — she usually agreed to come for tea or coffee. Checking *that* box. Miranda would hesitate upon entering, Rose was sure she sensed disbelief, the way she appraised the shabbiness she saw. *People live like this! My own mother! My own former self!* No matter how hard Rose worked to hide what was broken or breaking, Miranda would find the house's weakness. The tap, the roof. Or, "Have you thought of having the house insulated with this new cellulose stuff? It would stay so much warmer." Sure, Rose silently replied, with ten spare grand I'd love to insulate my house with cellulose.

Anika, only five, picked up on these cues. "Your house smells funny, Grandma." Mold spores, dust, dead mice, live mice. Anika was terrified of the noises in the walls. "Those are the mice," Miranda would say. "It's really their house, but they let Grandma live here."

Rose prepared the tea, she had bought eclairs from the organic baker in East Burke at huge expense — half her food budget for the week; worth it, though, for even Miranda approved of them. Anika was outside picking dandelions. "Leave her," Rose urged, for it was lovely to see a little girl in the garden again. "How's everything?"

"*Busy.*" Miranda was always busy, CFO of a tech firm outside Boston, God-knows what they did, though Miranda had calmly explained it to Rose a number of times, something about wearable medical devices. Miranda was on a plane half the time, she had an excellent nanny with a salary twice Rose's, plus benefits. She also had a housekeeper to vacuum the cream carpeting. Miranda had a sense of noblesse obligée toward these women, she valued their hard, simple work for it allowed her to do her own hard, complicated work. Miranda sipped her tea. "And you, Mom?"

"Yes, everything's fine." No mention of the car, the melting credit card, the humiliations — no proof for Miranda of her mother's incompetence.

Miranda shifted, pursed her lips. Rose guessed, then, there was a specific reason for the visit, and why Anika should be left to the dandelions.

"I want to ask you about my father."

The bad penny. Rose pointlessly rearranged the eclairs.

"We don't know 100% that he's dead," Miranda said.

"Well. Legally, he's dead."

"That was you."

"Because no one had seen or heard from him for a decade. It seemed likely."

"But he might not be dead."

Rose watched Anika, the bright posy in her hands, she'd gathered so many dandelions and Rose wished she'd stop because the bees required the flowers. Rose considered: what is it Miranda needs now? What is it I must pluck from my wallet like a silk scarf, the magic trick of ski lessons or the field trip to Montreal? What is it I must give without a hint of the cost?

With one hand, Rose smoothed the frown line that tended to tighten between her eyebrows. Her voice was careful, practiced: "I think it was difficult for you not having a father."

"That's not the point," Miranda said. A fly buzzed against the window pane. "I'm hiring a private detective."

"If that's what you need to do." Another fly, then three. Bluebottles. Rose thought about the mouse trap she'd set — and forgotten — in the pantry. "It's your money."

Clink went the cup on the tray. Miranda exhaled. "It's not about money. It's about my father."

Of course this conversation had to be had, it had festered for years like the dead mice. "Is there something specific I can tell you about him that will help you?"

"Oh, Mom." A patient sigh. "That's part of the problem. I only know him through what you've said about him, which isn't much. I mean lacrosse, he liked books. That's not much, is it?"

"He was secretive. And I was very young. I didn't ask the questions I should have."

Miranda only half-listened. "Plus, I don't know why he left."

"He didn't leave, he went to prison." Rose poured another tea. She was drinking fast.

"And when he got out? Did you try to find him?"

Rose pressed her lips together. "No. I was glad he was gone."

"Not a letter, nothing? I mean, you were just OK with not hearing from him?"

"He'd made life so difficult for us. You don't remember."

"Is it possible he decided not to come back?" Miranda

interjected. "Maybe — that's it, maybe he thought we didn't want him."

For a long moment, there was silence. Rose ate the eclair, the cream inelegantly spurting out the far end. Surreptitiously, she wiped her sticky hand on the couch. "You think he decided not to come back because I was unwelcoming?"

"Maybe, Mom, maybe. He was ashamed and he thought we didn't want him. And if he made that decision, he could still be alive, and I can find him."

"Find him?"

"Why not? It's easy to find people these days."

"I don't think —"

"It's possible, Mom. It is just possible that my father is alive."

Rose nodded, trying to give the impression of calm attentiveness while scurrying around her brain to see if she should or could concoct a different, new story that might satisfy her daughter — not just satisfy but alleviate. *Alleviate* the belief that someone was to blame, perhaps Miranda herself, the two-year-old child she'd been that last time she saw her father, the brief trial, the sentencing, the unbelieving, incredulous man in shackles being taken away. Oh: they hadn't loved Bennett enough. Hadn't welcomed him with confetti and bunting. Rose summoned conviction: "He would have come back if he could. For you. For *you*. He loved you. He adored you."

"Then why didn't he come back?" It was almost a whine. Miranda suddenly seemed a child again, the trappings of her success were a dress-up, a costume.

"I don't know."

Miranda folded her hands, simply yet perfectly manicured. "I used to believe he was going to walk through the door. One day.

And he'd take me in his arms and give me the biggest hug. There was one time —"

Rose sat very still. She felt the hair raise on her arms.

"— when I was sure he was home. I almost asked you. But I remember thinking you'd tell me if he was back. And it was right around the time Billy died and you were so sad."

A blob of eclair cream shimmered in Rose's lap — too big to dab away discreetly. Should she take the blame — *Yes, that's it, I told him to stay away and he did.* It was, ironically, the lesser lie. But entirely insufficient. She knew her daughter to be willful — take credit for it, you raised her, Ginny had said.

"I'll do whatever I can to help," Rose spoke quietly. "But I'm concerned for you, for your expectations."

Miranda slipped back into her form-fitting CFO-skin. "They're my expectations. Mine."

"You're right, they are."

"We should go."

"No. Don't. I haven't even seen Anika."

But Miranda was standing, she was hugging Rose, and Rose found herself still incredulous that she came only to her daughter's shoulder; Miranda had Bennett's height. Rose wanted to hold on, for the hug to last and deepen, so she could smell her daughter, so that some layer of her might stay on the surface of Rose for days to come. Yet Miranda stepped back, she always did. She was so elegant, so matching in navy blue and white. "It's not about you, Mom, it's not about anything you did wrong."

There was silence. And then the drip of the tap, that ruthless metronome.

Rose stood watching their car recede and she felt a sudden panic; she must run after them and call them back and find the words, the sentences that could be bundled into a sufficient and sensible explanation. Yet the car kept going.

*   *   *

The name rang no bell. Rose stared at the package sent by C. Barrow, an address in Santa Fe, New Mexico. She guessed newsprint, magazines — perhaps some kind of solicitation? She almost threw it away.

By now the rain had turned to snow, and there was a prediction of several inches overnight. It would be interesting driving the rental — a Ford Focus with summer tires — down the hill in the morning. Snow this late in the spring always made her fret for the birds who had just arrived, for the trees just daring to bud, and the creatures of the woods and earth who had already endured the winter and were frantically searching for forgotten stashes. Spring is more lethal than winter.

Pouring another wine, Rose sat down at the kitchen table and opened the package. Photographs. Of her as a teenager. A dozen. And a note. From someone called Chris. *Chris?*

Dear Rosie,

I didn't know I'd kept these, but somehow they have stayed with me through many moves (and lives) in an old shoebox. I am down-sizing, attempting Zen, and was about to throw them out. But I thought you might want them, or at least it should be up to you to do what you wish with them. I don't know what I feel looking through them. Mostly old. Maybe a little bewildered by how much passes through us. I hope you are well.

Yours,
Chris

The deck of pictures were from the days when people used film and sent the rolls away in their neat black canisters, the magic metamorphosis in a dark room, moments fixed in time, and returned in the bright yellow envelopes. Rose stared at herself in many attitudes — dress lifted in the breeze, clutching a hat, making a face with an ice cream, laughing. Beautiful. How had she not realized her own beauty when she'd had it? Yet, she could not remember believing herself beautiful. As Nick had said: *You were a babe.* Her high breasts, her brown skin and dark hair — it felt almost impossible that once she had been inside that body. And Chris was right — what to feel? Old, bewildered. As if dementia had already set in and she knew she should remember him precisely but only felt a wild, grappling — a kind of vertigo. What was lost, fallen away — *how much passes through us.* Chris? High school Chris.

Re-reading the letter, she decided he'd taken time to write it, he'd wanted the right tone — to convey his care, still. As if the bright pieces of the past should be handled gently, polished like pebbles, even if merely decorative at this point. He hadn't thrown out these pictures, these memories, but kept them through many moves. And many lives. Which meant, what? Different jobs, different women — children, griefs, divorce. But why send them to her — why the need to contact her? And how had he found her? Was it creepy, stalker-y — or just Facebook?

It's easy to find people these days, Miranda had said.

Rose reached for the one photograph of Chris with her — skinny, young, as if he hadn't had his growth spurt. Peering closer, now with her reading glasses, she recalled him more precisely, or rather an aura of him: comfort. He'd been funny and gentle and smart, qualities which made him unpopular. He'd wanted to be an artist — and that had been the plan, to go to Parsons together. But he'd changed his mind, something like that, and gone out West, one of those Californian universities — Berkeley, Stanford.

Rose finished her wine, and went to bed.

Yet she was writing a letter to him in her head, lying in the dark, composing and editing, so she got up and came back to the table, pen and paper.

Chris, she wrote. *Thank you for the package. I hope you are well, too. Wellness is increasingly important, isn't it? I am well.*

She almost signed off. Then:

If you ever come to Vermont, let me know. We could meet for a drink.

In hopeful wellness,
Rose

*   *   *

Bob was busy shredding documents, Rose could hear the whir of the machine. He was hunched over it, she could just see the bald pate of his head, his soft, rounded shoulders. He'd been shredding for nearly ten minutes. She knocked and said, "Bob?" Knocked again, louder, and then finally hammered with the palm of her hand and shouted above the shredder, "Bob!"

He whipped around with the exact look of a child caught out, it was such a caricature, Rose nearly laughed out loud.

"Jesus Christ, Rose, I didn't hear you."

"I'm sorry," she made no attempt to appear so. "I just need you to sign a couple of checks for suppliers."

"Sure." He pivoted his chair to face her, and the shredder fell silent. He was looking at her, and she was careful not to let her eyes slide to the shredder.

"Just these three."

Bob signed, the onerous task of lifting a pen.

"Great, thanks." She turned the page of the checkbook. "And just these two more."

He was so careless. Had Andy been on the take — not just cooking the books for the company, but fixing his own little deal? Handy Andy padding his paltry income. His — ha ha — *poultry* income.

Rose made $2,654.65 a month after state and federal taxes. Which, after all her bills and expenses, left her with exactly $26.28. This never seemed to materialize as actual money — a twenty, a five, a one and the change; she couldn't splurge on dinner in the town's one pizzeria, she certainly couldn't afford a two-grand car repair. Most months, she squeezed by — she bought the cheaper meat, the discount bread. She'd even given up Netflix DVDs and took her chances with the tatty collection at the library. To pay back her *emergency loan* from Bob, she withheld her usual retirement savings and she ate eggs, beans and frozen spinach, reducing her general expenses to $736.

When — only the day before — she had replaced the money in the petty cash, she had wanted very much to tell someone — *Look, I'm honest!* But no one had witnessed her decency as she slipped the bills back into the zippered bank purse during lunch. No one even knew the money had gone. After she'd replaced it, she noticed that the spider plant above the safe needed watering, so she took it into the bathroom, soaked it under the tap for several minutes. No one had thanked her. The plant had not looked greener, merely dangled the same timid tendril. The afternoon sun had come through the blinds, illuminating the dust motes in the air, and Rose had stood in the unremarkable stillness, stricken with the idea that she was as vital as a chair — and perhaps less relevant.

Now, the ennui overcame her again — something like finding grit in the bed; a tedious surface discomfort that didn't even have the energy to plunge into existential despair. Suddenly, there was a thud on the window by her desk, and Rose looked just in time to see a small shadow fall. She ran out and found the bird, a robin. It was inert, but she couldn't tell if it was dead. Carefully, she examined it — how beautiful it became in her hands, so perfect a machine of life, the spare and necessary lines of it. Lifting it to her face, she smelled the bird: a faint dusty odor. She had imagined something more voluptuous. The way a dog can smell an entire story, she'd wanted to know where it had come from, the scent of pine or sea air or wood smoke, the storms and cats it had evaded. Pressing her ear to its chest, she wondered if she might detect a heartbeat. In the second of that action, the bird revived, and with a horror of her — a wild misunderstanding of her intention — it screamed and pulled away, for a moment its twiggy claws tangled in her hair and she felt the wings beat about her head, she entered into the panic with the bird, flapping and scratching and when she reached her hand up to try to free it, the bird pecked her palm savagely. In the next second, it was released, and flew away on certain wings, calling out a harsh rebuke.

The wound was a perfect sharp "V" pointing to a tiny glob of blood. The blood genuinely surprised Rose, as if she'd forgotten her own blood. It had been years since she'd menstruated. Perhaps, she mused, this was why men are so careless — they are not reminded, monthly, of the frailty of the human form. They are not reminded, every day in magazines, on TV, on the internet, of their aging and their defects — cellulite, small breasts, floppy breasts, stretch marks, wrinkles. Men are not oppressed by the clocks of their bodies, decisions that must be made by a certain time. Bob could therefore steep in the delusional brew of his own mind, imagining himself desirable, virile. But women are trapped by form, by time — when they begin to menstruate, when they stop, and all the individual months in between that mark the ascendency of their fertility and its decline and its stuttering failure, culminating in the sweaty self-immolation of menopause.

Rose wrapped toilet paper around her hand. She took a breath. The ruckus, the parade began to quiet, and then packed up the big top altogether. And when Bob had also left, Rose carefully removed the lid off the paper shredder. The narrow strips of paper had delicately folded upon themselves, and she was therefore able to scoop out the top sets. These were jumbled, but not beyond repair — no more difficult than a 100-piece jigsaw. She taped the pieces back together, two entire pages and one half. She considered scrounging around for the other half, but what she had was sufficient.

Big bear,
Am a little Goldelocks. Only 13. Have no sexual experianse other than touching my self. I get myself wet so wet but don't know what to do with wet soft tight pussy. I really want my first time to be with older guy who is experiansed. I dont like young guy, they are just look to please their own penis...

Why had he printed this stuff out? He'd grown up when there were porn magazines. *Penthouse* and *Tits*. Maybe he needed to clutch something while he... while he...

Rose abruptly aborted the thought before it congealed into

an image. She remembered Billy telling her how male turkeys are so insane with lust during mating season that they'll court anything vaguely resembling a female. *Sticka coupla feathas to a cadboward box and ya gotta tom goin crazy.*

Though the pixilation and the shredder left much to the imagination, the pictures did not. Rose could make out various young girls in short skirts or baby doll nighties. Logging on to his computer, she was surprised to find she could go right to his home page. She checked his favorites bar — the guy was a moron — because he'd starred several sites as favorites: lolipop, naughteen, daddydome. On daddydome, the subjects (objects?) were teenage girls.

Looking through the site, she wondered who these girls were. Obviously, they were avatars — "Dainty Debbie" was not a 15-year-old gymnast who wanted to show off her flexibility; more likely a Ukrainian housewife or a medical student in Delhi trying to pay his bills. But the pictures themselves, even if altered, were of real young women, somewhere. And Bob crept into that narrow, fictitious space, knowing that it was safe and dark, for he'd never really be called upon to satisfy a beautiful, tender, expectant 13-year-old. *"I want slow and gentle, who will apreshiate my virgin, because I will never ever forget my first time,"* Goldelocks wrote. *"I know it will hurt. Please gentle —"*

Or maybe.

Thought Rose.

Maybe this is a trajectory.

Taking out her phone, she took a screen shot of Bob's favorites bar.

The note read:

Dear Rosie,

It was a nice surprise to get your reply. I wasn't sure you'd write back. As a matter of fact, I will be in Boston for a series of meetings the first week of June. Would you like to meet? My schedule is restrictive during the day, but I'm free in the evenings. It's very old-fashioned to write like this, so here's my email chrisbarrow@windmere.org.

Hope to see you—

Chris

Windmere, Rose typed. Windmere Cruises popped up, Windmere Realty, Windmere Dry Cleaners, Windmere Condominiums, *2,367,046 additional pages.* She added *Christopher Barrow* but nothing relevant came up. She switched the search to images — cruise ships, happy couples on cruise ships, idyllic Caribbean islands… she scrolled down to the one photograph of a middle-aged man; but this turned out to be Charles Windmere of Barrow Island, Michigan. Still, Rose scrutinized him, if only to help her imagine Chris at the same age.

Dear Chris,

Here I am on email, then. It's strange to think we are so old this wasn't invented when we knew each other.

Yes, let's try to meet. If you give me a time and place I'll do my best to be there.

But then how to end it? Warm regards? Best? Yours? Cheers? She couldn't use *Hope to see you* because he'd used that. At last she just wrote her name. Rose. Not Rosie. So he'd know there was a difference.

* * *

"Rose?"

She held the phone awkwardly, her other hand scrabbling for the light. "Yes?"

"It's Nick."

"Nick, yeah, hi." The light on now, she could see the clock: 02:37. "Is everything all right?"

Stupid question. A phone call at this hour was never all right.

"Uh, I've, uh, been arrested."

Rose swung herself upright now, feet on the floor. Christ almighty, the house was cold, rain drooling down in the dark outside. She thought about the traitorous roof. Then Nick, the dark hair falling in his eyes. "For what? Where are you?"

"I'm at the state police."

"Why?"

"Killing a moose."

"You ran into it?"

"We shot it."

"But it's out of season."

"Yeah."

"Have you called your dad?"

"No."

"You probably should."

"Can you come?"

"I really think you should —"

"Please. Rose."

"Now?"

There was silence and then the softest sniffle, softer than a mouse's, so she barely heard it. "Nick?"

Was he even still there?

"Nick?"

Very quietly, "I told Tyler not to shoot."

"I'll be there as soon as I can."

A red dawn leered over the Kirby Mountains to her east as she drove to St. Johnsbury, to the state police barracks just beyond the Comfort Inn.

A woman sat behind the bullet-proof glass, and Rose wondered: if it was bullet proof, how could it really be glass?

"Can I help you?"

"I'm here for Nick Booth."

Checking a list, finding the name. "And what do you want with Mister Booth?"

"I'm his ride."

"You his mom?"

"No."

"Aunt?"

"Friend."

The woman looked Rose over: what kind of an older woman *friend* came to the cop shop at dawn. "Hang on. He's not done bein' processed." Rose waited, scanning the "Wanted" posters hanging in the lobby. All these "adult, white males" she thought, all their mischief. Assualt, assault and battery, domestic assault, attempted homicide.

At last, a series of unseen doors clicked and buzzed, and at last Nick appeared. He was thin and pale, as if vampires had been at him. Her instinct was to rush and embrace him; but she checked herself. She stood, waiting.

"Sorry," he mumbled, then half-cocked a smile. "And thanks."

Rose took him for breakfast at the P&H Truck Stop a few exits down the interstate. Nick was ravenous, she ordered another round of waffles for him, she stuck to tea and a toasted muffin. "What about Tyler?"

"Oh hessh swill inwar."

"Don't talk with your mouth full."

"He's still in there."

Rose adjusted herself. If she wore glasses, she would peer at him over them in a Mother Superior way. "What were you thinking?"

Nick was about to put another forkful in his mouth. He stopped, the fork hovering for a moment, a drip of maple syrup descending onto the plate. "Thinking?" Nick put the fork down. "Now, that's the problem right there."

"Tell me then."

He took a breath, with the sleeve of his sweatshirt, he dabbed away the drip of syrup at his mouth. "We were just driving. Up past Willoughby, you know the road goes right along the lake. We were drinking but we weren't tanked, not even really buzzed. And this moose came out of the dark and stood there in the middle of the road and Ty stopped. And she was caught in the headlights, she didn't move, she just looked at us. Ty took down his rifle, and I said, 'Don't.' I guess I could have stopped him or at least clapped my hands or shouted so the moose ran away. But I was kind of like her, I just sat there, like there was something inevitable, like we'd all waited our whole lives to be in this one place. I can't explain it. But it's what I mean about not thinking. It was all happening outside of me, somehow, forces were directing me, like I couldn't stop. I didn't understand what I was supposed to do. He shot her. But didn't kill her. Even at that close range. So he had to get out and shoot her. And then —"

Nick paused, he pushed his plate away.

"It was terrible."

"It was Tyler not you —"

"No — I should have stopped him. Why didn't I? I kept just not stopping him and then just doing what he said. We hitched that poor cow to the back of his truck with a bunch of chains, we were going to tow her to Brownington, he's got a cousin there, but by the time we got to the turn off, the moose was all fucked up, just this bloody stumpy thing on the chain. So we dumped her and figured no one had seen us." He swallowed and looked down.

"How did the cops find out?"

"Maybe Tyler said something to his cousin. I dunno. Fish and Game put a reward out. Someone told them."

"What happens now?"

"Tyler says we should deny it. There's no proof."

"It doesn't matter what Tyler says."

The waitress came with the coffee refill, gestured to Nick's plate, "You done with that, hon?"

"Yeah," Nick said.

"No," Rose said. "You should eat more."

Nick made a stab at a pancake, drove it into the pool of maple syrup, making circuits around the plate. This went on for far too long. Rose waited, she sipped her tea, she finished the last crust of her muffin. Then she became aware of Nick, his face still down, his shoulders shuddering.

"Oh," she said.

And he looked up at her, eyes pooled with tears. "She had milk, Rose. Her tits were full of milk."

For a moment he seemed to broach the hill of his tears, to regain control, he sniffed hard and blinked. But then the features of his face contracted in on themselves and he started all over again.

Quietly, she invited him: "Is there something else?"

He bit his lip to stop it from juddering. "My dad, Rose. I don't want to be him in twenty years. Those poor fucking chickens. I want to leave, I want to just get in my car and drive away. So fucking far away." Dabbing his face with a napkin, he tried another laugh. "I can join the military, I guess. That's what Tyler's going to do. But I'm not a huge fan of killing. Or dying."

Her hand went to his face, but then she was instantly aware of a wider perspective, who might be watching, who might casually see this interaction, and she pulled her hand away. *Leave,* she wanted to tell him, she wanted to shout. *Just leave!* But she'd never left, had she?

Last spring, she'd found a dead snowshoe hare under her porch. The body was perfectly preserved, freeze-dried, so she could see the buckshot that mortally injured it. How it must have run, panting and bleeding through the snow, to find refuge. It must have collapsed in exhaustion, and perhaps died quite quickly, drowsy from the cold and the loss of blood. It lay in an attitude of action, legs stretched out, ears back, still running — a permanent and futile pose of escape.

"What if I never get away from here? What if I end up in chat rooms with underage Russian girls? What —" Taking a deep inhale, he wiped his nose on his sleeve. "Sorry —"

"It's OK, Nick."

"No —"

"Finish your pancakes."

"Diane Polinski. Hi." Her hair was short. She extended her hand. Rose noted that she wore a large man's watch. "Thanks for meeting with me."

"Of course."

They sat in the corner booth at the Bagel Depot. Diane took out a notebook and sharpened pencil and put them carefully on the table. Then she placed her smart phone in alignment. "OK if I record this?"

Rose shrugged, "If that's helpful, sure."

"It just means we're clear. What you say. What I say. No ambiguity."

Right, Rose thought. Because the spoken word is never ambiguous. "Before you turn it on —" she announced. "I just want to say one thing." And when Diane gave a small nod, Rose went on: "I understand my daughter's need for closure. And I hope that's what's happening here. That it's not about false hope. Or money."

"Ms. Kinney told me you'd probably say that."

Ah, Rose thought. Diane wants to make sure I know there'd been a lot of discussion behind my back. "Got it," Rose said. No ambiguity.

Diane pressed *record*. "I guess we just start with why you're so certain Bennett Kinney is dead."

"Do you have some reason to think he isn't?"

"This," said Diane. "Will be smoother if you just answer my questions."

Rose attempted contrition. "He didn't just go out for a cigarette for thirty years."

"Did you look for him?"

"No."

Diane tilted her head, waited.

Rose complied: "I didn't have the time, I was working three jobs. It wasn't like now when you just Google." Then she looked directly at Diane. "And I couldn't afford a private detective."

"What about his family? Did you contact them?"

"I didn't know them."

"None of them — parents? Siblings?"

"I think there was a sister."

"Her name?"

Rose shrugged.

"Can you speak out loud, please?"

"I don't know."

"Where was he born?"

"No idea."

"And no one ever contacted you from his family?"

"Never."

"Did you wonder why?"

"No."

This sounded implausible to PI Di, who frowned.

So Rose said: "For the record, you're frowning. And I'm answering. I never wanted to see my grandmother again. I wanted nothing to do with her. I assumed that's how it was for Bennett."

"I hear *assumed*. Did you ever have a conversation about it with Bennett?"

"He said his mother committed suicide."

"*He said?*"

Rose pointed to the phone and made a cutting motion. Diane obliged and turned the recorder off.

"He was a liar. Whatever he told me about his family, I never questioned it, because who lies about their family? Who lies about their mother committing suicide? Bennett would. Do I want Miranda to know that about him? That he was a liar as well as a drug trafficker? No."

Diane took a sip of her coffee and winced. "Miranda wants to know what there is to know. It's her right, as an adult."

"You have kids?" Rose asked, and when Diane gave a slight shake of her head, she went on. "You never stop protecting them. Making it right for them. Her father was a first-class asshole. Let me be clear. What does she gain by knowing that?"

"Control. Over her own past. I'm going to put this back on now." Diane jabbed her phone, sat back in a show of patience.

"There was a family issue with money. I think. They'd had money. Bennett said his father lost it all." Rose made a laugh she hoped would be light and dismissive. "But who knows."

Diane wrote quickly, concentrating. "Did you want him to come back?"

"No."

"Why?"

"He'd gone to jail for running drugs."

"Maybe he was rehabilitated."

Rose imagined roaring out in wild amusement. Instead, she said, "Look, I never saw him after he was released and he never contacted me."

"Huh." Diane chewed her pencil thoughtfully. "Because there's some confusion with the dates and maybe you can help me out. According to Miranda, you'd told her he was dead when he was — as I discovered — still in prison. And then he got out, and he allegedly disappeared and you declared him dead."

Rose sighed softly. "Yes, I see what you're doing. You think there was a pattern. Malice. Intention. But I just was making decisions as they came. I told her Bennett was dead because it seemed the easiest explanation at the time. She was a small child. I thought that was best."

"Easier to tell her her father was *dead*?"

"His dealer was a pedophile who wanted to take photographs of her, then a baby of two, to pay his drug debt. My only desire was to protect Miranda. It still is."

Diane nodded, then waited.

"I'm glad he's dead," Rose added. "For the record."

"You had no contact with him when he was in prison, and you had no idea when he was getting out?"

"None, and no."

"And he never contacted you when he got out?"

"No. As I've said."

"Not in May 1993?"

"No. I never heard from him."

"And that was your sole reason for declaring him dead? That he didn't show up, he didn't give you a call?"

"Yup."

"You had no other evidence?"

"Listen, Bennett always came back. It was how he kept control. By leaving and then coming back whenever he felt like it. I could never just get on with my life. Sooner, later, he'd appear, not out of love or duty or even homesickness but to fuck it all up." Rose flattened her hands on the table, she spoke slowly. "The only reason he would not come back was if he was dead."

"Right, hmmm. Interesting." Diane shifted in her seat, writing manically, then stopping, Columbo like, with the pencil to her lips: "So, there's a couple of odd things I'd like to go over. Like phone calls. I obtained your phone records."

"You can do that?"

"It's not difficult. The old phone companies disbanded, their records are available."

Rose was suddenly on fire, her face flushing, sweat pricking her underarms. She yanked off her sweater. Diane was studying her, interpreting this fluster. "Menopause." Rose took a long drink of water. "Go on, you were saying, the phone records."

"You had the phone installed in 1992."

"Sounds about right."

"And the bills at that time itemized every number you dialed."

"Probably, yes."

"So —" Diane brought out photocopies of the bills. "If you see here, in May of 1993, there's a cluster of phone calls to a number in Maine."

Rose felt herself frown, then applied a more placid veneer. *Maine*, she was thinking, what about *Maine*?

"Who do you know in Maine," Diane wanted to know.

"No one." The heat had subsided, Rose pulled her sweater back on, she was thinking about her daughter — why didn't she just ask for the phone records — and who had phoned who in — "*Maine*?"

"Kennebunkport," Diane clarified.

"I don't know anyone in Kennebunkport."

"Not a business or a person? Do you recall?"

"The Kennedys? The Bushes?"

Diane managed a tight smile. "You see the problem, right? Who would have been calling Kennebunkport from the phone in your house? If not you."

Rose's bra strap dug into her shoulder. "Maybe it was an error on the bill."

"Did you question it at the time? Did you call the phone company?"

"Do I remember calling the phone company 30 years ago to complain about a bill?"

"You're a book-keeper."

"Now. I wasn't then."

"But you were careful with money?"

"Did Miranda say that?"

"I just assumed from what she told me that things had been tight."

And what had Miranda told Diane? Rose thought she'd hidden their poverty so well.

"So if you'd got a bill and there were charges you didn't recognize, you'd probably flag it, right? Out-of-state calls weren't cheap in those days."

Rose tried to scroll back in her mind. She really had no recollection of the phone bill or the item *Kennebunkport*. Briefly, she wondered if Diane was making it up, a clever trap. In the days following Billy's and Bennett's deaths, she'd felt chaotic, filled with grief and fear, heavy with the weight of both their bodies, she'd had trouble getting out of bed and putting on her shoes. But Hook had stuck her long cold nose into the covers and regarded Rosie without pity. She needed to be let out to pee.

"The other odd thing —" for the detective believed she was on to something — "is that your neighbor Williamina Mix disappeared a day after the last phone call to Maine."

Rose gave an impression of thinking back. "I remember when she disappeared. I reported it to the police. I don't know the exact date. By May sounds about right."

"It's just a coincidence?" Diane leaned back, her hands braced against the table corners, triangulating her body. "The two disappearances?"

"I'm sorry, I don't follow you."

"They both disappeared, Bennett and Williamina, around the same time. Bennett was paroled the week before."

"I don't know when he was paroled. We weren't communicating." Rose idled her gaze in neutral.

"You had him declared dead."

"After seven years. I felt we needed closure."

"We?"

"For Miranda. Better a dead father than one who decided his daughter wasn't worth coming home for."

"But the seven years, Rose, the seven years is a very specific time, it's the legal minimum for such a declaration in Vermont, and you sought it seven years after Williamina Mix's death — *after the phone calls to Maine* from your house. After Bennett's parole."

"Exactly seven years?" Rose frowned. "To the day?"

"Not exactly."

"Roughly?"

"Within a year."

Rose looked exasperated. "Within 365 days of the seven year anniversary of his parole that I didn't know about, I filed a declaration of death form. And that's a coincidence?"

"I still don't understand why you bothered. Was it money? Insurance? Why not just accept that he was missing?"

"I've answered that question."

"His sister lives in Maine."

"Does she?"

"Kennebunkport, in fact."

Rose nodded.

"So maybe you heard he was getting out and you got in touch with her."

"I don't even know her name, let alone her number."

Now Diane smiled. "Then who phoned her in May 1993? The, ah, 5th, 6th and 7th."

Bad penny, Rose thought, you bad, bad, rotten goddamned penny.

"Do you think he isn't dead?" she burst suddenly out. "It halfway wouldn't surprise me that he was living in the Virgin Islands running a bar or shacked up with a rich widow in New Orleans. If he is alive, if you find him, please let me know. Eighteen years of unpaid child support would come in handy."

"Miranda told me you'd be like this."

"Like what?"

"Evasive."

"*Evasive?*" Rose felt the word like a hard slap. "How about just sad that I'm not having this conversation with Miranda?" Blowing out her cheeks, she went on: "This is years ago, *decades ago*, I don't remember exactly what happened or what I thought, but I was alone, Bennett abandoned me with a baby in the middle of nowhere in the middle of winter with no money and no car. I was 20."

Diane ignored this, she had her own pitiless agenda. "Williamina Mix. Cause of death is listed as suicide."

"That's right."

"But if the body was never found, how could anyone conclude that she killed herself?"

And here Rose faltered. Diane had at last found her heel, the deep hole where the lies slithered in.

"Hi, Rose!" It was Tony, the mechanic, his fat hand on her shoulder. "How's it going?"

"Fine, Tony. How about you?"

They chatted back and forth a moment more, the weather, his daughter's wedding in the summer. Diane distracted herself by checking her phone, this habit of young people to look busy and important at all times.

Then Tony moved off and Rose returned her focus to the detective: "You've obviously noticed that my daughter is very successful. And she's only just getting started. She's going to be very rich and very powerful. I'm sure you're asking yourself what you really want from her, long-term, and how you might get that."

Diane was so earnest. "Miranda Kinney is my client. My job is to provide her with the information she's asked for."

"I really have to get back to work now." Rose pushed her chair back. Billy wasn't in Heaven. Billy wasn't an angel standing in judgement of Rose's lies. There were no witnesses. Yet Rose felt her treachery afresh — she felt the rotten, fungal-infested wood of her soul, she felt what lies did to the liar. She took a deep breath and said: "Billy killed her dogs, Diane. She shot them. And then she went into the woods. Deep into the woods somewhere. With her gun. And she never came out."

Now she stood and began to gather her things. Diane was in no such hurry. "It's just so weird," she tapped her pencil. "Two people you know go missing within a short period of time, and yet there are no bodies."

"Weird? Huh," Rose puffed out her cheeks. "Weird is all you've got? What the hell do you think life is?"

Out the door, warm sunshine. Safe in her car. Ignition on. The engine sounded good with its new catalytic converter. Rose backed out, then pulled forward and away from the Bagel Depot. Turned right, maintained speed. She stopped at the road works near the supermarket. The town was finally putting in a traffic light. Her car was warm from the sun, she cracked a window. Bennett. She hated him, the hate still glowed hot and nuclear.

Then a wave of exhaustion came over her with such smothering force she leaned her head forward onto the steering wheel.

WHUMP! Her head flew up and back, the blasting, disconcerting sunlight. Instinctively, she slammed on the brake. A man was walking toward her. "Stupid bitch!" he was screaming, the way people scream these days, full of personal affront. "Fuckin' dumb, stupid fuckin' bitch you fuckin' rear-ended me!"

Insurance, she thought. Five hundred deductible.

*　　*　　*

It took her an hour to untangle the disparity in April's accounts. At last, she turned to the hard copies and realized that Silas had typed in $1056.94 instead of the correct amount, $156.94 on the invoice. She tidied up the errors, the columns were so neatly arranged. For this reason, she loved accounting — the numbers obeyed if you treated them well. Life in Excel was neat and tidy, ordered and predictable. If things didn't add up, the mistake could be pinpointed and corrected. Numbers were guileless.

Checking her email, she felt a little lift seeing one from Chris.

Rosie,

Is Boston too far? How about June 13, 7 pm, the Copley Plaza Hotel? I'm staying there. So we can eat at the hotel restaurant or find something in the area. What do you prefer?

Chris.

She replied:

That would be great. The hotel is fine. I'll see you then!

And worried about the exclamation mark. Was that too much enthusiasm? Too young? The equivalent of a skirt above the knee? She took it out, then reinserted it. Chris hadn't seen her since she had the skin of a peach, so she really shouldn't worry about age-appropriate punctuation.

On a piece of scrap paper, she wrote:

Haircut and color $100
Mani/Pedi $50
Facial?
Eyebrow shaping $25
Cash to have on hand $100
Clothes $200
Shoes $150
Ins. deductible for car $500
Total $1225.

Scrolling back into the accounts, she changed the $156.94 back to $1056.94, then went to the petty cash sheet and deducted $900. There. Seamless. From the petty cash, she took five hundred in twenties and fifties.

A few hours later, she stood at the bottom of the steps leading up to Le Petit Choux Boutique in Montpelier. Expensive clothes have a scent, she thought, as she entered in: wool, linen, cotton, cashmere, leather, suede are nothing like the smell of hands and detergent in a thrift store or the cleaning solvent mixed with cheap vanilla candles at Penney's. The subtle perfume of the cashier — and was that Aveda shampoo? Plus a bouquet of lilies on the counter.

A woman of her own age materialized from the racks: "How may I help you today?"

The saleswoman was calculating, scanning Rose from head to foot, identifying the cut and quality of her clothes. Was she a shoplifter? Was she a rich person dressed eccentrically in cheap clothes?

Her voice sounding suddenly too loud, Rose affected a breezy tone: "Just looking." The saleswoman stepped back, but Rose knew she was being followed; suspicion was upon her as she touched the fabrics, as if staining them with her dirty hands, as if her breath might undo the stitching. She'd gone from invisible to visible, and she did not dare to turn the tags face-up to see the prices.

The clothes made her feel hungry. The textures, the colors, the delicate buttons and hand-stitched hems. What was she doing? Stealing money to impress a man she hadn't seen in nearly four decades. Who'd asked her merely for dinner. Who thought she still looked as she had. Or had aged in a graceful California way.

Oh, but *here*: regard the bias cut of this linen dress, the dark coffee brown of the dye, so beautifully sophisticated. Elegant. Perhaps with this wide, striped scarf? The coveting was almost sexual. Rose wanted to put these beautiful dresses and slacks and skirts in a huge pile and roll around in them, she wanted to rub the soft suede trousers all over her breasts, to nuzzle the cashmere cardigans and suck on the shell buttons.

"Let me help you." The saleswoman's lipstick was immaculately applied. Meekly, Rose followed her. Inside the spacious changing room, she slipped out of her clothes. Here, the lighting was flattering and Rose re-appraised herself. How well the clothes fit, designed for the long lines of her body. She turned side to side, her hands running over the taut linen skirt. But this would wrinkle badly, so she swapped it for a light-wool mix in a dove-grey — a softer silhouette, more appropriate for the evening anyway. And beautifully elegant with the cream chiffon blouse. Though the blue was lovely.

Willfully, she averted her gaze from the price tags, and surrendered to the carnal wanting. She wanted, she wanted, the wanting of a hungry baby; she knew the wanting, yearning was completely irresponsible and unreasonable, but still she proceeded to the checkout, to the smiling, grateful saleswoman — "Oh, that shirt looks so amazing on you! I'm so glad you decided to go with it."

In this moment, she could flee. Run. She might even admit, "I've made a terrible mistake, I'm sorry, this isn't me, I can't possibly afford these clothes." Or she might simply buy one item. But there was a demon in her fighting against the years and years of pinching pennies, squeezing them like discount oranges.

"Your total today is four hundred and forty-three and nineteen cents."

Today. Rose liked that, the idea that she might come back tomorrow or next week and it would be *today* all over again. Then her gut contracted, she felt the first ember of another hot flash. Do not blush. This is nothing to you, a mere *today*. Reach into your thrift-store bag and pull out the envelope of money. Cross off *haircut and color* and *eyebrow shaping*, cross off *shoes*. Those serviceable black pumps from the second hand shop in Littleton will do.

Do not flinch, do not smile. Pay the lady.

Clearly, the saleswoman was not expecting cash, and yet here it was, a little stack of 20s. Rose watched her take the bills, test their authenticity with a magic marker, and hand over the change.

*   *   *

We've made this world in our own image. We desire only to undo nature, our own nature. The roads, highways, power lines, factories, shopping malls, houses — we think it's improvement, civilization; but perhaps it's self-hatred, a death wish. Rose had lived for so long in the Kingdom that the vast sprawl of outer Boston's suburbia shocked her. The ubiquity made it pointless. Why so many Staples? What were people doing in a giant warehouse containing stationery? How many different kinds of pens did humanity need? Cars flew by her, beeping, yet she was doing 15 over the speed limit. Drivers were on their phones — she could see them! What was so important, why were they so busy that a call could not wait? The roadside was littered with dead animals, raccoons, deer, toads, foxes — the sleek, perfect beasts who live in mute accompaniment with our world, rendered into litter, there among our beer cans and coffee cups. One raccoon lay face down, arms stretched forward in ghastly supplication.

Rose clung to the steering wheel, a drowning sailor with a floatation ring. She had forgotten this America, for her life had existed within a narrow set of compass points. In thirty years, she'd gone no further than Littleton or White River Junction or Burlington. She'd actually had to practice walking in the black high heels, wobbling back and forth across the kitchen. Her feet had shaped themselves to winter boots and Sketchers, the sensible footwear for seasons of mud and snow. Affordable. And unremarkable. She didn't want Fate to notice her, she didn't need drunk hunters to know she lived alone at the end of the road. Like Gran, she'd shunned joy, as if it necessarily trailed disaster. How cautiously she had moved through the days.

It occurred to Rose that she had imprisoned herself, like a Puritan in penance.

He would ask how she was, he would ask what she did, if she was married, if she had kids. They would circle each other, trying to smell the stories of their lives.

"I'm an accountant," Rose heard herself. "Not what I expected to be. But it's a good living."

Correction. "Book-keeper. It's a steady living."

If he asked about Vermont, she'd explain she'd moved there with Bennett, as if it had been a lifestyle choice. And then, of course, the tragedy of his death, yes, it had been difficult, but she'd had Miranda to raise, Miranda had been her focus.

Everything had been Miranda. Every job, every second job, every dollar, every dime, watching her sleep, her hair splayed on the pillow and all the love Rose had stored up for her entire un-loved life fell on that child. She'd stuffed Miranda full of love. She would have thrown her body across a bomb for Miranda.

In a way, she had, for Miranda never knew about their financial problems. Their *poverty*. The grinding quality of it — the grating. Like running a cheese grater back and forth over your knuckles. It was reflexive to look at every price tag, then pick the cheaper brand.

Rose tilted her face in the mirror, touched up her mascara. "I find the work interesting, actually. Making the numbers work." What else? What else did Rose do? Walk in the woods. She should be grateful for dullness, dullness was a goal, an aim, in mid-life; because change was bad — change was cancer, the default of a mortgage, untreatable gum recession. Change was PI Di.

"I have a small book-keeping business," she rehearsed. "Good business clients and a few private ones. And I can arrange my own schedule. I like to have time to go to my studio in the afternoons." She waited a beat, then gave herself a deprecating smile, "Yes, I keep up with my art. Small showings mostly. But I did have one in Montreal recently."

Rose realized she had actually been speaking out loud. And she was not alone. Another woman — young, beautiful in a pale blue silk sheath dress — emerged from one of the stalls in the cavernous marble bathroom. She washed her hands, careful to avoid the crazy talking-to-herself lady at the next sink. *Basin*, Rose corrected herself. She glanced again at the woman and felt immediately unclean. Wrinkles, dry skin, the little pad in her underwear in case she didn't make it to the toilet on time. The *W.C.* And her shoes. So obviously not the same caliber as her fine, new clothes. The shoes were scuffed at the heel, frumpy. Suddenly, Rose hated her shoes, she raged with regret that she hadn't bought a new pair. The fake black suede had looked fine in the dull light of her kitchen; but here they looked cheap, tatty, they were funeral shoes, and the one wear had done them in.

In contrast: this elegant, shining woman in her pale blue, the clean scent of the very rich. Her arms were firm, the skin like satin, lightly bronzed. Glowing. Look at the sapphire bracelet, worth many, many thousands, a sly link of them around her lovely narrow wrist. Delicate hands with pale peach gloss, a flickering of rings, a massive diamond. Look, oh look at her shoes: silver sling-backs with knots of pearls across the toes, Cinderella shoes.

Out she drifted, her elegant slippers floating her across the floor.

Well, Rose thought, she still pisses, she still had to wipe her ass.

Alone again with the mirror, Rose reappraised. No lipstick. It frayed in the lines above her mouth. She dabbed on more cream then a touch of lip balm. What might it be to live in a culture without the judgement of mirrors — a remote island, the deepest forest, where your only reflection was in water? How would that shift your sense of self as a woman? You'd not see yourself so directly, your age thrown back at you like a cream pie. Instead, you moved from tier to tier, respected for your age, or perhaps more honestly side-lined. What was that tribe that took you out and left you to be eaten by animals when you were no use anymore? No dying of hair or lifting of face, no Botox or filler. Hillary Clinton, Elizabeth Warren — for Christ's sake, serious women and look at their blond hair! Did men actually believe a 70-year-old woman still had naturally blond hair? Nancy Pelosi. Brunette at 79. Grey, what would society make of them?

Rose tidied her hair. She'd spent money on it, a fawn color, and a layered cut that kept falling into her eyes. Setting out across the lobby, she wondered if she was overdressed for a hotel restaurant — the bored and lonely business diners. She wondered if she was overdressed for Chris. He'd see she'd tried too hard, he'd just be in jeans and a tee-shirt, making a statement about his casual success. Or: he'd see the dress and then he'd see the stupid shoes.

There was a private party in one of the banquet rooms. Wealthy people filtering in. A going away party. The woman in the blue silk dress was merging into the human traffic, lots of kiss-kiss and "Oh, hello!" Rose passed them, feeling a wave of heat come over her. Not now, fuck's sake, she thought. Paused. Let the heat recede. Tried to smell herself surreptitiously, the sweat under the deodorant. All this fussing had made her ten minutes late.

The restaurant had high ceilings, the tall windows framed

with red velvet drapes. Tables with white tablecloths, waiters in black. She scanned the room which was half full of diners.

"Rosie. Rosie."

She turned toward the voice, but the strong evening light through the windows almost blinded her. To the right, she could just make out the silhouette of a middle-aged man coming toward her. She squinted, the backlight obscured his face and glinted off his glasses. His silhouette was lean. Closer in, she could see he was wearing a jacket and jeans, a white collared shirt, his hair had receded, his face slackened, there were lines around his dark eyes. He was taller than she remembered. "Hello across nearly four decades," she said brightly.

He looked at her askance. "I'm sorry, I think you have the wrong person."

"Rosie!" she heard again, and quickly attuned to the voice.

A woman was waiting for her.

The woman stood, smiled. A great confusion came over Rose, as if someone had suddenly turned out the lights. Somehow she'd gotten the wrong Chris. Chrissie? Christine? Christina? Had there been one in high school? Not to be rude she smiled back, waved, began a stiff walk toward this Chris, her thighs rubbing, suddenly too tight in the skirt, compressed by the rubbery compression underpants. She was hobbled and she was freshly seared from the hot flash. All elegance fell from her, sloughed like dry skin, her shoes clomped and the right one was already grating against her heel.

Chris was smiling, a woman slightly older than herself, but well-manicured, a little too much make-up — though it was expertly applied. Chris was not pretty, Rose could tell she never had been, and the face, even accounting for age, she could not recall. Chris has obviously done well for herself, or married well.

The cut of her clothes, the nice jewelry — a wonderful silver and turquoise necklace: Rose took it all in. The scent of perfume, of make-up. Nothing cheap.

The thought struck her: of course! This was Chris's *wife*! Which was slightly irritating — not because Rose had imagined, at all, a romantic reconnection, but — to be honest — she had relished spending time with a man who had, many years ago, loved her. Now it would be a meal of chatting.

Smiling back, Rose approached to shake the woman's hand. Close in like this, she realized there was something familiar about her. "Hi, I'm Rose."

The wife smiled back, "I know. I'm Chris. Christianne. Now."

Rose felt her face fall — the expression as a fact, the heavy, loosening skin of her face slip from the scaffold of her skull. Practically right off her head. She was gawping.

"I know it's a shock." The voice really too deep for a woman, but then older women spoke at a lower octave. The testosterone, apparently. "I made the change."

The change. Which was what they used to call menopause. *The Change.* Ambushed by her own hostility, Rose thought: Well, Chris-*tianne,* your change is more than a few hot flashes and an inability to drink red wine.

"Have a seat," Christianne was saying, smiling. "Do you drink? I've a nice Sauvignon Blanc I've already started in on."

"That would be very nice. Thank you." Rose folded her limbs into a sitting position on the chair. She touched the cutlery, which was very shiny and clean. No globs of dried food. Miranda was always finding some tiny crusty bit on her spoon or in between the tines of the fork, her expressions of disgust and pity in dialectic battle; she was chronically unable to overlook these faults, these lapses of her mother's.

"I'm sorry, I should have warned you," Christianne began.

"No, it's —"

"Fine that I'm a woman now?"

Like an app on Nick's phone — you could add cat's ears, you could change your nose, you could become the opposite gender with a single tap. Christianne put her hand on Rose's wrist. Manicured, be-ringed with turquoise and silver; but still in the knuckles and the knob of the wrist bone, the hand of a man. "I was afraid you wouldn't come. There's really no polite way to say, 'I've changed gender since you last saw me.' People get freaked out. They run a mile."

Rose said: "I'm not exactly who I was then, either."

Christianne gave a grateful smile. The waiter appeared, brandishing menus, filling their glasses. Rose took a sip. Lovely, crisp. Bennett would have approved. She took another, bigger sip.

"You live in Santa Fe. I used to dream about Santa Fe."

"Come and visit. I have a lovely house. In the foothills of the Sangre de Cristo's. Plenty of room."

"I had a thing about Georgia O'Keeffe. I was going to be an artist."

"You *were* an artist."

"I just had ideas —"

"You were very talented, Rosie. You didn't keep up with it?"

"It wasn't possible. I had a child to raise."

"Alone?"

"Mostly."

"That must have been difficult."

Rose glanced at Christianne and wondered if she knew or could guess how difficult, or if the words were reflexive, and his — her — idea of difficulty had the hiring of a new nanny. Then Rose wondered if the hardness showed, and Christianne could see the wear on her face, she was a tire worn through to the tread. "I managed."

"How is your grandmother?"

"Dead."

Rose's tone was unsentimental, and Christianne raised an eyebrow. Suddenly, Rose remembered the two of them spying on Gran through the kitchen window, Gran muttering to herself, putting the dishes away. And she and Chris had run away into the dark, laughing, free and feather-light, still capable of flight from that place, and Gran must have heard their laughter echoing back to her in reproach. The young don't know, the young have no idea, they think they'll get away with it.

"The other day I realized she was only 60 or so when I left Lowell, but she seemed ancient."

"It's happened, hasn't it!" Christianne laughed. "When I went to get my flu shot last year, the kid at the pharmacy said he was sorry but I'd have to wait, and I asked why, and he told me that people over 65 need a different vaccine."

"Ouch."

"The really good thing about being old is that no one questions my gender. It's of no interest or use to anyone."

"At least you don't have hot flashes."

"Or periods. You know, I always wondered about that. What it felt like, having blood come out."

"When did you — did you —" Rose began and meant to abandon the direction but Christianne immediately finished for her: "Have the chop?"

Rose wouldn't have chosen those words.

"Would you like me to explain?" Christianne touched his hair — *her* hair, which was surprisingly thick and not obviously a wig. "So we can move past the elephant."

Taking silence as affirmation, she went on: "It's like a door that never quite fits the frame. No matter how hard you try or which carpenter you hire to make the adjustment. And over the years, with all the weather of life, that fit gets even worse and you realize, it's the wrong door for the frame, completely wrong. It will never fit. Three divorces and I finally went to therapy thinking this was just a mid-life crisis, some bullshit that could be solved if I took testosterone pills or bought a new car."

Christianne paused to sip her wine, her lipstick staining the glass. Her lips were surprisingly full, unnaturally full, Rose noted as she watched them move; so it wasn't just the penis that had been tampered with.

"We got there slowly. There was the moment, the pivot, when I realized: it wasn't that I wanted to *be* a woman. But I *was* a woman. Just not technically."

"So," Rose clung to her wine glass, curious about the technicality of being female. "Technically?"

"Technically. The boy bits, gone."

"And —"

"Vagina. Yes. Hand-crafted in Denmark. And these, too." Christianne made a gesture over her breasts. "Transgender people often want huge boobs. I wanted your size. Is that odd? Yours were the first I ever touched, they were perfect."

"Not anymore."

"Well, mine are!" Christianne gave them a gentle lift with her hands and then took up the menu. "Let's order. Food for all this wine."

Both of them retrieved their reading glasses from their handbags, and they had a little titter. The menu was almost indecipherable, years since Rose had looked at one, held one in a leather binding, rather than a single laminated page that listed pizza and poutine. *Coulis? Radicchio?* There were no prices, which made Rose nervous. Obviously, if you ate here you didn't worry about the price of food or wine, you could afford whatever you wanted.

"I think the duck looks really promising," Christianne said.

"I was just thinking that."

Christianne lowered the menu. "One of the things, when I became a woman, I had to learn to speak like a woman, so I started listening to the way women talk. I realized women often preface their sentences with 'I think' or 'I feel.' Instead of just saying —" she deepened her voice, almost comically: "'The duck looks promising,' it has to be —" a high voice now: "'I think the duck looks promising.' As if we wait to be corrected, because our thoughts are not facts or our preferences need objective approval."

Rose lowered her own voice, "Bring me the lamb."

They laughed.

As they waited for the meal, they spoke in general terms, recapping years — Christianne had two children, one was a doctor, the other a teacher in a troubled inner-city school. Her third wife had not taken the transition well: "She thought she disgusted me, she thought it was all a lie, the years of marriage, but it wasn't that at all. It was nothing to do with her. And that alienated her even more." Chris had made a fortune in Silicon Valley, but hated it — the culture, the greed. "And it was certainly not somewhere I wanted to become this new Chris. People identify as liberal but they are actually very intolerant. So, I moved to Santa Fe and opened a gallery." Christianne smiled. "I could do a show of your work."

"That's all gone now." Rose waved her hand dismissively. The wine was going slightly to her head.

"Your art wasn't a useless penis, Rosie. You got a full scholarship to Parsons, for God's sake. I remember you had the spirit of a true artist."

Had she? And how, exactly, had Chris seen this spirit, as they bumbled to Dairy Queen or Moorehouse Lane, two awkward outcasts in his mother's Ford Fairmont?

Their food came, presented like a palette of color and texture. Rose felt her mouth water. Making sure she held fork and knife as she knew she should — rather than the sloppy manners of her long spinsterhood — Rose dabbed a small cut of the lamb in the *jus d' currant rouge*. Flavor exploded. She rolled the meat from one side of her tongue to the other, it was so tender it was already dissolving. The pique of the currants, salt, pepper, butter, the gentlest tide of something spicier — a chili of some sort. Complementing this: a creamy polenta and a tidy cupcake of collards.

"How is it?" Christianne enquired.

"Amazing. There's no food like this where I live."

"Something I can say for Santa Fe — incredible cuisine."

Should this be their discussion then? *Cuisine?* Surely they couldn't continue to talk about Chris swapping a penis for a vagina. Which — now that Rose was thinking about it — involved severing, wounding, gouging, stabbing, drilling into the flesh to make a hole, a tight, smooth hole. And what? Labia? They would be beautiful, small pale labia, of course, because the doctor would undoubtedly be a man; the labia of a young woman, a girl, even. Not the unwieldly flaps of a middle-aged woman.

"What sort of art do you have in your gallery?" Rose said. But she couldn't help thinking: What happened to the penis and the balls? Were they left in a bag? In a landfill?

"Contemporary. A few really fantastic new artists. I amazed myself slightly by having an eye."

The waiter refilled their glasses with the silvery wine. Rose made sure not to gulp. Christianne obviously drank wine like this every night.

"Tell me about Miranda."

Rose spoke of the big house in Marblehead, the nanny, the demanding job. "She's done it all herself."

"Married?"

"No. PhD. CFO. IVF. Her life is these acronyms. Like Brownie badges."

Christianne was alert to the churlishness.

"I just feel, sometimes, like her whole life is a reprimand to me," Rose confessed.

"Is it?"

The answer was *Of course not*. Yet Rose found herself hanging limply between the words and the sentiment.

"My wife struggled with that," Christianne said. "She just wanted some small acknowledgment from her children that her careful mothering meant something."

"Did she get it?"

"I thought so. But just not in the form my wife wanted or needed."

Rose drew up an image of Miranda, tall and bold and certain. What was it like to be so certain? She felt herself smile: "My daughter kicks ass."

"Good for her!" Christianne raised her glass.

They spoke about Santa Fe.

Christianne said: "I love the mountains. I love the history. The landscape that you just walk out into. But a lot of it is rich old white people with too much money, having colonic irrigation and culturally appropriating Native American spirit ancestors or whatever. I find it ridiculous, but I also realize, I'm rich and white, and an appropriator, too."

A moment passed. They finished their food, Rose careful not to scrape the plate too loudly. "Why did you contact me?" Rose asked. "I don't really think it was to return those photos."

The waiter was there again. Did they want another bottle? Rose demurred — she had to drive. He cleared their plates, asked about dessert. After conferring, they decided on the crème brûlée and the raspberry mousse, and they'd split.

"Did you learn that from women?" Rose asked.

"Oh, yes. As a man I never wanted to share my dessert. I felt I'd hunted it and killed it, it was mine."

Those years and years ago, parked in his car on Moorehouse Lane, the warm summer dark when there were still lanes and fields in Lowell, Chris had made her laugh. He'd been an incredible mimic, he could reproduce Miss Vickers, the uptight chemistry teacher, with deadly accuracy. And Rose remembered how Rosie had felt safe with Chris. Maybe because of the femininity hidden within him.

"To answer your question —" Christianne was neatly dividing the desserts. "I think — right, 'I think' — I *think* it was because we'd been happy together. You and I. We were in a little cocoon. Everything before and everything around and everything after were so complex and sometimes cruel and almost belligerently confusing. You were like this lovely night light."

Rose felt startled — the idea that she could have given anyone light all those years ago when she'd been bumping around in the dark, someone always changing the position of the furniture so she could never find her way. Christianne seemed to have known an entirely different version of her, a talented, clever, light-filled

Rosie with amazing breasts. To deflect, Rose said: "Couldn't you have just started wearing women's clothes?"

"No."

"Do you sleep with men?"

"Once."

"Did he know?"

"I'd paid him. So he didn't ask. I just wanted to know what it felt like."

Rose could not quite explain the anger she felt rising. The audacity — perhaps — required to hire a prostitute, because that is what men do, they hire women for sex and don't care what they feel or think, don't consider their repulsion, and they deny it has any value. The joke she'd heard Bob snicker to Silas: "What do you call the useless flesh around a vagina? *A woman.*" Haw haw.

"And what did it feel like?" The heat began now, the furnace heat sweating and staining the lovely silk $259 blouse.

"Wonderful. It felt absolutely wonderful."

Rose put down her fork. "Good for you."

Christianne heard the tone. Maybe this had happened before, the easy chat, the appearance of tolerance and acceptance. "Let's talk about something else."

"What? Talk about what?" Rose challenged her now. Her hair was sweating for God's sake, her eyebrows, behind her ears! "My tits look like something that got left in the microwave for too long."

"Rosie —"

"No. *Rose.* You think you're so good at listening but you didn't hear. All I could do to change myself was to drop the 'i.'" She pushed the chair back, she frantically fanned herself with the starch-stiffened napkin. The sweat was dripping down her back, pooling in the heavy-duty waistband of the compression pants that now felt like tightly wrapped cling film. She was a human sauna.

"Being a woman is not about having tits and a cunt and a manicure. *Chris,* you're from the other side, you probably took your daughter up the aisle and *gave her away* —"

People were looking at her, Rose knew but did not care. Christianne, though, was averting her gaze.

"— to her husband. Do you know what that means? Do you even know there was no such thing as 'marital rape' until 1983? The law didn't recognize that a man could rape his wife, because the law — written by rich white men like you, *like you were until very recently* — saw women as chattel —"

In a flash Christianne flung her glass of water in Rose's face.

"Stop!"

Rose stopped.

Christianne was shaking, her eyes brimmed with tears. "Do you think I need a lecture?"

Rose wiped the water from her face.

"This isn't a statement I'm making." Christianne's voice was slow and even. "It's my life."

Slowly, elegantly, she stood. "Don't worry about the bill, it's on my room." She rounded the table and walked away, the broad shoulders in a tailored cotton blouse above the narrow hips in a sleek suede skirt and the hairless, muscular calves funneling to narrow ankles, the big feet in Italian sling-back sandals, so very nearly pulling it off.

For a long moment, Rose sat. Around her, the other diners carried on, tilting in to discuss or chuckle, the old trannie and her old friend having an argument. The internal heat had diffused, but of course she was soaking wet with water and sweat. She reached over and finished Chris's glass of wine in one slug.

The waiter came. "Will there be anything else, madame?"

"No. I think that's been quite enough." And there it was, the insertion of 'I think,' bracketed with a question. So she said, louder, deeper: "It's been quite enough." She drained her own glass and stood. Lacking Christianne's practiced slink, Rose tramped out in her thrift-store shoes, her thrift-store bag briefly catching on the back of a chair. She didn't bother to apologize to the occupant. Fuck these people, anyway, with their *coulis* and their soup spoons. Bennett telling her to scoop the soup away from her, tilting the bowl delicately, and absolutely no slurping.

In the lobby, people spilled out from the private party. Glittering, laughing. She noticed their teeth, because the teeth of rich people are different to the teeth of the poor. Rich teeth are white and straight and gleaming. These teeth were snapping all around her, bright as flashbulbs, and for a moment she was bewildered. Somehow, the group had pulled her into their eddy — her hair, her clothes, she was one of the tribe.

"...lovely bistro on the Ile St. Louis..."

"...Bunny is expecting to hear from you the moment you get to Vienna..."

"...Cap d'Antibes..."

"...Darling..."

"...Hobie, old chap..."

"...do you know Fritz and Wally..."

Rose turned, hooked like a fish by the name. And there he was, with his age app switched on. On his body, he wore a full old-body suit, a prosthetic body that rounded his shoulders and flattened his ass. Hobie's chin jutted more than she remembered, his hair was thinner but still substantial for an old man. On his arm was the woman from the bathroom, dazzling in her pale blue sheath dress.

They swept past Rose, so close she could smell their lavender soap — it came wrapped in paper from a special *savonnier* in France — they moved on their tide of tidings, fluid, lubricated by vintage port and private healthcare. *Polo refers only to ponies.* The room behind them was almost empty — a stooped white-haired woman was rummaging around in her handbag, the wait staff were clearing up the dishes. Rose picked up a napkin. Its silver letters said: BON VOYAGE HOBIE AND BIZZA!

"Personally, I don't care for travel these days." The woman had arrived at Rose's side. "In my day, there was only one cabin. And it was slanted. The cheaper seats were always down in the rear. Gravity, my husband used to say, you can't fight it. Now, well! People travel in their *pajamas.*"

Rose looked non-committal.

"But he's got to keep up with her, you see. She's so much younger. Good luck, good luck, I say."

"Where are they going?"

The woman sized her up, just like Chip at the club all those years ago. Perhaps she was blind, perhaps she saw only the expensive clothes not the shoes, and so she engaged: "'Round-the-world. Europe. Kenya. Honk Kong. She's from Australia, that's where they're ending up."

Out the door, in the lobby, Rose could just see the back of their heads, Hobie's white hair, Bizza's thick brunette mane swept into a bun. They were chatting, laughing with their friends. From this angle, Rose could see Bizza's profile; she was — in fact — closer to her own age: note the slight slackening of the skin around her jaw line when she tilted her head down. Hobie did not see Rose, he did not sense her. And anyway, he would not remember her. He would not remember the power he'd had. Possibly, he had even intended to help her — but like that, with his pocket money for an abortion?

Rose sat in her car in the crepuscular gloom of the parking lot. She was unable to sort out her feelings, perhaps because of the wine, but she suspected there was no sorting out — neat little plastic tubs of laundry, whites, coloreds, permanent press, regret, blame. For a very long time, her life had been incredibly still — mid-pond on a summer day. She had, herself, made sure of this: the steady jobs, the careful spending, the careful friending. The years of raising Miranda had left her exhausted, though she'd been unable to calibrate at the time. Not merely the anxiety about money, but actual, physical exhaustion; the healthcare jobs, the waitressing, the kitchen work that required her to be on her feet more than eight hours a day, sometimes 12, then driving home in the dark, Miranda curled up in the back seat, only to get up six hours later to take her to school. The pretense had cost her, too: the lie that Bennett had left money for Christmas and birthday presents. And that he wasn't dead and buried in the basement. Rotting in the earth beneath their feet. All that Miranda never knew, all that she must never know. Rose blew the fringy bit of her new hairstyle out of her eyes — it was supposed to cover her frown lines. She wanted a drink, this would be the time to have a flask of brandy. She put the keys in the ignition, and the car beeped at her, seatbelt, engine, car door, all different beeps. So she pulled out the keys. And sat.

Why — the question like a loud bell kept ringing — *why* become a woman? What on earth appealed to Chris? She thought her body was hers — that was the difference, for she'd created it. Chris-Christianne would never have the visits to the doctor, feet up, splayed open, lit up, sometimes a medical student nervously peering in, oh yes, step right up, step right up and look inside, a circus exhibit. Breasts squashed in a machine, the delicate tissue flattened like pita bread. Women's bodies are communal, they always have been, a father gives away his daughter as a spare hammer or chain saw. A grandmother sends her granddaughter up the stairs and along the hall to help pay the bills with her seven-year-old body. *Does that feel good. Do you like it when I do this.* No question mark attached! Tampons, douches, diaphragms, penises, fingers, speculums — all go into your body, in and out, in and out, like a busy parking spot. Until no one wants it anymore and it's more like an abandoned shopping mall, windy and weedy. Ginny's mother had been having problems with her vagina actually falling out like a sock — apparently, this is common for women in their 80s — and the mother had taken the doctor's advice and simply had her vagina sewn shut and that was the end of that. Yet Christianne had chosen to make one. The idea of womanhood was entirely different for her, not merely the form but the context.

A couple sauntered past her car, arm-in-arm. Their laughter echoed around the cement walls. The man's hand drifted down onto the woman's ass and gave it a squeeze.

Rose exhaled. Perhaps what really made her angry with Christianne was her ability to transform — to have such a clear vision of her authentic self. Perhaps it hardly mattered that she'd cut off her penis and dug a hole in the flesh between her thighs; these were either physical mutilations or corrections. She was free in a way Rose wished to be free.

Grubbing around in her handbag for her phone, she rang the hotel and asked for Christianne's room. She picked up, but said nothing. Rose imagined her there, in her room, mascara running down her face, feeling defeated and sad and old. She'd taken the same kind of preparatory care Rose had.

"I'm sorry," Rose began. "I can't take it back and I can't even say I didn't mean some of it. But you don't deserve to be hurt like that."

The silence continued.

"I'm in my car, here in the hotel parking lot, and I want to drive to Lowell right now and I'm wondering if you'll come with me."

Christianne sighed softly. "I'll be at the front of the hotel."

The drive was mostly wordless and this heightened Rose's awareness of the woman sitting next to her: the shifting of silk, the clink of bracelets, the lemony scent of lotion. She could even hear Chris's stomach gurgle. When Rose pulled off Route 3, Christianne murmured a soft, ambiguous, "Oh."

In the darkness, street-lit, neon-winking, blind-alley-ed, Lowell emerged around them, the way a dream transforms the familiar into the strange and absurd and unpredictable, and Rose found herself in the landscape of de Chirico, the shadows in the wrong places or not where she remembered them. Within them lurked the misshapen flotsam that sometimes emerged when she couldn't sleep.

Rose and Christianne knew the roads, a grid laid down over which humanity had hung its shabby, transitory décor. Trees had been cut down, there was a parking garage where the Dairy Queen had been, yet the schools, the parks remained, haplessly pinned in time and space. The town retained its deeper sensibility — the slipperiness of its exits, its horizontality. The idea of a dream was persistent and filled Rose with unease. She was so very far from home and suddenly sure something terrible was about to happen.

"I want to turn around," she said.

"No." Christianne was firm. "I need to know that this place is real. We were here."

They drove on, turn upon turn through this facsimile town, arriving by unspoken agreement at Chris's house, or where it had been, for now there stood a brown brick office building, the suites for various doctors of internal medicine, their titled names illuminated on a white sign under a fake carriage light. Christianne got out and stood, peering at the sign and then the office block, short-sighted in middle-age, her silk shirt sticking to her narrow back. Above her, the night frayed into a dull brown sky, pocked by plane lights, absent of stars. Far-off traffic hummed along the interstate and the busy main roads, and, occasionally, a car closer by, the noise un-zippering and zippering the air of the still, abandoned street.

At last Christianne returned to the car, folding herself into the front seat with considered femininity — her hand flattening her skirt along her buttocks before sitting.

"Are you OK?" Rose ventured quietly.

"I'm glad the house is gone, I'm glad it's obliterated." Christianne exhaled. Her eyes sparkled, tears accumulating. "That little boy. He was so unhappy."

As teenagers, they had never spoken of childhoods, for the whole purpose of being 16 had been to abandon the past like a sacked town, just as they never spoke of their home lives — for they were leaving that, too, discarding the adults who held the car keys and locked the doors and who had incrementally diminished over years to their actual life-size. Neither Rose nor Rosie knew what had really happened to Chris, though Rose sensed some sly brutality, some bruiseless damage that injured the deeper tissue of the child. The shouting, drunken parents, the deep-space silence Chris had sometimes entered. Rose put out her hand, and Christianne returned the gesture. They held hands as once they had, back then unable to fathom the super-power of their connection.

"Where is he?" Rose asked.

Christianne put her hand on her chest, which heaved with a sudden sob. "Safe."

"Your house now," she said. Yet Rose faltered. Dread scrolled down from the sky, that suffocating fabric unpinned and smoth-ered her face.

"Come on, I'll drive." Christianne was already getting out of the car. They switched places, and Chris removed her high heels. "These bastards," she hissed. "Are dead. And we're not."

Gran's house remained, wedged as always within a row of similar architectural refrain. It was painted white now, and Rose considered the effort it must have taken the owners to obscure the dark brown. Otherwise, the house was anonymous, the own-ers gave no outward hint of their political or financial status. There was no evidence of children or pets. Instinctively, Rose glanced up to the second floor, not to her room — for that was at the back — but the lodger's room. Gran would not take pets or children. These lodgers had moved on a secret tide, the swift, merciless currents of their adult lives swept them in, then out, in mystery and melancholy. The Giggle Man had been among them, and if she looked up she might see him move into the frame of the window, his narrow grey face, she now remem-bered the angularity of it, the froth of eyebrow, for she had glimpsed the wiry hairs emerging like restless antennae as he had peered down at her. He'd been so deliberate, so careful to avoid her genitals. That way he couldn't be accused of sexually molesting her. It was just tickling, he could say, just tickles and giggles. All anyone heard was her laughter.

Rose pressed herself back into the car seat as his gloved hands moved up her legs — oh, her body remembered with spiteful and treacherous accuracy! — he pricked and squeezed her bare legs and even a violent Charlie horse upon her thighs and the relentless playing on her bare torso and armpits *do you like it when I do this* as if she could say *No*. But then Christianne's voice was commanding, suddenly male: "You're here with me, with me. Rose. Look, look at me." And Rose saw the familiar face, the boy who'd held her and whom she'd held in return, and she leaned forward and kissed him, and Christianne kissed back with familiarity, tongues flickering, mouth hard to mouth as if resuscitating, half-laughing and amazed by the sizzling of flesh, the vibration of nerves through the spine and the groin.

With perfect synchronicity, they pulled back from the sudden connection. Christianne began to laugh, and Rose, too. They laughed at themselves, the wild hysterical laughing that The Giggle Man had once plucked from Rosie, and yet this was different, welling from some other place in her body, from her feet, from her ears — some outer extremity working its way along the wires within, thrilling and curative as the kiss, she couldn't stop laughing and neither could Christianne, and they were howling, hooting, teeth flashing in the street light, hands flapping, until at last they faltered and gasped to silence. Christianne lifted her hand to Rose's face. "We're so done here."

As they drove away, Rose realized she'd wet herself slightly while laughing. Did Christianne have this problem? Did she still have a prostate? Rose remembered the old people she'd once cleaned and tended. Decrepitude was entirely democratic.

Beside her, Christianne was tilting slightly forward to gauge her way through the fast traffic and Rose took a deep breath. Lowell devolved behind them. As they merged into the tunnels of downtown Boston, Rose said, "Thank you, Christianne." She was nervous that Christianne would invite her up to the hotel room, the intimacy of the previous hour would be misconstrued and turn awkward. Yet when they arrived, Christianne got out and handed Rose the keys, they shared the briefest hug.

"Keep in touch," Christianne said, then turned and sauntered up the hotel steps.

By the toll station on the Massachusetts-New Hampshire border, Rose was sobering up, the window open, the take-away coffee in her right hand; not drunk but heightened by the rush of chemicals within her body and brain. She thought of the credit card machine —

Processing...

Processing...

The intensity of the evening had a physical impact. Her limbs ached, most acutely in the joints, and she felt a solid pressure in her upper abdomen, as if her diaphragm was weighted like a stone, making breathing difficult. She turned on the radio. *My Angel is the Centerfold.* She remembered Bennett, the last time she'd driven this way. The J. Geils Band, wasn't it? *Na na nanna nananana.* Were they even still alive? Tottering onto a stage somewhere in tight jeans, their lives a constant reprise. The least that Rose could say was that her life wasn't an endless repetition. Past Concord the reception faltered, and she was left with the long highway, her eyes sketching the darkness for deer and moose.

An hour later, she'd entered the narrow slot of Franconia Notch where 93 filtered down to one lane, winding through high black mountain towers. This late, there was very little traffic. By Littleton, she desperately needed a pee. Just off the highway, there was an Irving gas station. She entered the bright space, considered what she should buy, not only because she felt it rude to use a toilet for free, but because the frivolity of gas station fare suddenly appealed. Doritos or gummy bears? A York Peppermint Pattie? She glanced over the healthy snacks, and wondered, what was the point? You could buy complete and utter crap in here and no one would judge. She bought iced tea and a bag of Sour Patch Kids. By the time the tea hit her bladder and the sugar hit her bloodstream, she reckoned, she'd be home.

There was one other customer: a young woman, dark-haired, squeezed into a pair of jeans she'd bought when she was 20 pounds lighter. Lots of earrings. She was buying car oil, attempting to ask the cashier which kind she needed. "The 10-30 or the 10-15?"

He shrugged, "Dunno."

Yet in her desperation she persisted: "Do you know how much I need to put in?"

"Sorry, ma'am. I don't know anything about cars."

Ma'am? She was a girl, hardly older than he was.

"It's probably 10-30," Rose intervened. "That's what my car takes."

The girl turned to her. "Do you know about the oil light? It's flashing." She turned her head aside, made a correction in her tone so that she did not sound afraid, merely tired. "I'm just trying to get home."

"Your insurance might cover a tow."

"I don't have insurance."

"Isn't there anyone you can call?"

But no, there wasn't, Rose already knew the answer. No

boyfriend, no husband, no trustworthy dad, no friend. Not at this hour, not in her current life.

Rose said, "How far are you going?"

"Just through the Notch."

"I'd take you if I was going that way. But I'm heading north."

"That's kind. Thank you. It's not far, I think if I put oil in, I'll make it. Don't you?"

"The 10-30 should be fine. Maybe two quarts."

"What's a quart?"

"The small size bottle. Then take it to your mechanic in the morning." Although, Rose knew, this girl didn't have a mechanic.

"Thank you — really."

And because she knew, Rose said, "Do you have the money for the oil?"

The young woman hesitated. "I have some."

A crumple of dollar bills, a clink of coins.

Rose gave her a twenty, the last of the money she'd taken from Bob.

*　　*　　*

A pair of ravens turned in the sky, falling and soaring up, flipping and pirouetting.

In the distance, thunderstorms loomed over the Presidential Range. Rose had hiked them once with Miranda on a school field trip. She'd enjoyed the walk, but there were too many people. Absurd to be in a wilderness and syphoned onto a worn, narrow path, nodding "Hello" and "Lovely day" every other minute. Rose preferred the mountain at her back door. Diminutive though it was, after three decades there were still drainages to explore and a rumored granite mine she'd yet to discover. The mountain continually changed: ice storms laid waste to the tall old trees, or loggers did. The beavers abandoned one set of dams and formed others. She was especially glad of small discoveries: a particular wild apple mysteriously favored by morels; the old fence lines of barbed wire enfolded in the tough bark of a huge maple tree.

Ginny was lagging today, and Rose pretended to retie her shoe. They continued along the ridge, ending at a rocky outcrop from which the very edge of Vermont tilted into New Hampshire. Here and there, a metal roof glinted, and there were open patches of farmland. But mostly it was forest rising into mountain.

"It still amazes me that almost none of these trees are more than a century old," Rose said. "Back then, the land had been stripped, acre by acre, of trees with the girths of houses, all in the name of sheep. Most of the wildlife vanished then, too. The wolves, cougars, and bobcats hunted to extinction, the moose and deer pushed into the remnant woods. The towns along the river and the railway had been built on wool money — fine libraries and town halls, churches, and mansions. Then the bottom fell out of the wool market."

"Larry says it'll happen with oil." Ginny sat down and took out her water bottle. "All our destruction, those awful tar sands, and all the fortunes built on oil. Sooner or later, we'll find some other source of energy."

Rose took the rock beside her friend. "Try buying lamb around here now."

"Costs a fortune!"

They sat for a while watching the ravens in the gyre. Then Ginny said: "I'm dying."

Which Rose at first thought was just Ginny saying she was

hot or thirsty. Because Rose wanted to talk about Christianne, and her conflicting emotions and maybe even about the trip they'd taken to Lowell. Already, the evening — only a day before — hardly seemed real. One of those distant roofs, glittering in the sun, far away. "No, you're not," she replied.

Though she knew.

In the silence that followed, she knew, and the way Ginny kept watching the ravens. And all the way back, for months, Rose had known simply because she and Ginny never talked about the cancer. It was ironic: the most important things weren't discussed. Somehow, the time wasn't right, or the words could not be found. But possibly, Rose was just too afraid to ask.

Ginny's hand was on her arm. "Rose."

Rose surfaced, turned.

"Larry and I are moving to Martha's Vineyard. We've rented a house right on the sea. Outrageously expensive." She laughed softly. "But you only die once."

"When?"

"Three months. The doctors say anyway."

"I mean, when are you leaving here?"

"End of the week."

"I should have asked you. You were going to Hanover for treatment, and I should have asked how it —"

"No. It was me. I didn't want to talk about it. I just wanted to come on our walks. They mean so much to me."

Rose's mouth was dry with outrage. Ginny had been too happy, and Fate couldn't bear happiness — Ginny's wasn't even garish happiness, but the simple kind. Ginny in her garden, Ginny making jam. Even her marriage to Larry wasn't extrovertly happy — just two people who shared the crossword and liked the same books. "Can I visit you?" she asked.

Ginny shook her head. She wasn't crying. Dying of cancer was beyond tears. Cancer was spilled milk. So Rose fastened herself inside.

"What can I do to help?"

Ginny took her hand. "You've already done it. You've been a great friend. You love me. And you value me."

The ravens turned high above them, an impeccable choreography. "Don't you wonder about their synchronicity?" Rose said. "How are they communicating so instantly?"

"Thank you," Ginny whispered.

*   *   *

INTERSTATE KILLER STRIKES AGAIN — Body of woman found near Franconia Notch.

Rose grabbed the paper, read on:

The body of an unidentified woman was found by a Franconia Notch Park Ranger on Friday morning. Police are treating it as a suspicious death, possibly connected to two other similar murders of women in the North Country-Northeast Kingdom area.

"We are asking anyone who was driving through the Notch area of I-93 on Thursday night to please contact us," said Col. Tim Ludlowe of the New Hampshire State Police.

Col. Ludlowe also warned that the perpetrator or perpetrators are still at large, and that women should be vigilant when traveling on I-93 and I-91, especially at night. He was unable to give out further details of the crime, but stressed the possibility of a connection to the recent murders of Bonnie Duprea, 25, and Alexa Moore, 32. Duprea's body was discovered earlier this year at the northbound rest area on I-91 between Barnet and Wells River. Moore's body was found three weeks ago just off the southbound I-91 exit ramp for Bradford.

While Col. Ludlowe would not say why police thought the crimes were connected, he did state: "We do want people to be aware that the person or persons committing these terrible crimes are still at large. We believe women driving alone at night are particularly vulnerable and ask you to take precautions if at all possible."

New Hampshire State Police and Vermont State Police have now formed a joint task force, according to Ludlowe, including crime scene and profiling experts from the FBI.

No details have been made available regarding the cause of death of any of the three victims, nor have the police disclosed why they believe the deaths are connected. However, the victims are all women, and it has been determined by this newspaper that Moore was traveling alone.

Moore, of Sutton, was driving back from Dartmouth-Hitchcock Medical Center in Lebanon, NH, where she works as a radiologist. She was seen by co-worker Eileen

Walsh at approximately 5:15 p.m. "Her car was parked two down from me and we waved and said something about the bad weather," says Walsh.

Moore's family, including her husband, Justin Moore, and the couple's two children, alerted police when Moore had not returned home by 10 p.m. and could not be reached on her cell phone. Her body was found the following morning by Tessie Deveraux of Bradford as she drove to work at Farm-Way. "I thought it was old carpeting or a bag of clothes."

Sweat prickled in Rose's armpits and this triggered a hot flash. She fanned herself with the newspaper as the heat rushed to her face and scalp, then spread over her chest and torso in a chokehold. What if, she was thinking, what if it was the young woman in the Littleton gas station? Rose called up the memory, she wanted to be clear so that details did not slip, did not rearrange themselves. She shut her eyes to see the young woman — overweight in her jeans and sweatshirt, her hair was dark, tied back in a messy knot. She'd had a crescent of earrings. That was all.

*   *   *

At the state police, there was now a man at the reception counter. Rose spoke through the glass: "I need to speak with Detective Lieutenant Fornier, please. It's about the death, the murder in the Notch."

Fornier provided a no-nonsense shake that Rose reckoned she'd spent some time perfecting. Everything this woman did must be considered in the context of the masculine world in which she operated. She'd be labeled a *dyke* if she didn't sleep with a male colleague, and a *slut* if she did. She could be those things regardless; she was also probably a cunt and a bitch and possibly the object of masturbatory fantasies and, at the same time, deeply respected. Her office was devoid of the personal, not a book, not a photo, not even a coffee mug. She was giving nothing away.

Rose introduced herself, and Fornier gestured to a chair opposite her desk. "Whatcha got, Ms. Monroe?"

Rose told her about the scene at Irving, describing the young woman.

Fornier nodded, took a couple of notes. "And this was what time?"

"1:30, maybe 2 a.m.?"

"What were you doing in Boston?"

"Dinner, with a friend."

"You usually drive back late like that?"

"No. I don't usually go to Boston at all."

"You look familiar. Have we met?"

"I work for Bob Booth. You came to speak with him a few weeks ago."

"Right. I remember." Fornier performed a tidy smile. "Now, the Irving gas station in Littleton. So, that was it, just the chit chat about the oil?"

"Yes. And I gave her a twenty. She didn't have enough money."

"Did she appear scared, nervous?"

"I asked her if she had anyone to call, you know, to come and get her. But she didn't seem to."

"You mean she said that she didn't or you didn't see her make a call?"

"I didn't see her make a call. It was my impression that she didn't have anyone."

"What gave you that impression?"

"I don't know. Maybe, if she did have someone, she'd have already called them? She just seemed alone."

"There was no one with her?"

"Not in the store. Maybe in her car. But I just don't think so. It's just... by *alone*... I mean..." Rose circled back to where she'd started. "She was a young woman who didn't have anyone to help her out in the middle of the night, not a safe person, she just didn't."

"And do you have any memory of someone else, other than the cashier, either in the building, or outside?"

"It was so late, I don't think so, just her car."

"You saw her car?"

Rose thought, then shook her head. "I don't know. It must have been there. I think I would have wondered if I came out and didn't see another car."

Had the killer been there? In the deep well of shadows beside the gas station, the glint of headlights, the glint of steel-rimmed glasses? Had he watched Rose walk out, watched the young woman walk out, had he taken his pick?

"Was it her — was she the one who was killed?"

Fornier's exhale was carefully neutral.

But Rose knew. Her breath rushed out of her. "Did she have kids?"

"I can't discuss this. Her identity hasn't been made public yet."

"If I'd taken her — I could have taken her —"

"It doesn't work like that."

Abruptly, Rose stood. "But it does. That's exactly how it

works. If I'd just helped her, taken her where she needed to go, a young woman in trouble, it would have been an hour out of my way, and I had that choice, and I sensed her distress, she didn't have anyone and I let her go. And she's dead. She died in a horrible way."

Briskly, the cop handed over her card. "Thank you for coming in today, Ms. Monroe. We may be in touch if we have further questions. And give me a call if you remember anything else, anything at all." Then she was on her phone: "Fornier. Yep. Hi, Bert, about those reports —"

In the hallway, Rose looked properly at the card — the full title: Detective Lieutenant Pamela Fornier, Major Crimes Unit, her phone number, email, the state shield. Even the card was impressive. Rose turned back and pushed open Fornier's door.

"Is Bob Booth involved in this? Is that why you wanted to speak to him?"

Fornier was cupping the phone, irritated by the interruption. "I can't discuss an on-going invest—"

"But I work with him," Rose said briskly. "I want to be safe."

"Oh, you're safe from him," Fornier said.

"Because I'm old?" From the loam of her mind sprouted the phrase, *I don't like old meat.*

Fornier regarded her, not quite objectively, for Rose felt a momentary kinship — this tough woman's particular journey and the choice she'd made to wade into the deep mud of human depravity. What kind of woman — person — did this willingly? Pam Fornier knew what men did to children, what parents did to children, what happened to women on dark roads. She knew the seams of the human body, the ways in. She knew, too, how the perpetrators often got away. Maybe she even saw them walking around, buying coffee, pumping gas, free, due to some legal technicality or recanted testimony or silenced witness. Maybe she thought about those she'd put away and secretly wished them all the pain in the world. Maybe she thought about those she had saved, too stunned and broken to thank her.

"The cases are not related. Totally separate incidents of male dickery."

The Franconia Notch is grand geology, slicing between the steep ski runs of Cannon Mountain and the bulky high-rise of Mt. Lafayette. The White Mountains prickle outward, wilder and steeper to the north, more subdued to the south, where they cede to the suburban outflow of greater Boston. Rose always felt she'd entered another country here — Norway or Scotland — especially when the mists crowded the mountain tops. Fens, she would think, fjords, and just beyond, down a lonely track, there'd be a hamlet where few people spoke an English she could understand, there'd be old men with crooks and glasses of whiskey in a pub.

The road syphoned into one lane, there was no shoulder, so the girl wouldn't have stopped here, Rose surmised, she'd have forced her crappy, broken car on, begging her vehicle, chugging and spluttering, and then she'd have seen the exit for the Mt. Lafayette trailhead.

Rose imagined she was the girl, there was no cell reception here. At first, she parked right by the rangers' station, under the bright security light, but then she decided she'd try to get some sleep even though it was cold. Maybe the girl had something else in the car to keep her warm, a thrift-store coat, a borrowed jacket. Her failing car crabbed to a far corner of the parking lot where it was darkest and the girl turned the engine off.

How quiet, even in this mid-summer mid-afternoon, Rose

thought as she sat in her own car. The parking lot was full of cars, but most of the hikers were still out for the day. A family of four was arguing as they stood around the open hatchback of their SUV. The sky was reduced to a slice between the shouldering mountains, it was deeply shadowed already. The river, running fast just beyond a narrow stand of woods, drowned out the sound of the highway. At night, here, it must have been fiercely dark. But also, the girl might have found it peaceful, accepting defeat with the stars above and the wild river beside. She let go of the struggle, of the mess of her life and hassle of the car, she'd just wait until the morning and deal with it then.

A flock of blue jays startled Rose, shrieking out of the thick copse of spruce. She watched them vanish again, toward the river. That night, heads tucked, feathers fluffed against the mountain cold, they'd have heard when the girl arrived, the riotous midnight noise of her broken car. They'd have listened to see if it concerned them, this matter from the world of men, and as it did not, they'd turned back to sleep.

Maybe the girl did manage to sleep, a jagged dozing. The headlights from another car woke her. Or maybe the man did, already there, slipping into the seat beside her because she'd forgotten to lock the doors. Slipping in the seat beside her, slippery as oil.

Getting out of the car, Rose perused the perimeter of the parking lot, and at last she found what she was looking for: a torn ribbon of police tape. A sharp note of victory — she was right, this was the place. In the woods, she could see the trampled ground and even a coffee cup — some litterbug cop. The girl hadn't got far, 50 yards out of her car, sprinting into the darkness, shouting for help, and the jays heard and the man heard, but there was no one else.

How did he kill her? Did he rape her first? She had the idea that men who raped wanted women to carry the knowledge of rape with them as they lived on. Rape was like a tattoo, like a branding. No, she thought, the girl wasn't raped, she was just scared, she suddenly wanted her life more than anything, the dull days, the angry bills, the anxious dawns — suddenly, these were beautiful and glimmering. The girl had stumbled, the smell of pine needles, the taste of earth as if this were a summer picnic, she saw the sinewy roots of the dark trees, the gracious curve, and she grabbed on. Persephone. Beyond her, the inky river hurried by, the fat trout slumbering in the eddies.

And suddenly Rose wondered about Bennett. If he'd understood, just for a moment, that she was killing him.

*　　*　　*

"Some lady here to see you." Nick swung open the door.

It was PI Di. She nodded at Rose. "Sorry to bother you at work." She wasn't sorry at all, she was determined, she wanted Rose to know this.

"Have a seat." Rose gestured to an empty chair near her desk.

Diane sat. "This won't take long." Which made it sound like an unpleasant medical exam.

"Did you find Bennett?"

"I think we both know I didn't."

I think Rose noted, and suddenly wondered if they were lovers, her daughter and this woman. Perhaps Miranda had been gay for years and her decision to have a child by IVF wasn't the lack of a decent man, as Rose had supposed, but her dislike of them entirely.

Then Diane went on, barely able to contain her self-satisfaction. "Some new information has come to light."

"Has it?"

"I intend to search the house where you live."

The awkward wording had been carefully chosen. Rose grew alert. "Don't you need a search warrant or something?"

"I just need the home owner's permission." Diane was pleased with herself.

"Why would I give you permission?"

"You don't know, do you?"

Rose waited for what was about to come. The other shoe on the millipede.

"The house isn't yours."

The smile twitched as Diane proudly unfolded a piece of paper — a child with a gold star on her book report — and slid it across the table. It was the title deed. Rose read the owner's name: Barbara Elizabeth Kinney.

Not Bennett Edward Kinney. Rose almost laughed. Yet she did not touch the paper, she knew her hands would shake.

"I've been in touch with Barbara. She's his sister in Kennebunkport," Diane said. "I'm meeting with her next week."

"Why?"

"Why? I'm sure she'd like to know what happened to her brother. I'm sure she'll give her blessing for a warrant."

Rose kept her voice steady: "What do you expect to find in the house?"

"I don't know."

"There's nothing."

"Then we'll find nothing."

"Mice."

"Then we'll find mice."

How badly Diane wanted to defeat her, as if they were competing for Miranda's love. "Diane," she said carefully. "Do you have some other motive?"

"What do you mean?"

"You're trying to prove something, personally, to my daughter."

Diane leaned back, shook her head with full intent to condescend: "I'm a professional private investigator. I've been hired by Miranda Kinney to find out what happened to her father."

"Then why do you ask all these questions about who he was?"

"In my experience — which I must tell you is extensive — who the person was is usually connected to what happened to them."

Your experience. Oh, couldn't Di see her own self, projected forward in time with the magic time app? What would it be? A dead child, infertility, depression, brain cancer? Or maybe just Miranda. Miranda will run back and forth over Diane's heart like a power-sander. *Poor you,* Rose thought, *you still have extensive experience to happen to you.* "Bennett liked Miles Davis."

"Miles Davis?"

"Maybe that says something about him. The kind of man who likes Miles Davis. Personally, I can't stand it."

"Maybe Miles Davis killed him," Diane said.

"Maybe."

They regarded each other in silence.

"Something happened in May 1993," Diane said at last. "I'll find out what."

"And that's the crux, is it? The moment that defined Bennett Kinney was some hour in May decades ago? Not all the shit trailing behind him, a leaky sewage truck spewing through the years. Let me tell you, Diane, in my extensive experience, people seldom get the end they deserve. It's completely random. Bennett probably slipped on a banana peel and, bam! Instant death. Or, yes, he's running a writer's workshop in Iowa under a phony name with phony credentials telling his bullshit story about Truman Capote. And they all think he's *wonderful*."

Standing now, Diane leaned in. "His mother did commit suicide. He was 21."

"How?"

"Cut her wrists." Turning away from Rose, moving through her shoulders with a swagger of assurance, Diane left the title deed on the desk. At the last moment, she made one last riposte: "Miranda's just trying to find out about her dad. That's all."

Through the slatted blinds, Rose watched Diane walk to her car. She was swinging her keys, she drove a Jeep Wrangler, black with tinted windows, she slipped on her shades. *Dad.* Had Miranda used that word? Not *father*, the remote giver of genetic material. But Dad. Dadadad. Dad to give whiskery kisses and fix a broken bike, Dad to stand between a girl and the leering men of the world.

Glancing down at the deed, Rose studied the name. Barbara Elizabeth. She knew if she compared it to the deed Bennett had given her, she'd see a faint outline of Wite-out perhaps an unevenness in the letters where Bennett had typed his own name — Bennett Edward over Barbara Elizabeth.

Boomerang Bennett.

Which would be worse for Miranda? The cops finding her father in the cellar, his skull with a bullet hole? Or realizing that he'd been there all along, buried in the earth, a dozen feet beneath the kitchen table where she'd done her homework and blown out the candles on her birthday cakes? Rose's mouth filled with saliva. Stop the ruckus, stop the noise. She swallowed hard and did a Google search.

As Miranda herself had said: You can find people these days, there's always a trace.

Barbara · Elizabeth Kinney. A registered Republican. Kennebunkport, ME.

"You OK?" Nick was hovering.

Rose turned, smiled. "Fine, yup."

"Who was that?"

"A private investigator, actually."

He leaned on her desk, an antidote to Diane. "You a dangerous criminal, Rose?"

Then Bob's voice came on over the intercom. "When you two have finished your tea party, Nick, we're going to have to lock down shed 4, there's an eye infection. Nasty."

Ignoring him, Nick whispered to Rose: "He's such a dick."

She whispered back, "What qualities make someone, specifically, a dick?"

"That is a good question, Rose. Dick versus asshat."

"Asshat is not my generation."

"Asshat is an asshole who's also stupid. You know, maybe they can't help it, being low IQ."

"And *dick*? What defines someone as a *dick*?"

"A dick, Rose, a dick will go out of his way to fuck you over."

"It's about intention, then."

"Exactly. A dick plans, a dick means what he does."

Was this the final verdict, then? Bennett had been a dick? *Dickery*, Fornier had coined a word. But *dickery* didn't begin to describe the extent of his deception, the pathology of his lies. If she was a murderer, so was he. And it mattered, surely, the innocence of the victim, as much as the intention of the murderer.

Billy had walked across the field, burning with indignation and toughness and her desire to protect Rosie and Miranda — her family. Bennett laughed at her — *You don't even know who Ezra Pound is. I used to visit him in the insane asylum and we'd play cribbage* — and his greasy bullshit lies slid right down the silver armor of Billy's love. She had challenged him, and he'd simply taken something — a skillet, a bottle, a hammer — and smashed in her head. The way he'd driven over a body in the road and kept going. This was the man Miranda was so set on finding out about.

Suddenly, from Bob's office, the wild blaring of an air horn. Rose and Nick looked over and he let off another blast.

Nick whispered: "I'm planning my escape, Rose. Gonna light out for the territories. You wanna ride shotgun?" He gave her a quick smile, but his voice had held an odd tremor. Of panic or despair. Or something worse, for she recognized the pusillanimity.

*   *   *

Perhaps Andy had done it this way, perhaps Bob himself — though Rose doubted he had the cunning. The accounts were like a cave system in porous rock, full of corners and pockets in which to hide or get lost. She transferred small amounts from four different accounts, crossing the transactions with other transactions so that a cursory glance would give the impression of balance. She took several larger amounts from Bob's personal account, shifting money back into the account, then out again, winnowing it into the accounts payable. From this she made cash withdrawals over five days, amounts that mirrored amounts she paid by check for actual invoices. On the statements, the transactions would look like self-corrected bank errors, and the accounts would show that the money was still there. In total, she had stolen $13,497.50.

She counted this out at her kitchen table, stacks of hundreds, the 20s, the smaller bills, the change. And put it into a brown paper bag. One day they might come for her, they might hunt her down, but she would be hard to find, an invisible middle-aged woman living a quiet life under a different name, Betty or Sue. One day she'd find a way to tell Miranda, explain: this was the choice I made, the choices, I made them with the best data available to me at the time, I made them because of everything already stored in the museum of my cells, I made them because of you.

The night was warm, Rose decided to stay awake, to be with herself — Rosie-Rose, the last night of her sentence. The prisoner did eventually grow accustomed to the prison; and, even to feel affection for the inanimate objects within it. The house had kept her dry and mostly warm, it had at least sheltered her from the storms. At the kitchen table, she had fed Miranda for 18 years; the rich venison, the wild forage, the day-old bread, the discount vegetables — misshapen or bruised, but in sufficient quantities so that the child grew tall and strong and bold. There had never been hunger at this table.

Thank you, table.

The bed Rose had slept in, Hook once curled warm and snoring at her feet, expanding in the night so that Rose was crowded to one side and the dog splayed out in comfort. Rose was used to that bed, the slant to the left, the sink-hole mattress. The bed had molded itself around her body like a sarcophagus. Rose knew — there was one certainty: she did not want to die an old woman in that bed. She was grateful, though, for the sleep she'd had. Thank you, wonky bed. Thank you, cool sheets and warm blankets and lumpy pillows. The chair by the stove: Miranda used to sit on her lap, they'd wrap themselves in blankets, and Rose would read — *Goodnight Moon*, *The Tale of Peter Rabbit*, *Treasure Island*, *The Hobbit*. There had been a pivot — no, rather a slow arc through a series of points on a graph, and Miranda had sat on her lap less, she'd been too big, too heavy. Miranda's need for affection was replaced by the desire for individuation; childhood was one long trajectory away from the womb. And Rose had let her go, that was the great proof of mother love — the relinquishing. One day, Miranda would learn that, too.

The stove. Rose put her hand upon the cast iron beastlet. It was cold, hibernating through the summer. No one would use it again, no one would notice the design crafted by a 19th century Vulcan on the sides — along the ribs; and the elegant handle, rounding into the palm with the ergonomic and perfect design of a bone into a socket.

Stove — she began:

Stove,

You have kept me alive. Cold winter storms, colder springs — you kept me bodily warm. You could be relied upon, mute and stolid. If I tended you as you required, you always bloomed back your warmth. You did not fail, the failing was always mine: damp wood, insufficient kindling, my haste. You taught me to value the steady.

Goodbye, dear Stove. Thank you.

Absurdly, her eyes were tearing. The stove, an inanimate con-glomeration of molecules, made no reply, did not arch its back to her touch as beloved Hook had done. But perhaps — per-haps, something of her life was embedded within its atoms after all. Who really had the final say about life's energy — not just movement, construction and destruction — but what was felt with intensity, what energy came out through the pores of the skin and into the air. The residue of love and hate, despair and hope, and the vast steeps in between these treacherous antipodes — perhaps drifted, alighted, and was absorbed. Why not? Why not consider the air filled with the invisible pollen of emotion? Why not consider the absorbency of every object, flesh or earth or steel or wood? And the re-spooring, out again, out-out — like downy seeds, Nature's relentless recycling through different forms, perhaps transforming even the densest hate and grief into something digestible, restorative.

She put the matches she used to light the stove in her pocket.

And she thought of the young couple renovating Billy's house and barn. She wanted them to bring noise and children and chaos into it, for the garden to bloom and surge. There should be laughter again in this quiet valley in the lee of the mountain.

Goodbye.

In her hand she held the green Lanvin dress and slipped it over her head. She was too fat for it, across the back, the zipper wouldn't rise. But it still fit her smoothly across the hips. The glorious color, the filmy texture — in a sense, her trousseau.

And then she stepped outside.

To the woodshed where she found a red plastic container of fuel for the chain saw. From this position, she saw the house before her. It was like a Wyeth painting: a sense of unease pinned the beauty like a moth so that her eye didn't simply slide over the easy prettiness, but was drawn in, fascinated by the mystery that waited within. Rumors, stories were like the chipped paint and the cracked windows, so much a part of the place. Life had happened here. Death, too. Not just during her tenure, but for nearly two centuries.

Rose went back into the house, down into the basement. She

stood on Bennett's grave. He would be bones now. Maybe little bits of mummified skin. Teeth. A few strands of hair. But he was nothing else, not a ghost, not a spirit, neither guilt nor sadness.

Looking around for a rag, she didn't see any on hand, so she tore off the hem of the Lanvin dress and stuffed one end into the neck of the fuel container and lit the other with the matches. The silk burned slowly but surely. *Nothing that a match and a gallon of gasoline won't fix*, Bob had said. Well, on this occasion, Bob was right. Thank you, Bob.

Upstairs, in the kitchen, she turned on the gas cooker, all four burners. They hissed eagerly, exhaling their toxic, eggy scent. Then she went out the front door, closing it firmly behind her. She was pleased for all the care she'd taken over the years to shore up the insulation, the weathering seals on the windows and doors. She thought about how one day she'd paint it. Heavy oils, thick brushstrokes. She'd paint it from memory, the only place it would still exist.

The Tercel with its new catalytic converter started instantly, and the hills bowed up into the morning sky, jade green sails of earth and rock that caught the wind and pitched the planet forward. Up there in the rustling green, smothering green of trees, so much moved and lived in secret; the woods had chosen what to reveal to her — glimpses, shadows, paw prints. Not one creature, not one trout lily or mushroom or rock up there would miss her or even note her absence. And yet how much she had depended upon those things, they had been her outer hearth, they had kept her soul warm and her belly full in the leanest days. One last glance, and then she swung the Tercel onto the road and she did not look in the rearview mirror.

Down the hill, the channel of her days, the road grooved as ice upon granite, the greenhouses, the small, fervent church, the corn fields, hay fields, cows. This early, only the farmers were out in the fields and the shift workers on the roads. She turned at the traffic light, not left to the interstate, but right. *Right*.

Through the sleeping, slow-stirring town, out the other side.

No one had arrived — Silas was due in half an hour, at six. Rose had the place to herself. She parked and walked directly to the sheds. The huge fans hummed eternally, the smell was as sharp as old cheese, old shoes. Closer, closer than she had ever been, and at every step she retained the ability to turn back. What would she gain, other than a vision she'd never be able to erase? She couldn't change a thing, couldn't make anything better, she wasn't going to save a single chicken. Turning back, turning away now isn't the same as denying, she decided. Denying is the resort of the weak, the incapable, the lazy. It's adult pretending. Santa Claus exists and the lodger is a nice man who makes Rosie laugh.

Thus, Rose kept going, feeling queasy, another hot flash rising from her low back, her nose pricking with the oncoming stench of the sheds. No surprise awaited her — she wasn't going to discover that Bob was growing marijuana instead of chickens, or some vast meth lab or sweatshop of illegal Guatemalans dutifully sewing underwear. She opened the door.

They had minds, they had existential awareness of themselves as individuals. This was the worst of it. They did not aspire, they did not know that other chickens had better lives, they did not know green fields existed or the sunny farmyards of children's books. They did not believe in heaven or hell, they had no hope nor concept of hope, and yet they were hopeless. They were miserable, because true misery — this kind of daily, joyless, mechanical living — is not a comparison but an inescapable condition, a docile acceptance. The hens laid egg after egg after egg, each taken from them, day upon day upon day. And the end of their obedient servitude was death, a twirling of Silas's wrists to break their necks. To Silas and Bob, they were simply reproductive systems. But they were chickens with chicken brains, and in that chicken brain an egg was tended and then it hatched into a chick and the chick was tended and a chick was loved with all of a chicken mother's capacity. The hens' misery was not just one of physical discomfort — the claustrophobia, the raw-pecked backs and necks, the clipped-off beaks, the ceaseless, staring light — but of thwarted mother-love; this primal force that makes all life possible: the desire of the mother to bear and tend her young.

Rose sank to her knees in sorrow.

"Rose?"

She stumbled upward, not quickly, for her knees were stiffer these days. Nick stood before her. He looked confused. He was wearing his overalls open to the waist, and she silently noted the beautiful, firm symmetry of his form, the smoothness of his skin. He was marble and godlike in this Hades.

"What are you doing in here?" he asked.

"I was —"

She looked away, gathering herself like a loose spool of middle-aged wool. The ragged green dress. The early hour. She looked like a crazy lady. She sprang for the door, escaping out into the morning. He followed her. "Rose — what're you here for?"

She said, "You're not on duty until ten. You're not supposed to be here."

"The eye infection," he explained. "I have to treat them. I feel sorry for them." Then he touched her arm, "Rose —" and all regrets flared within her. She wanted to touch him right back, lay her hand upon that smooth, warm chest. She wanted to kiss him and fuck him and have him plow into her 17-year-old body — to experience the deep, unashamed lust she'd never had, and never would. She was ugly now, a saggy carapace.

"I'm leaving," she said.

"Why?" He frowned. "Is it my dad? Did he fire you?"

"No."

"So, like, leaving here, this particular shithole, or what?"

"This town."

He turned his head, she noted his profile, the slanted cheek-bones, the straight nose. Then, he regarded her almost angrily: "But you're my friend, Rose."

"I am. But I have to go."

"Where?"

"Far."

"*Where?*"

"Far, far."

"You're not going to kill yourself, right?"

"Not that far."

"Can I come with you?"

She felt the time, and she could feel Silas nearing them and how this singular moment was already fraying at the edges.

Nick said again: "Please, Rose, can I come with you?"

She thought: maybe all that happens in life is that you get to see your own life from a different perspective, up instead of down, or inside out, like a reversible coat.

"Wait here," she said and ran to the car, and got the brown bag. Then she ran back to him. "Listen, Nick. Can you listen? Because I'm going to tell you something important."

He nodded.

"There are moments, fulcrums upon which our entire lives depend. When we're young we don't see these, we don't understand their rarity. We think we have endless possibilities. We don't understand the suction of time. And I'm telling you now, this is one of those moments and in the future you'll look back and see it so clearly." She felt the bag's weight — the weight of her own plans, gas, food, several months of rent, of the new start, where she wasn't yet sure, but *far, far.* "I'm giving you money, enough for you to leave and go anywhere you want. It's money, that's all, not a perfect, tragedy-free life."

He opened the bag. "Holy shit."

"Don't tell anyone where you got it, don't let anyone take it from you. Go to a bank in another town, open a safety deposit box and keep it in there."

She leaned in, kissed him chastely on the cheek like an auntie, and then fled. She passed the fire trucks roaring out of their station and heading up to Kirby Mountain where a house was burning to the ground, a propane-fueled explosion.

Stopping at the last traffic light before the interstate, she fished around in her bag, found her phone and Pamela Fornier's card. With a light patter of her fingertips, she attached the screen grab of Bob's favorites bar — *daddydome* and *naughteen.*

And sent it.

* * *

Kennebunkport began like any other town on the Maine coast, with a seafood restaurant and a liquor store. Yet as Rose moved closer to the center, she noticed the differences. For instance, there were rust-mottled cars like hers, and there were extremely expensive cars. The serfs and the nobility. Nothing in between. The roads were immaculate, there was no McDonald's, no Pizza

Hut. The chain drugstore was a quaint white-clapboard house with window-boxes containing real red geraniums.

Do the very rich even know what the rest of America looks like? she wondered. Possibly, they think it's the same, only with smaller houses, and thus their failure to comprehend the populist calls for better healthcare and schools; to the rich, poverty is merely a matter of scale, and not wintering the polo ponies in Boca. Or it is inner cities burning in protest, self-immolation displayed through the long lens of a CNN camera. On the other side of the equation, most poor have no idea of how the rich really live — they cannot comprehend the vast amounts of disposable income, most of which has been dubiously gained or merely inherited or made from the blood and toil of the poor, if not here, then some other blighted country. They cannot comprehend the power that money brings, the choices, the options. The poor lack imagination: what do a million grains of sand look like? What about a billion? Jeff Bezos, a trillionaire. A trillion what? Stars? Dollars? How? And why? What could possibly be the point of that much money? The poor blame themselves for being poor, the rich take credit for being rich.

Her directions took her through town, toward Cape Porpoise. Behind the walls and fences were not mere houses or even mansions. An entirely different noun was needed to accurately describe the multiple buildings, tennis courts, pools, croquet lawns, staff quarters: *compounds*. Not for chickens or survivalists in army fatigues, but for leisure, for comfort. Private movie theaters, indoor pools, guest houses, boat houses. Most of the owners were here for a month or less, because there were new WASP frontiers — ranches in Montana, tents in Serengeti, villas in Costa Rica. And in between, they lived in their residences in Manhattan, Greenwich, Southport, Old Lyme, Marblehead, Chesapeake Bay, and, if absolutely necessary, San Francisco.

527 Queens Road was worth millions — *millions*. Once, a simple lobster shack, it was now a carefully weathered cottage with a cerulean-blue front door, extensive decks, and private ocean frontage. On the land side were the property's real assets — a dozen acres of hay fields, though Rose doubted these were hayed in the way real farmers hay: to feed their livestock through the long winter. She suddenly thought of Hobie's van Eyck — how these fields were the same thing: the way WASPs surreptitiously signal their wealth to other WASPs. Bennett semaphoring with silks scarves. That had been funny, hadn't it?

The drive curved through the fields — a tidy track with a grass strip up the middle to retain the "rural" charm of the property. Her tires made a pleasing sound on the gravel, a democratic sound — exactly the same as the hunter-green Jaguar parked in front of the house. As she got out, Rose peered inside the car: buttery leather seats, walnut dash, an overflowing ashtray.

Her knock on the cottage's blue door triggered the crazed yapping of multiple small dogs. She could hear them skidding and skittering on the floor on the other side of the door. Shortly, there was the sound of human footsteps, a woman's rebuke: "Fuck's sake, Minty, get out of my way!" The voice was posh, almost British, the way actors used to speak in old movies.

The woman opened the door, the dogs surged around Rose. They were Jack Russells mainly, but Rose spotted the odd tawny fur-ball. A Yorkie? "Bloody dawgs!" the woman shouted. She was mid-70s, tall, her thick silver hair held at bay by a wide velvet hairband. She stank, even from a few feet away, of booze and cigarettes. She squinted at Rose — as if at a prescription bottle, not just to read the tiny writing but to ascertain the contents. Her voice rose above the barking, "Are you lost?" The "o" sounded as if she was rolling marbles in her mouth.

"Barbara?"

"Rather, I believe the question is, who are you?"

They were speaking above the yipping dogs.

"Rose Monroe." And because this was an entirely insufficient resume, she added: "I knew Bennett. A long time ago."

"What?" *WOT?* The insane barking.

"Bennett. A long time ago. More than 30 years ago."

Suddenly, the dogs surged away from them like a school of fish taking fright; they dashed into the field in a tight pack. Rose and the woman were left in silence.

"Neighbor's cat. Hope they kill it. Can't stand the things. Murder all my birds."

Sure enough a cat flew vertically into the air, pivoting like an acrobat, before disappearing into the grass again. It was going to have a very close call.

"Bennett. Bennett? Bennett. Bennett?" The woman seemed to be trying to place him.

"Are you Barbara Kinney?"

The woman resumed her squint. "Why?"

"It's about Bennett. I just want to talk with you. I won't be more than ten minutes."

She gave Rose a look from top to toe. "Is that a Lanvin? I once had one just like that. Come in, then."

Barbara led her down a hall lined with dark grey bead-board and framed watercolors of seascapes. The paintings were able, though trite. The hallway opened into a living area with a full glass front to the sea. It was a different house here — modern, full of light. The furniture was either utilitarian or valuable antique. There were books everywhere, stacked on an elegant tiger mahogany table, in columns on the floor, stuffed into floor-to-ceiling bookcases. Persian rugs covered the wood floor. These were of quality but Rose smelled dog urine. The dogs had circled around from the field to the deck and were hurtling themselves against the glass doors. Barbara let them in, they surged onto the furniture, occupying every seat.

"Anywhere," she waved an arm. "Just shove them awf."

One of the brown tufty dogs curled its lip at Rose, but she was not deterred.

Barbara wore no jewelry and her clothes, on closer inspection, were dirty with food and dog hair. The room gave other clues: books, cigarettes, an open bottle of sherry, a TV in pole position with the comfiest armchair, a bird guide, stacks of unopened mail. Barbara had never been beautiful, but she was tall and strong, she had an athlete's frame. She resembled Bennett, and in this female form, Rose clearly saw Miranda — the thick hair, the shape of the occipital bones, the jawline, the oceanic eyes. The resemblance, once detected, was eerie and contaminating. The tributaries of DNA ran concurrently through the Kinney veins, and Rose had the sudden impression she'd merely incubated Miranda for this powerful genetic lineage; it wasn't until now, seeing Barbara, that Rose realized how little Miranda looked like her.

"Wot's this about Bennett?" Barbara took a sip from the delicate crystal glass of sherry on the table beside her. It didn't occur to her to offer anything to Rose.

"You're his sister?"

Barbara frowned, she did not encounter strangers, not out here on this rarified shore, not here in her lonely life. At length she said, "Wot's he done?" A barely detectible twitch at the edge of her mouth.

"I lived with him in Vermont. In your house."

"My house?"

"The farmhouse in Kirby."

A long scavenging of the memory. "Oh! You mean Aunt Kit's place. She married some kind of farmer." At the close of every sentence, Barbara's jaw thrust slightly forward and up, and Rose recalled this affectation in Bennett. "I just sort of got it in a will and didn't think anything about it, never wanted to go. Vermont! Why would I? Never been a skier." She settled her eyes on Rose. "What on earth was he doing there?"

"We lived together. Bennett and I. We had a child. Miranda."

"*Miranda?*" Barbara sounded incredulous.

"She turns 30 this year."

A pause. Barbara thinking. "Is this about money?"

"No —"

"Because he's dead."

"How do you know that?"

A choppy laugh. "He stopped asking for money."

"When — do you remember when, exactly?"

"So if it's money you're after —"

"No. It's not money. It's just —" What? Just what? Rose suddenly floundered. The vast and uncontrollable future circled, she was its prisoner once again, brought here by the folly of her decisions. It was impossible to explain or warn, or to ask Barbara for an alliance against Diane. If PI Di wished, if she bullied and manipulated, she would get her warrant, the house — what was left of it — would be searched, and if the police searched hard enough, the can of gasoline, the shards of human bone might be discovered and DNA'd. Then — then — a net would cast upon the land, and Rose brought to justice at last: a murderer in chains. The maudlin story would appear in the local paper,

Diane would be victorious, and Miranda would know what had happened to her father. But that terrible, pointless knowledge was not the same as the truth.

Two dogs suddenly exploded into a fight. Like a whirling, furry ouroboros, it was impossible to tell where one ended and the other began. Barbara hurled a book at them with surprising accuracy. "Knock it *awf*! Little turds!" Yelping, the culprits diverged onto separate chairs, one dislodged a fat black duck decoy. Now Rose noticed: the room was filled with duck decoys — it was like a Magic Eye, she just hadn't seen how they were placed among the books, on top of magazines, cluttering up the windows. Had he made them? Ducks, whimbrels. When had he been here? How long had he stayed? Was this their childhood home? Questions arrowed through time. Where and how had he learned to lie? And why? Who had he loved? Had he found his mother on the bathroom floor, bleeding out? Had he gone to Paris? Studied history at Oxford? What had he been like as a child? What about the Picasso and Truman Capote and Cuba?

"May I use your bath —" and she remembered "— your W.C.?"

"Down the hall, awn the left."

Down the hall. *Awn* the left. Facing the fields. First room. Wall to wall copies of *National Geographic*, decades of them. *Awn* the left. Second room: bathroom, smell of urine and potpourri. *Awn* the left. Third room. An unmade bed, disarray, men's clothes, boxes of papers and books. She recognized the Harris Tweed, the worn brogues and Brooks Brothers shirts. Bennett. She smelled him. For a brief, terrifying moment she thought he was alive, and this another ruse. And she felt exactly as the young girl she'd been in his wake, the painful insufficiency of self. She'd clung to him like a buoy in a storm, only to discover he'd had no anchor. He was barely afloat himself.

There is no sharp end of life, Rose thought. There isn't even direction — no culmination of knowledge or grand arrival. Every moment is continually being lived and relived. There's no closure, no past. There's nothing tidy or succinct. Even forgiveness is just emotions shapeshifting. It's all overflow, a chaos of conflict and definition. It's just constant wading.

Her ankle hurt, a sharp pain.

She looked down. There was a dog. Attached by its mouth. She left it there, grateful for the pain, for she saw, now, the room was dusty, cobwebbed, abandoned decades ago. She dragged the dog, which made low growling sounds, the little needle teeth embedded in her flesh, just as well, it was anchoring her. Rose stood in the room, she touched the tweed, and then she clutched it in her fist with something that felt mostly like hunger but might have been anger or some other human inconsistency. She had loved him, or tried to, and in moments he may have loved her, and in their stumbling they had made Miranda. Then as now, he was as unknown to her as a far galaxy, mysterious as unnamed stars, and yet she realized she had no curiosity. None at all. She did not care to know — not denial; rather, a banal disinterest. The questions — and their answers — were not hers anymore.

Miranda's just trying to find out about her dad. That's all, Diane had said.

That is all.

The facts of Bennett's death may be revealed or they may not, Rose could do nothing either way, and there would be other discomforts in Miranda's life that she could neither prevent nor alleviate. She could not protect her daughter anymore, and she must not try. Miranda was a strong tree, grown with good light on rich soil, well-tended, and she would absorb the barbs of life's wire within her bark. She knew her mother loved her.

Rose turned and staggered back down the hallway, towing the dog.

In the living room, Barbara was pouring herself another drink, the booze right there by her chair so she didn't even have to stand up, simply move a decoy to the side. Then she lifted her eyes, deep Atlantic blue, and Bennett looked out through them. "You wanted to talk about my brother."

"Actually about his daughter. Miranda. She wants to know more about him. His family, his history. You. She doesn't even know you exist."

"You're sure this isn't about money?"

"It isn't —"

"— becawse with Bennett it was always about money, he only ever telephoned when he wanted some."

May 1993, Rose thought. But it didn't matter. She smiled, extending warmth: "She looks like you."

"Her name — Miranda —" Barbara began, then fortified herself with another go at the sherry. "Bennett chose it?"

Rose affirmed. "From Shakesp —"

"Our mother was Miranda."

There was a brief pause, while Rose absorbed this. Of course, of course. She said: "She was a painter."

"How did you know?"

"The watercolors," Rose made a small gesture to the hall. "They're very good."

"They are not," Barbara declared. "But they are all that remains."

The remains: what is left, what you gather and take with you for the rest of your journey or what you leave for others to find.

Rose rushed on, as if downhill and certain of her course: "Miranda wants to know about her father. She has a child, Anika, with the same eyes, your eyes and Bennett's, and they also live by the sea. Bennett loved the sea and maybe the whole story of us would have been different if we'd lived by the sea instead. I've made a terrible mess, but she's my daughter, *my daughter,* and I want her to be happy, whatever that is I'm not sure, only as a mother, what I really want is to not hurt her."

Barbara turned the sherry glass in her fingers and Rose was now writing Miranda's number on a scrap of paper, handing it to the old woman. "Will you call her, Barbara? Will you call her soon? Now? Will you tell her who you are, and tell her to come here, take her into Bennett's room, tell her about him?"

Barbara took the paper, held it. "He just disappeared, you know. I wouldn't lend him any more money. There comes a point… one just can't anymore…" She trailed off and glanced at Miranda's number.

"Tell her about your mother. What a wonderful artist she was. Take her down to the beach and walk with her. Tell her about Bennett when he was a child."

Then the dogs barked. They leapt up and shrieked, racing to the French doors, tiny paws battering the glass. A gull had landed on the deck and was sauntering back and forth, mocking them. Rose moved the other way, quickly down the funnel of sad sailing pictures toward the front door, aware that Barbara was struggling up from the chair on stiff knees. Flinging open the door, Rose gulped the hay-perfumed air.

Barbara arrived, the tide of dogs at her feet. "Rosie," she said. "Yes, I think he mentioned you."

Was there more? Rose waited for the next sentence, for quali-fication. He loved you. He hated you. He said he was going to see you and he never came back.

But that was it. *Mentioned.* Rosie had been mentioned.

*   *   *

Approaching Bridgeport, a sign tempted the motorist: "VISIT THE PEZ MUSEUM! OVER 1500 PEZ DISPENSERS ON DISPLAY!"

Rose remembered the exit off the interstate, left, then straight on. Nothing was familiar: the low-slung buildings, the small businesses — a cleaners, a carpet store — had all been replaced by big box malls and office buildings. For some reason she thought of Joseph Conrad — "The horror, the horror!" The horror now was the leveling of the dark and wild forests for this ubiquity. The virus of ubiquity. The Farm Shop restaurant was now Friendly's, and jammed between a carpeting store and a car wash on the busy Boston Post Road. She parked in the center spaces, where there would be the most traffic and she thought a casual viewer would be less likely to notice her Vermont plates. Inside, she ordered an omelet, paid cash.

Outside, the late afternoon was still hot. She began to walk. Half a mile past Friendly's, she entered a Dollar General and purchased a flashlight and a pair of black panty hose. By six, she'd reached the Southport train station. Almost nothing had changed, the quaintness retained by the very rich, their own lie that all is well in the world: the over-priced pharmacy on the cor-ner, the post office, the small café — though this had probably changed hands and served something other than Chock Full o' Nuts filter coffee.

Bearing left through an avenue of trees, she came out at the Pequot Yacht Club, and left again around the harbor. At dusk she reached the Mill River bridge. Cars drove past, Mercedes, BMWs, Audis. Then the road swung up, onto Sasco Hill. Here, surely, it was always such summer, the rich could buy year-round summer. Towering maples shaded the narrow street. Prim green verges, immaculately tended, backed onto high walls that hid the mansions beyond. She heard the droning choir of lawnmowers. The sea could only be glimpsed through the trees and walls — a titbit, a hand-out, a donation to the poor — blue and glimmering and set upon with yachts. Not yachts: *boats*.

By the time Rose reached the entrance to the country club, it was sufficiently dark. Now she cut down the access road, keeping clear of the clubhouse. Laughter and the sound of plates, glasses, silverware clinking, clattering, tinkling drifted through the open windows, a smell of cooking — hamburgers, chicken. Across the golf course itself, she was able to chart her way between the higher ground of the ridge of Sasco Hill and the low, moon-glimmering sea. The sand bunkers glowed among the dark pools of the fairways and the putting tees. Her eyes had adjusted to the darkness, and Rose felt a deep, atavistic pleasure in being out and alone in the night. She still knew the way.

Another forty minutes of walking had passed when the golf course gave way to the narrow strip of stony beach. The sea timidly pulled at the shore, polite little wavelets left offerings of twigs, seaweed, and bottle caps. Rose followed the arc of the land. Not far ahead was Hobie's boathouse. The lights were on, the doors to the upstairs apartment wide open. Closer, she could hear music — Miles Davis or someone similar, and it still seemed to her neither raucous nor serious nor emotive. The music was a language she had never understood, she had no ear for it. Perhaps Bennett was there now, a silver mane of hair, an expensive red wine in hand, reading *The Stranger*.

No: he was dead, she had killed him, she had done her time, 30 years, three hots and a cot. She was now paroled.

A dozen yards before the boathouse, Rose turned onto the lawn, edging along the cedar hedge that ran straight uphill toward the main house. A few lights were on, though only downstairs, and Rose tried to remember the rooms. The main reception hall, the dining room, Hobie's office were all dark, so she supposed it must be the kitchen alight. All the doors and windows were closed, the house shut-up. No one was home.

Bats sliced the air, cut from black cloth, the night's own curtain, and the lawn was already damp underfoot. Rose noted the flower beds, the drooping heavy heads of hydrangeas and plump roses and frothing hollyhocks. The effect was as she remembered: of floral bounty barely restrained. But now the curation seemed absurd — these ludicrous flowers that could not survive without tending. Why not let the garden go, wild flowers, wild bees, dandelion, weeds, moles, voles, groundhogs, foxes, wasps? What was wrong with people — this relentless domestication?

Creeping right up against the house, she supposed she should look for cameras. But if there was a fancy security system, she certainly wasn't going to outsmart it. Now was the time for Fate. She jiggled the door to Hobie's office. Locked. Around she slunk to the front door, and this too was locked. Here, though, she could glance in. The interior had been violently redecorated in minimalist white — surely, the forceful hand of Bizza.

Rose kept going, she was light and happy, like a child playing hide-and-seek. She'd never felt so careless. She pulled the black panty hose out of her pocket and slipped them over her head. The waist band came over her chin, and the empty legs hung limply, swinging as she turned her head. The fabric flattened her nose. It didn't inhibit her breathing, but it was hot, so she pushed the elastic back up, more of a demented beret look than mask.

The kitchen door was open.

Though Rose had never seen the kitchen, it was obvious Bizza had imposed her will upon it. White countertops, white cabinets, and white tiling: it looked like the cafeteria on a space ship. A white oven. In the corner, the white fridge hummed. Rose listened for any other sound. Perhaps somewhere an alarm was ringing shrilly. She might be shot. In the bowels of the house, a vent of some kind sighed.

Had Mitzi died? A battle with breast cancer? Or was she in exile, a gated community in Palm Springs? Golf, followed by water aerobics and lunch, an afternoon lecture on paleo-arctic human migration, more golf, dinner at 4:30, then mahjong and martinis until everyone passed out.

The reception room was a white marble quarry, the hallway that had once been filled by hunting prints now exhibited huge black-and-white photographs. Rose paused to examine them, unsure what she was looking at — slashes of black across white. Sensing it might be human flesh, she turned her head sideways, as if a different angle might make the difference. The legs of the panty hose fell across her face, and she pushed them aside like recalcitrant bunny ears. Reaching the end of the hallway, she realized these were all extreme close-ups of vaginas. Or one vagina from many different perspectives. Bizza's?

At last, Rose had arrived at her destination. Mitzi's gorgeous blue had been murdered by screaming white. White sofa, white arm chairs, white tables, white floor, a lunatic asylum or a bad dream. White was the Chinese color for death. For bones, ash, nothingness. For reasons known only to Bizza, the curtains were black. Hobie must loathe it. For a moment, Rose stood looking out the window at the dark garden, sloping down to the dark sea.

Now the heat started in the flesh behind her face, burning her face off like the scene in *Raiders of the Lost Ark* when the Nazi in the black coat melts from behind his face; then around her entire skull, the blood searing between bone and skin, her hair must be standing on end, her scalp was actually sweating under the panty hose. *Oh for God's sake*, she thought, *for fuck's sake, not now!* At the same time her torso was the surface of the sun, her clothes were going to melt off her, she was immolating, and all that would be left was a small clump of smoking ash on Bizza's white floor. And then, just as suddenly, the heat left, a menopausal ghost vacating the cask of her body like an exorcism. She could smell her own sweat, beads trickling down the groove of her back.

She exhaled, then laughed, a short guffaw which sounded extraordinarily loud in the quiet room, the quiet house. Her stomach made a low, creaking sound like a door hinge, and she realized she was hungry. She turned, her eyes scanning the darker section of the room. The painting was there! How lonely it seemed, the only painting on the vast wall. It had survived the great white spell Bizza had cast upon the house and the aggressive swarm of giant vaginas. Hobie, she knew, Hobie had resisted. He wasn't going to move this painting for Mitzi, he wasn't going to move it for Bizza.

The girl and her husband looked back at Rose from their frame. She was younger than Rose remembered, and he was older. He looked more bored than ever, as if he was posing only for her, he was indulging the wishes of his young wife; but really, he had much more important things to do — businesses, travels. The girl stared at the painter, the viewer, eagerly; she had ambitions. But when the painting was done she was disappointed. She'd expected it to be bigger, wider, brighter, more flattering — not only of herself, but of her life. Her husband looked so dull, so grumpy. Behind them, in the sunlit door beyond the kitchen, the maid stood with the dead hare's long satin ears in her work-reddened hands.

Gently, Rose lifted the picture off its hook. Hobie had hung it himself with a hammer and a small nail, not even a proper picture hook that braced itself back against the wall. It could have fallen at any time. The weight of it was about the same as a carton of eggs. She lifted it close to her face, inhaled. The sharp odor of gesso and oil were still there, 500 hundred years later.

"You'd better put that back."

The voice made her jump, like a slap. A house-keeper? Rose clung on to the painting, keeping her gaze fixed on the young girl at its heart. She seemed to be amused, now, and somehow pitying. Rose thought of Nick. The young do not believe it will ever happen to them — this sagging, this wrinkling, this ennui grinding the days like meat.

"No, I will not," Rose said. She pulled the panty hose back down over her face.

"I've called the police."

Rose turned to face the woman. She was in a bulky satin dressing gown, her wrinkled face glistening with cream. Pointless, Rose thought with a savage thrust, no cream is going to give you smooth skin.

"You're stealing my painting."

Rose took a few steps forward. She was in a movie, everything was going to work out, the bold are always rewarded. She was a little surprised herself that she believed this quite so fervently. Her time had come.

"It's not your painting," she said.

"The police will be here any minute," the woman countered.

"Mitzi?" Rose wondered aloud.

"Who are you?" Mitzi demanded.

Far off, but incoming, the sound of sirens. Rose dashed forward, holding the painting tight, shoving Mitzi aside, running down the hall. Vaguely, she heard Mitzi tumble and cry out. Her focus was her trajectory through the house. Her legs seemed to expand and her heart grow large, she was sucking great quantities of air. Down the stairs, through the bar — all of this white, white, white! My God! Mitzi had erased every trace of her life with Hobie! The room to the left, once his study, was painted black.

The sirens were closer now, but so was she. The latch was simple, it clicked open and Rose was outside, the cool air, the sea scent. Just as the red and blue strobes hit the front of the house, she was down the garden, the painting firmly under her arm, she was ducking into the cedar hedge, the rich smell of cedar, the gummy residue of the branches flashing across her face, snagging on the panty hose. Rose plunged on through the night garden, she was in the rough grass that led down to the dark sea and the limitless ways beyond. Obligation fell from her, hate and doubt, and love, too, and she ran, her body was light-boned, long-limbed, unburdened. She was free as a hare, she was bounding.

ACKNOWLEDGMENTS

This book is for Kate Shaw, my one and only agent, who has been with me since the start in 2002. Kate has perfect instincts — not just as an insightful and bare-knuckle reader of manuscripts, but, like a badass PT trainer, she knows when to cajole, when to reassure and when to make me do the literary equivalent of 100 push-ups. Thank you, Kate. My thanks also to Detective Corporal Matthew Knisley with the Montpelier Police Department for background info, and Steve Gabrault for turning Rosie into a hunter; any mistakes noted by pedants are completely mine. My mother, Rosalind Finn, and Hope Bentley read cronky early drafts and gave crucial feedback. There is no one of this planet I would rather work with than Eric Obenauf and Eliza Wood-Obenauf at Two Dollar Radio. I'm continually amazed by their commitment, kindness and style, and am proud to be among the exceptional talent they publish. Eliza is a brilliant copy editor: thank you for your care, sharp-eyes, curiosity, and patience with my spelling. Eric: I *love* the cover. Gratitude and love to my husband, Matt, who keeps the faith in my writing and our marriage when I falter; and our daughters, Molly and Pearl, shining star, deep blue sea, who allow me to love them wildly and sometimes messily. Their forgiveness of my maternal short-comings is curative, miraculous. I know a dark and a powerful circle has been broken.

The Hare is also for my sister, Catriona.

Two Dollar Radio
Books too loud to Ignore

ALSO AVAILABLE
Here are some other titles you might want to dig into.

THE GLOAMING A NOVEL BY **MELANIE FINN**

After an accident leaves her estranged in a Swiss town, Pilgrim Jones absconds to east Africa, settling in a Tanzanian outpost where she can't shake the unsettling feeling that she's being followed. *The Gloaming* is a thrilling, haunting new work of guilt, atonement, and finally, hope.

* *NEW YORK TIMES BOOK REVIEW* NOTABLE BOOK OF 2016
* *THE GUARDIAN'S* "NOT THE BOOKER PRIZE" SHORTLIST
*VERMONT BOOK AWARD FINALIST

"Deeply satisfying." —JOHN WILLIAMS, *NEW YORK TIMES*

"In this richly textured, intricately plotted novel, [Finn] assures us that heartbreak has the same shape everywhere."
—LISA ZEIDNER, *NEW YORK TIMES BOOK REVIEW*, EDITORS' CHOICE

THE UNDERNEATH A NOVEL BY **MELANIE FINN**

The Underneath is an intelligent and considerate exploration of violence—both personal and social—and whether it may ever be justified. With the assurance and grace of her acclaimed novel *The Gloaming*, Melanie Finn returns with a precisely layered and tense new literary thriller.

"A musk of sex and menace soaks three narrative strands, expertly braided… Finn puts her readers on the knife's edge."
—*KIRKUS REVIEWS*, STARRED REVIEW

"*The Underneath* is an excellent thriller… Finn's third novel proves that she's deeply original, a writer who's not content with rehashing old tropes." —MICHAEL SCHAUB, *STAR TRIBUNE*

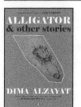

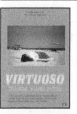

Books to read!

SAVAGE GODS MEMOIR BY **PAUL KINGSNORTH**

→ **A Best Book of 2019** —*The Guardian*

← "[*Savage Gods* is] a wail sent up from the heart of one of the intractable problems of the human condition: real change comes only from crisis, and crisis always involves loss." —Ellie Robins, *Los Angeles Review of Books*

SAVAGE GODS ASKS, can words ever paint the truth of the world—or are they part of the great lie which is killing it?

THE BOOK OF X NOVEL BY **SARAH ROSE ETTER**

→ **Winner of the 2019 Shirley Jackson Awards for Novel**
→ **A Best Book of 2019** —*Vulture, Entropy, Buzzfeed, Thrillist*

← "Etter brilliantly, viciously lays bare what it means to be a woman in the world." —Roxane Gay

A SURREAL EXPLORATION OF ONE WOMAN'S LIFE and death against a landscape of meat, office desks, and bad men.

TRIANGULUM NOVEL BY **MASANDE NTSHANGA**

→ **2020 Nomo Awards Shortlist**
→ **A Best Book of 2019** —*LitReactor, Entropy*

← "Magnificently disorienting and meticulously constructed." —Tobias Carroll, Tor.com

AN AMBITIOUS, OFTEN PHILOSOPHICAL AND GENRE-BENDING NOVEL that covers a period of over 40 years in South Africa's recent past and near future.

THE WORD FOR WOMAN IS WILDERNESS
NOVEL BY **ABI ANDREWS**

← "Unlike any published work I have read, in ways that are beguiling, audacious…" —Sarah Moss, *The Guardian*

THIS IS A NEW KIND OF NATURE WRITING — one that crosses fiction with science writing and puts gender politics at the center of the landscape.

AWAY! AWAY! NOVEL BY **JANA BEŇOVÁ**
TRANSLATED BY **JANET LIVINGSTONE**

→ **Winner of the European Union Prize for Literature**

← "Beňová's short, fast novels are a revolution against normality." —Austrian Broadcasting Corporation, ORF

WITH MAGNETIC, SPARKLING PROSE, Beňová delivers a lively mosaic that ruminates on human relationships, our greatest fears and desires.

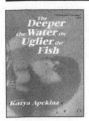

THE DEEPER THE WATER THE UGLIER THE FISH NOVEL BY **KATYA APEKINA**

→ 2018 *Los Angeles Times* Book Prize Finalist

→ A Best Book of 2018 —*Kirkus, BuzzFeed, Entropy, LitReactor, LitHub*

← "Nothing short of gorgeous." —Michael Schaub, NPR

POWERFULLY CAPTURES THE QUIET TORMENT of two sisters craving the attention of a parent they can't, and shouldn't, have to themselves.

THE BLURRY YEARS NOVEL BY **ELEANOR KRISEMAN**

→ A Best Book of 2018 —*Entropy*

← "Kriseman's is a new voice to celebrate."—*Publishers Weekly*

THE BLURRY YEARS IS A POWERFUL and unorthodox coming-of-age story from an assured new literary voice, featuring a stirringly twisted mother-daughter relationship, set against the sleazy, vividly-drawn backdrop of late-seventies and early-eighties Florida.

PALACES NOVEL BY **SIMON JACOBS**

← "*Palaces* is robust, both current and clairvoyant… With a pitch-perfect portrayal of the punk scene and idiosyncratic, meaty characters, this is a wonderful novel that takes no prisoners." —*Foreword Reviews*, starred review

WITH INCISIVE PRECISION and a cool detachment, Simon Jacobs has crafted a surreal and spellbinding first novel of horror and intrigue.

THEY CAN'T KILL US UNTIL THEY KILL US ESSAYS BY **HANIF ABDURRAQIB**

→ **Best Books 2017:** NPR, *Buzzfeed, Paste Magazine, Esquire, Chicago Tribune, Vol. 1 Brooklyn,* CBC (Canada), *Stereogum, National Post* (Canada), *Entropy, Heavy, Book Riot, Chicago Review of Books* (November), *The Los Angeles Review, Michigan Daily*

← "Funny, painful, precise, desperate, and loving throughout. Not a day has sounded the same since I read him."
—Greil Marcus, *Village Voice*

WHITE DIALOGUES STORIES **BENNETT SIMS**

← "Anyone who admires such pyrotechnics of language will find 21st-century echoes of Edgar Allan Poe in Sims' portraits of paranoia and delusion."
—*New York Times Book Review*

IN THESE ELEVEN STORIES, Sims moves from slow-burn psychological horror to playful comedy, bringing us into the minds of people who are haunted by their environments, obsessions, and doubts.

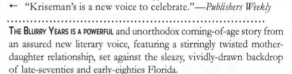

Books to read!

Now available at **TWODOLLARRADIO.com** or your favorite bookseller.

FOUND AUDIO NOVEL BY N.J. CAMPBELL

← "[A] mysterious work of metafiction... dizzying, arresting and defiantly bold." —*Chicago Tribune*

← "This strange little book, full of momentum, intrigue, and weighty ideas to mull over, is a bona fide literary page-turner." —*Publishers Weekly*, "Best Summer Books, 2017"

SEEING PEOPLE OFF NOVEL BY JANA BEŇOVÁ
TRANSLATED BY **JANET LIVINGSTONE**

⇢ **Winner of the European Union Prize for Literature**

← "A fascinating novel. Fans of inward-looking post-modernists like Clarice Lispector will find much to admire." —NPR

A KALEIDOSCOPIC, POETIC, AND DARKLY FUNNY portrait of a young couple navigating post-socialist Slovakia.

THE DROP EDGE OF YONDER
NOVEL BY **RUDOLPH WURLITZER**

← "One of the most interesting voices in American fiction." —*Rolling Stone*

AN EPIC ADVENTURE that explores the truth and temptations of the American myth, revealing one of America's most transcendant writers at the top of his form.

THE VINE THAT ATE THE SOUTH
NOVEL BY **J.D. WILKES**

← "Undeniably one of the smartest, most original Southern Gothic novels to come along in years." —— Michael Schaub, NPR

WITH THE ENERGY AND UNIQUE VISION that established him as a celebrated musician, Wilkes here is an accomplished storyteller on a Homeric voyage that strikes at the heart of American mythology.

SIRENS MEMOIR BY JOSHUA MOHR

⇢ **A Best of 2017** —*San Francisco Chronicle*

← "Raw-edged and whippet-thin, *Sirens* swings from tales of bawdy addiction to charged moments of a father struggling to stay clean." —*Los Angeles Times*

WITH VULNERABILITY, GRIT, AND HARD-WON HUMOR, Mohr returns with his first book-length work of non-fiction, a raw and big-hearted chronicle of substance abuse, relapse, and family compassion.